Henry Augustus Wise

Captain Brand, of the Centipede

Henry Augustus Wise

Captain Brand, of the Centipede

ISBN/EAN: 9783337086237

Printed in Europe, USA, Canada, Australia, Japan

Cover: Foto ©Andreas Hilbeck / pixelio.de

More available books at **www.hansebooks.com**

CAPTAIN BRAND.

CAPTAIN BRAND,

OF THE

"CENTIPEDE."

A PIRATE OF EMINENCE IN THE WEST INDIES:

His Loves and Exploits,

TOGETHER WITH SOME ACCOUNT OF THE SINGULAR MANNER
BY WHICH HE DEPARTED THIS LIFE.

BY

HARRY GRINGO,

(H. A. WISE, U.S.N.),

AUTHOR OF "LOS GRINGOS," "TALES FOR THE MARINES," AND
"SCAMPAVIAS."

"Our God and sailors we alike adore,
In time of danger—not before;
The danger passed, both are alike requited:
God is forgotten, and the sailor slighted."

WITH ILLUSTRATIONS.

NEW YORK:

HARPER & BROTHERS, PUBLISHERS,

FRANKLIN SQUARE.

1864.

CAPTAIN BRAND,

OF THE

"CENTIPEDE."

PART I.

CHAPTER I.

SPREADING THE STRANDS.

> "Shout three times three, like Ocean's surges,
> Join, brothers, join, the toast with me;
> Here's to the wind of life, which urges
> The ship with swelling waves o'er sea!"

> "Masters, I can not spin a yarn
> Twice laid with words of silken stuff.
> A fact's a fact; and ye may larn
> The rights o' this, though wild and rough
> My words may loom. 'Tis your consarn,
> Not mine, to understand. Enough—"

It was in the year of our Lord eighteen hundred and five, and in the River Garonne, where a large, wholesome merchant brig lay placidly on the broad and shining water. The fair city of Bordeaux, with its great mass of yellow-tinted buildings, towers, and churches, rose from the river's banks, and the din and bustle of the great mart came faintly to the ear. The sails of the brig were loosed, the crew were hauling home the sheets and hoisting the topsails with the clear, hearty songs of English sailors, while the anchor was under foot and the cable rubbing with a taut strain against the vessel's bluff bows. At the gangway stood a large, handsome seaman, bronzed by the sun and winds of about half a century, dressed in a square-cut blue jacket and loose trowsers, talking to the pilot—a brown little Frenchman, in coarse serge raiment and large, clumsy sabots. The conversation between them was carried on partly by signs, for, in answer to the pilot, the other threw his stalwart arm aloft toward the folds of the spreading canvas, and nodded his head.

"*Fort bien! vite donc! mon Capitaine*," said the pilot; "the tide is on the ebb; let us go. Up anchor!"

"Ay, pilot!" replied the captain, pulling out his watch; "in ten minutes. The ladies, you know, must have time to say 'good-by.' Isn't it so, my pilot?"

The gallant little Frenchman smiled in acquiescence, and, taking off his glazed hat with the air of a courtier, said, "*Pardieu!* certainly; why not? Jean Marie would lose his pilotage rather than hurry a lady."

Going aft to the raised cabin on the quarter-deck, the captain softly opened the starboard door, and looking in, said, in a kindly tone,

"It is time to part, my friends; the pilot says we are losing the strength of the tide, so we must kiss and be off."

Two lovely women were sitting, hand clasped in hand, on the sofa of the transom. You saw they were sisters of nearly the same age, and a little boy and girl tumbling about their knees showed they were mothers—young mothers too, for the soft, full, rounded forms of womanhood, with the flush of health and matronly pride tinged their cheeks, while masses of dark hair banded over their smooth brows and tearful eyes told the story at a glance. They rose together as the captain spoke.

"*Adieu, chère Rosalie!* we shall soon meet again, let us hope, never more to part."

"Adieu, Nathalie! adieu, dearest sister! adieu! adieu!"

The loving arms were twined around each other in the last embrace; the tears fell like gentle rain, but with smiles of hope and trustfulness they parted.

"Ay," said the sturdy skipper, as he stood with eyes brimful of moisture regarding the sisters, "ay, trust me for bringing you together again. Well do I remember when you were little wee things, when I brought you to France after the earthquake in Jamaica; just like these little rogues here"—and he laid his brawny hands on the heads of the children, who clung to each other within the folds of their mothers' dresses; "but never fear, my darlings," he went on, "you will meet happily again. Ay, that you shall, if old Jacob Blunt be above land or water."

A boat which was lying alongside the brig shoved off; the little boy, who had been left on board, was held high above the rail in the arms of a sturdy negro, while the mother stood beside him, waving her handkerchief to the boat as it pulled rapidly away toward the shore.

"Man the windlass, lads!" cried the captain. "Mister Binks, brace round the head yards, and up with the jib as soon as the anchor's a-weigh."

The windlass clinked as the iron palls caught the strain of the cable, the anchor was wrenched from its oozy bed, the vessel's head fell off, and, gathering way, she moved quietly down the River Garonne.

CHAPTER II.

CALM.

"It ceased: yet still the sails made on
 A pleasant noise till noon—
 A noise like that of a hidden brook
 In the leafy month of June.
Till noon we quietly sailed on,
 Yet never a breeze did breathe;
Slowly and smoothly went the ship,
 Moved onward from beneath."

THE great lumbering brig, with yards square, mainsail hauled up, and the jib and trysail in the brails, lay listlessly rolling on the easy swell of the water, giving a gentle send forward every minute or so, when the sluggish sails would come with a thundering slap against the masts, and the loose cordage would rattle like a drum-major's ratan on a spree. The sea was one glassy mirror of undulations, shimmering out into full blaze as the rising sun just threw its rays along the crest of the ocean swell; and then, dipping down into the rolling mass, the hue would change to a dark green, and, coming up again under the brig's black counter, would swish out into a little shower of bubbles, and sparkle again joyously.

Away off in the distance lay the island of Jamaica—the early haze about the mountain tops rising like a white lace veil from the deep valleys below, with here and there a white dot of a cluster of build- ings gleaming out from the sombre land like the flicker of a helio- trope, and at intervals the base of the coast bursting forth in a long, heavy fringe of foam, as the lazy breakers chafed idly about the rocks of some projecting headland. Nearer, too, were the dark succession of waving blue lines in parallel bars and patches of the young land wind, tipping the backs of the rollers in a fluttering ripple of cats'- paws, and then wandering sportively away out to sea.

On board the brig, forward, were three or four barefooted sailors, in loose frocks and trowsers, moving lazily about the decks, drawing buckets of water over the side and dashing it against the bulwarks, while others were scrubbing and clearing up the vessel for the day. The caboose, too, began to show signs of life, and a thin column of smoke rose gracefully up in the calm morning air until it came with- in the eddying influence of the sails and top-hamper, when a bit of roll would puff it away in blue curls beyond.

Abaft stood a low, squat-built sailor at the wheel, his striped Guernsey cap hanging on one of the spokes, and his body leaning, half asleep, over the barrel, which gave him a sharp twitch every now and then when the sea caught the rudder on the wrong side. Near at hand, with an arm around an after topmast backstay, and head resting over the rail, was the mate, Mr. Binks, with a spy-glass to his eye, through which he was peering at the distant hills of Jamaica. Presently, as he was about to withdraw the brass tube, and as the old brig yawed with her head inshore, something appeared to arrest his attention; for, changing his position, and climbing up to the break of the deck cabin, he steadied himself by the shrouds, and rubbing his eye with the sleeve of his shirt, he gave a long look through the glass, muttering to himself the while. At last, having apparently made up his mind, he sang out to the man at the wheel in this strain:

"Ben, my lad, look alive; catch a turn with them halliards over the lee wheel; and just take this 'ere glass and trip up to the fore-yard, and see what ye make of that fellow, here away under the eastermost headland."

Ben, without more ado, secured the spokes of the wheel, clapped his cap on his head, hitched up his trowsers, and, taking the glass from the mate, rolled away up the fore-rigging. Meanwhile Mr. Binks walked forward, stopping a moment at the caboose to take a tin pot of coffee from the cook, and then, going on to the topsail-sheet bitts, he carefully seated himself, and leisurely began to stir up the sugar in his beverage with an iron spoon, making a little cymbal music with it on the outside while he gulped it down. He had not been many minutes occupied in this way when Ben hailed the deck from the fore-yard.

"On deck there!"

"Hallo!" ejaculated Mr. Binks.

"I see that craft," cried Ben; "she's a fore and after, sails down, and sweeping along the land. She hasn't got a breath of wind, sir."

"Very well," said Mr. Binks, speaking into the tin pot with a sound like a sheet-iron organ; "come down."

As Ben wriggled himself off the fore-yard and caught hold of the futtock shrouds to swing into the standing rigging, he suddenly paused, and putting the glass again to his eye, he sang out:

"I say, sir! here is a big chap away off on the other quarter, under topsails. There! Perhaps ye can see him from the deck, about a handspike clear of the sun"—pointing with the spy-glass as he spoke in the proper direction.

"All right!" said the mate, as he began again the cymbal pot and spoon music; "becalmed, ain't he?"

"Yes, sir; not enough air to raise a hair on my old grandmother's wig!" muttered Ben, as he slowly trotted down the rigging.

The sun came up glowing like a ball of fire. The land wind died away long before it fluttered far off from the island, and, saving the uneasy clatter at times of the loose sails and running gear, all remained as before. It was getting on toward eight o'clock, and while the cook was dishing the breakfast mess for the crew beneath an awning forward of the quarter-deck, the captain came up from his cabin below. The stalwart old seaman stepped to the bulwarks, and, shading his eyes with his hand from the glare, he took a broad glance over the water to seaward, nodded to the mate, and said, in a cheerful voice,

"Dull times, matey! No signs of a breeze yet, eh?"

"No, captain," said Mr. Binks; "dead as ditch water; not been enough air to lift a feather since you went below at four o'clock. But we have sagged inshore by the current a few leagues during the night, and here's old Jamaica plain in sight broad off the bow."

"Well, it's not so bad after all, a forty-four days' passage—so I'll tell my Lady Bird passenger."

Going to the latticed door of the deck cabin, the jolly skipper threw it wide open, clapped his hands together thrice, and then, placing them to his mouth like a speaking trumpet, he bellowed out, in a deep, low roar,

"Heave out there, all hands! Heave out, Lady Bird and baby! Land ho!"

There came a joyous note from a soft womanly voice within a screen drawn across the after cabin, mingled with a little cooing grunt from a child, and presently an inner door swung back, and the sweetest little tot of a boy came tumbling out into the open space, and sprang at once into the captain's arms. The little fellow buried his brown curly head into the old skipper's whiskers, and then, kicking up his fat naked legs, he laughed and chattered like a magpie.

"Aha! you young scamp, this small nose smells the oranges and cinnamon, eh? And dear lazy mamma shuts her pretty eyes, and won't look for papa, and so near home, too!"

Here Madame Rosalie's low sweet voice trilled out merrily in a slightly foreign accent, while the contralto tones vibrated on the ear like the note of a harp.

"Ah! *bon capitaine*, how could you deceive me? Still, I forgive you for telling me last night that we were so far from Kingston. When you know, too," she went on in her Creole accent, "how I love and want to see my dear husband these last four years, since you carried him away in your good big ship. But never mind, my good friend, I shall pay you off one of these days; and now send, please, for Banou to dress his little boy."

Scarcely had the worthy skipper reached a bell-rope near at hand, and given it one jerk, than the cabin door opened, and in stepped a brawny black, whose bare woolly head and white teeth and eyes glittered with delight. There was that about his face which indicated intelligence, courage, devotion, and humanity—those indescribable marks of expression which Nature sometimes stamps in unmistakable lines on the skin, whether it be white or black. He was below the middle height, but the large head was set with a great swelling throat on the shoulders of a Titan. His loose white and red striped shirt was thrown well back over his black and broad chest; and putting out a pair of muscular arms that seemed as massive and heavy as lignum vitæ, the boy jumped from the captain to meet them; and then sticking his little soft legs down the slack of Banou's shirt, he ran his rosy fingers in his wool, and shouted with glee.

"Oho!" said the black, as he passed his huge arms around the little fellow, and smoothed down his scanty night-dress as if it were the plumage of a bird, "oho! little Master Henri loves his Banou, eh? Good, he take bath."

Bearing his charge out upon the quarter-deck beneath the awning, he pulled a large tub from under a boat turned upside down over the deck cabin; and then, while the young monkey had scrambled round to his back, and was beating a tattoo with his tiny fists on his shoulders, Banou caught up a bucket and proceeded to draw water from over the side, which he dashed into the tub. When he had nearly filled the tub he felt around with his black jaws as delicately as if he was about to seize a musquito, and, clutching the kicking legs with one hand, he spun the little fellow a somersault over his head, and skinning off at the same time his diminutive frock, plunged him into the sparkling brine, singing the while in a laughing chant:

> "Dis is the way strong Banou catch him,
> First he strip and den he 'plash him;
> Henri he jump and 'cream for his moder,
> But Banou lub him more dan his broder!"

Here the brawny nurse would souse him head over heels in the sparkling water, lift him up at every dip, rub his black nose all over him, making mock bites at the little legs and stomach; and, finally, holding him aloft, dripping, laughing, and struggling, go on with his refrain:

> "What will papa say when he sees him,
> Picaninny boy dat is sure to please him?
> Big Banou he rub and dress him,
> But little Henri he kick and pinch him!"

All this time the men seated forward on the deck, pegging away deep into their mess-kids, would pause occasionally, shake their great tarry fingers at the imp, and chuckle pleasantly with their mouths full of lobscouse, as if the urchin belonged to them as individual property.

"What a tidy little chap he'll make some of these days," said Ben, "a-furlin' the light sails in a squall! My eye! wouldn't I like to live and see him!"

"No, no, messmates," replied that worthy, as he crunched a biscuit and took a sip of coffee out of the pot, "that 'ere child will, some of these times, when he's growed a bit, be a-wearing gold swabs on his shoulders, and a-givin' his orders like a hadmiral of a fleet!"

"Quite right, my hearty! It'll never do for sich a knowin' little chub to spend his days along shore a-bilin' sugar-cane on a plantation, and a-footin' up accounts; for, ye mind, he was like the chip as was

> "'Born at sea, and his cradle a frigate,
> The boatswain he nursed him true blue;
> He'll soon learn to fight, drink, and jig it,
> And quiz every soul of the crew!'"

While these old salts were thus carving out a destiny for the youngster, the black gave him a·final souse in the tub, and then holding him up to drain, as it were, for the last time, exclaimed, while his face lighted up with pleasure,

"Oho, my little massa! what will papa say to-morrow when he sees his brave Henri?"

"Ah! how happy he will be, Banou!" said the lovely mother, who had just come on deck, as she kissed the mouth of the young scamp, while the black wrapped and dried his little naked body in a large towel.

"Ah! yes, my mistress, we all will be happy once more to get home to master on the plantation."

"Tell me! tell me, good *capitaine*," said she, turning in a pretty coquettish way to the skipper, "when shall we get in port?"

It was a sight to see her, in the loose white morning-gown folded in plaits about the swelling bosom, her slender waist clasped by a flowing blue sash, the dark brown satin bands of her hair confined by a large gold filigree pin, and half concealed by a jaunty little French cap, with the ribbons floating about her pear-shaped ears; and while her soft, dark hazel eyes were bent eagerly toward the solid old skipper, her round, rosy, dimpled fingers clasped a miniature locket fastened by a massive linked gold chain around her neck. Ah! she was a sight to see and love!

"Tell me, *mon cher Capitaine* Blunt, how many hours or minutes will it be before I shall behold my husband?"

The good-natured skipper laughed pleasantly at the eagerness of his beautiful passenger, and opening his hands wide, he gave vent to a long, low whistle, and replied,

"When the wind comes from good San Antonio, my Lady Bird—
when the sea-breeze makes—then the old brig will reel off the knots!
But see! just now not a breath to keep a tropic bird's wings out.
There, look at that fellow!"

High up in the heavens, two or three men-of-war birds, with wide-
spread pointed wings, and their swallow tails cut as sharp as knife-
blades, were heading seaward, and every little while falling in a rapid
sidelong plunge, as if in a vacuum, and then again giving an almost
imperceptible dash with their pinions as they recovered the lost space
and continued on in their silent flight.

"That's a sure sign, Madame Rosalie," continued the skipper,
"that the trade wind has blown itself out, and the chances are that
this hot sun will drink up the flying clouds, and leave us in a dead
calm till the moon quarters to-night. What say you, Mr. Binks? am
I right?"

"Never know'd you to be wrong, sir," said the mate, with an honest intonation of voice, as he tried to stare the sun out of countenance
in following the captain's glance.

"*Hélas!*" said the young mother, with a little sigh of sadness, as
she stood peering over the lee rail to the green hills and slopes of the
island, standing boldly out now with the lofty blue mountains cutting the sky ten thousand feet in mid-heaven; "so near, too; and he
is thinking and waiting for us!"

"Come," exclaimed the skipper, heartily, "the youngster wants
his breakfast!"

"WHEN THE WIND COMES FROM GOOD SAN ANTONIO, MY LADY-BIRD—"

CHAPTER III.

HIGH NOON.

> " No life is in the air, but in the waters
>> Are creatures huge, and terrible, and strong ;
> The swordfish and the shark pursue their slaughters ;
>> War universal reigns these depths along.
> The lovely purple of the noon's bestowing
>> Has vanished from the waters, where it flung
> A royal color, such as gems are throwing
>> Tyrian or regal garniture among."

High noon! Still the stanch old brig bowed and dipped her bluff bows into the long, easy swell of the tropics; the round, flat counter sent the briny bubbles sparkling away in the glare of the noontide sun; the sails flapped and chafed against the spars and rigging, while the crew sheltered themselves beneath the awnings, and dozed on peacefully.

Off to seaward a few dead trade-clouds showed their white bulging cheeks along the horizon, and occasionally a fluttering blue patch of a breeze would skim furtively over the backs of the rollers; but long before they reached the brig they had expended their force, and expired in the boundless calm.

Not so, however, with the large sail that had been seen from the brig in the early morning. For, with a lofty spread of kites and a studding-sail or two, she at times caught a flirting puff of air, and when the sun had passed the zenith she had approached within half a mile or less of the brig. There was no mistaking the stranger's character. Her taunt, trim masts, square yards, and clear, delicate black tracery of rigging, shadowed by a wide spread of snow-white canvas over the low, dark hull—which at every roll in the gentle undulations exposed a row of ports with a glance of white inner bulwarks—while the brass stars of her battery reflected sparks of fire from the blazing rays of the sun, showed she was a man-of-war.

"She's one of our cruisers, I think, sir," said the mate, as he handed the spy-glass to the captain; "but Ben here believes contrariwise, and says she is a French corvette."

"Have to try again, Mr. Binks; for, to my mind, she's an out-and-out Yankee sloop-of-war. Ay! there goes his colors up to the gaff! so up with our ensign, or else he'll be burning some powder for us."

Even while they were speaking a flag went rapidly up in a roll to the corvette's peak, when, shaking itself clear, it lay white and red, with a galaxy of white stars in a blue union, on the lee side of the spanker; while at the same instant a long, thin, coach-whip of a pennant unspun itself from the main truck, and hung motionless in the calm down the mast. Her decks were full of men, standing in groups under the shade of the sails to leeward; and on the poop were three or four officers in uniform and straw hats. One of these last stood for some time gazing at the brig—one hand resting on the ratlines of the mizzen shrouds, and the other slowly swinging a trumpet backward and forward. Presently an officer with a pair of gleaming epaulets on his shoulders mounted the poop ladder, touched his hat, and waved his hand toward the brig. A moment after—

"Brig ahoy!" came in a sharp, clear, manly tone through the trumpet.

"Sir?"

"What brig is that?"

"The 'Martha Blunt!' named after my dear old wife, God bless her! and myself, Jacob Blunt, God bless me!" added the jolly skipper, in a sotto voce chuckle to the fair passenger who stood beside him.

"Where are you from, and where bound?" came again through the trumpet.

"Bordeaux, and bound to Kingston. We have a free passport from Sir Robert Calder and Admiral Villeneuve."

There was a wave of the trumpet as the speaker finished hailing, and then touching his hat to the officer with the gold swabs, and pausing only a moment, he moved to the other side of the corvette's poop.

"It would be no more nor polite in him to tell us what his name is, arter all the questions he's axed."

"Don't ye know, Mr. Binks," broke in the captain, "that the dignity of a man-of-war is sich that it wouldn't be discreet to tell no more than that she has a cargo of cannon balls, and going on 'a cruise' any wheres? which ye may believe is as much valuable information as we might get out of our own calabashes without asking a question."

"You are allers right, Captain Blunt, but I did not tax my mind to think when I spoke them remarks," said Binks, deferentially.

The cruiser, however, seemed more communicative than the mate gave her credit for, and a moment after the officer with the trumpet sang out,

"This is the United States ship 'Scourge,' from Port Royal, bound on a cruise! Please report us."

And again, after a few words apparently with the officer with the epaulets, the trumpet was raised to his lips, and he asked, "Have you seen any vessels lately?"

The skipper was on the point of answering the hail, when his mate said, " Beg pardon, Captain Blunt, but Ben and me made out a fore-and-aft schooner airly this morning, with sweeps out, pulling in under the outermost headland there," pointing with his horny finger as he spoke.

" Nothing, sir, but a small schooner at daylight sweeping to windward."

" What ?" came back in a clear, quick note from the corvette.

" Small fore-and-after, sir, with sails down and sweeps out, close under the land."

In a moment two or three officers on the cruiser's deck put their heads together, several glasses were directed toward the now dim mirage-like shadow of the island, and the next instant the sharp ring of a boatswain's whistle was heard, followed by a gruff call of, " Away there ! Ariels, away !"

Immediately a cluster of sailors, in white frocks and trowsers and straw hats, sprang over the ship's quarter to the davits ; and then with a chirruping, surging pipe, a boat fell rapidly to the water. The falls were cast off, the cutter hauled np to the gangway, and soon an officer stepped over the side and tripped down to the boat. The white blades of the oars stood up on end in a double line, the boat pushed off, the oars fell with a single splash, and she steered for the brig. Descending down into the gentle valley of the long swell, she would disappear for an instant, till nothing but the white hats and feather blades of the oars were visible ; and again rising on the crest, the water flashed off in foam from her bows as she came dancing on.

In a few minutes the coxswain cried, " Way enough," and throwing up his hand with the word " Toss," the cutter shot swiftly alongside ; the boat-hooks of the bowmen brought her up with a sudden jar, and the next moment an officer with an epaulet on his right shoulder and a sword by his side stepped over the gangway. The skipper was there to receive him, to whom he touched his cap with his fore finger ; but as his eye glanced aft he saw a lady, and he gracefully removed his cap and bowed like a gentleman to her. He was a man of about eight-and-twenty, with a fine, manly, sailor-like figure and air, and with a pair of bright, determined gray eyes in his head that a rascal would not care to look into twice.

" I am the first lieutenant of the 'Scourge,' sir," he said, turning to the skipper, " and if you will step this way, I'll have a few words with you."

This was said in a careless tone of command, but withal with frankness and civility. The captain led him aft toward the taffrail, but in crossing the deck the little tot of a boy followed closely in his wake, and getting hold of the officer's sword, which trailed along by its belt-straps on the deck, he got astride of it, and seized on to the coat-skirts of the wearer. The little tug he gave caused the officer to turn round, and with a cheerful smile and manner he snatched the urchin up in his arms, kissed him on both cheeks, and as he put him down again and detached his sword for him to play with, he exclaimed,

"What a glorious little reefer you'll make one of these days! Won't you?"

"*Oui! oui! mon papa!*" said the little scamp, as he looked knowingly up in the officer's face.

"Excuse my little boy, sir," said his mother, who was in chase of him; and then turning to the child with a blush spreading over her lovely face, "It is not your papa, Henri! papa is in Kingston."

"Ah! madame, I love children. I had once a dear little fellow like this, but both he and his sweet mother are in heaven now. God bless them!"

A flush of sadness tinged his cheeks, and he passed his hand rapidly across his eyes, as if the dream was too sad to dwell upon; but changing his tone, and while with one hand he patted the little fellow's head, he went on: "Madame lives in Jamaica?"

"Oh yes; I was born there, but my parents were destroyed by an earthquake when I was quite a little child, and this good captain here carried my sister and myself to France soon after, where Monsieur—" here she hesitated and blushed with pleasure—"where I married my husband, who is a planter on the island. Perhaps you may know Monsieur Jules Piron?"

"Piron!" said the navy man, with warmth. "Ay, madame, for as fine a fellow as ever planted sugar! Know him? Why, madame, it is only a week ago that a lot of us dined with him at his estate of Escondide; you know it, madame? in the grand piazza which looks down the gorge. But he behaved very shabbily," said the officer, as his face lighted up gayly, "for he kept a spy-glass to his eye oftener than the wine-glass to his lips, in looking out seaward, and in talking of his wife and the little boy he had never seen."

"Oh, monsieur! you make me so happy," said the lovely woman, as with sparkling eyes and heaving bosom she cried, "Banou! Banou! this gentleman has just seen your good master."

The black, who had been standing near and guarding every movement of his little charge, who was trailing the sword about the deck, immediately approached the officer, and, falling on his knees, seized his hand and drew it toward his face.

"Ah! madame, I see that kindness meets with a return as well from a dark as a fair skin," said the officer, in a low tone, as he gently withdrew his hand from Banou's grasp.

"But," he continued, turning toward the skipper, as the clear sound of the cruiser's bell struck his ear, I must not forget what I came for."

"You say, captain, that you saw a schooner at daylight, eh? This way, if you please"—as he raised his cap to Madame Piron and walked over to the other side of the deck.. "What was she like?"

"She was reported to me by the mate," replied Jacob Blunt.

"Please send for him."

"Oh! Mr.—a'—"

"Binks, sir," said that individual, touching his hat and making an awkward scrape at a bow.

"Well, Mr. Binks, did you clearly make out the vessel you saw this morning under the land?"

"Can't say exactly, sir, as·I did; but Ben Brown there was on the fore-yard, and he got a good squint at her."

"Ah! can I see the man?"

The mate straightway went forward, and, after a few pokes about the lee waist, Ben was roused out from under the jolly-boat and came rolling aft.

"*You* saw the schooner, eh?" said the lieutenant, as if he was in the habit of asking sharp questions and getting quick answers.

"Yes, sir," said the squat seaman, as he hitched up his knife-belt, and wiped his mouth with the back of his hand, and took off his cap.

"Where?"

"Here away, sir," with a wave of his paw, "just clear of that bluff foreland where the gap opens with the Blue Mountain."

"How was she rigged?"

"Bare sticks, sir, not much of a bowsprit, and no sail spread. I see her first by the flash of her sweeps in the rising sun, as she was heading about sou'-sou'-east into the land."

"Two masts, you say?"

"Ay, sir; but I thought as 'ow there was a jigger-like yard a-sticking out over her starn, though I wasn't sartin."

"So!" said the lieutenant, in a musing tone, and with rather a grave face and compressed lip; "that will do; thank you, my man." Then placing his hand on the skipper's shoulder, he drew him to one side, out of ear-shot, and said,

"Captain Blunt, are you much acquainted in these latitudes?"

"Oh yes, sir, me and my old brig are regular traders here, from Bordeaux to Jamaica, and so home to England."

"No treasure, I presume?" went on the officer, with a smile.

"Why, lieutenant, none to speak of, p'raps; just a handful of dollars and a guinea or two in the bag for a few sacks of sugar or coffee, or a pipe of rum, or sich like, on my own account."

"Well, my friend, there is probably nothing to fear, but if the breeze springs up, keep as close to the corvette as you can, and I shall ask the captain to keep a look-out for you during the night."

"By the way"—the officer continued in a low tone as he moved toward the gangway—"in case any thing should happen, you had better hoist a lantern at your peak or in the main-rigging—we have sharp eyes for ugly customers,. and one or two of them have been particularly troublesome of late hereabouts."

Turning for a moment to bid adieu to the fair lady passenger on the quarter-deck, and recovering his sword after a playful struggle with the youngster, he buckled it around his waist, and, stepping lightly over the side and into the boat, the oars fell with a single splash, and the cutter shot rapidly away toward the corvette.

CHAPTER IV.

SUNSET.

"Light is amid the gloomy canvas spreading,
  The moon is whitening the dusky sails,
From the thick bank of clouds she masters, shedding
  The softest influence that o'er night prevails.
Pale is she, like a young queen pale with splendor,
  Haunted with passionate thoughts too fond, too deep;
The very glory that she wears is tender,
  The very eyes that watch her beauty fain would weep."

Not a breath from the lungs of Æolus. The sun went down like a globe of fire; but just as it touched the horizon it flattened out into an oval disk, and, sinking behind a dead, slate-colored cloud, shot up half a dozen broad rose and purple bands, expanding as they mounted heavenward, and then fading away in pearly-tinted hues in the softening twilight until it mingled in the light of the half moon nearly at the zenith. There lay the island, too, now all clear again, with the blue tops of the mountains marked in pure distinct outline, and falling away from peak to peak on either hand, till the sea flashed up in sluggish creamy foam at the base. The man-of-war birds came floating in from seaward, high up, like black musquitoes, with their pointed wings wide spread and heading toward the land, but now with never a quiver to their silent pinions. A school of porpoises, too, broke water from the opposite direction, and, crossing and recrossing each other's track, came leaping and puffing over the gentle swells until they struck the brig's wake, when they wheeled around her bows, dashed off on a swift visit to the corvette, and then, closing up in watery phalanx, went gamboling, leaping, and breaking water again to windward. Presently, along the eastern horizon, the banks of clouds, which had been lying dead and motionless all the sultry day, seemed to be imbued with life, and, separating in their fleecy masses, mounted up above the sea, and soon spread out, like a lady's fan, in all directions.

"Ho! ho!" shouted Captain Blunt, clapping his hands, "what said I, Madame Rosalie, when we saw the sun setting up his lee backstays a while ago? A breeze, eh? Come, Mr. Binks, be wide awake! We shall be bowling off the knots before the watch is out."

The mate caught the enthusiasm of the skipper, and, jumping up on the break of the deck cabin, he sang out,

"D'ye hear there, lads? give us a good pull of the topsail halliards, and round in them starboard braces a bit! That's your sort! Well, the head yards! That'll do with the main! Up with the flying jib, and trim aft them starboard jib and staysail sheets! There! Belay all."

Meanwhile the corvette, with her lofty dimity kissing the sky, caught the first light airs before the slightest ripple darkened the surface of the water; and with her helm a-starboard, and her after yards braced sharp up, she silently swung round on her heel, while the spanker came flat aft, like a sheet of white paper, and with the headsails trimmed, she slowly moved athwart the stern of the brig. The sharp whistles of the boatswain and his mates, piping like goldfinches, were the only sounds that were heard; and as the cruiser moved on in her course, the declining moon cast a mellow light over the folds of her canvas, and, like a girl in bridal attire, she threw a graceful shadow over the smooth and swelling waters away off to windward.

The sails of the brig, which had begun to swell out in easy drooping lines, fell back again flat to the masts as the ship crossed her wake. But as the corvette passed, the officer of the watch on the poop raised his cap to the lovely woman who was standing out in graceful relief on the upper cabin deck, with her little boy held up beside her in the sturdy arms of the black, and placing the trumpet to his lips, said, in a distinct voice, as if addressing the skipper,

"We shall go about at midnight. Remember the directions I gave you this morning. *Bon voyage, madame!*" He shook his trumpet playfully at the boy, who put out his chubby arms with delight to the speaker, and then hammered away with great glee on the crown of his bearer's head.

"Thank you, sir," said Captain Blunt, who was leaning over the rail; and then turning to his mate, he added,

"Them Yankees, Mr. Binks, always treats a merchantman like gentlemen on the high seas, and I never knew one on 'em to turn their backs on friends or foes. What a pity they ever cut adrift from the Old Country! Howsoever, matey, it can't be helped, and you had better up with the port studding-sails, hang out all the rags, and make the old drogher walk."

Now came the rippling breeze all at once over the sea, fluttering furtively for a minute or two, so as to make the topsails of the brig swell out and then fall back in a tremulous shiver; but again bulging forward in a full-breasted curve, the vessel felt the tug, and began to dash the spray from her bluff bows till it fell away beyond the lee cathead in flying masses of foam. The studding-sail booms rolled out, the sailors busied themselves aloft in making the additional sail, and by-and-by the old brig floundered along, the bubbles gurgling out ahead in the ruflled water, tipping over astern as the crests broke on her quarter; at times plunging her bows into the rolling swell, but coming up sturdily again, and so on as before.

Meanwhile the corvette had edged away in a parallel course with the brig, running past her at first as if she were at anchor, when she let her topgallant-sails slide down to the caps, and, with the weather clew of her mainsail triced up, she held way with the brig a mile or more to windward.

The moon was sinking well down in the west, and the clear, well-defined crescent was occasionally obscured by the light fleecy clouds moving under the influence of the trade wind, when, toward eight bells, the moon gave one pure white glimmer, threw a rippling flood of light over the waves, and sunk below the horizon. Still the stars twinkled and the planets flamed out like young moons—masked at intervals by the darkening clouds as they swept overhead in heavy masses—and tinging the sea with shade, which would again break out in phosphorescent flashes as the waves caught the reflection.

"Now, Madame Rosalie," said the kind old skipper, "it is nearly midnight; take your last snooze in the old barky, and wake up bright and happy for Port Royal and—you know who, in the morning."

The charming woman had been watching, with soul-rapt gaze, the lofty hills of Jamaica from the last blaze of the setting sun, and until the moon too had vanished and left only a dim blue haze over the island. She started as the captain spoke, gave a deep sigh, kissed her hand to the good old skipper, said "*Bon soir, mon ami*," and with a smile she entered her cabin.

The black was seated within the partition of the apartment, a small swinging cot, urging it gently to and fro, and watching over his little charge.

"Good-night, Banou," she said, in patois French; "you may go to bed, and I will take care of my little boy."

The black grinned so as to show his double range of white teeth beneath the rays of the cabin lamp, and without a word he moved silently away. The lady stood for a few moments gazing lovingly at the sleeping child, and then drawing the miniature from her bosom, she detached it with the chain from her neck, and after pressing it to her lips, she leaned softly over the cot and fastened it around the little sleeper. As light and zephyr-like as was the effort, it caused the little fellow to stir, and reaching out his tiny arms, while a baby smile played around the dimples of his cheeks, he clasped his mother's neck.

Ah! fond and devoted mother! That was the last sweet infantile caress your child was ever destined to give you! Treasure it up in joy and sorrow, in sunshine and gloom, for long, long years will pass before you press him to your heart again!

CHAPTER V.

DARKNESS.

"The busy deck is hushed, no sounds are waking
  But the watch pacing silently and slow;
The waves against the sides incessant breaking,
  And rope and canvas swaying to and fro.
The topmost sail, it seems like some dim pinnacle
  Cresting a shadowy tower amid the air;
While red and fitful gleams come from the binnacle,
  The only light on board to guide us—where?"

On went the "Martha Blunt" with no fears of danger near. The bell struck eight, the watch had been called, and the captain, taking a satisfactory look all around the horizon, glanced at the compass, and, with a slight yawn, said,

"Well, Mr. Binks, I believe I'll turn in for a few hours; keep the brig on her course, and at daylight call me. It will be time enough then to bend the cables, for I don't think we shall want the anchors much afore noon to-morrow. Where's the corvette?"

"There she is, sir, away off on the port beam. She made more a few minutes ago, and now she appears to be edging off the wind, and steering across our forefoot. I s'pose she's enjoying of herself, sir, and exercisin' the crowds of chaps they has on board them craft."

"Well, good-night, matey"—pausing a moment, however, as the honest old skipper stepped down the companion-way, and half communing with himself, and then, with his head just above the slide, he added, "I say, Mr. Binks, there's no need, p'r'aps, but you may as well have a lantern alight and bent on to the ensign halliards there under the taffrail, in case you want to signalize the corvette. Ah, Banou! that you, old nigger? Good-night!"

So Captain Blunt went slowly down below, and at the same time the black went aft, coiled himself down on the deck, and made a pillow of the brig's ensign.

Mr. Binks wriggled himself upon the weather-rail, where, with a short pipe in his mouth, he kicked his heels against the bulwarks, and while the old brig plunged doggedly on, he indulged himself with a song, the air, however, being more like the growl of a bull-dog than a specimen of music:

> "If lubberly landsmen, to gratitude strangers,
>   Still curse their unfortunate stars;
> Why, what would they say did they try but the dangers
>   Encounter'd by true-hearted tars?
> If life's vessel they put 'fore the wind, or they tack her,
>   Or whether bound here or there,
> Give 'em sea-room, good-fellowship, grog, and tobaker,
>   Well, then, damme if Jack cares where!"

"What d'ye think of that, Ben?" said Mr. Binks, as he finished his ditty, and sucked away on his pipe.

"Why, Mr. Mate," replied Ben, as he gave the wheel a spoke or two to windward and glanced at the binnacle, "the words is first-rate, but it seems to me your singing gear is a bit out o' condition, and I thought you wos a prayin'; but the fact is," concluded Ben, apologetically, "that whenever I hears grog and tobaker jined together, I likes to see them in my fist."

"Oh! you would, eh? Well, shipmate, turn and turn about is fair play; so here, just take a pull at the pipe, and I'll step to the cuddy for the bottle, and we'll have a little sniffler all around!"

Saying this, Mr. Binks swung off the rail, handed Ben the pipe, and after an absence of a few moments, he returned with a square case-bottle and a pewter mug.

"Now, Ben," said he, "this 'ere is not a practice, as you know, I often is guilty of; but you bein' a keerful hand and a stiddy helmsman, and port here close aboard, I've no objections to take a toss with ye." Then pouring out a moderate quantity of the fluid, the mate handed it to Ben, who, taking the pipe out of his mouth, and with one hand on the king-spoke of the wheel and one eye at the compass card, threw his head back and pitched the dram down his throat.

"My sarvice to ye, sir!" said Ben, as he smacked his lips and then shut them tight together, fearful lest a breath of the precious liquid might escape; "a little of that stuff goes a great ways."

Mr. Binks hereupon measured himself off an allowance, and touching Ben on the shoulder, raised the pewter to his lips. Before, however, draining the cup, he tuned his pipes once more, and croaked forth in this strain:

> "While up the shrouds the sailor goes,
>   Or ventures on the yard,
> The landsman, who no better knows,
>   Believes his lot is hard.
> But Jack with smiles each danger meets;
>   Casts anchor, heaves the log,
> Trims all the sails, belays the sheets,
>   And drinks his can of grog!"

"Here comes the corvette, sir!" broke in Ben, as he stood on tip-toe, holding on to the spokes of the wheel, and taking his eyes off the binnacle a moment to get a clear view over the rail. "Here she comes, with her starboard tacks aboard, athwart our bow, and moving like an albatross!"

The man-of-war had for an hour or more crept well to windward, and then, wearing round, she came down close upon the wind under royals, and her three jibs and spanker as flat as boards. As she whirled on across the brig's bow, a few cables' length ahead, the sharp ring of the whistles was again heard, and the moment after the head-sails fluttered and shook in the wind, the sheets and blocks · rattled, and with a clear order of "Mainsail haul!" the after-yards swung round like magic, the sails filled, and without losing headway the head-yards were swung, and she gathered way on the other tack. On she came, with the spray flying up into the weather leech of her foresail, the dark mazes of her rigging marked out in clear lines against her white canvas, and the watch noiselessly coiling up the ropes on her decks. As she pushed her sharp snout through the water, and grazed along the brig's lee quarter, an officer on the poop gave a rapid and searching glance around, peered sharply along the brig's deck, waved his trumpet to the mate, and resumed his rapid tramp to windward. In ten minutes after she had passed the brig's wake nothing was seen of her save a dark, dim outline; a light halo reflected on the water from her white streak, and an occasional luminous flash of foam as it bounded away from her lean bows.

Half an hour went by. The mate was sitting on the weather rail droning out an old sea-song to himself, and the four or five men of the watch were dozing away along the bulwarks. Presently, however, Ben, the helmsman, happened to let his eyes wander away from the compass-card for a moment, as he steadied the wheel by his legs and bit a quid from his plug of niggerhead to last him to suck for the remainder of the watch, when, glancing beneath the bulging folds of the lee clew of the mainsail, he clapped both hands again on the steering spokes, and shouted,

"Mr. Mate, here's a sail close under our lee beam!"

"Where?" said Binks. But, before he had fairly time to run over to the other side of the vessel and take a look for himself, a quick rattle of oars was heard as a boat grated against the brig's side, and, before you could think, a swarm of fellows started up like so many shadows above the rail. In five seconds they had jumped on the deck, Ben fell like a bullock from a blow from the butt-end of a pistol, the helm was jammed hard down, the lee braces let fly, and, as the old brig gave a lurching yaw in bringing her nose to windward, the weather leeches shivered violently in the wind, and, taking flat aback, the studding-sail booms snapped short off at the irons, and, with the sails, fell slamming and thumping below.

Meanwhile the mate had barely time to spring to the companion-

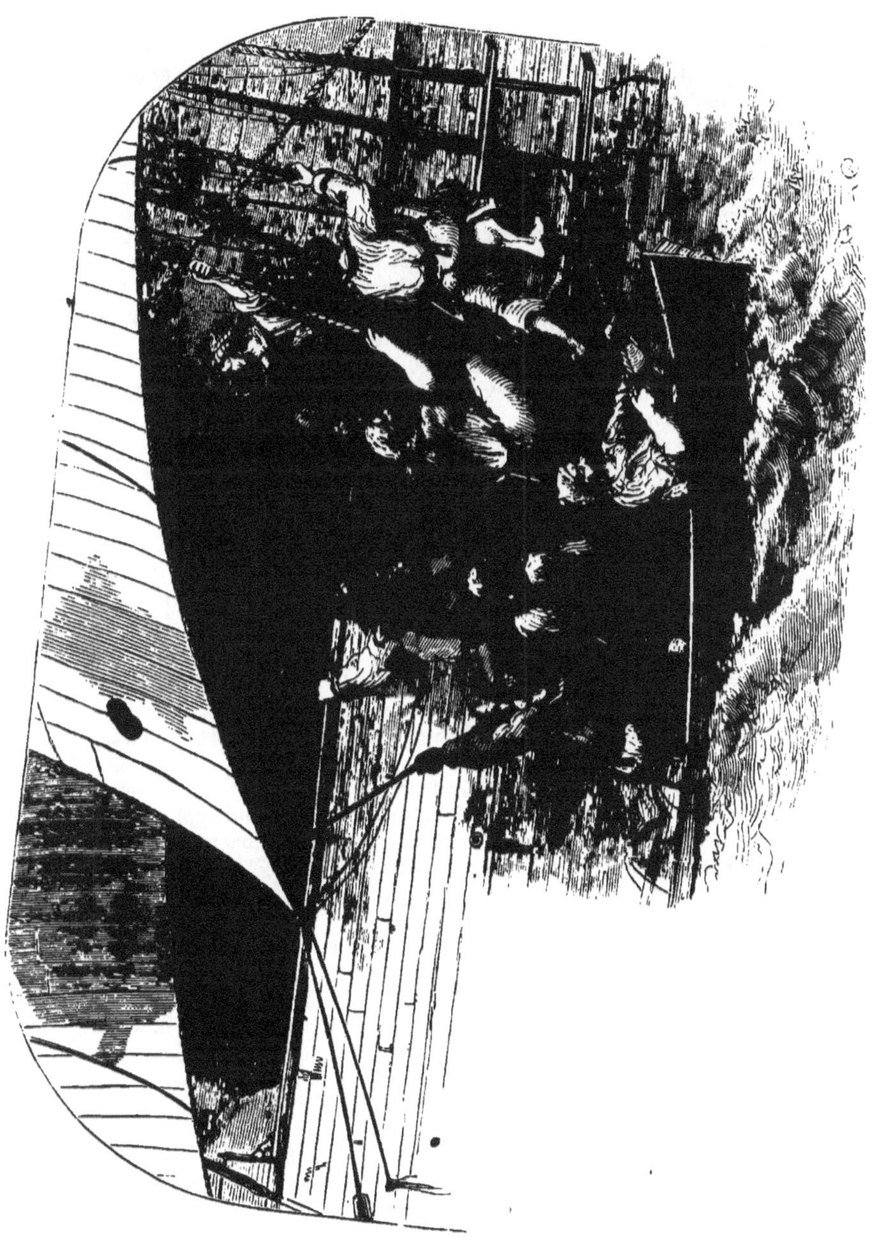

way and sing out, "We're boarded by pirates, Captain Blunt!" when he, too, received an ugly overhand lick from a cutlass on his skull, and went senseless and bleeding down the hatchway like a scuttle of coals.

At the first noise, however, the black Banou sprang to his feet, and, as he caught a glimpse of the fellows swarming over the side, he snatched hold of the ensign halliards where the signal lantern had been bent on, and in an instant it was dancing away up to the gaff, shrouded from view to leeward of the vessel by the spread of the spanker. In another moment the black leaped to the deck cabin and darted through the door. But in less time than it has taken to tell it, the "Martha Blunt" had changed hands.

There, on the quarter-deck, stood in groups some sixteen barefooted villains, in coarse striped gingham shirts, loose trowsers, and skullcaps, and all with glittering, naked knives or cutlasses, and pistols in their belts and hands. In the midst of this cluster of swarthy wretches, near the companion-way, stood a burly, square-built ruffian, with a pistol in his right hand, and his dexter paw pushing up a brown straw hat as he ran his fingers across his dripping forehead and a tangled mass of carroty, unshorn locks. There was a wisp of a red silk kerchief tied in a single knot around his bare bull neck; the shirt was thrown back, and exposed a tawny, hairy chest, as a ray of light flashed up from the binnacle. He looked—as indeed he was—the lowest type of a sailor scoundrel. His companions were of lighter build, and their dress, complexion, and manner—to say nothing of their black hair and rings in their ears—indicated a birth and breeding in other and hotter climes.

"Well, my lads," said the big fellow, who seemed to be in command, "the barkey is ours, and we've cheated that infarnal cruiser handsomely. Go forward, Pedro, and gag them lubbers, and then tell the boys to trim aft them jib sheets; and round in them afterbraces, some of you, so we can keep way with the schooner and take things easy."

Here he laughed in a husky, spirituous, low chuckle, and then went on: "This will make up for lost time, *amigos! Christo!* there may be some ounces on board. But who's left in the boat, Gomez?" This was addressed to a bow-legged, beetle-browed individual, with a hare-lip, which kept his face in a perpetual and skeleton-like grin, who hissed out from between his decayed front tusks,

"*El Doctor Senor, con tres de nosotros.*" "*Bueno!* all right; three of the chaps will do to look out for her; but tell the doctor to drop the boat astern, and veer him a rope from the gangway. There! that's well! with the braces! Keep her off a point; so—that'll do."

As the orders were promptly obeyed, and the crew of the brig gagged, and the vessel surged slowly on her course, the same speaker turned to his men and said,

"Now, my hearties! let's have an overhaul of the skipper. Hand him up here, will ye? or, never mind," he added, "I'll just step down and have a growl with him myself."

As the mate pitched head foremost down the companion ladder, two of the pirates jumped after him, and, dealing him another cruel stab with a knife deep into the back, they passed on into the lower cabin. There was a brief struggle, the sound of voices mingled with curses and threats, and then all quiet again.

In pursuance of his expressed purpose, the stout ruffian slewed himself round, took a sweep about the horizon, then sticking his pistol in its belt, he slowly descended the ladder, gave the wounded and dying mate a kick, and with a hoarse laugh entered the cabin.

There, on a small sofa abaft, between the two stern air-ports, sat Captain Blunt. Blood was trickling down in heavy drops from a lacerated bruise on his forehead; but, notwithstanding the swelling and pain of the wound, his features were calm, stern, and honest. On either side of him sat as villainous a brace of mongrel Portuguese or Spaniards as ever infested the high seas; and his arms were pinioned by a stout cord to the bolt above the transom.

"My sarvice to you, sir!" said the leader of the gang, with a devilish smile of derision, as he stuck his arms akimbo and squirted some tobacco-juice from his filthy mouth across the cabin table at the pinioned prisoner.

"I s'pose you know by this time that you're a lawful prize, captured by an hindependent constable of the West Indies, notwithstandin' ye had sich safe escort and convoy all the arternoon?"

Here he chuckled, squirted more juice over the table, then dropped down on a sea-chest cleated to the deck, took off his hat, and scratched his yellowish red hair. The poor captain said not a word, but shook a great clot of blood from his brow.

"Well, now, my old hearty, the first thing for you to do is to poke out your manifest, and any other little matters of vallew ye may have stowed away; and be quick, mind ye, for you haven't much time to sail in this 'ere craft. Howsoever, I s'pose ye can swim?"

"You'll find the manifest and the ship's papers there, inside that instrument-box; and all the money in the vessel is in that locker; and I trust in Heaven it may burn your hands to cinders, you devils!"

"Ho! smash my brains! keep a stopper on your jaw, or I'll squeeze your dead carcass through that 'ere starn port."

The fellow rose as he spoke, and, stepping up to the narrow state-cabin near by, he jerked open the upper drawer of a small bureau affair, and pulling out a canvas bag, sealed at the mouth, tossed it on to the cabin table. The coin fell with the heavy dead sound peculiar to gold, and the ruffian, after taking it up again and weighing it tenderly, growled out, "This chink will do for a yapper, at any rate! So now let's have a peep at what the cargo consists on."

Then stepping a second time to the berth, he gave a kick to the instrument-box, the lid flew off, and diving in his fist he drew out a bundle of papers. Once more seating himself at the table beneath the swinging lamp, he clumsily undid the papers and spread them before him.

"What a blessed thing is edication," muttered he to himself, "and what a power o' knowledge reading 'riting does for a man!" Putting his fat stumpy finger on each line of the manuscript as he slowly began to spell out the contents, he began, "Man-i-fest of Brig 'Martha Blunt'—Ja-cob Blunt, master;" here he paused, and, squirting more tobacco-juice over at the skipper, as if to attract his attention, he suddenly ejaculated, "Hark ye! Master Blunt, what was the name of that man-o'-war vessel as was lyin' by you this morning?"

"The 'Scourge,'" replied the skipper, faintly, as he shook another great drop of blood from his brow.

"The what? The 'Scourge!' That Yankee snake! Smash my brains! D'ye know that that ship has been a hangin' about the north side of Cuba for ever so long, interruptin' our trade? And you an Englishman, to go and ax him to purtect ye! take that!"

Here he snatched a pistol from his sash, and, taking aim full at the skipper's breast, he pulled the trigger. Fortunately, the weapon snapped and did not explode. The ruffian held it a moment in his hand, and then letting it rest upon the table, he said, with a horrible imprecation,

"Ye see you wos not born to be shot; but we'll try what salt water will do for ye by-and-by."

Taking out his knife at the conclusion of this speech, he picked the flint of his pistol, opened the pan, shook the priming, and then shoved the weapon back in his belt. The mention of the "Scourge," however, had evidently caused him some trepidation, for when he resumed the perusal of the manifest it was in a hurried, agitated sort of way, and not at all at his ease.

Smoothing the papers again before him, he went on, making running commentaries as he read: "Eighty-six cases of silks—light, and easily stowed away; twenty-nine tons bar iron; sixty-four sugar-kettles! it will help to sink the brig; forty pipes of Bordeaux; two hundred baskets Champagne; three hundred and fifty boxes of claret—sour stuff, I warrant you; two casks Cognac brandy—but I say, you Blunt," said the fellow, looking up, "where's your own private bottle? It's thirsty work spellin' out all this 'ritin', and my mouth's as dry as a land-crab's claws. Howsoever," he continued, as he caught the glance of satisfaction which came over the swarthy faces of his companions beside the captain, "wait a bit, and we'll punch a hole in a fresh barrel presently."

Having run through the manifest, he opened another paper and exclaimed, "Hallo! what have we here? List of passengers—Madame Rosalie Piron and—ho! that's a French piece, I knows by the name. Where is she? Hasn't died on the v'yage, has she? D'ye hear there, ye infarnal Blunt?"

The captain's face was troubled, and his head dropped down on his breast without replying; but one of the scoundrels at his side struck him a brutal blow with the back of his knife-hilt on the mouth, and jerking up, he said, with an effort,

"Yes, we have a female passenger on board, with a helpless child; but I pray you, in God's name, to leave the innocent woman in peace. You've robbed and ruined me and my poor old wife—turn me adrift if you like, drown or hang me, but don't harm the poor lady."

The tears blinded him as he spoke, and mingled with the bloody stream which trickled down his cheeks. The ruffian's ugly-face and bloodshot eyes lighted up with a devilish and sinister satisfaction as the skipper began his appeal, but before he had well finished speaking he broke in,

"Avast your jaw! will ye? You'll have enough to look out for your own gullet, my lad, without mindin' any body else's; so turn to and say your prayers afore eight bells is struck, because there's sharks off Jamaiky."

Then addressing his own scoundrelly myrmidons, he exclaimed, "Look out sharp for that old chap, my lads, while I goes to sarch for the woman passenger!" As he turned, however, to leave the cabin, one of his subordinates began to rummage about in a locker, when the burly brute said, "Tonio, don't get to drinkin' too airly, boy, for ye know it's agin the law till the prize is snug in harbor, or sunk, as the case may be."

"*Si, señor,*" replied the man, with a nod and a grin, and he resumed his seat again; but no sooner had their leader left the cabin than a bottle and glasses were placed upon the table, and they fell to with a will, complimenting the bound and wounded prisoner by pitching the last drops from their tumblers into his face.

CHAPTER VI.

DANGER.

"What tale do the roaring ocean
  And the night wind, bleak and wild,
As they beat at the crazy casement,
  Tell to that little child?
And why do the roaring ocean
  And the night wind, wild and bleak,
As they beat at the heart of the mother,
  Drive the color from her cheek?"

IN all this time so little noise had been made that even the watch below, in the brig's forecastle, were snoozing away without a dream of danger; though, had one of them shown his nose above the fore-peak, he would have either been knocked down and murdered like the mate, or, with a gag in his jaws, been hurled overboard. When the leader of the pirates stepped again on deck, he said to his companions, who were still clustered around the companion-way,

"Well, my boys, we have 'arned a good prize—a fine cargo of the real stuff—silks, wines, and what not, besides a few of the shiners!" Here he jingled the bag of gold and dollars in his paws, and then threw it, with an easy, indifferent toss, on to the slide of the companion-way.

"But what think ye, lads?" he continued, in a hoarse whisper, "there's a petticoat aboard! and, as sure as my name's Bill Gibbs, here goes for a look; for there's nothing like lamplight for the love-ly creeturs!"

As he slewed round on his bare feet to approach the entrance to the deck cabin, a move was made in the same direction by two or three of the wretches of his band; but, shoving them roughly back with his heavy fist, and clapping a hand to his belt, he said, in a threatening tone,

"None o' that, my souls! I takes the first look myself; and if I think her beauty'll suit the chief, why—I shall be able to judge, ye know, whether she'll go furder on the cruise or swim ashore with the rest of the lubbers at daylight to Jamaiky. Keep your eye on the schooner, Pedro, and don't make no more sail! D'ye hear?"

"Ay, ay, *si señor!*" quoth that worthy, as he and his followers fell sulkily back. It took but three strides for Mr. Bill Gibbs to reach the cabin door, when, finding it hard to open, after several trials at

C

. the knob, he placed his burly shoulder against the edge of the panel-work, and, throwing his powerful weight upon it, the door yielded with a snap of the lock, and he pitched forward full length upon the cabin floor. The noise startled the lady within, and speaking as if half asleep, she called,

"Banou! Banou! what is the matter?"

"*Mon dieu, madame!* we are prisoners in the hands of pirates!"

Before more words were uttered, Mr. Bill Gibbs, who by this time had regained his feet while giving vent to a volley of blasphemous curses, roared out as he beheld the black, "Ho! nigger passengers, hay? A mounseer of color, as I'm a Christian! I say, cucumber shins, is that 'ere woman as is talkin' as black as you be?"

He was not left long in doubt concerning the color of the person he alluded to, for at the instant the state-room door flew open, and the lovely woman, in her loose night-dress and hair streaming in brown, heavy silken tresses over her fair neck and shoulders, with a pale and terror-stricken face, stood before him. Speechless with agony, she gazed at the coarse ruffian, who had, at the moment, reached the swinging cot which held the little boy, and while he was in the act of looking at the sleeping child, the mother uttered a fearful cry and the boy awoke.

"Sarvice, madam! don't be scared! come and take the little chap! I ain't goin' to hurt him—that is, if it be a him."

The frightened mother, spell-bound at first, needed no second bidding, and, forgetful of her disheveled dress, sprang forward, and with outstretched arms, bare to the shoulder, was about to snatch her child. The pirate, however, with his red eyes gleaming with unholy fire, threw his great arm around the lovely woman's waist, and with a hoarse, fiendish chuckle of triumph, attempted to draw her toward him. But, quick as lightning, two black, sinewy paws clutched him with such a steel-like grip about the throat that his sacrilegious arm dropped by his side, and he was hurled violently back against the cabin bulkhead. Then standing before him, the negro glared like an angry lion roused from his lair as he looked round inquiringly at his mistress.

"Ho!" sputtered the ruffian, as he pulled a pistol from his belt, "ho!" you mean fight, do ye?"

"*Banou! mon pauvre Banou!*" screamed the terrified woman. "Yield! Oh, sir, spare him! Don't harm us, and we will give you all we possess!"

The burly scoundrel hesitated a moment, and balanced the cocked pistol in his hand, as if undecided whether to blow the black's brains out on the spot where he stood; and then shoving the weapon back in his sash, and keeping a wary eye on his assailant, he exclaimed in an angry tone,

"Well, come here, then, my deary, and give us a kiss for this nigger's bad manners."

Moving forward as he spoke, he caught up the little boy from the cot, tore the gold chain and locket from his neck, which he thrust into his pocket, and shook him roughly at arm's length, in hopes, perhaps, of enticing the tender mother within his merciless grasp. But again the black interposed his heavy frame before his mistress.

"What! at it again, are ye? Well, then"—fumbling with his left hand for his pistol—"say your prayers, ye imp of darkness."

The black seemed, however, in no mood for praying; and putting forth his slabs of arms like the paws of an alligator, he tried to grapple his foe by the throat. The cries of the mother now mingled with those of the child as he put out his little arms to shield his black protector. The ruffian, foiled in his purpose, with baffled rage evaded the negro by stepping to one side; and as he did so, he hurled the helpless child with great force from him. The large cabin windows at the stern were open to let in the breeze'; and as the brig sank slowly down with her counter to the following waves, and gurgled up as the sea eddied and surged around the rudder, the faint, plaintive cry of the little boy arose above the seething waters—a light splash followed—and the mother had lost her child!

"Oh, monster!" cried the heart-broken woman. "Oh, my boy! my boy! May Heaven curse you forever!" as she sank down senseless on the deck.

The awful howl of vengeance which burst from the deep lungs of Banou came simultaneously with the report of the pirate's pistol, the bullet from which struck the black hard in the left shoulder; but putting out for the third time his sinewy arms, and this time with an iron grip that only left the ruffian time to yell with a stifled curse for help, he was hurled headlong, smashing through the latticed cabin door, and fell stunned upon the outer deck. In an instant half a dozen pistol balls whistled around the negro's head, and the knives of the pirates flashed from their sashes as they rushed forward to bury the blades in his body; but leaping to one side, and while two more bullets were driven into him, he seized an iron-shod pump brake from the bulwarks, and, with a mighty bound, whirled it once with the rapidity of thought high above his head, and brought it down on the leg of his prostrate foe. Such was the force of the blow that it smashed both bones, and drove the white splinters through the brute's trowsers, where they gleamed out red and bloody by the light of the binnacle lamp. Even then, wounded, and the blood flowing from several places, and though almost encircled in the grasp of the scoundrels, Banou made good his retreat to the cabin, and planted his powerful body firmly against the door.

With a volley of polyglot curses and yells in all languages, two or three of the pirates stopped to raise their fallen leader, while the others, leaving the wheel and vessel to herself, rushed in pursuit of the black. Scarcely, however, had they made a step, when their ears were saluted by a stunning crash from a heavy cannon, and the peculiar humming sound of a round shot as it flew just above their heads between the brig's masts.

There, within half a cable's length to windward, loomed up the dark hull of a large ship. The crew were evidently at quarters, with the battle lanterns lit and gleaming in the ports, while the rays shot up the black rigging and top-hamper, and spread out over the sails in fitful flashes as she slowly forged abreast the brig, with her main top-sail to the mast. For a minute not a sound was heard, though the decks were full of men, some with their heads poked out of the open ports beside the guns, or swarming along over the lee hammock nettings and about the quarter boats; but the next instant there came in a voice of thunder through the trumpet,

"What's the matter on board that brig?"

There was no answer for a few seconds, until a choking voice, as if with a pump-bolt athwart the speaker's mouth, mumbled out,

"We're captured by pi—"

A dull, heavy blow cut short these words; and though the reply to the hail could hardly have been heard on board the ship, yet, as if divining the true state of the case, loud, clear orders were given—

"Away, there, third and fourth cutters! away! Spring, men!"

Then came the surging noise of the whistles as the falls dropped the boats from the davits; then the men, leaping down into cutters—silently and quick—no sound save the clash of a cutlass or the rattle of an oar-blade as they took their places and shoved off. Again an order through the trumpet—

"Clear away the starboard battery! Load with grape! Sail trimmers! stations for wearing ship! Hard up the helm! Fill away the main-yard!"

The "Scourge" had by this time forged ahead of the brig, her sails aback or shivering, as she came up and fell off from the wind, and the boats dancing with full crews toward her. No sooner, however, had the presence of the unwelcome stranger been made known on board the brig than the pirates seemed seized with a panic, and, without a second thought, they scudded to leeward, where their boat had been hauled alongside, and forgetful or indifferent for the fate of their companions below, though dragging the while their maimed comrade to the rail, they lowered him into the boat, jumped in themselves, and pulled away with all their strength toward the schooner near. They were not, however, a moment too soon; for as the last of the band disappeared, their places were supplied by a crowd of nimble sailors to windward, headed by an officer with his sword between his teeth as he swung over the bulwarks. The first sound which greeted the new-comers was from below, and from the throat of the honest skipper. Down the open companion-way leaped the officer, with half a dozen stout, eager sailors at his heels, and dashed right into the lower cabin. There was the brave old skipper, with but one arm free, shielding himself and struggling—faint and well-nigh exhausted—from the knives of the drunken brace of rascals who had been left to guard him. A pistol in the hands of one of this pair was pointed with an unsteady aim at the officer as he entered, but the ball struck the empty rum-bottle on the table and flew wide of its mark; and before the smoke of the powder had cleared away, a sword and cutlass had passed through and through both their bodies, and they fell dead upon the cabin floor.

While Captain Blunt found breath to give a rapid explanation of the trouble, and while the brig was once more got under control and the wounded cared for, we will take a look at the man-of-war and the part she bore in the business.

At the first sound of the warning gun from the cruiser the schooner began to show life; and drawing her head sheets, she wore short round on her heel, with every thing ready to run up her fore and aft sails, and a stay-tackle likewise rove and hanging over the low gunwale to hook on to the boat and hoist it in the moment it came alongside. Meanwhile the "Scourge" had shot ahead of the brig, and wearing round her fore-foot, with her starboard tacks on board, she emerged out beyond, like a hound just slipped from the leash. As she cleared the brig, the schooner lay with bare masts about three cables' length to windward, and the rattle of oars told that her boat had just scraped alongside. At that moment a clear, determined voice shouted through the trumpet,

"Level your guns! Take good aim! Fire!"

A brilliant series of sheets of flame burst forth from the corvette's battery, lighting up the water and jet black wales, and away aloft to the great towering maze of rigging and sails to the trucks, with the topmen clustering to windward, and their very eyes and teeth lit up in the glare; then, too, the crews of the guns, in their trim frocks and trowsers; the marines on the top-gallant forecastle, with their firelocks and white cross-belts; and abaft a knot of officers on the poop, with night-glasses to their eyes, all standing out as clear as day in the sudden flashes from the cannon. Then followed the concussive roar, and the next instant you could hear the hurtling rush of the iron hail as it flew singly or in bunches through the air, or skipped in its deadly flight from wave to wave, until it went crashing into the pirate's boat, slapping with heavy thumps against the schooner's side, or furrowing along her decks; while a shower of white splinters flew high over her low rail, and told how well the iron had done its bidding.

Then, with many a groan and imprecation, the shattered and sinking
boat was cut adrift, and, a moment after, the sails of the vessel were
spread, the sheets hauled flat aft, and, taking the breeze, she heeled
over till her lee rail was all awash, and away she walked, right up to
windward.

But again came the clear, commanding tones on board the cruiser,
mingled with the jumping of the crew and ramming home the charges
in the guns:

"Load! round shot! Run out! One point abaft the beam! Fire
as you bring the schooner to bear!"

Out belched the red flames; the heavy globes of iron, like so many
black peas in daylight, sung their deadly note as they darted on their
way, and the corvette gave a little heel to leeward as the shock of the
explosion was felt. One shot dropped within fifty yards of the low
hull of the schooner, bounded just clear of her after deck, knocked
off the head and shoulder of a man at the tiller, and then went skipping away over the water like a black foot-ball. Another messenger
cut off the schooner's delicate fore-top-mast as clean as a bit of glass,
bringing down the gaff-top-sail, and, what was equally pleasant, the
fellow who was setting it—pitching him over and over like a wheel,
until he fell, a bruised and lifeless lump of jelly, on the oak bitts at
the foremast. Before, however, they were treated to another of
these metallic doses, the pirates had got their craft in splendid trim;
and with every stitch of her canvas spread, and tugging and strain-
ing, she rushed on with the heels of a race-horse, within three points
of the wind. The "Scourge," too, was now close hauled, her yards
braced as fine as needles, and crowded with every inch of sail that
would draw; while every ten minutes or so she would let slip two
or more guns from a division at the chase. But the uncertain gloom
of starlight, and the darkening effect of the passing trade clouds,
made the little vessel a very difficult object to see; and though one
of the last balls struck her on the narrow deck, passed through that
and the water-ways, and out to windward, spoiling two of her timbers, and no end of planking, yet this was the last damage she received. Her crew, also, had got as well as could be out of harm's
way — both the sound and wounded — and were lying quietly as
possible deep down in the vessel's run. When daylight broke the
breeze began to slacken, but she was by this time hull down from
the corvette, a long way beyond the reach of her long eighteens in
the bow-ports, and eating her way to windward, with no chance of
being taken.

"It's no use," said the captain of the corvette to his first lieutenant, as they stood watching the receding chase. "We may as
well give it up; she has the heels of us in this light wind, and will
soon be out of sight. I think, however," continued the captain, with

a smile, "that ho'll remember tho 'Scourgo' when ho meets her again. This is tho second timo we havo chased that fellow; and this heat, by tho way the splinters flew, wo must havo peppered tho skin off his back."

Shutting up tho joints of tho spy-glass which he held in his hand, he took hold of tho man-ropes of tho poop-ladder, and as ho put his feet on tho steps, ho said,

"You can go about, Mr. Cleveland, and run down to tho brig."

CHAPTER VII.

THE MEETING AND MOURNING.

"Moan! moan, ye dying gales!
The saddest of your tales
Is not so sad as life!
Nor have you e'er began
A theme so wild as man,
Or with such sorrow rife.

"Then, when the gale is sighing,
And when the leaves are dying,
And when the song is o'er,
Oh! let us think of those
Whose lives are lost in woes—
Whose cup of grief runs o'er!"

THE afternoon following the night when the foregoing events transpired, the "Martha Blunt" sailed slowly along the sandy tongue of land which separates Port Royal from Kingston, and dropped anchor in the harbor. As the cable rumbled out with a grating sound through the hawse-hole, and the crew aloft were furling the sails, a large, gayly-painted barge, pulled by a dozen blacks shaded by a striped awning, shot swiftly alongside. Jabbering were those darkies, and clapping their hands, and shouting joyously. A rope was immediately thrown from the gangway of the brig, and a tall, handsome man, with a broad Panama hat, loose white jacket and trowsers, sprang with a bound up the side, and leaped on deck.

Captain Blunt stood there to receive him. A broad white bandage was passed around his head, and the tears trickled slowly down his bronzed and honest cheeks. Just beyond him, under the shade of the awning, lay Banou, stretched out at full length on a mattress; while Ben, the helmsman, was kneeling beside him, fanning his hot and fevered face with his tarpaulin. A yard or two beyond, on a broad plank resting on trestles, lay the mate, Mr. Binks, cold and rigid in the grasp of death, with the union jack folded modestly over his corpse. The black breathed heavily and in pain; but when he caught sight of the gentleman as he stepped on deck, a deathly blue pallor came over his countenance, and, closing his eyes, the hot salt tears started in great drops from the lids.

"My God! captain," said the gentleman, with a bewildering stare, "what's all this? What has happened?"

The old skipper merely made a motion with his hand toward the cabin, and, leaning painfully against the rail, wept like a child. The gentleman's blood forsook his cheeks, and, with his knees knocking together, he staggered like a drunken man toward the cabin door. A few minutes later he emerged, bearing in his arms the sobbing, drooping form of his wife. Starting from his close embrace for a moment as he bore her to the gangway, she gave one shuddering, terrified, searching gaze over the blue water to seaward, and then, with a wailing cry of agony, that would have shaken the hardest heart, she fell sobbing again into her husband's arms.

The voices and joyous shrieks of the negroes in the barge alongside subsided into low moaning groans; four or five came up, and carefully lowered Banou down; then all got into the boat, and she moved mournfully away toward the shore.

CHAPTER VIII.

CAPTAIN BRAND AT HOME.

"From his brimstone bed at break of day,
A-walking the Devil is gone,
To visit his snug little farm the Earth,
And see how his stock goes on."

UPON a broad, flat, rocky ledge, near a small. landlocked narrow inlet of one of the clustering Twelve League Keys on the south side of Cuba, stood a red-tiled stone building, with a spacious veranda in front, covered by plaited matting and canvas curtains triced up all around. The back and one side of the building rested against a craggy eminence which overlooked the sea on both sides of the island, and commanded a wide sweep of reef and blue water beyond. A few clumps of cocoa-nut-trees and dwarf palms, with bare gaunt stems and tufted tops, stood out here and there along the rocky slopes, while lesser vegetation of cactus and mangrove bushes were scattered thickly over the island, cropping out with jagged edges of rock down to the sandy beaches of the sea-shore. A deep narrow inlet of blue water lay pure and still near the base of the rocky height, where, too, was a shelving curve of white sand, sprinkled about by a few mat sheds, while on the other side the rocks arose to an elevation of a hundred and fifty feet, forming a precipitous wall to the water. The inlet here took a sharp turn, scooped out in a secluded basin, and then narrowing to less than forty yards in width, it wound and twisted for a good mile in a thin blue channel to the open sea. Half that distance farther out was a roaring ledge of white breakers, where the long swell came hammering on it, bursting up in the air in brightish green masses, and then tumbling over the reef and bubbling smoothly on toward the shore. On a level with the water no channel could be discerned through the ledge; but, looking down from the heights around the inlet, a narrow blue gateway was marked out, skirted on the surface by frothy crests of dead foam, and near where flocks of cormorants and gulls were riding placidly on the inner side of the ledge. The island itself was about two miles broad and seven long; and about midway of its width the inlet formed a forked strait, one branch finding its way to the north, between a low succession of sandy hummocks, where the water was too shallow to float a duck, and the other finding an outlet, scarcely

a biscuit-toss wide, between two bluff rocks. With the trade wind this passage was safe and accessible; but on the change of the moon, with a breeze and swell from the south, the sea came bowling in, in boiling eddies and whirlpools, and it required a nerve of iron to attempt an entrance. Just within this narrow mouth, on a flat beveled ledge of rock but a few feet above the water, was a small battery of two long eighteen-pounders, and two twenty-four pounder carronades mounted on slides and trucks, with platforms laid on a bed of sand. Near by, beneath a low shed of tiles and loose stones, were a pile of round shot, nicely blacked, and some stands of grape and canister in canvas bags and cases, together with a large copper magazine of cartridges. Seated a little way off on a low stool was a dingy Spaniard with a telescope laid across his knees, which every little while he would raise to his eye and take a steady glance around the horizon to seaward. At other times he would roll and light a paper cigar, murmuring some low ditty to himself as he sent the smoke in volumes through his nose. A small brass bell hung beside the shed near the battery, together with a telegraphic card, which was connected by a wire strung on low posts, or hooked from rock to rock to the stone building away up at the basin. To return, however, to the building: the veranda rested on square rough masonry full twenty feet from the ground, which was loopholed for musketry, and with but one narrow slip of a doorway that fell like a portcullis, banded and strapped with bars and studs of wrought iron. Within this stone inclosure was a large and roomy vault, half filled with cases, barrels, and packages, and at the upper angle was a narrow subterranean vaulted passage, barred also by an iron-bound door, which led to a succession of whitewashed chambers—dark, damp, and gloomy— and then on, in a fissure-like pathway, to another equally strongly secured outlet on the other side of the crag. Leading to the veranda was a tautly-stretched rope ladder lashed to eye-bolts let into the natural rock below, and hooked on to the edge of the floor above. This was the only approach to the main floor of the building from the outside, though within were heavy trap-doors like the hatches of a ship, which communicated to the chambers beneath. The whole structure was of stone and tiles, roughly built, but yet strong and durable, and capable of resisting any assault, unaided by cannon, that could be brought against it. The floor was divided into four rooms, the smallest used for a kitchen, the next for a magazine of small arms, and the third a spacious bedchamber, which opened into a large square apartment facing the veranda, and which deserves more notice.

The lofty ceiling came down with the slant, showing the bare red tiles and heavy square beams which supported the roof. In one of the stoutest of these beams was an eye-bolt and copper-strapped block, through which was rove a long green silk rope, with one end secured by a cleat on the wall, and the other dangling loose, and squirming, whenever a current of air struck it, like a long, slim snake. Around the sides of the room, which were paneled with cedar, stood four or five quaint ebony armoires, and as many cabinets, clocks, and bookcases, with here and there a woman's work-stand, some of them curiously inlaid with pearl and silver. The walls were hung with a great number of pictures of all kinds of vessels—generally, however, of the merchant description—under full sail, with vivid light-houses in the distance, and combing breakers under the lee; and all portraying gallant crews and buoyant freights, which probably had never reached their destinations. Among this gallery of marine display was a broad framing of the "Flags of All Nations;" and codes of signals, too, in bright colors, hung beside them. Farther on, in a pretty panel by itself, surrounded by an edging of mother-o'-pearl, was a triple row of female miniatures, a number of them of great beauty, and many executed in excellent taste and art. In one corner was a large chart-stand, covered with rolls of maps and nautical instruments, while above were suspended, by white rope grummets, a pyramidal line of spy-glasses and telescopes of all sizes and make. Near the centre of the apartment stood a large round dining-table, on which was laid things for a breakfast, a box of cigars, and a small silver pan of live coals. There were but two windows to this room, both hung with striped muslin curtains, the casements going to the floor, and looking out upon the veranda; and but two doors, one leading to the kitchen, and the other to the sleeping-chamber on the opposite side.

Presently this last door opened, and, pushing aside a blue gauze curtain which hung before it, an individual of about eight-and-twenty years of age stepped languidly into the room. He was a tallish man, over six feet in stature, rather spare in build, but with great breadth of shoulders, and though pale, apparently from long illness, yet he was evidently very active and muscular when his nerves were called into action. Had it not been for a downward choleric curve to his large nose, and a little parting at the corners of his wide mouth and compressed lips, the face might have been thought handsome. The eyes were light blue, set close together, but hard and stony, with no ray of mercy or humanity in them. He wore no beard, and his light brown hair was thin and dry, and carefully parted at the side. He was dressed in a snow-white pair of loose drilling trowsers, cut sailor fashion, straw slippers, and silk stockings; and above he wore a brown linen jacket with large pearl buttons, and pockets. As he entered the room he held a delicate cambric handkerchief, with a fine lace border, in his hands, which he seemed to regard with curious interest as he lounged toward the windows of the veranda.

"I wish I could remember," he muttered musingly to himself, "which of those sisters this bit of cambric belonged to, marked with an E.—Ellen or Eliza—hum! They *would* die—silly things!—tried to stab me! Ho! what fun! Never left me even a miniature, either, for my collection. '*Buéno!*' There's more fish in the sea—and under it too!" he concluded, with an unpleasant elevation of his eyebrows.

By this time he had approached the open window, and, shoving the delicate fabric daintily in his pocket, he gave a slight yawn and looked out. Before him lay the deep blue basin of the inlet, with a couple of boats hauled up on the shore; a few idle sailors moving about, or squatted beneath the sheds playing cards or sewing. Without letting his eye rest more than a moment on this scene, he turned and gave a long, earnest gaze between an opening of the rocks to seaward. Then, with an angry frown, he approached the table, poured out a cup of black coffee, threw rather than dropped in a lump of sugar, and sat himself down for his morning's meal. He had scarcely, however, gulped down his cup of coffee and choked after it a slice of toast, than he pushed away the breakfast things, snapped his teeth together like a steel clasp, biting a tooth-pick in twain by the effort; and then, tossing the pieces away, he dashed his hand into the cigar-box, extracted one, touched it to the pan of coals, and began to smoke savagely. At first the grateful smoke appeared to soothe his chafed spirit, for he threw himself lazily into a large cane-bottomed settee, and, stretching out his legs, seemed to enjoy the tranquil scene around him with uninterrupted pleasure. But soon a scowl darkened his face; he dropped his cigar on the floor, and springing to his feet as if touched by a galvanic battery, he snatched down a telescope from the wall, steadied it at the window-sash, and peered again long and anxiously to windward. He saw nothing, however, save the long, glassy, unbroken undulations of a calm tropical sea, rolling away off beyond the ledge under a burning sun; no sign of a breeze—not even a cat's-paw; and only now and then the leap of a deep-sea fish sparkling for a moment in the air, and some sluggish gulls and pelicans sailing and diving about the reef for their prey. Shutting up the glass with a crash that made the joints ring, he strode to the settee, where hung several knotted bell-ropes, and, seizing one, gave it a sharp jerk. Then putting his ear to an aperture in the wall, where was a hollow cane tube like the mouth of a speaking-trumpet, he listened attentively till a hoarse whisper uttered the word,

"*Señor.*"

Putting his mouth to the tube, he said,

"Can you make out the 'Centipede' from the crag station?"

"Not sure, sir, this morning; but last evening, at sunset, I saw a sail which I took to be her. The sea-breeze is just beginning to make, and if she's to windward of Punta Arenas she'll soon heave in sight."

D

This colloquy was held in Spanish; and when the signal-man had ceased speaking, the interlocutor lit another cigar mechanically, kicked a foot-stool out of his way like a foot-ball, and thus communed with himself as he rapidly paced between the table and the veranda:

"Fourteen weeks ago yesterday since the schooner was off Matanzas; not a word of news to cheer me through all that cursed fever; the spring trade done, and the track deserted by this time!"

Then pausing in his walk, he stopped at the chart-stand, and unrolling a map, he went on:

"Where, in the devil's name, could she possibly have gone to? She might have been to Cape Horn and back before this. Miserable fool that I was to trust the craft with that thirsty, thick-headed Gibbs! *Diavolo!* he may have been captured, and if he has, I hope his neck has been stretched like a shred of jerked beef."

Even while he was talking a bell struck near the settee, and, putting his ear again to the tube, the hoarse voice said,

"I can make her out now, *señor.* She's just caught the strong young breeze, and is, hull up, coming along with the bonnet off her fore-sail and a reef in her main-sail! There's a felucca to windward of her, which I take to be the 'Panchita!'"

"Ah ha!" laughed the individual in the room. "The 'Centipede' is safe, then; and I am to have the pleasure, too, of a visit from the Tuerto, the mercenary old owl, with his account of sales and his greed. But let me once catch him foul, and, my one-eyed friend, I'll treat you to such a dance that you won't need shoes!"

Here he glanced with a meaning look at the silk rope swaying from the beam above his head, and the laugh of satisfaction which followed was not one a timid man would care to hear in a dark night; nor did it come from his heart, as any one might have discovered from the ferocious gleam of inward passion which shot out in the cold sparkle of his eyes and flitted away over his grating teeth.

Controlling his feelings, however, and stepping out on the veranda, he drew aside the curtains and sung out to the men in the huts, "One of you fellows, tell the boatswain I want him."

The men started up, and a moment after a man in a blue jacket stood out from one of the sheds and threw up his hand to his straw hat.

"Get together the people! Let run the cable at the Alligator's mouth, and have three or four warps ready for the schooner when she passes the point! The 'Panchita' is coming too, so look out, and have enough lines to tow both vessels in case the breeze fails. Tell Mr. Gibbs to moor close under the other shore in the old berth, and to come to me when he's anchored! D'ye hear?"

All this was said in a sharp tone of command, and by the alacrity with which the orders were executed the men seemed to be accustomed to a master who knew how to rule them.

THE "PANCHITA."

CHAPTER IX.

CAPTAIN AND MATE.

"So I hauled him off to the gallows' foot,
And blinded him in his bags;
'Twas a weary job to heave him up,
For a doomed man always lags;
But by ten of the clock he was off his legs
In the wind, and airing his rags!"

A COUPLE of hours had passed since the occupant of the stone building had last spoken to his subordinates down at the inlet, but the interval he devoted to a minute inspection of weapons in the armory adjoining his bedroom. They were all in excellent order, of the best make, and very neatly arranged in stands and cases around the room. When he emerged again, after locking the door, he held an exquisite pair of small pistols inlaid with gold in his hand, which he gently polished with his cambric handkerchief, and then slipped them into his trowsers pockets. Then he held short dialogues with the voice at the signal-station, and, without looking out of the window, he informed himself of what was doing outside, and what progress the vessels made toward their haven. When, however, the schooner poked her slim, low black bows, with her sails down, around the point, he gave one stealthy peep, or glare rather, at her. He took all in at that glance, from the patches of sheet-lead nailed over the shot-holes in her side, to the sawed-off stump of the fore-top-mast; and then he remarked the absence of the boat which was carried amidships, and the few men moving about her deck. Ay! he took it all in with that one comprehensive glance, and when he had done, he raised his fore finger quivering with anger, and slowly and unconsciously passed it with an ominous gesture across his throat.

Soon was heard a sullen plunge as an anchor was let go, and the splashing of the warps upon the water as the stern of the "Centipede" was being moored to the rocks, to make room for her companion the felucca, now shortly expected.

"Mr. Gibbs is coming on shore, *señor*, and he seems to have a wooden leg," came through the tube. "The doctor is coming with him, and there is a little boy in the boat."

"Ho!" muttered the man in the saloon, "where was that brat picked up?"

Nothing more was said. The tall man lit a cigar, threw himself into an easy attitude on the settee, opened a richly-bound volume, and waited. Ten minutes may have gone by when the trampling of feet was heard on the smooth rocks outside the building, and the voice of Mr. Gibbs exclaimed,

"Easy, will ye? Doctor! Don't ye see it tears the narves out of me to hobble with this broomstick-handle of a leg! There! Stop a bit! How in thunder am I to climb this ladder? Oh!" Here a low howl of pain. "Another shove. Easy, old Sawbones! So—give us another push, will ye? All right! There, that'll do."

The next minute Mr. Bill Gibbs stood on the broad piazza, and, with the assistance of a crutch, he hobbled to the entrance of the apartment, and only pausing to recover his wind and compose his features, he pulled off his straw hat and entered.

"So ho! Mr. Gibbs," said the man on the settee, as the burly, lame ruffian darkened the entrance, laying the book down as he spoke, and waving his delicate handkerchief before him.

"So ho! Mr. Gibbs, you've come back at last! Delighted to see you. I am, 'pon my soul. Ah! one of those stout pins gone? Why, how's this? Some little accident? Santa Cruz rum and a tumble down the hatchway, perhaps, eh? D'ye smoke? Take a cheroot. Put that bag on the table."

All this was said in a gay, gibing tone, with an indifference and *sang froid* that a tight-rope dancer might have been proud of; and as he ended, he threw a handful of cigars across the table, and pushed the pan of coals toward his visitor. Before, however, Gibbs had time to utter a word in reply, his companion, while lolling over the settee, caught up an opera-glass from the table, and, placing it to his eyes, went on:

"Ha! ho! the fore-top-mast of my pretty long-legged schooner is gone. Pretty stick it was! I suppose, Master Gibbs, that *you*"— he nodded fiercely without removing the glass—"cut it up for that lovely new leg you've mounted. Ay, my beauty!" again apostrophizing the vessel, which lay like a wounded bird in the calm inlet before him; "but where's my handsome barge, that used to cover the long gun? Ho! stormy weather you've seen of late."

During all this one-sided conversation Gibbs had managed to wriggle his mutilated body on to a wicker chair, where he steadied himself with his crutch, evincing manifest signs of choler the while by running his fat fingers through the reddish door-mat of hair, hitching up his trowsers, and rapping nervously his timber stump of a leg on the floor, until at last, unable, apparently, longer to control himself, he burst out, with his bad face suffused with passion,

"I say, Captain Brand, it's time to end them 'ere gibes. What's took place is unfortinate; but, howsoever, I has a bag of shiners and a wooden leg to show for it, and d—n the odds."

"Stop, stop, my bull-dog! Don't be profane in my presence, if you please. We are both Christians, you know, and friends too, I hope."

This was said in a very precise, emphatic, and clear enunciation, and without apparent heat; and Captain Brand smiled too—but such a smile, as his wide mouth came down with a twitch at the corners, and left a sort of hole, where the cigar was habitually stuck, to see his teeth through.

"And now, my friend, suppose you give me some little account of your cruise, and fill up, if you can, any chinks that I haven't seen through already," he concluded, throwing his legs again over the back of the settee, and elevating his eyebrows as the cigar smoke curled in spiral wreaths around his face.

Mr. Gibbs hereupon settled himself more at ease in his chair, laid his crutch across his knees, and began:

"I s'pose, sir, you got the news I sent in a letter from Matanzas, after we'd been chased out of the Nicholas Channel by that Yankee corvette?"

Captain Brand nodded at the eye-bolt which held the green silk rope from the ceiling, as if calculating mentally the strain it would bear, merely as a matter of philosophical speculation, perhaps.

"Well, arter that—and a very tight race it was—we ran down to the Behamey Banks. There we picked up a Yankee schooner loaded with shingles and lumber; and as the skipper was sarsy, I just made him and his crew walk one of his own planks, and then bored a couple of holes through his vessel, arter taking out some water which we stood in need of. You hasn't a drop of summut to drink, has you, Captain Brand? becase it makes my jaw-tackle dry to talk much."

The captain merely motioned with a wave of his cambric handkerchief to an open liquor-case which stood on a cabinet near, and to which Mr. Gibbs hobbled; when, seizing a square flask of crystal incased in a network of frosted silver, he returned with it to the table. Had Mr. Gibbs chosen he might have brought with the flask a small, thimble-shaped liqueur glass; but he did not, and contented himself with a china coffee-cup which stood on the tray before him. He seemed a little near-sighted too; and as he inverted the flask, gave no heed to the quantity of fluid he poured into the cup. But he took care, however, that it did not run over; and then, raising it with a trembling hand to his lips, he said, "My sarvice to you, Captain Brand," and tossed it down his capacious throat. The captain gave no response to this compliment, but as Mr. Gibbs put down the coffee-cup he said blandly,

"Thank you; but suppose you put that flask back in the case. I am rather choice with that brandy; it was a—given to me by a— person who was a—unfortunately hanged, and a—I rarely offer it a —the second time."

Puffing his cigar as he spoke in an easy manner, he then turned round to listen to Mr. Gibbs's narrative. Becoming more genial as the brandy loosened his tongue, Mr. Gibbs continued:

"Well, sir, from the Behameys we ran to leeward, nearly to the Spanish Main, in hopes, perhaps, of finding some stray fellow as was bound to Europe; but we see nothing for days and days, and weeks and weeks, till finally the water fell short again, and we beats up and runs into Santa Cruz. There, as luck would have it, Eboe Pete and French Tom got into a bit of a scrimmage up on a gentleman's plant- ation arter sunset, and was werry roughly handled by a patrol of so- gers as happened to be near. I believe as how Eboe Pete died that night; and I heerd, too, that French Tom had his skull cracked; and what does he go for to do but make a confession to the author- ities that the 'Centipede' was a pirate!

"Well, captain, the moment that information reached me, and see- in' a sogers' boat gettin' ready, and the sogers running about the water-battery of the fort, than I just slips the cable, and runs out to sea like a bird; and, Lord love ye, sir! the way they pitched round shot arter us was—was—" Here Master Gibbs paused for a simile, and the captain observed with a hacking, cough-like laugh,

"You saved the water-casks, though?"

"Why no, sir; and we was forced to go upon a 'lowance of a pint a water a man!"

"Ho!" rejoined the listener. "Capital! Didn't suffer, I hope? Go on."

"Howsomever, I says to myself, the captain wants a good valy'ble cargo, and so we beats up again and stretches away back along the coast of Jamaiky, on the look-out for any think that might be comin' that 'ere way. Well, sir, d'ye see, airly one morning, as we was a lying as close as wax under the land, we spies a big brig becalmed off to seaward; but we diskivered at the same time that same Yan- kee cruiser as was in chase of us off Matanzas. I know'd as how you would be displeased at any risks being run, so we keeps clean and snug inshore, under a pint o' land, till set of sun, and until arter the moon went down. Then the breeze sprung up fresh from the old trade quarter, and says I, now we'll make a dash at that 'ere drogher, and squeeze him as dry as bone-dust; more pertikerly, ye see, captain, since the corvette, arter dodgin' about him all day, had yawed off, and, with his port-tacks aboard, was beatin' to wind'ard."

Here Mr. Gibbs's auditor took the cigar from his mouth and rolled his light blue eyes at him, puffed a thick volume of smoke through the corner of his mouth, but said never a syllable.

The narrator gave a wistful look at the brandy-flask, drained the last few drops from the coffee-cup, pushed out his timber leg, and resumed:

"So you see, sir, as I was a sayin', I says to myself, I'll get the boat in the water with the lads, and, to make sure of all being conducted shipshape, I'll go myself."

"Oh!" said the captain, as his eyebrows went up and the corners of his mouth came down, with the faintest breath of a sardonic smile, while he lit a fresh cigar, "oh! you did!"

"Ay, sir! So we let the old drogher go bouncing on past us, at about the rate of five mile in four hours, when we crossed his wake under the jib, and then we ups with the fore and main-sail, got a pull of the sheets, and—"

Captain Brand shook the point of his curved nose at the speaker, who checked himself, and, giving an emphatic rap with his crutch on the floor, went on with—

"Beg parding, sir; but, Lord love ye! we just walked up under his lee, and afore he know'd where he was, we boarded him, knocked over two or three chaps, and had the skipper lashed down in his cabin as quick as winkin' and as quiet as could be. Ay, sir, we had it all our own way; but during the scrimmage wot should I see (here he inclined his head out like a loggerhead turtle) but the lovelyest young 'oman as ever I clapped eyes on!" Here his timber stump grated nervously on the floor. "Says I, that's just the craft, with such a clean run and full bows, as would please Captain Brand"—at which that individual rolled round on his elbow and brought his eye to the opera-glass in the direction of the schooner.

"She isn't there, captain!" parenthesized the narrator, following the motion with his head. "So I just fisted hold of her to hand her tenderly into the boat, with a bag of shiners as was found on board, when, so help me—— —beg parding, sir—if a dwarfed giant of a nigger didn't take an overhand lick at me with an iron pump-break, and nearly cut this 'ere larboard pin in two pieces; and, smash my brains!" he continued, shaking his broad paw aloft with rage, "but what does I do, with all the pain from the clip that da— (beg parding, sir) give me, I slams away with a pistol bullet through the nigger's head—"

"Didn't I see a little boy on board the 'Centipede?' Perhaps I was mistaken, the sun blazes so fiercely, eh?" broke in Captain Brand, though the sun didn't blaze with a fiercer light than shot out of his deadly cold blue eyes.

"Ho, ay, sir! that young imp was a bitin' at my t'other leg like a bull terrier pup, while the nigger was attackin' me, and then he goes and crawls out of the cabin winders, and was fished out of the water by the chaps as wos towin' astarn in the boat."

"Oh, really! how very fortunate!" muttered the captain; "go on; don't stop, I pray you, Master Gibbs."

"Well, sir, I knows very little what happened arter this, for the young 'oman was a screamin' and our chaps a cursin' about the decks, when all of a sudden I fell off into a faint like, and the same time a heavy gun came slamming into our very ears; and there was that infarnal corvette agen bowlin' down within five cables' length of the brig, her battery all alight and the whistles a callin' away the boats, in as violent a haste as any think I can remember," said Gibbs, as he paused to catch his breath.

"You must have kept a sharp look-out, though?" But, without heeding this remark, the burly scoundrel went on—

"Well, Captain Brand, the boys tumbled me over the side—"

"Not forgetting the little bag of shiners!" sneered his auditor.

"Tumbled me into the boat, sir, and then pulled like mad for the schooner. I know'd, d'ye mind, captain, or leastways I felt sartain we could show any think afloat our heels, and so away we scrambles aboard, and off we splits. But ye must see by this time, sir, the corvette had come down and rounded to on the weather beam of the drogher, acting like a screen for the schooner close under his lee. It wos only a minnit, though, while he was holding some jaw with those lubbers aboard the brig, before he filled away again, and wearing sharp round her bows, he diskivered us sartain. I don't think, as matters stood by this time, that our boat was a boat-hook's length from the schooner when I jist see a burst of red flashes from the man-o'-war's starboard ports, and heerd an officer roar out, 'Give him the whole three divisions of grape!' when I'm da—your parding agin, sir; I'm blest if ever I heerd sich a rain of cold iron in all my sea-goin' experience. Ay, sir, by G—gracious, sir, if about two bushels of them grape didn't riddle the barge like the nozzle to a watering-pot, and same time tore seven of our noble fellows all to rags—"

"You saved the boat, of course?" suggested his companion, in a kind voice, but with a frightful sneer.

"Why, captain, we unfortinately lost her; for ye see, arter tumbling me aboard the schooner, and arter bailing nigh as much blood as water—"

"Capital! excellent! best joke I ever heard," broke in Captain Brand, with a hollow laugh of much enjoyment.

"Arter bailin' as much blood as water, and finding the man-o'-war was heaving in stays to slam another broadside into us, we cut the boat adrift, and then got the sheets flat aft, the gaff-top-sails up, and away we drove with a crackin' breeze right up to wind'ard, like a swordfish. Lord love ye, sir! we walked away from the cruiser, a eatin' the wind out of him like a knife, and notwithstandin' he hove more or forty round shot at us, ho only knocked away the fore-top-mast and some other triflin' little damage about the hull, and"—he hesitated—"Lascar Joe's head."

"That counts off about half your crew, eh?" said Captain Brand, smiling in his peculiar manner. "Well, what next?"

"Why, sir, the next mornin' Belize Paul—as is part doctor, you know—said as how my leg was to come off below the knee, and arter givin' me a sip or two o' rum—"

"Bottle," interjected the captain, twisting the beak of his nose in a puff of smoke.

"—Rum, why, smash my brains, sir, if he didn't hack it off with a wood-saw!"

"Well, what next?"

"Then, sir, ye see, we run the schooner down Cape Cruz, where we kept werry snug and quiet till sich times as the old one-eyed Diego judged the coast clear to return to head-quarters."

"Well, what then?"

"That's all, Captain Brand!" concluded the narrator his garbled yarn, as he again had recourse to scratching the door-mat on his head, and cast a thirsty look at the brandy-flask.

"That's all, is it?" hissed the man with the iron jaws, in a tone of concentrated passion, as he sprang with a single bound from the settee, and clutched Master Gibbs with both hands around his hairy throat until his face turned livid purple and his eyes started from the sockets. "That's all, is it, you drunken beast? That's all you have to tell after idling away the summer, losing anchors and boats, and more than half my crew, and bringing a hornet's nest down about our ears! That's all, is it? And what would you say, now, if I should order the doctor to cut off your other leg close behind your ears, you beast?"

In the last stages of suffocation, the man was hurled on his back to the floor, and there lay, bleeding a torrent from his mouth and nose. His superior stood over him for a moment and put his hand in his trowsers pocket for a pistol, and then he glanced rapidly at the green rope squirming from the beams above; but, changing his purpose apparently, he strode back to the settee and shouted "Babette!"

Presently the door opened from the passage leading to the kitchen, and there appeared a large, powerfully-made negro-woman, with her arms akimbo, and a pair of bloodshot eyes gleaming from beneath a striped Madras turban wound round her head.

"Babette!" repeated the captain, resuming his seat and his habitual polite air and voice, " serve out a barrel of Bordeaux and a beaker of old Antigua rum to the ' Centipede's' crew to drink my health; and I say, my beauty! have a pig or two killed; tell the boatswain to haul the seine, and have a good supper for all hands to-night.

And, Baba"—he went on as if he had just thought of something—
"there's my friend Gibbs lying there—I believe he has fallen down
in a fit—be very careful of him—a bed in the vault—a little biscuit
and water—he may be feverish when he wakes up, you know. And,
Babette, old girl, if you are in want of kindling wood, you may as
well use that timber leg of our friend Gibbs! I don't think he'll
want it again. There! *doucement*, Baba!"

The negress gave a deep grunt of assent, and, seizing the senseless
body lying on the floor, she dragged it out of the room. Returning
a few moments after, she wiped up the blood with a cloth dipped in
hot water, and finally disappeared.

CHÁPTER X.

AN OLD SPANIARD WITH ONE EYE.

"I fear thee, Ancient Mariner!
I fear thy skinny hand!
For thou art long, and lank, and brown,
As is the ribbed sea-sand."

"The 'Panchita' has passed Mangrove Point," came in the hoarse whisper from the signal-man. "You can see her now from below, sir."

Captain Brand put on a fine Panama hat, and stepped out on the veranda, where, with a cigar in his mouth, he leaned over the balustrade, and kept sharp watch on every thing that was going on below him. In a few minutes a long pointed brown bowsprit protruded itself beyond the wall of rocks, followed by a great triangular lateen sail, bent to a yard a mile long, and tapering away like a fly-fishing-rod, where, at the end, was a short bit of yellow and red pennant. As her bows came into view they showed above a curved prow falling inboard, with a huge bunch of sheepskin for a chafing-mat on the knob, and a thin red streak along the wales, on a lead-colored ground, above her bottom, which was painted green. As more of her proportions came into the picture, you saw a stout stump of a mast, raking forward, with short black ropes of purchases for hoisting the single yard, and heavy square blocks close down to the foot of the mast. When this great sail had come out from the screen of rocks, another light stick of a mast stood up over the taffrail, with another lateen sail and whip-stalk of a yard, to which was bent the Spanish Colonial Guarda Costa flag. In fact, she was a Spanish felucca all over, from stem to stern, and truck to water-line. A few dingy hammocks were stowed about halfway along her rail, and there were a good many men moving about her decks in getting the cable clear, and a lot more clinging like so many lizards along the bending yard, and all in some attempt at uniform dress, in readiness to roll up the sail when the anchor was down. There was a long brass gun, too, burnished like gold, on a pivot slide, with all its equipment, trained muzzle forward in front of the main-mast. No sooner had she sagged into the open basin, with her immense sail hanging flat and heavy in the light air, than a boat from the schooner boarded her, and presently she let go an anchor. There were a few coarse compliments and greetings exchanged between the crews of the two vessels, and some rough jokes made, as the last comer veered out the cable, rolled up his sails, and set taut his running gear in quite a tidy and man-of-war style.

"Go on board the felucca, José, and give my compliments to Don Ignaçio, and say I shall be happy to see him," cried Captain Brand from the piazza to a man at the cove; "and tell him," continued he, "that I should have called in person, but I can't bear the hot sun since I caught the fever. Take my gig."

This was said in Spanish, and when he had finished speaking he shaded his face behind the curtain and scowled.

"You're a bird of ill omen, my one-eyed friend; but one of these days I'll wipe out old scores, and new ones too, perhaps," Captain Brand muttered to himself; and, from his murderous expression of face, he seemed just the man to carry out his threat. Meanwhile, a light whale-boat of a gig, manned by four men and a coxswain, pushed off from the shore, and in three strokes of the oars she was alongside the felucca. The coxswain stepped over the low rail, and, walking aft, turned down a cuddy of a cabin, took off his hat, and delivered his message. A minute later he again got into the boat, and pulled to the cove, where he said to the captain,

"Don Ignaçio says he'll come in his own boat when he's ready."

"*Bueno!*" was responded aloud; and then to himself: "Don't ask or receive favors, eh? What an old file the brute is!"

He said no more, but watched. Presently a small man came up out of the cabin of the "Panchita," but so very slow, and with such a quiet motion did he emerge, that one might suppose it was a wary animal rather than a human being. He was scrupulously neat in attire—a brown pair of linen trowsers, a Marseilles vest with silver filigree buttons, an embroidered shirt-bosom with gold studs, and a dark navy-blue broadcloth coat, with standing collar and anchor gilt buttons. His head-gear was simply a white chip hat, with a very narrow brim and a fluttering red ribbon; but beneath it his coal-black hair behind was chopped as close as could be, leaving a single long and well-oiled ringlet on each side, which curled like snakes around a pair of large gold rings pendent from his ears. His complexion was dark, bilious, and swarthy, with a thin, sharp nose, and a million of minute wrinkles, all meeting above, at the corners, and under a small line of a mouth; quite like rays, in fact, and only relaxed when the lips parted to show a few ragged, rotten pegs of sharp teeth. But perhaps the most noticeable feature in his face was his eye—for he had but one—and the spot where the other is seen in the species was merely a red, closed patch of tightly-drawn skin, with a few hairs sticking out like iron tacks. His single eye, however, was a jet black, round, piercing organ, which seemed to do duty for half a dozen ordinary glims, and danced with a sharp, malevolent scrutiny, as if the owner was always in search of something and never found it, and every body and every thing appeared to slink out of its light wher-ever it glanced around. His age might have been any where from forty to sixty. As he stepped on deck, clear of the cuddy cabin hatch, his sinister optic played about in its socket—now scanning the long brass gun, the half-furled sails, the crew, the ropes, or taking a steady, unwinking glance at the midday sun, and then shining off to the shore, and sweeping in the "Centipede," the little pool of blue water, and the mouth of the inlet. Feeling apparently satisfied with the present aspect of affairs, he slowly pulled out a machero from his waistcoat pocket, plucked a cigaretto from the case, and then proceeded delib-erately to strike a light. Even while performing this simple opera-tion, his uneasy orb, like unto a black bull's-eye, traversed about in its habitual way; and when he raised the spark of fire with his brown, thin hand, and the claws of fingers loaded with rings, he seemed to be looking into his own mouth. Nodding to a fellow who stood near, with a crimson sash around his waist, he inclined his eye toward the shore, blew out a thin wreath of smoke from his lungs—all the while his vigilant organ shining like a burning spark of lambent jet through the smoke—and merely said,

"The boat!"

In a moment a small cockle-shell of a punt was lowered from the stern of the felucca, when, stepping carefully in, he seized a scull, and with a few vigorous twists pushed her to the landing at the cove.

During all these movements of the commander of the felucca Cap-tain Brand was by no means an inattentive observer; and, indeed, he was so extremely critical that he stuck the tube of a powerful tele-scope through an aperture of the curtains around him, and not only looked at his cautious visitor, but he actually watched the expression of his uneasy eye, and almost counted every wrinkle—finely engraved as they were—on his swarthy visage; but, if Captain Brand's own visage reflected an index of his mind, he did not seem over and above pleased with what he saw.

"Has a bundle of papers under his arm! I can see the hilt of that delicate blade, too, sticking out from his wristband. Ah! I've seen him throw that short blade from his coat-sleeve and strike a dollar at twenty yards! Wonderful skill with knives you have, Don Igna-çio; but you never yet tried your knack with *me!* Oh no, my Tuer-to—bird of ill omen that you are! We can't do without one another just yet, so let us wait and see what's in the wind!"

Soliloquizing these remarks, Captain Brand withdrew his telescope as the commander of the felucca approached, and, with a cheerful smile, waited to receive him. A few moments later the one-eyed individual mounted the rope-ladder stairway, carefully feeling the strands, however, and looking suspiciously around him as he stepped lightly on the piazza.

"*Ah! compadre mio!*" exclaimed Captain Brand, in Spanish, as he seized his visitor by the flipper, and squeezed his fingers till the pressure on his valuable rings made him wince, as he was led into the large and spacious saloon, while at the same time the captain gave him a hearty slap between his narrow shoulders.

"*Ah! compadre!* How goes the friend of my soul?"

The small man gave no symptoms of joy at this warm greeting; but, screwing his wiry frame out of the captain's caresses, his eye flashed like a spark of fire quickly up and down and all around the apartment, as if making a mental inventory of the furniture, and not omitting his tall companion, from the crown of his head to the toes of his straw slippers, when he quietly remarked through his closed teeth,

"*Como estamos?*"—"How are we?"

"Ah, Don Ignaçio, *poco bueno, poco malo!* Half and half. Just getting well over that maldito attack of Yellow Jack."

"Hum! more bad than good. No? I've brought you some letters from the agent at Havana."

"Thanks—thanks, my friend. Ho! Babette! Babette! Some anisette for Don Ignaçio. *Presto!* my good Baba. There—that will do!" he said, merrily, as the liquour and glasses were placed on the table. "And don't omit the turtle-soup for dinner, and tell Lascar Joe to make it. Ah! I forget—the best cook I had—the devil's making soup of him now. However, do the best you can, my Baba, and let us have dinner about sunset."

Then turning to his visitor, with a graceful bow and a laugh, he added, "And we'll have the doctor to join us, and tell how he cut off our poor friend Gibbs's leg with a hand-saw. *Dios! amigo!* Capital joke, 'pon my honor!"

Captain Brand's honor! Lord have mercy upon us! And he had very few jokes, and never told one himself.

"Hum!" replied the Tuerto, in the pause of the conversation. "There's better jokes than that to hear. *Mira!* look!"

With this brief rejoinder he threw a bundle of newspapers on the table, and, pulling out a packet of letters from a breast pocket, pitched it toward his host. Then helping himself to a thimbleful of anisette, he took off his narrow-brimmed chip hat for the first time, polished up his eye a bit with the knuckle of his fore finger, and looked at his companion fixedly.

"Letters, I see, from our old friend Moreno, at Havana," said Captain Brand, as he sat down on the settee, and with a pretty tortoise-shell knife cut round the seals. "Ah! what says he? 'Happy to inform you,' is he? 'Packages of French silks seized by custom-house on account of informal invoice and clearance.' Why didn't the fool forge others, then? Well, what next? 'Schooner "Reel," from Barbadoes, with cargo of rum and jerked beef, wrecked going into Principe, and crew thrown into prison on suspicion of being engaged in—' Oh! ah! served them right, when I ordered them to St. Jago —delighted they must be! 'Bills for advances and stores now due, please remit, per hands of Don Ignaçio Sanchez—'"

Here Captain Brand caught a ray from the one eye of his companion, which he returned with interest; and then laying the letters down on the table with the softest motion in life, he exclaimed, with a sigh,

"Not the best news in the world, as you say, *compadre;* all those rich goods, and those bags of coffee, and pipes of rum gone to the devil. But these are little accidents in our profession."

"*Como?*" said Señor Ignaçio, "*our* profession?" shaking his fore finger before his paper cigar in a deprecating manner. "Speak for yourself, *amigo.*"

"Ah! true," the other went on—"my profession. The freedom of the seas, the toll of the tropics, the right of search, and all that sort of buccaneering pastime, is liable, you know, to the usual risks."

Here he inclined his head to one side and gave a slight clack to his lips, as if to illustrate in a humorous way a man choking to death with a knotted rope under his ear. "However, we must be more cautious in future and retrieve the past disasters, for there are still on the sea as good barks as ever floated."

Captain Brand said this as if he were a merchant of large means and strict integrity, and was about to enter into some shrewd commercial speculation.

"Hum!" murmured Señor Ignaçio, while pouring out another little glass of anisette. "*Amigo mio!* you had better read the papers from Havana before you talk of another cruise."

"Oh! delighted to read the news—quite refreshing to get a peep at the world after being cooped up here for months! Another French revolution! Bonaparte alive yet! A Patriot war! Nelson and Villeneuve! All interesting."

Thus glancing rapidly over the prints, pausing at times at a paragraph that arrested his attention, then tossing a paper away and taking up another, till suddenly Captain Brand's hand shook with passion as he read aloud,

"His Britannic majesty's squadron has been augmented on the West India station. The brig 'Firefly,' corvettes 'Croaker' and 'Joker,' touched at Nassau, New Providence, on the 2d instant, bound to leeward. We also learn that the United States have fitted out a squadron of small vessels, called the Musquito Fleet, to search for the noted pirate Brand, who has so long committed atrocities

among the islands.   He was last chased by the American corvette
'Scourge,' off Morant Bay, on the east coast of Jamaica, but escaped
during the night.   The following day a shattered boat was picked
up, which had been cut adrift from the piratical schooner, containing
several dead and dying bodies of the pirates.   One of the latter gave
such information to the captain of the 'Scourge' as leads to the hope
that Brand's retreat may soon be discovered and his nest of pirates
be destroyed.   Recent advices from Principe state that a vessel loaded with valuable merchandise struck on the Cavallo Reef and went
down.   The crew, however, five in number, were rescued, but on
landing were identified by the mate of the English bark 'Trident' as
a portion of the men who robbed that vessel and murdered the master and several of the passengers.   Our readers may remember that
among the latter were two sisters, who leaped overboard and were
drowned, to save themselves the horror of a more cruel fate.   The
men alluded to, who were wrecked in the brig off Principe, were sent
in chains to Havana, and were yesterday publicly garroted in the
Plaza of Moro Castle."

"HE TOUCHED THE BELL OVERHEAD AS HE SPOKE, AND, PUTTING HIS MOUTH TO THE TUBE, ASKED, 'ANY THING IN SIGHT?'"

CHAPTER XI.

CONVERSATION IN POCKETS AND SLEEVES.

"He holds him with his skinny hand :
'There was a ship,' quoth he.
'Hold off! unhand me, graybeard loon!'
Eftsoons his hand dropp'd he."

CAPTAIN BRAND laid down the paper without a sign of outward emotion, and nodded his head several times at the one-eyed man facing him. He then extracted his perfumed handkerchief, examined the cipher in the corner, and waved it before his face. Don Ignaçio pulled out a red silk bandana, and polished his eye as if it were the lens of a spy-glass. At length the former spoke:

"*Amigo mio!* The nets are spreading, but the fish are not in them yet!"

"No, *amigo!*"

"Ah! *compadre, viento y ventura poca dura!* the fair breezes have chopped round in our teeth. Success, my friend, creates jealousy, envy, hatred, and malice. Now here were we swimming along as quietly as sharks under water, only coming up for a bite occasionally, when on come those villainous swordfishes, and wish to drive us away."

Captain Brand gave expression to this pious homily in a tone of virtuous reproach against the world at large, and as if he were a very much maligned and ill-used gentleman. He touched the bell over-head as he spoke, and, putting his mouth to the tube, asked,

"Any thing in sight?"

"Nothing, *señor.*"

"Telegraph the man at the Tiger-trap station to keep a bright look-out, and direct the gunner to keep the battery manned day and night! Tell the boatswain to set taut the chain on the other side at the Alligator's mouth!"

Don Ignaçio gave a rather suspicious glimmer at his vessel as this last order was given, and smiled; that is, if a one-sided twitch to the wrinkles about the line of his mouth could be tortured into a smile. His companion seemed to divine what was passing in the Don's mind, for he added politely,

"The cable won't interfere with the 'Panchita!'"

"No, *amigo ;* the felucca is anchored just *out*side of it." The

Tuerto was not a man to leave any thing to chance, and he had taken the precaution to be on the safe side of the pirates, either as friends or enemies. He had indeed been as near an approach to a pirate himself as could be, and had only abandoned the business for a profession quite as bad, where there was less risk and more profit. In other words, he was now a colonial officer in command of a Guarda Costa, winking—but without shutting his eye—at piracy whenever he was well paid for it; and he invariably was well paid for it, or else he made mischief. Withal, he was as crafty and determined an old villain as ever sailed the West Indies. He had amassed a large fortune, and owned several tobacco estates—pretty much all his wealth acquired by the easy trouble of holding his tongue. Yet his greed was insatiable, and he probably would have sold the fingers from his hands, and his legs and arms with them—all, save his single black ball of an optic, which was invaluable to him—for doubloons. In fact, this feverish thirst after gold which always raged in his hot veins had induced him to pay Captain Brand a visit, and we shall see with what result. The truth is, however, that Captain Brand was the only man of his numerous villainous acquaintance afloat for whom he felt the least dread. He knew him to be bold, skillful, and wary, and so the Don had a tolerably positive conviction that, should he play him false, his own neck might get a wrench in the garrote while he was throwing the noose for his coadjutor.

To return, however, to the pair of worthies sitting in conclave in the pirate's saloon: the captain, resuming the conversation, observed in a careless tone, quite as if the subject under discussion was a mere ordinary matter,

"When will this swarm of hornets be down upon us?"

The Spaniard blew a thick puff of smoke from his cigarette, and still holding it between his teeth, while his eye glittered through the murky cloud, he replied,

"Perhaps a fortnight, a little more or less. I left St. Jago five days ago, with orders from the Administrador to run down this side of the island, and procure information for the English consul."

"Any cruisers down that way?"

"Ay! the corvette 'Scourge,' and the 'Snapper' schooner; they arrived the night before I sailed."

"Did you happen to see their officers, *amigo?*"

"*Oh si!* I had a long talk with the captain of the corvette at the custom-house."

"Holloa! and you told him—"

"Yes; I showed him a chart of the Isle of Pines, and pointed out how to get into the old hole."

Here the pair laughed short laughs, when Brand continued his questions with,

" And how did he take the bait ?"

" Hooked him; for I heard him order his first lieutenant to be ready for weighing at daylight, and say that my description tallied with that of the dying man they picked up in the 'Centipede's' boat," replied the Tuerto, with a chuckle.

"*Bueno!*" exclaimed the pirate, as his face assumed an unwonted sternness, while he rested his cheek on his left hand with the elbow on the table, and slipped his right into the pocket of his trowsers.

"*Bueno! amigo mio!* But how do I know but you may have made a little mistake, and described another haunt besides the Island of Pines, off in this direction ?"

There was the faintest click of a noise in the captain's pocket as he spoke, but not so faint but that it vibrated on the ear of the Spaniard, and, pushing back his chair a foot or two from the table, he raised his right hand, the fore fingers and thumb slightly bent inward, but grasping a jewel-hilted knife, whose dim blue blade glimmered up the loose sleeve. There was nothing threatening apparently in the movement, though the two villains looked at each other with a cold, murderous, unflinching glare.

The Don was the first to break the silence; and he said, in a low, hissing tone,

"*Maldito!* Because I had a little account of plata to settle with you before the men-o'-war should roast you out. But beware, *Capitano, mio!* I left a little paper at St. Jago with directions where to find me in case I did not return in a certain time."

" Ho, *compadre*, how very cautious with your friends! Why, what has put such thoughts into your head? *Diavolo!* we have stood by one another too long to separate now. There, my hand upon it."

Saying this, Captain Brand's whole manner changed, and, drawing his hand from his pocket, he reached over toward his companion. The Don, however, watched him narrowly, and his eye shot out a wary sparkle as he withdrew his hand, when, cautiously putting forth his own left, he touched his cold, thin brown fingers to those of the man before him. This operation ended, he quietly sipped a few drops of anisette, and rolled and lighted another paper cigar.

. " Well, *amigo*, let us now proceed to business," said Brand, gayly, "for dinner will soon be ready, and we have no time to lose. How stands the account ?"

" The papers are on board the felucca, and it will be more convenient, when the settlement is made, to come on board with the money. How would to-morrow morning do? There's no hurry."

" Just as you choose, friend of my soul! The doubloons, or the silk, or broadcloth are ready for you at any moment. Pay you in any thing except the delicious wines of France. *Bueno!*" he added, pulling out a splendid gold repeater, with a marquis's coronet on the chased back. "And now, *amigo*, accept this little token into the bargain."

Don Ignaçio's fiery eye twinkled with greed, but it was only for a moment, when, giving a quick glance at the coronet and coat of arms, he waved his fore finger gently to and fro, and shook his head.

"What! No? Why, you know it once belonged to the Captain General of Cuba, old Tol de rol de riddle rol—what was his name? He gave it me, you know, together with some other trinkets, for saving his life—a—you remember? Very generous old gentleman— nobleman indeed—he was. May he live a thousand years, or more, if he can!"

Ay, Don Ignaçio did remember the circumstance attending that generous transaction, and he remembered to have heard, also, that the Captain General made a present of all his money and jewels with the point of a broad blade quivering at his throat. He said nothing, however, in allusion to this interesting episode, but he smiled meaningly, and went on with his cigar.

"Not take it, eh? Well, *amigo*, I must look you up something else; but now for dinner. Babette, clear away for dinner. Here are the keys of the wine-cellar. The best, my beauty, and plenty of it." Then turning to his companion: "Suppose we take a stroll to the Tiger's Trap; the sun is sinking, and a walk will give us an appetite for the turtle-soup—*vamanos!*"

CHAPTER XII.

DOCTOR AND PRIEST.

'"But soon I heard the dash of oars,
I heard the pilots' cheer;
My head was turned perforce away,
And I saw a boat appear.

"The pilot and the pilot's boy,
I heard them coming fast;
Dear Lord in heaven! it was a joy
The dead men could not blast."

WHILE Captain Brand and Don Ignaçio Sanchez walked pleasantly along the pebbly shore of the clear blue inlet to the Tiger's Trap, let us, too, saunter amid the habitations which sheltered the pirate's haunt.

Apart from the mat sheds of the shelly cove of the basin, where the "Centipede" and "Panchita" were anchored, there was a nest of red-tiled buildings which served the crew of the former vessel for a dwelling when in port. It was pleasantly situated on a little sandy plateau, within a stone's-throw of the water, and shaded by a cluster of palm-trees; while in the rear was a dense jungle of canes and bushes, through which led numerous paths to a small lagoon beyond. The buildings were of one story, constructed of loose stones, the holes plastered with yellow clay, with broad, projecting eaves extending over roughly-built piazzas. They stood in a double row, leaving a stone pavement yard between, where one or two cocoa-nut-trees lifted their slim trunks like sentinels on guard. Two of the largest of these huts were mere shells inside, and used for mess-rooms, exposing the unhewn girders and roof above, but all whitewashed and tolerably clean. The floors were of rough mahogany boards, or heavy dark planks, and no doubt part of the cargo of some Honduras trader who had fallen into the pirates' hands. Around the sides of these mess-rooms were arranged small tables and canvas camp-stools, with eating utensils of every variety of pattern and value, from stray sets of French porcelain to common delf crockery. A large open chimney stood a little way off, where was a kitchen, in which the cookery was carried on, under the superintendence of a couple of old negroes. Beyond the mess-rooms were the sheds used for sleeping apartments, with lots of hammocks of canvas and straw braid hanging by their clews from the beams, quite like the berth-deck of a ship of war. Bags and sea-chests stood out from the walls, with bits of mirrors here and there, some with the glasses cracked, and others in square or round gilt frames. All, however, was arranged with a certain degree of order, and the floor was clean and well scrubbed. Another detached building, much smaller than the rest, was divided by a board partition into two rooms. The first was used for a store-room,· and was filled with bread in barrels, bags of coffee and sugar, hams, dried fruits, beans, salt meats, and what not, but every thing in abundance, and apparently the very best the market of the high seas could produce. A strong door protected this repository, with a wrought iron bar and padlock. ·The other portion of the building was more habitable. There were chairs and tables; a couple of upright bookcases with glass doors, one filled with books, odd numbers of magazines, and old newspapers, and the other containing a multitude of vials, pots, and bottles of medicine—a small apothecary's shop, in fact, together with two or three cases of surgical instruments. Two elegant bureaus, with rosewood doors and mouldings, like those furnished passenger ships to the East Indies, stood against the wall at either side; and near to each, in opposite corners, were low iron bedsteads, without mattresses or bedding, and merely stretched with dressed and embossed leather. For pillows were Chinese heel stools, and as for covering, the climate dispensed with it altogether. Hanging against the wall were a couple of brace of pistols and two or three muskets, and on the table stood a square case-bottle of gin, some glasses, and a richly-bound breviary clasped with a heavy gold strap; but in no other part of these huts were fire-arms ever allowed, and very rarely was liquor served out in more than the usual daily half-gill allowance. .

Seated at the table in the last room we have described were two men. One, the shorter of the two, was dressed in a long, loose bombazine cassock, girded about his waist by a white rope, which fell in knotted ends over his knees. Around his open neck was hung a ·string of black ebony beads, hooked on to a heavy gold cross, which rested on his capacious breast, and which the wearer was ·continually feeling, and occasionally pressing to his lips. His face was dark and sensual—thick, unctuous lips, a flat nose, and large black eyes—while a glossy fringe of raven hair went like a thick curtain all around his head, only leaving a bluish-white round patch on the shaved crown. This individual was the Padre Ricardo, who, for some good reasons best known to himself, had left his clerical duties in his native city of Vera Cruz and taken service with Captain Brand. One of the reasons for leaving—and rather abruptly, too—was for thrusting a cuchillo into the heart of his own father, who had reported him to his superior for his monstrous licentiousness. The padre, however, always declared that he was actuated entirely by filial duty in killing his old parent, to save him the pain and disgrace which would have followed the exposure of his son! He still clung, though excommunicated, to the priestly calling, and prided himself upon his fasts and vigils, never omitting the smallest forms or penances, and saying mass from Ave Maria in the early morning to Angelus at vesper time in the evening. For Captain Brand he was ready to shrive a dying pirate—and pretty busy he was, too, at times—or hear the confession of one with a troubled conscience in sound health; which, if important to the safety or well-being of the fraternity, he took a quiet opportunity of imparting to his superior in command. In these pursuits he not only made himself useful to Captain Brand, but he became more or less his confidant and adviser, and seemed to maintain his influence by ghostly advice over the superstitious feelings of the men. The padre, however, utterly detested the sea, and never touched his soft feet in the water if he could by any possibility avoid it; but since he had plenty to eat and drink on the island, and no end of prayers for his amusement when in charge of the haunt—as he was —to look out for the people who were left when the "Centipede" sailed on a cruise, he thus passed the time in a delightfully agreeable manner.

The companion who sat opposite to the padre was a tall, gaunt, cadaverous person, evidently of French extraction, with something kind and humane about his face, but yet the physiognomy expressed the utmost determination of character—such a heart and eye as could perform a delicate surgical operation without a flutter of nerve or eyelid, and who would stand before a leveled pistol looking calmly down the barrel as the hammer fell. His face was intellectual, and he never smiled. His whole appearance portrayed a thorough seaman. Where he came from no one knew; nor did he ever open his lips, even to the captain, with a reason for taking service among his band. All known about him was that he landed from a slaver at St. Jágo, and was engaged by Don Ignaçio to serve professionally with Brand in assisting the patriots on the Spanish Main. When, however, he reached the rendezvous of the pirates, and discovered that they were altogether a different sort of patriots than he had bargained for, he nevertheless made no objections to remain, and took the oath of allegiance, only stipulating that he should not be called upon to take an active part in their proceedings. Here, then, he remained for nearly three years, attending to the sick or wounded, taking no interest in the accounts of the exploits of the freebooters around him —rarely, indeed, holding speech with any one save his room-mate, the padre, or occasionally a dinner or a walk with Captain Brand. On the last expedition, however, of the "Centipede," he had been induced to go on board, so that he might become a check and guard over the brutal ruffian who had been placed temporarily in command; but, as we have already seen, his influence had been of little avail.

There was yet another occupant of the room inhabited by the doctor and Padre Ricardo; and a low moaning cry caused the former to rise quietly from his chair and approach the low iron bedstead on his side of the lodging. There, beneath a light gauze musquito-net, lay our poor little Henri—his once round, rosy, innocent face now pale and thin, with a red spot on each cheek, and a dark, soft line beneath the closed eyes. Uneasily he moved in his fitful slumber; and putting his little hands together as if in prayer, he murmured, "Oh mamma, mamma!"

Beside the bed stood an unglazed jar of lemonade, together with a vial and a spoon. The doctor drew nigh, and, gently pushing aside the curtain, stood looking at the child for some minutes. Presently the little sick boy feebly stretched out his delicate, thin limbs, and unclosed his eyes. Oh! how dim, and sad, and touching was that look, as he gave a timid, half-wild stare, and then, closing the lids tight together, the hot drops bubbled out and coursed slowly down his tender cheeks.

The doctor, with the gentleness of a woman, bent over him, and taking up his poor, limp little hand, he remained feeling the fluttering pulse and catching the hot breath on his dark cheeks. As if communing with himself, while a glow of compassion lighted up his careworn visage, he muttered,

"By the great and good God, who hears me, if I save this child I will restore him to his heart-broken mother!"

He sank down on his knees by the bedside as he made his vow, and letting the little hand rest on the bed, he buried his face in his large bony hands. What thoughts passed through that man's mind none but the Almighty knows; but when he arose his stern features had resumed their wonted expression, and, pouring a little lemonade in a glass, he held it to the sleeper's lips. Then moving noiselessly back to the table, he said, in a low tone,

"Padre, the boy will live. His fever is leaving him, and he will get well."

"*Ave Maria! Santissima!*" ejaculated the padre, crossing himself and kissing his cross; "I pray for him. You must give him to me, doctor. I will make him a little priest, and he shall swing the censer and chant the Misericordia when I get the new chapel built."

"Time enough to think of that, *mi padre*, when he gets strong again. But just now all the prayers *you* can say for him will do him no good, and so I hope you won't put yourself to the trouble."

"*Cierto, amigo*, doctor; but don't sneer at the prayers of the

Church. They do good; they ease the soul and soothe the pangs of Purgatory."

"Ah! and how long do you expect to stop in Purgatory?"

"*Ave purissima!* What a question to ask your pious and devout Padre Ricardo!"

"Question the devil when you want fire," retorted the doctor, as he opened a book lying on the table before him, and put an end to the dialogue. His companion quietly helped himself to a measure of pure gin, and unclasped the covers of his richly-bound missal.

Scarcely, however, had their conversation ceased, when a hoarse hum of many voices was heard in the direction of the sheds without, mingled with shouts in all tongues and uproarious laughter.

"*Peste!*" said the doctor, looking out of an open window; "the people have knocked off work and are coming home to their supper. They seem to have brought some of the crew of the felucca with them too. We shall have a loud night of it, for the captain has sent them a pipe of wine and a barrel of rum to carouse with."

"*Pobre çitos!* they have had a hard time of it during the summer —short of rum, and water too, I hear, and they need refreshment and repose. So many of my poor flock killed, too, by that savage American corvette, and I not near to administer the last consolations and holy rite!" sighed the padre, as he kissed the crucifix and bowed his head. "There is Lascar Joe, too, among the missing! He refused the sacrament, infidel as he was, the day before he sailed; but what turtle-soup he made!" The padre hereupon sighed deeply again, but whether for the loss of the Lascar or the soup, no one knows.

The noise without increased—the rattle of crockery, the clinking of glasses, the moving of feet, and all the sounds of hungry, boisterous sailors at table. Soon, too, a shout or cheer would be heard, then a verse of a song, roars of laughter, and now and then the tinkle of a guitar struck by vigorous fingers in waltz or fandango.

"*Merçi!*" muttered the doctor, as he looked compassionately at the sick child on the bed; "those noisy wretches will, I fear, disturb the little boy, and it's as hot here too, padre, as the place we all are going to."

"It *is* warm, my son!" he replied, as his thick unctuous lips parted with a smile at his companion's allusion to another and a hotter place; "but I think our good *capitano* would have a cot slung for my little priest in the saloon of the big building there. It is always cool on the crag, you know."

"Ah! perhaps he will," said the doctor, reflectively; "I'll see about it."

Stepping again to the bedside of the little sufferer, he laid a hand gently on his forehead, where the soft curls lay in confusion about his temples, and then quickly touching his pulse, he regarded him

attentively for a few moments, while at the same time a light glow
of perspiration came faintly over the innocent face and spread itself
down the neck.

"His fever is breaking! *Grace à Dieu!*" whispered the doctor to
the padre; "his breath is regular and cool, and he is sleeping sweetly. Now, if you like, we will go to see the captain, and, if he con-
sents, I will carry the child when he wakes to the dwelling."

The doctor carefully closed the door of the room, as he and his
companion stepped out into the open court-yard, and moved toward
the spacious sheds beyond.

CHAPTER XIII.

A MANLY FANDANGO.

" While feet and tongues like lightning go
  With—What cheer, Luke? and how do, Joe?
  Dick Laniard chooses Meg so spruce,
  And buxom Nell takes Kit Caboose."

" Now around they go, and around and around,
  With hop, skip, and jump, and frolicsome bound,
        Such sailing and gliding,
        Such sinking and sliding,
        Such lofty curvetting
        And grand pirouetting,
  Mix'd with the tones of a dying man's groans,
  Mix'd with the rattling of dead men's bones."

TWILIGHT had taken the place of the red sun, the stars came timidly out one by one, and then in sparkling clusters the brilliant constellations illumined the blue heavens as the rosy twilight faded again away. Then the ripple of the inlet came with a tranquil musical sound upon the white pebbly beach, the lizards in the holes and crevices of the rocks began their plaintive wheetlings, the frogs and alligators joined in the chorus from the low lagoon in the distance, and the early night of the tropic had begun.

But louder far than the hum of the insects and reptiles, and brighter than the lamps of heaven, arose the wild shouts and songs of the pirates carousing, where the torches and wax-lights lit up the scene of their orgies with the glare of day. The great mess-room was a blaze of light from candles and lamps, stuck in brackets or gilt sconces about the walls, or hanging awry in broken chandeliers from the lofty beams. The remains of their feast had been cleared away, and the tables were covered with bottles, cups, and glasses, with boxes of cigars and pans of lighted coals. At one end of the room was a large table, on which was laid a black cloth with a broad silver border—sometimes used by the padre on great occasions—and covered with cards and piles of Mexican or Spanish dollars. At the other end was a raised platform, where four or five swarthy fellows with guitars in their hands were strumming away in the clear rattling harmony of Spanish boleros and dances, shrieking out at intervals snatches of songs in time to the music, or twirling the instruments around their heads in a frenzy of excitement. At the tables,

too, were more of the excited band, vociferating with almost superhuman fluency in various languages their exploits, pausing occasionally amid the hubbub to clink their glasses together, and then chattering and yelling on as before. In the centre of the apartment were
some half dozen of the same sort, either spinning around the floor in
the waltz, or moving with a certain air of careless, manly grace one
toward another in the gavotte or bolero. There were at the least
some sixty or seventy of these fellows in the room together, most
of them above the middle height, with finely-developed muscles,
broad shoulders, bushy whiskers, and flowing hair. They came apparently from all climes, from Africa to the Mexican Gulf, and their
features and complexions partook of every imaginable type, from the
light skin and florid complexion of the Swede, to the low brow, oval
olive cheek of the Mediterranean, and the coal-black hue and flat nose
of the Bight of Benin. Their dress was uniform—frock collars cut
square and thrown well back over their ample chests; their nether
limbs incased in clean duck or brown linen trowsers, with silk sashes
around their waists, and large gold rings in their ears. Mingled here
and there in the moving throng, or leaning over the large table with
the black cloth cover, were a few fellows in the uniform rig of the
Guarda Costa, in navy jackets and black silk belchers around their
throats; but all were without weapons of any description, and were
enjoying themselves each after his fancy. Sentinels stood at the
doors of the mess-room with drawn cutlasses over their shoulders,
so that in case of a violent quarrel or row, in dance, drinking, or
gaming, the culprits might be cared for.

While the uproar was at its height, and the lofty tiled roof was
ringing with the gay and ribald songs and shouts of the excited
crowds, two persons appeared in the doorway at the middle of the
room, and entered. In a moment, as the busy revelers beheld them,
the dance ceased, the music of the guitars died away in a tinkling
cadença, the glasses stopped clinking, the dollars no longer chinked,
and the songs and shouts were hushed. You might have heard a
real drop for a minute, until one of the individuals who had entered
slowly walked forward a few paces and threw his right hand aloft in
salutation. Then burst forth a hoarse, simultaneous shout of

"*Viva nuestro amigo! Viva el capitano!*"

Captain Brand did not pause until he had reached the centre of
the great hall, where he stood calmly looking around upon the
swarthy groups, who crowded about in circles at a respectful distance from him; and then amid the silence he spoke up, in a frank,
off-hand manner,

"Well, my men, I am glad to see you all once more around me.
You have not been so successful as I hoped, but we must take the
good and ill luck as it comes, and I have no fault to find with you.

The times, however, are bad enough; for I have certain news that our retreat here, where we have so long been hid, may be discovered"—the villains around held their breath and let their cigars lie dead in their mouths—"but," went on their commander, "I shall do all that is prudent in the circumstances for the benefit of all of us; and when we leave here you will still have me for your leader, with my head, heart, and blade ever ready to advise or protect you." As he stopped speaking another cheer arose:

"*Viva, nuestro amigo! viva! viva! El 'Centipede' y el capitano! Hasta muerto!* Long live the captain! We stand by you until death!"

"Thank you, my friends; I have but one more word to say. The men who have the relief at the signal stations and the water battery must keep sober. Now go on again with the music."

The captain, however, did not immediately quit the hall, but, while the revel began once more with all its enthusiasm, he moved amid the crowd of its adherents and said a cheerful word to many.

"Ah! Pepe, your arm in a sling, eh! a graze of a grape-shot, eh? Why, Hans, you here! nothing can hurt *you!* Well, Monsieur Antoine, how well thou art looking; and that pretty sweetheart of thine at St. Lucie! Bah! never look sad, man; thou shalt see her again. What, my jolly Jack Tar! an ugly scratch, that, across your jaw—a splinter, eh? Never mind; a little plaster and half allowance of grog will put you all right again. So good-night, my friends. *Adios!*"

Saying these words, all addressed to the individuals in their different languages, he gave a graceful wave of his hand and passed out of the building. As he rejoined his friend, the commander of the "Panchita," who had waited at the threshold, while his wary glim of an eye searched the faces and read the thoughts of all the villains who clustered about the room—they both stepped out into the court-yard and sauntered pleasantly on toward the crag. They had not, however, proceeded many paces before they encountered the padre and the doctor.

"Ah!" exclaimed the captain, who was in advance, "how goes it with my doctor?" shaking his hand as he spoke. "Oh, *mi padre*, how art thou?" turning to Ricardo.

"*Salve!* my son; not been so well this morning, with the old rheumatism in my head."

"Drunk!" said sententiously the doctor.

Then again with a gay laugh to the other, "Well, my doctor, your first cruise has not been so pleasant in the 'Centipede' as I hoped it might be, but the next may be more agreeable."

"Perhaps so, Captain Brand; but I shall have a word or two with you on that subject to-morrow; and, in the mean while, *señor*, I brought a little boy back with me who is ill from fever, and my

F

quarters are so stifling hot, and the air from the lagoon is so bad, that I would like to stow him for a day or so, with your permission, in your quarters, where it is cooler."

"Certainly, doctor; why not? my house and all in it are at your service. By the way, I was about to ask you and the padre to dine with me and Don Iguaçio there. Will you join us? Yes? Then let us move on, for dinner must be ready by this time, and it would be a sin to keep Babette waiting."

Excusing himself for a few minutes, the doctor went for his sick charge, and returned with him in his arms to the pirate's dwelling.

CHAPTER XIV.

A PIRATES' DINNER.

'But the best of the joke was, the moment he spoke
Those words which the party seemed almost to choke,
As by mentioning Noah some spell had been broke,
And, hearing the din from barrel and bin,
Drew at once the conclusion that thieves had'got in."

WHEN the guests had assembled in the pirate's saloon it was some minutes before their host appeared. When, however, he did step into the room from his private apartment adjoining, he was altogether a different man in outward appearance than in the early morning. In place of the loose sailor summer rig which he then wore, he was now attired as a gentleman of elegant fashion of the time in which we write. His lower limbs were clothed with flesh-colored silk stockings, and fitted into a pair of pointed toed pumps with buckles of brilliants that a duchess might have envied. A pair of white cassimere breeches, which set off to advantage his well-shaped leg, were tied in a dainty bow of rose-colored satin ribbon below the knee, and fitted him like a second skin. His waistcoat was of rose-colored watered silk, embroidered with silver, and which, with its flaps and ample proportions, was halfway hidden by a dress coat of green velvet. This last garment had a sort of navy cut, with standing collar richly laced with silver, gold buttons in a double row of the size of doubloons, with loose sleeves and cuffs heavily laced with silver also. His linen was of the most gossamer fineness, the collar thrown slightly back and confined by a single clasp of rubies the size of beans, while below was a frill of cambric ruffles sparkling with opal studs framed in diamonds. The ruffles, too, at his wrist were of the most beautiful point lace, secured by royal brilliants, and he was altogether a dandy of such princely magnificence that the courtiers of the days of the old French monarchy might have taken him for a study. His manner, likewise, was every way in keeping with his splendid attire; and the ease and grace with which he excused himself to his guests for keeping them waiting certainly denoted a knowledge of a higher order of breeding and society than that in which his lot had been cast.

From the very moment of his entrance, however, Don Ignaçio had measured him at a glance. His single glittering eye of jet had taken

him in from the laced collar of his coat to the buckles of his shoes.
Not a jewel in his dress, from the flaming opals in his bosom to the
brilliant stones at his wrists, and down to the sparkling clusters at
his feet, did not his one uneasy optic drink in the flash and estimate
the value. Nay, he calculated by instinct the weight of the gold buttons on his coat and the price of the exquisite lace which fell in snowy
folds about his hands. Oh, a rare mathematician was Don Ignaçio!
What greedy thoughts, too, passed through that little Spaniard's
brain! "Ah!" thought he, "shall I take my debt in those priceless
gems, each one the ransom of a princess, which the old Captain General may one of these days reclaim? Hola! no! Or shall I receive
more negotiable commodities in gold, cochineal, or silks? Well!
Veremos! we shall see!"

The effect produced upon the good Padre Ricardo was altogether
different. As the captain entered with all his glorious raiment upon
him, he started back, and, bowing before him as if he were Saint
Paul himself, he seized his superior's white hand, and kissed it with
fervent devotion. Not satisfied with this mark of respect, he raised
his dingy paws, holding his crucifix before him, and murmured, in a
sort of ecstasy,

"*Mi hico! mi capitano! que brillante!*"—"My son! my captain!
what a brilliant being you are!"

Singularly in contrast, however, was the effect produced upon the
doctor, who merely raised his dark eyes in an abstracted gaze, gave
a careless and rather contemptuous nod of recognition, and then
turned to examine one of the richly-inlaid cabinets which adorned
the saloon. All these various phases of sympathy, attraction, or contempt flickered like a sunbeam into Captain Brand's reflecting brain,
as, with a delicately-perfumed handkerchief in one hand, and a gold-
enameled and diamond-incrusted snuff-box in the other, he bowed
gracefully to his visitors, and seated himself at table.

The table was now rolled out into the centre of the saloon, laid
with a snowy-white damask cloth, and covered with the equipage
for a banquet. At either corner were noble branches of solid silver
candelabra, which would have graced an altar, as perhaps they had,
and holding clusters of wax-lights, which shed their rays over the
display below. In the centre arose a huge epergne of silver, fashioned into the shape of a drooping palm-tree, whose leaves were of
frosted silver, and about the trunk played a wilderness of monkeys.
Beneath, around the board, were cut-glass decanters, flat bulbous
flasks of colored Bohemian glass, crystal goblets, delicate and almost
shadowy wine-cups from Venice, silver wine-coolers, all mingled in
with a heterogeneous collection of rare china and silver dishes. Such
wines, too, as filled those vessels! not a prince or magnate in all the
lands where the vine is planted could boast of so rare and exquisite

a collection. Pure, thin, rain-water Madeira, full threescore years in bottle! Pale, limpid Port, whose color had long since gone with age, and left only the musk-like odor; flasks of Johannisberg of pearly light; bottles of Tokay for lips of cardinals; tall, slim stems of the taper flasks of the Rhine; while the ruby hues of wine from the Rhone stood clustering about amid pyramids of pine-apples, oranges, and bananas, and all loading the air of the saloon with their delicious fragrance.

When the party had become fairly seated around the board, and while the host was bailing out the soup from an enormous silver tureen with a tea-cup—for it did not appear that he had ever been presented in the usual way with a ladle—fishing out the floating morsels of rich callipee, with the delicate frills of his sleeves turned back, he began the conversation in the Castilian language:

"Well, *amigos*, we are taking our last feast together, I fear, on this little cluster of rocks, for a long time to come."

"How!" exclaimed the padre, as he stuffed a wedge of turtle fat in his oily mouth, and opened his round black eyes to their fullest extent in manifest surprise.

"*Como, mi hico!*" he repeated, as he passed a dirty paw over his smooth chin, and looked inquiringly.

"Yes, holy father, our good friend Don Ignaçio here has brought us somewhat startling intelligence. Capital soup, this. I shall give Babette a dollar. Yes, the eagles and vultures are after us; all the West India fleet; the Lord only knows how many ships, and brigs, and gun-boats. Glass of Madeira with you, doctor?" wiping his thin lips with a corner of the damask table-cloth as he spoke; "and they have tampered, too, with my old friends the custom-house people. Take away the tureen, Babette—and, in point of fact, I shouldn't be the least surprised to see a swarm of those navy gentlemen off the reef here at any moment. A sharp knife, Babette, for these teal—a duck should be cut, not torn. Try that Moselle, Don Ignaçio; I know your fancy for light wines. This was given me by a Captain— 'pon my soul, I forget his name; he had such a pretty wife, Madame Matilde," glancing at the frame of miniatures on the wall; "sweet creature she was; took quite a fancy for me, I believe, and might have been sitting here at this moment, but a—really I forget her other name. However, it makes no difference: the wine is called Moselle."

Now be it here observed that Don Ignaçio drank very little wine or stimulants of any sort, and never by any chance a drop from any vessel which, with his single bright eye, he did not see his host first indulge in. This self-imposed sacrifice may have been owing to his diffidence, or modest deference to Captain Brand, or, perhaps, other and private reasons of his own; but yet he never broke through that rule of politeness and abstemiousness. Sometimes, indeed, he carried his principles so far as to refuse a meat or the fruits which his host had not partaken of, and always with a slow shake of his brown fore finger, as if he did not like even to smell the dish presented to him.

"What! not even a sip of that nectar, *compadre mio ?*"

The compadre shook his digit, and observed that drinking nectar sometimes made people sick.

The captain laughed gayly, and said, "Bah! learning to drink does the harm, and not the art, when properly acquired."

During all the foregoing interlude the doctor remained in his grave, calm humor, and only when the captain alluded to the lady whose husband's name escaped him did he show signs of interest. Then his eye followed the look toward the miniature, and his jaws came together with a slight grating spasm.

Padre Ricardo, however, was in excellent sympathetic spirits, eating and drinking like a glutton of all within his reach, and turning his full eyes at times, as if to a deity, upon his friend the captain. Once he spoke—

"But, my son, you were talking of leaving this quiet retreat, where we have passed so many happy hours."

"Yes, friend of my soul! Those fellows with commissions, and pennants at their mast-heads, and guns, and what not, seem determined to do us a mischief." The devout padre crossed himself, and pressed the crucifix to his greasy lips. "Ay! they would no doubt arraign us before some one of their legal tribunals. Put us in prison, perhaps; or maybe give us a slight squeeze in a rope or iron collar!"

The padre groaned audibly, and dropped the wing of a teal he was gnawing, forgetting, strange as it may seem, to cross himself.

"*Hola, mi padre!* cheer up! We are worth a million of dead men yet. The world is wide, the sea open, and with a stout plank under our feet and one of these fellows"—here he balanced a long carving-knife, dripping with blood-red gravy, in his hand—"in our belts, who can stop us?"

There was the cold, ferocious-eyed gleam of a dying shark in the speaker's eyes as he went on with his carving; but the priest gave a jerk of trepidation with his chin, and appeared anxious to hear more.

"Don Ignaçio, try a bit of this roast *guana ;* it's quite white and tender. No? Babette, give me some of that rabbit stew!" The one-eyed individual was likewise helped to some of that savory ragoût, and proceeded to pick the bones with much care and deliberation.

"Still *triste,* my *padre!* Come, come, this will never do. Join me in a bumper of this generous old Port. *Bueno!* may we attain the same age! By the way, where did this rich stuff come from?" holding up the decanter between the light and his face as he spoke.

Don Ignaçio's glittering optic pierced clear through the light ruby medium of the wine, cut-glass decanter and all, as he furtively watched his host, and was prepared to dodge in case the heavy vessel should slip out of the captain's hand. Such things had happened, and might again; besides, a hard flint substance with a multitude of sharp projections, two or three inches thick and five or six pounds in weight, falling from a height on a man's head, might kill him. The Don thought of all this, and twitched something up his sleeve with his hand under the table. But Captain Brand, it seemed, had no intention of smashing his elegant dinner set of glass, and putting down the decanter and raising a finger to his forehead, he said, "How did that wine come into my possession?"

. "Somebody gave it to you, perhaps. *Quien sabe?* (Who knows?)" suggested Don Ignaçio.

Without heeding the interruption, the captain's eye rested on the brilliant snuff-box on the table beside him, where the letter L was set in diamonds and blue enamel on the back, and catching it with a rap, his face lighted up, and as he took a pinch and passed the box to the padre, he exclaimed,

"Ah! now I remember, my old friend—the Portuguese countess from Oporto. *Dios! de mi alma!* (God of my soul!) what a stately beauty was her daughter!"

Here Captain Brand sneezed, and, drawing a delicately-perfumed lace handkerchief from his waistcoat pocket, blew his nose. Meanwhile the box went round the table; Padre Ricardo took a huge pinch with his dirty fingers, and feasted his eyes upon the precious lid. The doctor scarcely gave the elegant bawble a glance as he helped himself. The Don, however, examined it with the eye of a connoisseur, and not only that, but he threw a spark at the captain's flashy waistcoat, and thought he detected some other article in the capacious pockets vice the handkerchief. Perhaps he may have been mistaken and perhaps not, though he was so very suspicious an old villain that he sometimes did his friends injustice. Nor did he put his thin brown fingers, with the few grains of snuff he had dipped from the box, to his sheepskin nostrils till he had watched the effect it had produced on those around him.

"Ah! my friends, I remember distinctly now all about it," continued the captain, as he returned the kerchief and shook a few specks of the titillating dust from his point-lace sleeve; "it is about three years ago, just before you came to live with me, padre, that we fell in with a large ship bound to Porto Rico. She had been disabled in an awful hurricane, which had taken two of her masts clean off at the decks, and was leaking badly. We, too, had been a little hurt in the same gale, and having made a pretty good season, I was anxious to get back here and give the crews a rest. Well, we made out the ship about an hour before sunset, and it was quite dark before we came up with her. There she lay, rolling like a log, though there was not much sea on, and we could hear her chain-pumps clanking, and saw the water spouting out from her scuppers as pure almost as it went into her hold. As we came up alongside they hailed me for assistance, and said the ship was sinking, and could not live till morning.

"Of course I could give them no actual assistance, situated as I was"—here the narrator smiled as he glanced round upon his guests—"it would have been simply absurd, you know, the idea of my putting men on board to keep her afloat for the nearest gibbet. Bah! I did not dream of such ridiculous nonsense. However, I determined to make her a visit, and, if there should be any thing to save from the wreck in an undamaged condition, why, I should look around.

"Not too much of that Port, *mi padre;* think of your rheumatism in the morning! Doctor, you don't drink!

"Well, going on board, I found two lady passengers—the wife and daughter of an old judge of the island of Porto Rico, with half a dozen servants, who were all screaming, and praying, and beseeching me to save them—all but one, a tall, graceful girl, with a large India shawl wrapped around her shoulders, her white arms glancing through the folds, and a pair of dark, liquid, almond-shaped eyes, such as I had never before seen. The fact is, my friends, I had always before fancied blue. But there stood this girl, with eyes like a wounded stag, leaning up against the weather bulwarks near the open cabin door.

"Babette, take away all but the wine and fruit, and bring fire. Pass that box this way, if you please, *compadre!* Thank you."

Don Ignaçio seemed to have an affection for the trifle, and had counted the brilliants over and over again, and made a mental calculation of their weight and value; and when he did move it as he was desired, his greedy eye followed it with fascination.

"Yes, it's very pretty, and I set a great store by it," parenthesized the host, as he resumed his tale:

"The girl never screamed or even spoke, and, amid all the hubbub of a drunken skipper and a disorderly crew, she remained quiet and unmoved. To assure the people, I told them that I would stay by the ship and do what I could for them. At this the old lady clasped me around the neck, and kissed me, and blubbered over me more than ever she did, I imagined, to the old Spanish judge, her husband—imploring me too, by all the saints she could think of, to take herself and daughter out of the sinking vessel at once. You may believe that I would much rather have been treated in that way by the lovely girl with the wonderful eyes instead of the fat, rancid old woman beside her; but there was no help for it just then, and so I consented, with all the professions of sympathy I could make, to do as she desired."

Here the captain lit a pure Havana, and, after a few puffs and a sip of Port, continued:

CHAPTER XV.

DROWNING A MOTHER TO MURDER A DAUGHTER.

> "At last she startled up,
> And gazed on the vacant air
> With a look of awe, as if she saw
> Some dreadful phantom there."

"No sooner had I assured the old lady that I would transfer them to my vessel than her daughter made a step forward, and, letting her shawl fall upon the deck, she seized my hand with both of hers, and said, in a low contralto voice,

"'Heaven bless you, *señor!*'

"By the cestus of Venus, *caballeros*, the pressure of that girl's hand, and the deep, speaking look of gratitude she gave me out of her liquid eyes, quite did my business!"

"And the senorita's too, I think," chimed in the one-eyed commander, as he wagged his uneasy head at the narrator.

"*Quien sabe?*" (who knows?) went on Captain Brand: "at all events, I raised her soft patrician hand to my lips and kissed it respectfully. Ha! I noticed, too, as I released her round, slender fingers, that she wore a sapphire of great brilliancy—ay, here it is now. I keep it in remembrance of the girl."

Saying this, the host shook back the lace ruffles of his sleeve, and, crooking his little finger, exhibited the jewel to his guests.

"Go on, my son," said the padre, as his sensual face expressed his satisfaction at the recital—"*Vamonos!*"

"My holy father," responded the narrator, "beware of that wine-flask! You have grand mass to-morrow! it is the feast of our patron saint, you know."

"*Si! si! hijo mio!* your padre is always ready," crossing himself in a half tipsy way as he spoke—"*Vamonos!*" The doctor looked as cold as marble, and said not a word.

"Well, gentlemen," went on Captain Brand, "I soon got that ship in a tolerably wholesome state of command. I made my trusty old boatswain, Pedillo, lock the fuddled skipper up sound and tight in his own state-room, and the rest of my men took a few ropes' ends, and belted the lubbers of a crew until they went to work at the pumps with renewed vigor. I also insisted upon the scared male servauts of tho passengers lending a hand at that innocent recreation, for you see I had no intention of letting the ship go down—"

"With tho Capitano Brand in her," interrupted Señor Sanchez.

"No, by no manner of means; for the ship, I felt, was settling fast, and I could hear the loose cargo, which had broken adrift below in tho main hold, playing tho devil's own game; smashing and crushing from side to side as the vessel rolled, and coming in contact with the stanchions and beams, with a surging swash of water, too, which told tho tale without the trouble of breaking open the hatches. I took, however, the precaution to run my eye over the manifest to see if, perchance, there was any treasure in tho after run or any where else, as, in case there had been, I should have made some little effort to get at it. However, there was nothing on board but wine, dried fruits, and heavy bale goods, not worth tho time or trouble, in the aspect of affairs at that time, to save as much as a single cask or a drum of prunes. I glanced, too, at the clearance list, and saw that the names of tho passengers were La Señora Luisa Lavarona, and tho Señorita Lucia, lady and daughter, with half a dozen orders and titles, of the judge in *Puerto Rico*. *Bueno!* roll me an orange, if you please, doctor! Ah! *gracias*, thanks."

The doctor rolled the orange, and, had it been a grape-shot or any other iron missile, its aim would have gone straight through the captain's body, just above his left waistcoat pocket.

"In the mean while the old lady rushed around in a tremendous hurry, in and out of tho cabin, losing her balance occasionally in the lurches, ordering her maids to pull out trunks and boxes on to the deck; then giving me a hug to relieve her feelings, and praying and crying between whiles in the most whimsical manner. Not contented either with getting out a pile of luggage and chests that would have swamped a jolly-boat, she insisted upon waiting until a locker was broken open in the cabin pantry for the purpose of rescuing six cases of old Port wine, which had been, she told me, sent as a present from the Archbishop of Lisbon to his friend the judge. At this juncture I persuaded her to send her daughter and a few light articles first on board my vessel, when the boat would then return for herself and the remainder of their property. Accordingly, I carefully wrapped the lovely girl in shawls and cloaks, and got her over the side and down into my boat, pitched a few light caskets and cases in after tho young beauty, and then, with a quiet word or two into Pedillo's sharp ear, the boat shoved off. I suppose it may have been half an hour before my boat returned, and then I learned from the coxswain that he had shown his charge down into my private cabin, and she appeared as comfortable and resigned as possible. Well, we made quick work of it now, tumbled a good many things into the boat, when I myself got in to receive the old lady and her retinue. By tho way, among tho articles were the boxes of wine—this is some of it"—tapping the decanter, now nearly empty from the attacks of the priest—"and in my opinion it does great credit to the taste and judgment of that venerable archbishop."

"*Ave, purissima!*" said the padre, with a hiccough; "I shall be a bishop myself one of these days. *Ora pro nobis!*"

"You'll be a cardinal," gibed in the doctor, "if swilling wine will do it."

Captain Brand went on with his narrative:

"Where was I? Oh! ah! We were waiting alongside the ship, with her lower chain-plates not a foot above water, for the donna to be hoisted over the rail, since she would not permit any of her attendants to precede her—though Heaven knows they were anxious enough to do so. By this time, too, after my men had left the deck of the ship, the crew had somehow got hold of a barrel of wine, and, letting the pumps work themselves, were guzzling away in grand style. I began to lose patience at last, and shouted to the old lady to come at once, or I should be compelled to leave her. She merely leaned over the rail, however, and chattered forth that all she had in the world was at my service—of course, figuratively she meant—but she must stay another minute to find a jar of preserved ginger, which was her only cure for the cholic."

"You didn't take the offer of the old lady as a figure of speech, I presume?" asked the doctor.

"No!" muttered the one-eyed old wretch, with a sneer. "And that jar of ginger spared her any more attacks of cholic!"

"*Caballeros*, you are both right. I did accept the gift of her worldly goods in the frank spirit in which it was offered, without any reservation; and, to my almost certain knowledge, the Señora Lavarona was never more troubled with illness of any kind.

"The fact was, that, finding the ship fast sinking, and her crew becoming boisterous and rebellious as the imminent danger burst upon them, they proposed, since their own boats were stove, to take possession of mine! That *was* a joke, to be sure! A dozen drunken swabs, with naked hands, to capture ten of the old 'Centipede's' picked men, with a pistol and knife each under their shirts; and."—here the speaker laughed heartily—"and Captain Brand beside them! *Diavolo!* what silly people there are in this world!"

The good padre joined his superior in this ebullition of feeling, and seemed to enjoy the joke immensely, rolling his goggle-eyes and head from side to side, kissing his crucifix, and exclaiming, with devotion,

"*Que hombre es eso!*"—"What a man he is!"

"Well, *señores*, the next minute we let go the painter and floated astern past the ship's counter, and a few strokes of the oar-blades sent us dancing away to leeward, where the schooner was lying with

THE PIRATE'S PREY.

her main-sail up, and the jib-sheet hauled well to windward. We made no unnecessary noise in getting alongside, and it took no great time to get the boat clear, a tackle hooked on, and to swing her on board over the long gun. Then we drew aft the sheets, set the foresail, and the 'Centipede' was once more reeling off the knots on her course."

"But the ship, my son?"

"Why, my padre, I was so busy attending to the schooner, and afterward going below to break the sad news to my lovely dark-eyed passenger of the loss of her mother, that I had no time to devote to the ship. Pedillo, however, told me that he heard a good deal of frantic shrieking, and prayers, and cursing, with, for a little while, the renewed clank of the chain-pumps, but after that we had got too far to windward to hear more. About midnight, though, Pedillo and some of the watch thought they saw a white shower of foam like a breaking wave, and a great commotion in the water, but that was all. So, you see, what really became of that old craft we do not positively know; though for a long time afterward I read the marine lists very attentively, yet I never saw any accounts of her arrival at her destination.

"Perhaps," added Captain Brand, with a peculiar smile, as he lit a fresh cigar, "her arrival may have escaped my notice, as I hope it may, though I think not."

Don Ignaçio intimated, by waving his fore finger to and fro, that such a hope had no possible foundation in fact; and he stated, too, that he knew the underwriters had paid the full insurance on the missing ship.

"Ah! well, that seems to settle the matter, truly," murmured the captain, as if he had long entertained painful doubts on the subject, and now his mind was finally relieved.

"But, *hico mio!* Son of mine! *La Señorita*—hiccough—with the almond-shaped eyes—*Santissima!*—hic—how did she bear the—death of her—hic—mother?"

"*Por Dios, padre!* there was a scene which would have drawn tears from a—"

"Pirate," suggested the doctor.

The padre blubbered outright, and his round, tipsy eyes nearly popped out of his head.

"Ay, *monsieur*, even from mine! But to go back a little. When I had got all snug on board the schooner, I went below, and moved softly on tiptoe along the passage to the door of my beautiful cabin.

"You remember, *amigo*," said the narrator, turning toward Don Ignaçio, "how that cabin was fitted, and how much it cost to do it. I think you paid the bill for me? No?"

Oh yes, Captain Brand was quite right. Don Ignaçio remembered it well, and the bill was a thousand gold ounces, sixteen thousand hard silver dollars; and by no means dear at that, for the Don never allowed any body to cheat *him*.

"Cheats himself, though, sometimes. Don't charge more than the usual commission."

The one-eyed usurer looked wicked at this remark, but he said nothing, being occupied at the moment rolling up a paper cigar with one hand, and wetting the brown fore finger of the other.

"Well, *caballeros*, I peeped through the lattice-work of the cabin door, and there reclined my pretty prize—I recall her as if it were yesterday—on one of the large blue satin damask lounges of the after transoms. Her head rested on one of her round ivory arms, half hidden in the luxurious pillows; her shawl, too, was thrown back; and with a somewhat disordered dress, and a mass of glossy hair clustering in ringlets about her neck and white shoulders, I thought then, as I do now, that she was a paragon of loveliness. I saw her, as she thus reclined, by the light of a large shaded crystal lamp, which hung by silver chains from the cabin beams, and shed a rose-tinted effulgence over the whole apartment. When I first approached the door the girl was looking out of her own large liquid lamps, so superbly framed in a heavy fringe of dark lashes, in evident curiosity around the elegant cabin. Her looks wandered from the Turkey carpet on the floor to the beautiful silk hangings, that exquisite set of inlaid pearl ebony furniture, the display of knickknacks, and Dresden porcelain panels of the sides, and, in fact, nothing seemed to escape her; and the good taste of the fittings evidently met her approbation. At times, too, she would turn her gaze out of the narrow little window of the stern, and peer anxiously over the vessel's wake, which by this time was skimming along like a wild duck, and leaving countless bubbles behind her. At the first sound I made, however, in opening the door, she started up and stepped forward to meet me.

"'Oh, *Señor Capitano, mi madre!* (My mother!) What detains her? We seem to be going very fast through the water!'

"I gently took the girl's outstretched hands and led her back to the cushioned transom. Then I told her, as kindly as I could, that I did all in my power to save her good mother, but that the crew had mutinied—they had taken possession of the unfortunate ship—great confusion existed—and as I feared, you know, that my own boat would be swamped by remaining longer alongside, I was compelled to leave her to her fate.

"'But my mother, *señor!*' exclaimed the girl, with anguish; 'she was saved?'

"'No, *señorita*,' I said, 'she went down with the ship; but the last words she uttered—that is to me—were to invoke a blessing on my head, and to consign all she possessed to my care.' The poor thing swooned away as I uttered these words, and it was a long time before she came to again. When she did, however, regain consciousness, tears came to her relief, and I did all I could to soothe her distress by telling her that, if the wind came fair, she would in the course of a few days be restored to her father."

"But the wind didn't come fair, eh?" broke in Don Ignaçio, "and she didn't see—"

"No, *amigo*, the wind held steady from the opposite quarter, and I thought it better not to beat up with a fished fore-mast, and all that —and a—she did *not* see her father."

Captain Brand here wet his thin lips with a few sips of wine, said, "Babette, bring coffee!" and resumed his story.

"When the girl became a little more calm I induced her to retire to my stateroom, where I left her to sob herself to sleep. Don't spill that coffee, Babette, and put the liqueurs on the table. There, that will do, old lady.

"Well, *señores*, the next morning my pretty prize was too ill to leave her room; but, as I handed her a cup of chocolate through the door curtains, she thanked me with much gratitude for what I had done, and knew that her dear father, the judge, would bless me."

"So he will," snarled the one-eyed old rascal, "if he ever catches you, when he draws the black cap over your head."

"Possibly he may, though perhaps it will be some considerable time before he has that pleasure."

"Ah! *cuidado hico mio!* Take care of yourself, my son," hiccoughed the priest as he crossed himself. The captain gave a light laugh, sipped his coffee, and went on as if a dungeon, scaffold, and noose were the last things he ever thought of.

"I amused myself during the day in looking over the trunks, caskets, and what not we had saved from the sinking trader—presented to me, as you know, by the old lady who was on board. There were, of course, a great quantity of ladies' dresses, and a good many jewels and trinkets; among the latter this fine snuff-box here, which our friend Don Ignaçio so much admires, and which I set aside as an especial testimonial of the old lady's regard. Try another pinch, *amigo*? No? *Bueno!* I caused what I believed to be the daughter's elegant raiment to be placed in the after cabin. For three days I never even saw my pretty passenger, though I heard her low, sweet voice occasionally when I laid out something for her to eat in the adjoining cabin. She sang, too, some little sad songs with a voice which vibrated upon my ear like the notes of an Æolian harp sighing in the night wind. *Dios!* how I regretted then and afterward that I did not have a cabinet piano!"

"Presented to you," suggested the doctor.

"Yes, presented to me, so that she might have touched the keys with those ivory and rose-tipped fingers.

"So the time passed, the schooner flying on under whole sails, the wind about two points free, and the weather as fine as silk. It was the fourth evening, I think, after parting with the Oporto trader that I induced my fair passenger to come on deck and take a little breath of sea-air. You will observe, *caballeros*, that I did not make this suggestion in the daytime, because the 'Centipede's' crew, you know, were rather numerous, and some of them not so handsome in point of personal looks as ladies at all times care to behold. Besides, there were certain things about the decks—racks of cutlasses, lockers of musketry along the rail, and a long brass twelve-pounder, which is not altogether hidden by the boat, you know, and might have given rise to a little curiosity, or maybe suspicion, even in the mind of a girl, as to our character, pursuits, and so forth, which I should have been puzzled to answer. Therefore I chose a clear starlight night to pay my homage, and accordingly I went below about four bells of the first watch to escort the little lady to the deck. She was dressed, and waiting for me in the cabin; and if I was so struck with her beauty when I first saw her, my heart thumped now against my ribs like a volley of musket-balls against an oak plank. She wore a black silk robe, such as Spanish women wear at early mass, and around the back part of her head—where the hair was gathered in a glossy knot, and secured by a gold bodkin—fell the heavy folds of a black lace mantilla, the lower end fastened sash fashion around her lithe waist. She stepped, too, like a queen on a pair of slim, long, delicate feet, with arched ball and instep, as if she were in command of the schooner.

"By my right arm!" exclaimed Captain Brand, shaking that member aloft in a glorious fit of enthusiasm, "I am quite sure she had conquered me, and that was more than half the battle!

"Well, I led her to the quarter-deck, where some cushions and flags had been placed for her near the weather taffrail, and where she sat down. The schooner was at the time under the two gaff-topsails, the main boom and sheets eased off a little, those long masts, with the sticks above them running clear away up the sky, almost out of sight, bending like whalebone, and reeling over the long swell when the breeze freshened; and not a sound to be heard save now and then a light creak from the main boom as the broad white sail strained flat and taut over to leeward, or the rush of the water as it came hissing along from her sharp, clean bows, with a noise like a breeze through the leaves of a forest, away off over the counter into luminous sparkles as it swished out into our wake. The 'Centipede' was indeed doing her best, and you all know what that is, when we have been chased many and many a time by some of the fastest cruisers going.

"You remember, Don Ignacio, how the 'Juno' frigate nearly ran us under, and yet never gained a fathom on us in nine hours?"

"Ay, *amigo;* but, had she not carried away her fore-top-mast, in another hour there would have been nothing left of you afloat but a —hencoop perhaps."

"*Quien sabe, compadre?* If hads had been shads you would have had fish for your breakfast," rejoined the narrator; and then throwing back the lappels of his green velvet coat with an air of gentlemanly satisfaction, he hooked his thumbs in the arm-holes of his fine waistcoat, and went on.

"Well, *señores*, the graceful girl beside me never spoke scarcely for half an hour. I divined, however, what her thoughts might have been in dwelling on the painful scenes she had recently witnessed, and I held my peace also; for, you see, I have had considerable experience with women, and I have ever found that a man loses more by talking than by remaining watchful and attentive."

Captain Brand looked, as he gave utterance to this philosophical sentiment, as if he were a thirsty, cold-eyed tiger, lying in wait to spring upon an unwary passer-by.

"Yes, I waited, until at last she spoke.

"'*Capitano*,' she said, 'what a beautiful vessel you command, and how fast she sails!'

"What I replied, my friends, is neither here nor there; but I sank down on the cushions beside the lovely girl, and poured out a torrent of passionate words—which I really felt, too, at the time—as I don't think I ever uttered before or since. She was a little startled and nervous at first, but after a while I saw her stately head droop to one side till it rested on my shoulder; I stole my arm around her yielding waist and clasped her to my breast."

Here Captain Brand looked as if the tiger had already sprung upon the passer-by, and was sucking the blood, with his claws buried deep into the carcass.

"'*Señor*,' she murmured, in the low, sweet, plaintive note of a nightingale, 'I am a young and inexperienced girl, of an old and noble family; you have saved my life; my mother is gone, and I have no one to advise with, and, if my dear father smiles upon my choice, I will marry you; but do not, I implore you, deceive me!'"

"And you did not deceive her, I hope?" broke in the doctor, with a shiver of light from his determined eyes that was almost painful to see, so earnest and terrible it was, as he leaned forward with both of his clenched hands quivering nervously on the table.

Captain Brand looked at the doctor with rather a suspicious stare, and letting his thumbs drop from his armpits till they rested on the flaps of his waistcoat pockets, he replied, in a careless tone,

"Oh no, *monsieur*, I never deceived—a—that is to say, intentionally deceived a woman in all my life!"

"Let us hear more, my son," said the priest, thickly, who had now woke up from a short nap.

"*Bueno, caballeros!*" continued the narrator, as he tossed off a thimbleful of maraschino from a wicker-bound square bottle after his coffee. "Well, gentlemen, the young Portuguese damsel, Señorita Lucia, and I sat there under the weather rail till the first faint streaks of early dawn in the tropics began to announce the coming of the gray morning. Then she arose, and, leaning with a soft pressure on my arm, I took her to her cabin, kissed her sweet hands, and bade her good-night."

At this stage of the narrative Captain Brand threw himself triumphantly back in his large Manilla chair, and ran his white muscular hands through his dry light hair. Ay! the tiger had clutched his prey. An unprotected, young, and lovely girl had been won and lost, and her palpitating heart was soon to be torn from her tender body.

CHAPTER XVI.

NUPTIALS OF THE GIRL WITH DARK EYES.

"With a pint and a quarter of holy water
    He made the sacred sign,
And he dashed the whole on the only daughter
    Of old Plantagenet's line !"

"But the count he felt the nervous work
No more than any polygamous Turk,
    Or bold piratical skipper,
Who, during his buccaneering search,
    Would as soon engage a 'hand' at church
As a hand on board his clipper."

THE captain got up from his chair, stepped to the settee, and, pulling the signal-cord on the wall, held a short dialogue with the man at the station ; then, saying in a low, sharp whisper through the tube, "A bright look-out, Pedro !" he resumed his place at the table. The doctor had, in the mean while, got up and gone to the veranda, where, swinging in a Yucatan grass hammock, shielded from the night wind, lay his little patient sleeping soundly. Carefully closing the curtains again around him, he returned to his place. The padre was now all awake again, with his thick lips open, waiting for the captain to go on with his story. As for Don Ignacio, he never stirred body or limb, but his eye traveled about perpetually, and he observed the movements of his companions all at the same time. Still the hoarse roar of the pirates in their carouse arose from the covered sheds in the calm night, and the two solitary lights from each masthead of the felucca and schooner twinkled above the basin of the inlet.

"And now, *amigos*," began again Captain Brand, after he had assured himself that all was going on as he could wish without, "I shall inform you of the sequel of my adventure with the Señorita Lucia. The evening after the night on which I had declared my passion, we were seated at dinner in the after cabin. Such a choice little dinner, too, as only our late friend, Lascar Joe, could prepare ! Poor fellow, he'll never make another of those famous curries, though, no doubt, he'll find fire and pepper enough where he is, if the devil chooses to employ him. What a neat hand he was, too, with that spiral-bladed Malay creese of his ! Ah ! well—we were sitting over the dessert, and I was relating to my pretty passenger some account of my early days, and of my lady mother and my old squire of a father, omitting, perhaps, some few uninteresting details—"

Here the old commander of the felucca cackled, and his black, beady eye glittered as the thought flashed through his head as to what details his villainous compeer had omitted. How he forged his old father's name, which brought down his gray hairs in sorrow and disgrace to the grave; and how his poor mother, too, died of grief, together with other bitter memories, all of which Captain Brand, the pirate, omitted to mention.

"Yes, I related likewise some of my early privateering adventures, when all the broad Atlantic was alive with the fleets of France, England, and Spain; how I was captured by a Spanish brigantine"— omitting again to state that he got up a mutiny with the crew of that brigantine, poniarded the captain and mate in their sleep, and, assuming command of the vessel, changed her colors for a black flag, and began his career as a pirate in the Caribbean Sea—"and how I escaped. To all this she listened with great interest, her large eyes dilating, and her bosom swelling with sympathy as I proceeded, when suddenly the cabin door opened, and my ugly friend Pedillo put his head in, and gave me a warning nod.

"'What is it?' I said, rather sharply, to Pedillo; 'and how dare you intrude inside my cabin?' I fear, too, that I came very near doing a mischief to my boatswain; for I am rather impulsive at times, and by the merest accident I happened to have a small pistol in my pocket."

Don Ignaçio twitched his sleeve, and looked as if he believed such accidents as pistols being found in the narrator's pockets happened quite often.

"'Señor,' said Pedillo, 'there are two sail standing out from the lee of Culebra Island, and one of them appears to be a large—'

"I stopped any farther particulars from the lips of my subordinate by a motion of my finger, and then, kissing the hands of the girl, who was somewhat surprised at what had transpired, I left the cabin and jumped on deck.

"The schooner was now running down through the Virgin's Passage between St. Thomas and Porto Rico, with a fine breeze on the quarter, and the sun was just sinking behind the last-named island. I snatched a spy-glass from the rail, and looked ahead. There, sure enough, was a sixteen-gun brig on the starboard tack heading across our track, and a large frigate under single-reefed top-sails stretching away over to the opposite shores of Culebra, while they were telegraphing bunting one with another as fast as the bright-colored flags could talk. And, as luck would have it, as I swept the glass round, what should I see but a long rakish corvette in company with a huge whale of a line-of-battle ship, with her double tier of ports glimmering away in the slanting rays of the sun, both on the wind, and coming out from under the lee of Culebra Point, just a mile or two astern of us. By the blood of Barabbas, *caballeros*, we were in a trap for wolves, and the hounds were in full cry! I immediately, however, luffed the schooner up, and steered boldly for the frigate; and, as a puff of smoke spouted out from the lee bow of the admiral to windward, and before the boom of the gun's report reached us, I hoisted American colors. Seeing this, the brig hove in stays, and, perhaps being ordered to board me, came staggering along on the other tack across our forefoot, while the frigate went round too, and held her wind toward her consorts to windward. Now this was just the disposition which I wanted of the vessels, and it could not have been done better for my plans had I been the admiral of the squadron. In less than a quarter of an hour, the brig—and no great things she was, with a contemptible battery, as I could see, of short carronades—hove aback a little on the bow of the schooner, and gave us a warning of a twenty-four pound shot across our forefoot, to heave to also, at the same time hoisting the English ensign.

"So ho!" ejaculated Captain Brand, as he twisted the point of his nose, accompanied by a malevolent scowl, "*señores*, I at once hauled flat aft the fore-sail, dropped the main peak, and put the helm up, as if to round to under the brig's stern; whereupon my man-of-war friend dropped a cutter into the water, and she had just shoved off in readiness to board me, when, before you could light a paper cigar, I ran up the main peak, got a pull of the sheets, and the 'Centipede' was off again like a shark with his fin above water, heading for the narrow passage between Culebra and Crab Islands. It was at least five minutes before that stupid brig could believe his eyes, and ten more before he got hold of the boat again, when she filled away and began to pop gun after gun at me as fast as he could bring his battery to bear! There was only one shot that skipped on board us, and that only smashed both legs of a negro, and then hopped off through the fore-sail to windward.

"Had I not had a good dinner that day and pleasant society on board"—how peculiarly the speaker smiled—"I should perhaps have taught that brig such a lesson that he would not have cared to report it to his admiral. But as I knew I had the heels of him, and as the rest of the squadron were now crowding all sail and keeping off in chase of me, I ordered Pedillo, just by way of touching my hat and saying '*Adios*,' to clear away the long gun and return the brig's salute. The shot struck him just forward the night-heads by the bowsprit, and by the way the splinters flew and his jib and head-sails came down, I knew I had crippled him for an hour at least. At the same time, to prevent any mistakes as to our quality, and to satisfy the admiral's curiosity, we hauled down the Yankee colors and set our swallow-tailed flag!"

"Rather dark bunting! no?" edged in Don Ignaçio.

"Ay, *amigo!* as black as that eye of thine, though not half so murderous," retorted the pirate as he continued his narrative.

"*Bueno*, there came the whole of the squadron down after us, spitting out from their bridle ports mouthfuls of cold iron, which all went to the bottom of the Virgin's Passage, for not one came within a mile of the schooner; and then I led them such a dance through that intricate cluster of reefs and islets, that soon after dark they gave up the game, and I said '*Buenos noches*' to them all!"

Here Captain Brand paused, made a careful selection of a beautifully turned trabuco cigar from the box, shouted to Babette to produce some old Santa Cruz rum, sugar, lemons, and hot water — screeching hot, he said — at which the padre crossed himself; and then throwing his fine legs, incased in the lustrous silk stockings, on a chair beside him, and while his eyes gazed fondly on the brilliants sparkling in the buckles of his shoes, he resumed his tale.

"When I went below again, after every thing had become quiet on deck, I found my stag-eyed sweetheart waiting to receive me! How superbly she looked as she made a movement from the cushions where she had been reclining, and exclaimed,

"'Oh, *señor*, what has happened, and what was the cause of all that noise of guns, and those cries of agony I heard above?'

"'*Querida Lucia*, dearest,' I replied, 'we have been where there are — a — pirates, but fortunately have escaped, and the cries you heard were from one of my poor crew who got slightly wounded by a shot!'

"'Ah, *malditos piratos!* cursed pirates!' exclaimed the charming beauty, as she put both her hands in mine, 'and how thankful am I that you are not hurt!   But, *querido mio!* dear one!' she went on, 'when shall we get to Porto Rico and *our* dear father?   We must be near, for I heard one of your sailors shout to you the name of the island!'

"In reply, I told her that we had been near Porto Rico, but that — a — circumstances were such, on account of the dangerous pirates who infested those seas, that I felt obliged, for her safety — you understand — to run along by way of Hispaniola — she not having a very clear idea of the position and geography of those parts — and that our cruise might probably be prolonged for a few days more."

"And into h—, perhaps," said the doctor, with a hollow voice and a calm cold eye.

"Oh no, my friends, certainly nothing so bad as that.   Possibly to heaven! but, *quien sabe?* no one can tell!

"However," pursued the captain, "I soon succeeded in allaying her apprehensions, and then I threw myself at her feet, and implored her to risk her father's displeasure and to marry me at once; that she knew her father was cold, stern, and obdurate, and should he frown upon my suit I should die of despair!"

"*Cierto!*" murmured Ignaçio, with the grin of a skeleton.

"I used these passionate appeals and many more, until at last the fond girl yielded her consent to my entreaties.

"'But the priest, *querido mio!*' she exclaimed, as she rose and disengaged herself from my arms. I told her that I chanced to have one on board as a passenger, who would perform the ceremony.

"And so I had," added Captain Brand, "or at least a very near approach to one, for my ugly boatswain, Pedillo, had been bred up—as an acolyte—you comprehend—in the house of a rich old prelate of San Paulo Cathedral in Trinidad, to whom Pedillo, one fine morning, gave about eight inches of his cuchillo!"

"*Jesus Maria!*" exclaimed Padre Ricardo, starting back with horror, and telling his beads.

"Ay, *mi padre!* Pedillo assassinated the holy father, and plundered his cash-box besides; and so you see Pedillo was just the man I wanted."

Don Ignaçio nodded his wicked old head through a cloud of cigar smoke as a sign of approval.

"Accordingly, *señores*, the next day I made the trusty Pedillo cut off all the bushy beard about his ugly face, and had the crown of his head shaved besides—quite like that round, oily spot there on the top of good Ricardo's poll—and then he rigged himself out in a clerical gown, to which the trunks of my bride's old mother contributed, and, take my word for it, he was as proper and rascally a looking priest as could be found on the island of Cuba. He performed the ceremony, too, by way of practice, on Lascar Joe and the second cook beforehand, with as much decorum and solemnity, and gave as pious a benediction, as his old Trinidad uncle, the prelate, ever did. Well, that evening we were married."

"How many times has the *capitano* been married?" grunted out Don Ignaçio.

"Why, let me reflect," as he threw his cold, icy look at the frame of miniatures on the opposite wall. "You mean, *compadre*, how often the ceremony has been performed. Ah! I think on eleven occasions. No, it was only ten. Madame Mathilde had two husbands living when I made love to her, and declined to take a third. But then, you know, I have an affectionate disposition, and I can not set my heart against the fascinations of the sex."

He gave vent to these moral sentiments as if he really meant them to be believed and generally adopted by his audience.

"Well, that same evening I was married to the beautiful Señorita

Lucia Lavarona, though I am sorry to say that Pedillo did not perform his part of the business as well as I had expected of him, from his practice in the morning. He stammered a good deal, and when he raised the crucifix to the lips of the young girl, her innocent looks and maidenly majesty of deportment so struck my coadjutor with confusion that he let the crucifix fall to the deck at her dainty feet. This little incident caused me some displeasure; but, reflecting that the poet tells us

> 'A tiger, 'tis said, will turn and flee
> From a maid in the pride of her purity,'

I said nothing to the abashed Pedillo as I gave him back the emblem; but I favored him with a look, with my right hand in my pocket— this fashion."

Here the cold-blooded scoundrel dipped his thumb and fore finger into the flap of his waistcoat, while the commander of the " Guarda Costa" waved his brown digit before him, as if he knew what was there all the time.

"Ah! that restored my new-made priest to his senses, and he then got through the ceremony entirely to my satisfaction.

"However," said Captain Brand, turning with lazy indifference toward Padre Ricardo, " ever after this I resolved not to take the risk of such another chance of failure, and this is the reason why I first sought your services."

"*Gracias à Dios!* Thanks be to heaven, my son, that you found me!" said the sacrilegious wretch, as he bowed to his superior and sipped a glass of rum punch. "*Vamonos!* let us hear more."

"At the conclusion of our nuptials, while I held my sweet Lucia to my heart, and kissed her pale brow, and while tears of crystal drops, half in rapture and half in sorrow, dimmed her large, sparkling black eyes, she withdrew this royal sapphire from her slender finger, and gently placing the gem on mine—where you see it, *amigos*—she said,

"'My dear and only love, this is the talisman of my race. It has been for ages in my family, and it has been the guardian of our hope and honor. Receive it, friend of my heart, and be the protector of the young girl who yielded up to you her very soul!'"

The doctor started as if he had been stung by a scorpion; but Captain Brand, heedless or inattentive to the movement, went on:

"Yes, *caballeros*, those were her very words; murmured, too, in her low contralto tones with a pure, lisping Castilian accent, as she laid her stately head on my shoulder.

"Ay, those were rapturous moments; and it was in some degree —yes, I may say in truth—entirely her own fault that they did not last.

"Well, for some days—eight or ten, perhaps—with light baffling winds, we crept stealthily along the south side of St. Domingo; but the weather was delightful, and the time passed on the wings of a zephyr. In the warm, soft evenings, with the moon or stars shedding their pearly gleams over the sea, she sat beside me on the deck of the schooner, watching with girlish interest the white sails above her head, òr singing to me the sweet little sequidillas of her native land. And again, starting up from my arms, she would peep over the counter, trace the foam as it flashed and bubbled in our wake, or point to the track of a dolphin as he leaped above the luminous waves and went like a bullet to windward.

"I flatter myself, *caballeros*, that there have been periods in my career on the high seas, or on land, and may be again, for aught I know," continued the elegant pirate, as he crossed his legs and threw back the lappels of his velvet coat, so as to expose the magnificence of his waistcoat, and the frills on his broad, muscular chest, " when men of high birth and breeding, and lovely women too of noble lineage, have not thought it beneath them to dine with or to receive the homage of—a—Captain Brand.

"And, *por Dios!*"—the narrator did not consider it unbecoming his cloth and profession to swear in a foreign language—"*por Dios! señores*, I have known the time, too, when I have played whist with a French prince of the blood and two knights of the Golden Fleece."

"And you fleeced them? No?" muttered Don Ignaçio, with an envious glimmer from his greedy eye, as if no one had a right to rob the community but himself.

"And not only that," continued the captain, rapidly, "but the daughter of an English peer of the realm once proposed to run away with me. Ho! ho! yes, she actually proposed to elope with me; but as she was verging on fifty years, and only weighed fifty pounds, with never a pound in her pocket, I sighed my regrets. Ay, great compliment it was, but I declined the honor. You yourself, *compadre*, must remember how I was received by the people on the Buena Vista villa at Principe; how the obispo blessed me, the old general embraced me, and the beautiful marquesa, with the hourglass waist, smiled on me."

"*Cierto!*" That astute old Spaniard never forgot any thing, particularly a debt due to him; and he remembered, moreover, to have heard that when the noble *Mi Lord Inglez* left the villa one dark night, a good deal of plate, jewels, doubloons, and other valuable property disappeared with him. Ay, the sly old fellow had a faint recollection as well of seeing a heavily-armed schooner running the gauntlet through the forts before daylight, and that she left a certain bag of gold ounces for him—Don Ignaçio Sanchez—somewhere in a secret hole beneath a well-known rock inside the harbor. Oh, a won-

derful memory for matters of this nature had our rapacious one-eyed
acquaintance!

"Yes," went on his partner in many a scene of pillage and crime,
"I have every reason to know that I won the hearts, and purses too,
sometimes, of some of the fine people I met in refined society. But
yet there have been occasions when the game has gone against
me—"

Don Ignaçio's tenacious memory came again into play, and he
looked back to the time when he himself had cleaned his profuse
friend out of all his gains at the card-table, even to the buttons off
his coat; but he gave no sign of remembrance of those days, and only
blew a dense cloud of smoke from his thin yellow nostrils as the captain spoke.

"—Though those occasions have not been of frequent recurrence."

The good Padre Ricardo at this juncture hoped that, by Saint Barnabas, luck might, in all time to come, befriend his son and patron;
croaking, too, with a goblet of punch to his unctuous lips, "*Vamonos!* Tell us more of the adorable Doña Lucia!"

Captain Brand rapped his snuff-box, opened the diamond-crusted
lid, took a dainty pinch, laid his cambric handkerchief over his ker-
seymere breeches, and resumed his narrative.

"So passed the days, *caballeros;* and when, one morning, the high
mountains back of Port Guantamano were reported to me, I felt a
presentiment that my dream of bliss was drawing to a close. Indeed,
I might probably have remained at sea a week or two longer, but the
men were getting a little impatient, and I thought it better to sacrifice my own pleasure to theirs. That day we caught a cracking breeze
out of the Windward Passage, and toward midnight we came up
with this little sandy island here.

"The preparations for going into port excited the curiosity of my
bride; for, poor thing! she believed we were bound into Porto Rico,
and I had some trouble in inducing her to go below before we crossed
the reef. *Bueno!* the coast was clear, the signals were all right, and
an hour later the schooner had her anchor down and sails furled pretty
much in the spot where she now lies moored.

"While, however, we were sweeping up the inlet, I sent a boat
ahead, with directions for my tidy old housekeeper, Babette, to have
every thing prepared to receive her new mistress. Just then one of
those terrible thunder-storms came up; heavy masses of clouds obscured the sky, followed by such double-barrel shocks and intensely
vivid lightning as is only beheld in the tropics preceding the equinox.
The rain, too, came along in horizontal sheets, driven by a squall
which burst in fury over the island, and it seemed to me that all the
devils from hell were howling and shrieking in the air.

"Shielded from the storm by a large boat-cloak, I carried my beautiful bride, with her face nestling on my breast, to the cove, and then I bore her into this fine saloon.

"I shall never forget the sweet words she whispered, and the loving caresses she gave me on that little journey, even while the tempest almost dashed me to the ground, and the sharp flashes of lightning nearly blinded me. They were the last she ever lavished upon me."

No sigh escaped the lips of this cold-blooded monster as he uttered these words; no sign of feeling for the ruin of a gentle girl whom he had betrayed to his piratical den of infamy and crime—whose dream of life was destroyed like a crushed rose-leaf, and all her hope gone from that moment.

CHAPTER XVII.

DOOM OF DOÑA LUCIA.

"I went into the storm,
And mocked the billows of the tossing sea;
I said to Fate, What wilt thou do to me?
I have not harmed a worm!

"Thy dim eyes tell a tale—
A piteous tale of vigils; and the trace
Of bitter tears is on thy beauteous face;
Beauteous, and yet so pale!"

"Thus it ever is, *caballeros*, and ever will be," went on Captain Brand, in rather a reflecting strain. "There is a point to begin and stop, and an end to joy as well as grief. We should, however, take the world as it comes and as it goes. I do, and so do you, *compadre!*"—pitching a cigar spear fashion at Don Ignaçio to attract his attention—"and, therefore, we should never look too far ahead, and live only for the present.

"Indulging then in this train of thought, as I set down my lovely burden here, and the cloak fell from her shoulders, I was prepared for any thing which might happen. I wore a slightly different costume at the time than that she had been accustomed to see me in, as I always do when I think there might be a chance of a surprise or trap laid for us in entering the inlet. So, instead of fine linen and velvet, I had on a red flannel shirt, canvas trowsers, with a cutlass slung to my side, and a pair of pistols in my belt. I don't think I appear handsome in that rig, but the fellows at my back somehow think it is becoming to me, especially when we are engaged in a hand-to-hand fight! What say you, *compadre?*"

The Don said nothing, and merely waved his fore finger, as if dress was not a matter to which he devoted much attention. He thought, however, that sleeves should be cut loose for knives when the pockets were not too small for pistols; but he uttered no word.

"*Bueno!* There I stood"—pointing to the corner of the room as he spoke—"drenched with rain, and there stood my tall and lovely wife!

"The saloon was brilliantly lighted; a profusion of plants and flowers were clustered here, there, and every where, on cabinets and tables, in striking contrast to the display exhibited yonder in that armory, where pikes, muskets, and knives were gleaming through the open door.

"Quick as the lightning which was piercing deep into the inmost crevices of the rocks and lighting up the crag without; Lucia's dark eyes flashed around the apartment from floor to ceiling, from flower to blade, resting an instant on the frame of miniatures there—hers was not among the collection *then*; it is the one in the middle, doctor—"

There were no knives on the table, or else, from the deadly look the doctor gave, he might have perhaps sprinkled the narrator's heart's blood on the floor.

"—Until at last her gaze of terror rested on *me!* No one, I fancy, can tell the power of Spanish girls, who has never seen them when the whole passion of their souls, either in love or hate, comes pouring in a black blaze of jet from their gleaming eyes.

"Advancing a step toward me, with her white hands clasped together, she said, in a hurried, beseeching voice—and low as was the sound, I heard it distinctly during the crashing thunder which shook the rocks of the crag to their foundations—

"'*Señor!* where am I? My father! Who—who—in the name of the Blessed Virgin, art *thou?*'

"Again giving a look of the utmost horror around the room, she pressed her hands to her eyes, and said, in the same low, distinct tone,

"'Speak, *señor!* For the love of our holy Savior, speak!'

"I felt that the girl had saved me, by her own instinctive perception, a world of painful explanations, and I replied,

"'Lucia! I divine that all farther concealments are useless; you are in the haunt of the most noted pirate of these seas, and that man stands before you.'

"*Caballeros!*" continued Captain Brand, "had my pretty prize swooned away, or fallen down in a fit, or gone into hysterics and torn her hair out by the roots, I should not have been greatly surprised; but she did none of those things. On the contrary, she became as calm as marble—frightfully so, in fact—and pushing back the bands of her magnificent tresses from her pale forehead, she raised her round white arm aloft, with her slender fore finger quivering like the tongue of a viper in mid air, and then poured forth such a torrent of awfully impressive words that I quailed before her.

"Yes, *señores*, I am no coward, take me when you will; but on this occasion I must honestly admit that I stood powerless before the gaze and gesture of that slight, delicately-formed woman.

"'Pirate—wretch—monster! may the curses of hell be heaped upon thee! Murderer—betrayer! may thy heart be burned, and thy soul blasted forever!'

"I need not pain you, *señores*, by reciting the cruel words that came hissing through her closed teeth, nor yet farther describe the terrible concentrated gaze of hate and fury which streamed from those gleaming eyes. Suffice it to say, that though often afterward I was treated in the same manner, yet, on the occasion alluded to, I cut short the interview by summoning Babette to see her mistress to her chamber, and then, glad to escape, I went out of the house and attended to the duties which required my presence."

The padre, with his flat lips half open, eagerly drinking in—with his Santa Cruz punch—the words of his patron; the doctor, calm, unmoved now, and thoughtful; the one-eyed old rascal, still puffing his cigarettes and allowing no rest to his uneasy, suspicious optic, all sat listening, with each an interest peculiarly his own, to the fate of Doña Lucia. The narrator leisurely arose and held his hourly confab with the man at the signal-station, and then returning to his place, proceeded with his discourse:

"I shall pass rapidly over, my friends, many little incidents of a rather unpleasant nature which occurred here, in this my rocky re-- treat, for some months after the interview which I have described. I tried every argument and persuasion I was master of to bring my proud bride to reason, but to all my entreaties she turned a cold and chilling stare of obdurate hate. Day by day the intensity of her de-testation grew stronger and stronger, and seemed to have become a part of her nature. Yes; the gentle, yielding girl I had won on board the 'Centipede' had now become as stern and unbending as a rock, and my controlling power over her mind and love was gone. I left her entirely to herself for some weeks, until one day I thought her passion might have subsided, and once more, attired in a rich and splendid suit, I came in here, as she sat like a marble statue at table. She never looked up at my entrance, but her eyes shone like stars as she mechanically went through the forms of the dinner laid before her.

"'Lucia!' I said, gayly. No answer by word or look. 'Lucia! *querida mia!*' I repeated, and, sinking on one knee beside her, attempted to take her hand.

"By all the saints, *señores*, that came near—very near—being the last time that I ever should kneel to a woman; for with a movement so sudden that I had barely time to leap aside, she snatched a long pointed carving-knife from the table and lunged full at my throat! The blade just grazed my jugular artery, inflicting a slight wound. But she never turned round to see the extent of her effort, and again sat calm and rigid at the table.

"This was my last visit save one. I had long before abandoned these comfortable quarters entirely, and occupied the rooms you do, *mi padre*, out there among the men. In fact, my stern young bride was in entire command of the island; and even my good Babette here stood in such awe of her that she always crossed herself when called to approach her mistress.

"Month by month matters went on in this way, until the rainy season had gone, and I was preparing for another cruise in the schooner; but hour by hour the consuming passion which flamed in the veins of Lucia was doing its work. I sometimes beheld her standing out on the veranda, tall and stately as ever; and when the moon was at the full, it threw its light upon her wan and sunken cheeks, and thin, wasted frame. Ay, there she stood, like an almost transparent statue of alabaster, with her dark eyes shining with an unearthly light, turned in one long tearless gaze upon the ledge and combing breakers to seaward. It was singular, too, the effect she produced even upon the horde of these brave fellows of mine, for no persuasion could induce a man of them to come within pistol-shot of that part of the house while she was thus keeping her nightly vigils. And as for Pedillo, he acquired such a superstitious dread of the girl he had married, and lived in such a state of abject terror, that I had serious thoughts of shooting him through the head to avoid the contaminating influence he exercised over his comrades.

"Well, *caballeros*, late one Saturday night, while the men were carousing and drinking success to the coming cruise—we were to sail on the following Monday—and while I was returning from my usual stroll to the Tiger's Trap to see the battery in order and the look-outs wide awake, I met Babette toddling along, nearly out of breath.

"'What is it, old lady?' You know, *amigos*, that Babette never spoke a word in her life, but she made signs to let me know that I was wanted at the crag, and that there was no time to be lost. I quickened my pace, and, preceded by Babette, I once more darkened my own threshold. The curtains and hangings were all closely drawn in the saloon here, and it was dark as a tomb; but there was a light burning yonder in the passage leading to the chamber, and I made my way to the door.

"I shall never forget what I saw, though I should like to, as it comes to me sometimes in the night, or when I am left much alone by myself."

The pirate passed his hands over his eyes as if he saw something while he spoke, and then, letting his voice drop to an almost sepulchral pitch, he went on hurriedly:

"I stood at the door, *caballeros*, and looked in. On the bed, which was drawn to the middle of the chamber to get the air through the narrow loopholed windows, with the gauze curtains falling square on all sides, lay Lucia. Her attenuated frame scarcely presented an uneven surface beneath the snowy sheet which covered it. Her superb hair was spread in great black masses on the pillow, and her

pale marble face reposed there like an ivory picture in an ebony setting. Her eyes were wide open, large and luminous, and her thin
delicate hands were clasped around a silver and pearl crucifix, which
rested on her hollow breast. A single taper in a silver lamp threw
a lurid, flickering ray about the room, and beside it was Babette on
her knees quivering with terror, while from one of the loopholed windows a broad white band of moonlight streamed directly across the
pillow and face of the dying girl."

Captain Brand's face assumed a deathly pallor, and, with his icy
blue eyes fixed on vacancy, and his voice sunk to a hoarse whisper,
he went on:

"As I appeared in the portals of the door, Lucia slowly raised her
fore finger, and beckoned me to approach. I could no more have
resisted the summons than if a chain cable to a frigate's anchor had
caught me in its iron coils, and was dragging me to the bottom of
the sea. I moved to the foot of the bed.

"'*Pirato!*' came from her slightly-parted lips, in her old low and
distinct tones. '*Pirato*, behold your cruel work! Destroyer of mother and child—of soul and body—may the curses of a dying woman
and her unborn child haunt you by day and by night!' I was dumb,
and my pulse stopped beating.

"'*Ave Maria purissima!*' were the last words that came in a
sweet, pure whisper from her parted lips; she clasped the crucifix
tighter, and the spirit departed. I tore aside the gauze net to lay
my hand on her heart, when, on my soul! her right hand slowly relaxed its death-grasp on the crucifix, and, rising to a vertical line,
with the fore finger pointing upward, quivered in the light of the
waning moon, like, as it was, a supernatural warning! Yes, that
finger—"

"Mamma! mamma!" came in a weak, plaintive voice from the piazza, while the villain, with his hands before him as if to shut out a
frightful vision, and eyeballs starting from their sockets, was hoarse-
ly whispering to his horror-stricken audience the last warning of the
dead Lucia.

As the low moaning cry in the stillness which reigned around the
saloon struck his ear, he sprang with a bound to his feet, and, quick
as thought, with a pistol in each hand, he shouted, "Who's there?"

"It is the little sick boy, *señor*. Do him no harm at your peril!"
and the doctor stood towering before the pirate's leveled weapons.

"*Maldito* on the brat! Pshaw!" said Captain Brand, quieting
down, and returning the pistols to his pockets. "How nervous I
am! Excuse me, *caballeros*. I was thinking of something else."

CHAPTER XVIII.

END OF THE BANQUET.

"There was turning of keys, and creaking of locks,
As he stalked away with his iron box.
Oh, ho! oh, ho! The cock doth crow,
It is time for the fisher to rise and go.
Fair luck to the abbot, fair luck to the shrine!
He hath gnawed in twain my choicest line;
Let him swim to the north, let him swim to the south,
The *pirate* will carry my hook in his mouth."

In the pause which followed the dreadful episode just recounted by Captain Brand, the padre was occupied in pattering a prayer, counting his beads, and elevating his crucifix as if he was mumbling high mass at the altar. Don Ignaçio slowly waved his brown fore finger, and his single spark of glowing eye glared fiercely and fixedly at his host. A clammy sweat burst out on the pallid brow of the doctor, and his hands were clutched before him on the table like the jaws of a steel vice. And still the drunken shrieks and cheers of the piratical crew at the sheds arose wild and shrill in the calm night, making a gloomy echo for the banquet. The doctor was the first to break the awkward silence which pervaded the saloon.

"*Capitano!*" said he, in his habitual calm, deep voice, "with respect to what you said in the early part of the evening, of breaking up this establishment, what, may I ask, are your plans for the future?"

"*Gracias! amigo* doctor! Thank you, my friend, for changing the conversation. My plans! eh! ah! Well, they are these—"

Here Captain Brand's face assumed its usual expression; and entirely himself again, he went on to state, in a precise, business-like way, the views he had resolved upon for future action.

"—To-morrow, gentlemen, is Sunday. Those boisterous fellows out there, after mass, will need rest all the day. On Monday, however, I shall begin to change the rig of the schooner, fill up with provisions for a long cruise, take on board all the loose odds and ends we have stowed here, of course," he added, as he remarked an inquiring and a rather alarmed mercenary look from the Tuerto's glim— "of course, after having squared up all claims of our *compadre* there!"

"Hum!" croaked that sharp rascal, with a nod of satisfaction quite like an old raven.

"Then, *señores*, I shall burn or destroy the old sheds, and bury the cannon and heavy articles we can not find room for in the 'Centipede;' when, if nothing happens, we shall trip anchor and spread our sails for sea!

"Babette! Babette! Really I believe that dear old negress has fallen asleep. Babette! ah! there you are, my beauty! See if you can't give us a bowl of okra gumbo before we break up here!"

Babette had not been asleep. Oh no! She had her ear to the door of the saloon, and was listening to the sad history of Doña Lucia, and when her master came to the final scene the old woman fell on her knees and shivered all over, where she remained until the sound of the captain's voice again called her to her duties.

"And when we have left these quiet waters, my son!" broke in the padre, "what then?"

The fact was, that the carnivorous and vinous Father Ricardo knew that his stomach was not suited for high winds and rough oceans, and was hoping that some scheme might be devised to allow him to remain tranquilly on the island.

"Why, holy padre, I propose to steer clear of the West Indies by some unfrequented track, and, striking the broad Atlantic, stretch down the coast of Brazil. Perhaps we may double Cape Horn, and see what those miserable patriots are fighting for in Chili and Peru; then maybe across the Pacific, to the lovely islands and maidons of Polynesia; so on to the China Seas, where we may fall in with an outward-bound Canton trader, or a galleon with a ton or two of silver on board—who knows?—there is plenty of blue water and fine ships every where; so we must be content."

Padre Ricardo made the sign of the cross, kissed his thumb and fore finger, and, reaching his dirty paw over to the captain, shook hands with him.

"Ay, *amigos!*" continued the leader, without minding the friendly interruption; "yes, my friends, we shall, I trust, give the hounds in search of us the slip; and even should they scent out this retired little spot, they will have their trouble for their chase, and find nothing but a few stones and heaps of rubbish above ground."

"They may find some little matters below, though," chimed in the commander of the felucca.

"If they do," retorted the pirate, with a meaning scowl, "I'll put the spy who betrays it to such a torture as that he'll wish himself below ground when I come back here."

"*Cierto, amigo!* no fear of that!" muttered the Tuerto, with some little trepidation of manner. "*My* papers are white."

"Captain Brand," said the doctor, "my contract with you is nearly up, and since I only agreed—as you know—to enlist my professional services here on shore, I presume you will have no objections to permit me to depart with Don Ignaçio in the felucca."

It would be difficult to say what caused the flush of passion which overspread the leader's face as he listened to this simple request, but it was full a minute before he replied, and then, having weighed the matter carefully in his mind, he said, in a precise and determined tone, in French,

"*Monsieur le Docteur!* the compacts that I have made with all those that have taken service with me have never been broken except by death. I can not, therefore, consider your request, and I shall expect you to sail with me in the schooner."

Then he added, quickly, as he noticed a certain haughty expression in his subordinate's face, "Pardon me, *monsieur;* we had better not discuss this question now. Suppose you see me on the morrow."

"Willingly, *señor*, and you will find my resolution unchangeable." Rising as he spoke, he bowed to his companions at table, and saying "*Buenas noches!* (good night!)" he passed from the saloon to the piazza. There he paused a moment, as if communing with himself, and then approaching the grass hammock where the sick boy was sleeping, he gently took the little fellow up in his arms. The child murmured "Mamma, mamma!" and was borne away.

Captain Brand followed the doctor with his searching, sharklike eyes until he had left the apartment, and there was something that denoted danger in the look; but he uttered no sound, and, placing a finger on his lip, he nodded meaningly to the padre.

A moment after Babette brought in the steaming gumbo soup, and the pirate's feast was nearly ended. Don Ignaçio waited until his companions had swallowed a goodly portion of the grateful mess, when he too refreshed himself. Then making his salutations in his usual observant manner, he departed. He declined, however, the offer of his host's society to his boat, saying he had, he knew, half a dozen of the felucca's crew outside the building to guard his footsteps, and he would not put the *capitano* to the trouble.

When the padre rose to give his benediction to his patron, the captain took him impressively by the rope which girded his cassock about the loins, and giving it a sharp jerk or two, he said,

"My holy father, I think we shall have a sad duty to perform to-morrow. Our old friend Gibbs has behaved badly, and I shall punish him. He is now in the Capella dungeon. After early mass go and console him."

The padre returned a meaning smile, crossed himself, and slowly left the pirate alone in his saloon.

CHAPTER XIX.

FANDANGO ON ONE LEG.

"God! 'tis a fearsome thing to see
That pale wan man's mute agony—
Those pinioned arms, those hands that ne'er
Shall be lifted again—not even in prayer!
That heaving chest! Enough; 'tis done!
The bolt has fallen! the spirit is gone."

Day dawned in the east. The early spikes of morning shot up in rosy bands from behind the lofty hills of Cuba and announced the coming of the sun. The inlet and basin, framed in by their rocky walls, were still clothed in the gloom of night, and dimly reflecting the fading stars on the calm unruffled surface where the schooner and felucca were moored. Away off in the distance a dense white misty vapor hung flat and low over the lagoon and thickets of mangroves, with not a breath of air to disturb the noxious fog or quiver a leaf in the silent groves. The revels, too, of the drunken sailors had long since ceased; the sentinels, with their cutlasses in the sheaths, paced slowly to and fro before the doors of the sheds, and the lookouts at the signal-stations and battery peered through the early dawn to seaward; else not a sound or moving thing, save a teal or two fluttering with a sharp cry up and down the lagoon; the music of the tiny ripples lapping on the shelly beach; and the low roar, in a deep bass, breaking and moaning over the ledge beyond the island. Such was the appearance of things where our scene is laid in the Twelve League Group of Keys, on a Sunday morning, in the year of our Lord eighteen hundred and five.

Half a mile, perhaps, inland from the sheds where the sailors lived, and beneath the steep face of the ridge-like crag which split the island in two parts, stood a low chapel, built of loose stones nicely fitted together and roofed with tiles. A rough iron cross was fastened over the doorless entrance, and at the other end was a stone balustrade, with a rude painting of the Virgin over the altar, on which stood four or five tall brass candlesticks and a lighted taper. Outside the building was a narrow and secluded inclosure, surrounded by a low wall of coral rocks, with a few head-stones marked with black crosses— the graves of the pirates whose bones reposed beneath. At one end of this burial-place was still another subdivision, where stood ten upright flat white stones, on whose faces were rudely carved initial letters, with the years in which the eternal sleepers had been laid beneath the sand. Far and near sprang up close and almost impenetrable thickets of cactus,,whose sharp and pointed needle-shoots defied the passage of any thing more bulky than land-crabs and lizards. One or two narrow pathways had been cut out here and there, but they were overgrown again by the stubborn, hardy vegetation; and only with the risk of losing one's trowsers, and having one's legs cut in gashes, could a human being struggle through it.

Within the chapel kneeled a dozen or more of the "Centipede's" crew, the coarse and sodden faces and uncombed locks, from their night's debauch, in striking contrast to the place and the apparent devoutness of manner in. which they crossed themselves while the rites of the Church were going on. Before the altar stood Padre Ricardo, with his breviary on the chancel beneath the taper, and chanting forth from his deep lungs the services of the mass. In a few minutes the unholy hands and lips which performed the solemn ceremony ceased word and gesture, and with a sonorous benediction at the elevation of the Host, and a tinkle of a bell, the sailors arose from their knees and again staggered back to the sheds, to slumber through the day. When all had gone, the padre clasped his missal, tucked it into his bosom, and making the sign of the cross with a genuflexion before the Virgin, the sacrilegious wretch turned and left the chapel.

Pursuing the winding path which led to his own habitation for a certain distance, he then turned to the left, and carefully picking his way through the sharp cactus and Spanish bayonets along the face of the crag, he stopped at a yawning fissure which gaped open in the rock. Here, too, the same wiry vegetation had crept, and it was with great difficulty, and many an "*Ave!*" and "*Santa Maria!*" that the padre succeeded in passing into the dark, rugged mouth of the cavern.

"By the ashes of San Lorenzo!" he muttered, "there are serpents and venomous insects in this pit of purgatory. Oh, *misericordia!* what has pierced my leg? Why should my son drag me through this hole? Ah! blessed Saint Barnabas! a slimy reptile has crossed my instep!"

Feeling with his outspread hands in his fright, as he gradually made his way into the dripping cavern, getting narrower and lower as he proceeded, he at last, after stumbling prayerfully along for about a hundred and fifty yards, came to a loose pile of stones. Here opened another low narrow fissure on the left, and, in some doubt, he was about to enter; but the noise he made by stepping on a stone was answered by the hissing warning of a serpent, and the scared padre fell back at his full length in a pool of stagnant slimy water.

"*O Madre di Dios!* I am stung by a cobra! Holy Virgin! my new cassock ruined too! *Ave Maria!* light me out of this abode of the devil!"

Slowly recovering, however, from his fright, he once more regained his feet, and, after a few steps, which he was obliged to accomplish by scraping his crown against the jagged rocks above, his outstretched hands touched an iron-bound door.

"*Gracias à Dios!* Thanks be to all the saints, I am here at last; but, alas! curses on me, I shall be obliged to return by the same path unless my son allows me to escape by the casa."

Cautiously searching with his fingers as he muttered these words, he touched a bolt, and, grasping it with both hands, drew it partly out like the knob of a bell. Then, placing his ear to the door, he presently heard a rattling, creaking noise, as if a beam of timber, with pulley and chain, was being raised from behind the entrance. When the sound ceased the door yielded to the padre's sturdy shoulder, and there was just room to admit his portly body. Here the passage was wider, the rock evidently chiseled away by the hands of man, and on one side was an artificial chamber, blasted out of the solid rock, with a narrow door with heavy iron bolts on the outside. At this opening the padre paused and listened. No sound caught his ear at first, but as he clutched the bolt and it grated back in its bands, he was saluted by such a volley of frightful curses as to make him start back and cross his ample breast. It was the voice of Master Gibbs, lying there on a low iron settle in the noisome dungeon, with not a ray of light to cheer him, and only a jug of water and some weevily biscuit to save him from starvation. All through the day and during the long, long hours of the awful night, in pain and suffering from his lopped-off limb and bruises, had he lain on his hard bed with clenched hands, blaspheming and impotently raging in his agony and despair. No prayer, however, dawned in his ruthless heart, or was breathed from his brutal lips; but curses upon curses came thick and fast, till his tongue refused to give them utterance, and he fell back in utter exhaustion. As the noise, however, of the bolt struck his ear, he clutched the stone water-jug from the floor, and hurled it, with a yell of execrations, toward the door, where the fragments fell with a clattering crash on the stone pavement.

Grinding his teeth in his frightful passion, he howled,

"Let me but once put these hands on your bloodstained carcass, and if the mother that bore ye will know her spawn again, my name's not Bill Gibbs! Ha! you miserable swab, with your soft words and white hands! when I get out of this hole I'll blow you and your infarnal hounds to ——! Give me fair play, and, even on one of my legs, I'll cut the cowardly heart out of you, Captain Brand! Come in, will ye? ye son of the devil, and I'll bite the tongue out of your mouth by the roots!"

SHRIVING A SINNER.

Here the hoarse and panting wretch again ceased his roarings, and the padre timidly opened the door.

"Ha! who's that? Babette?"

"No, my son, it is your good Padre Ricardo, come to console you."

What the maimed villain replied to the priest, and what means the holy father took to allay the passion and assuage the sorrows of the man lying helpless in the dungeon, or whether successful in his mission, is not important to state in detail. An hour later, however, the priest seemed relieved in body and spirit as he retired from the loathsome hole, and shooting the bolt as he closed the door, cautiously felt his way along the dark and narrow passage. Presently, as he turned an angle, a ray of light from the loopholes of the great stone vault beneath the pirate's dwelling lighted his pathway; and a moment after, with a hearty sigh of satisfaction, he seized a cord above his head and gave it a jerk. A bell sounded above, and then a large, square-hinged trap-hatch fell down, swinging gently to and fro from the beams above. At the same time the padre put his arms about a square wooden stanchion which supported the floor of the saloon, and then painfully sticking his toes in some deep-cut notches at the sides, he slowly began to mount upward. When, however, his oily shaved crown appeared nearly at the level of the floor, a vigorous grasp was laid on his shoulders, and he was pulled up like a flapping lobster and rolled into the apartment. It was Captain Brand who kindly assisted the holy father, and it was the captain's hollow laugh which saluted him in his torn and soiled raiment, as, with difficulty, he regained his perpendicular.

"Laugh not, *hijo mio*, at my sorrowful plight," said the bruised Ricardo, with some asperity; "I have met with dangers of venomous serpents, and been stabbed cruelly by those villainous cactus."

"But I raised the beam, my padre, the moment you made the signal."

"You did, my son; but what I suffered in the cavern was as nothing to what I endured when I entered the dungeon of the English Gibbs. *Jesus Maria*, what an infidel he is!"

"You did not find his spirit subdued, then, by bread and water?"

"Far from it, my friend. He rages like a wild beast. He consigns your body and soul to everlasting torments! But, what is more impious still," went on the padre, as he crossed himself, "he damned your holy father, and hoped I would roast in hell!"

"But he confessed, Ricardo, and you gave him absolution?"

"If calling me thief and assassin, and hurling his stone water-jug at my head, be confession and forgiveness of sins, the ceremony has been performed. Ah! my son, he needs no more mercy in this world!"

"Of course not, my padre; and we will give him a short shrift and a long rope."

"Babette!" continued Captain Brand. "Ah! my Baba, you have not forgotten to feed our jolly Gibbs there below? No? I thought not. Well, then, it is Sunday, you know; give him a pint of pure rum for his morning's draught. And, Baba, my beauty, slip a pair of iron ruffles over his wrists, and then pass a cloth over those blood-shot eyes of his, and lug him here beneath this hatch. Go down by your own ladder, and be quick, my Baba, as I wish my breakfast presently!"

All this was said in a cool and rather an affectionate tone, as Captain Brand sipped a spoonful or two of chocolate from a cup of Dresden china. Then turning to the padre, he said,

"You would perhaps like a cordial, my father, to take the chill off your stomach? Yes. You will find some capital Curaçoa in that stand of bottles there."

The padre, forgetful of the dignity of his calling, shuffled with indecent haste to the spot indicated, and, without going through the form of filling one of the diminutive thimble-shaped glasses in the stand, he boldly raised the silver-netted flask to his lips, and sucked away until it was nearly empty. Then seating himself on the settee, he lugged out his illuminated missal and pored over its contents. Captain Brand occupied himself with opening the loop of the silk rope which fell from the ceiling, and securing the end firmly on the stout cleat at the wall.

So passed the time until a noise beneath the room of a voice in anger, and a body bumped and dragged along, once more attracted the attention of those in the saloon.

"Oh ho! is that you, Master Gibbs?" exclaimed Captain Brand, in a cheerful voice. "You have risen early; but stop that profane language, my friend, or you will never see daylight again!"

The maimed ruffian only muttered, "Your friend, eh? blindfolded and manacled!" And then, apparently abashed by the cool, commanding tone of his superior, he held his peace.

"Well, you are quiet, my lad. Now we'll see if we can't hoist you up here in the saloon."

"Thank ye, sir!" said Gibbs, aloud; and then he muttered to himself, "Let me jest get one grip of ye, and I'll show ye how quiet I'll be."

"Do you think we shall need assistance, my son?" whispered the padre into the ear of his patron.

"*Diavolo!* No. I never wanted help in these little affairs, except in the case of that violent Yankee whaler, who gave us much trouble, you know, and we were obliged to call Pedillo," replied the captain, in the same low tone. Then, raising his voice, he said,

"Hark ye, Master Gibbs! Babette will lift you off the stones, and the padre and I will raise you up to the room here. You don't weigh so much as you did before you had your leg hacked off with a hand-saw—ho! and I dare say you are as light now as a dried stockfish! Up with him, Baba! There—steady! all right—here you are!"

Saying this, Captain Brand, with the assistance of the stout negress and the padre, raised the once burly ruffian, with a vigorous hoist that made him groan, to the floor of the saloon, where they laid him out at full length on his back.

"Wait a moment, my hearty, till the hatch is raised, and then we will raise you. Unpleasant position, no doubt," continued Captain Brand, as the trap came up and was secured by a spring; "but then, you know, you *would* have that pin of yours cut off, and somehow you have been so careless as to dispose of the nice leg you had the other day, made out of the spruce fore-top-mast of the 'Centipede' —a very tough bit of a spar it was."

Here Master Gibbs grated his teeth and grinned hideously.

The captain smiled like a demon, and, approaching the prostrate cripple, said cheerfully—ay, in a frank and hearty tone—

"Now, my padre, place a comfortable chair for Master Gibbs, and we will help him to a seat."

The considerate Ricardo placed a large, roomy Manilla chair on the fatal trap, and then aided his chief in lifting their victim to the position assigned him. As they performed this operation, the captain, with the gentleness of a tiger before he strikes his prey, and with a wink to the padre, lightly passed the noose of the silk rope over the ruffian's hairy throat, where it lay like a snake with its slack coil squirming at the back of the chair.

"Now, Master Gibbs, I am about to remove this bandage from your beautiful red eyes," said Captain Brand, in his cold, chilling, deliberate manner, "and if you so much as move when daylight shines before you, I'll blow your brains out."

Here the pirate leisurely cocked a pistol close to his subordinate's ear, removed the bandage, and laid the weapon on the table within reach.

"No noise either, Master Gibbs!" continued Captain Brand, as he stirred up the remains of his chocolate and gulped it down; "for it is Sunday morning, and we must respect the feelings of our padre. You were unkind to him, he tells me, just now, and even said some disrespectful things of me. What have *I* done to vex you?"

The manacled wretch tried to raise his horny hands to his face when the cloth was removed from his eyes, and rub those organs, while he glared suspiciously around; but the captain pointed with his white finger in a threatening way to the cocked pistol, and Master Gibbs let his hands fall again.

I

"Well, Captain Brand, I s'pose now you're going to treat me as a faithful man who has sarved under you ought to be treated; and I'm willin' to forgive what has passed."

There was no look of forgiveness, however, in those brutal blood-shot eyes, nor much signs of repentance in those grinding teeth and compressed lips.

"Why, no, my Gibbs, *I* am *not* going to treat you as a faithful man, but I tell you what I will do"—here the captain moved his chair nearer till his straw slipper touched the spring of the trap—"I will drink a glass of grog with you in forgetfulness of the past and for-giveness for the future."

"Thank ye, Captain Brand; I do feel dry. That stuff Babette gave me a while ago didn't touch the right spot, and I'll be glad to jine you."

"Ah! *bueno*, my old friend; you *shall* drink something that *will* touch the right spot! What shall it be? you have only to name it."

"I'll take a toss of that old brandy you gave me the other day, if it's the same to you, sir."

"Oh, Master Gibbs, it's all the same to me. Delighted I am to oblige you! *Padre mio!* a glass of old Cognac for our friend—a tumblerful; a wine-glass will do for me."

The padre poured out the brandy as he was desired, handed the lesser glass to the captain, and the tumbler he placed in the locked hands of the victim. Slowly and painfully the subdued ruffian raised the glass to his mouth, careful not to spill a drop; then, before drain-ing it, he cleared his throat, while at the same time the captain rose to his feet, his right foot resting a little on the heel, and held the wine-glass before him.

"Now, then, Master Gibbs, for a toss that will touch the right spot."

"Ay, ay, captain!" said Gibbs; "and here's forgiveness for the future."

Scarcely had the words been uttered, and the liquor began to gur-gle down the hairy throat of the manacled wretch, than the pirate before him pressed his foot with a quick, nervous action on the spring.

Like a flash the trap fell, carrying chair and man with it. The hinges of the hatch creaked, the wicker-work chair fell with a bound on the stone floor below, the heavy beam overhead gave a jarring quiver as the strong silk rope brought up with a shuddering surge on the cleat where it was belayed at the wall, and with a gasping, choking cry of pain mingled with the ring of the shattered tumbler on the pavement, the ruffian of a hundred crimes fell full three feet, and hung struggling in the death agony. With almost superhuman force he raised his clenched hands and struck his forehead till the manacles were twisted like wire by the effort, spinning around too by the lopsided weight of his body, while the beam above yielded slightly to the strain, and the deadly cord, no longer squirming, but taut as a bar of iron, held the wretch in its knotted embrace, clasped tight around the throat. In a minute or two the hands ceased beating the inflamed face and head, and fell with a clank before the body; the legs gave a few convulsive twitches, a last and violent spasm shook the frame, and there Master Gibbs hung, a warm dead lump of clay.

While this murderous business was going on, and the poor crippled wretch was struggling in the jaws of death, the padre was chanting with his profane tongue from his open breviary the *Salve Domine*, and his patron coolly took down a telescope and swept it over the blue water to seaward. When, however, after a quarter of an hour had elapsed, and the body of their victim gave no more signs of life, the captain laid down the telescope as the padre closed his missal, and remarked quietly, while glancing critically down at the suspended body,

"He did not go off so easy as I had anticipated; his bull-neck is not broken, though the knot was perfectly well placed. However, he is stone dead, and we will lower him down. You, my padre, will bury him!"

"*Hijo mio!* son of mine! spare me that troublesome duty. Would you have me drag such a carcass through the cavern and consign him to consecrated earth, when he refused the last holy offers of salvation?"

"*Bueno*, my padre, I respect your feelings! You need not put him under the sand; take him merely to his late dungeon, and lay him decently on his bed."

"Thank you, my son; your orders shall be obeyed!"

Glad, apparently, to be relieved from farther exertion, though with manifest symptoms of disgust, the priest, more infamous even than the scoundrel he had assisted in hanging, clumsily descended the hatchway by the way he came up, and awaited the movements of his chief. The captain stepped to the wall, and, casting off the turns from the cleat, he slowly lowered the body down till it rested on the pavement.

"Unbend the rope from his neck, my padre, and hitch it on to that Manilla chair. There—all right! you may return this way and breakfast with me."

Saying this, Captain Brand rounded up the chair, detached the silk rope, hung the loop in its accustomed place, and then waited the reappearance of his confederate. Not many minutes elapsed before the padre, having performed the last rites, again ascended the stanchion, and was assisted above the floor by his chief. Then both together got hold of a ring-bolt in the trap, drew it up and secured the spring, placing square bits of mahogany over the countersunk apertures, so as to prevent accidental falls or hangings of themselves. Even while performing these mechanical operations, the priest puffed out an account of his proceedings below: how he had dragged the body to the dungeon; how, when there, he had inadvertently stumbled and fallen on the top of it; and that his lips—*maldito !*—came in contact with the open mouth of the late Master Gibbs; but when he had recovered from the horror of this frightful caress, he had said a short prayer and bolted the door.

"You have done well, my padre; and now let us break our fast. Babette, a couple of broiled snappers and a cold duck! Be lively, old lady, for I have business to attend to after breakfast. *Hola, mi padre*, will you wash your hands in water before sitting down? No! *bueno !* I will myself take a dip all over."

No, the oily Ricardo never washed his hands, save wetting the tips of his fingers in holy water in the chapel; and, indeed, he rarely touched water in any quantity either outside or in; and it was with a look of surprise, not unmingled with contempt, that he beheld his patron retire for a bath.

CHAPTER XX.

BUSINESS.

"He had rolled in money like pigs in mud,
  Till it seemed to have entered into his blood
    By some occult projection ;
And his cheeks, instead of a healthy hue,
As yellow as any guinea grew,
Making the common phrase seem true
    About a rich complexion."

THE business which Captain Brand alluded to when he was about to partake of breakfast with his friend the padre was, in the first instance, to arrange some matters in the way of payment of debts to his compadre, Don Ignaçio Sanchez, commander of the Colonial Guarda Costa felucca "Panchita."

Accordingly, when he rose from table, and after a whispered dialogue and reports as to the state of affairs in and around the den and island from the men at the signal-stations, he summoned Pedillo. When that worthy appeared below the veranda—for be it remembered that Captain Brand never permitted the inferior officials of his band to pollute his apartments, unless, perhaps, as in the case of his deceased subordinate, Master Gibbs, it was on urgent business—Captain Brand ordered his gig manned.

Pedillo threw up his hand in token of assent, and walked down to the brink of the basin to execute the command. Then, after a few minutes, Captain Brand lit a cigar, dismissed the padre, put on his fine white Panama straw hat, unlocked a strong cabinet with a secret drawer, glanced over a paper before him, and, making a rapid calculation, he caught up a heavy bag of doubloons, and left the house in charge of Babette. The captain always told his guests that his fellows had such love and respect for him that he rarely locked up his property, and never placed a guard at his door. The truth was, that his fellows—scoundrels, miscreants, and villains as they were—stood in such fear and dread of their leader, that they were glad to keep out of his way. Moreover, he never boasted or made any display before them, living on shipboard, as on shore, by himself, but always ready and terrible when the moment came for action; treating his crew, too, with the most rigid impartiality, adhering strictly to his promises and compacts with them, and never overlooking an offense.

So Captain Brand left his dwelling in charge of his dumb housekeeper Babette, and tripping down the rope ladder from the piazza in a clean suit of brown linen and straw slippers, his beardless face shaded by his broad-brimmed hat from the sun, and the bag of gold on his arm, he jauntily walked toward the cove.

"Ah! good morning, my doctor! Glad to meet you! How are the sick? 'Doing well, I hope!'"

"Quite well, sir; but I was about to call upon you in relation to the conversation we had last evening, and—"

"Pardon me, *Monsieur le Docteur*, but I have been very busy this morning, and am now going to see Don Ignaçio on matters of importance"—here the elegant pirate took the cigar from his thin lips and held it daintily between his thumb and fore finger in the air— "and really, monsieur, I am very sorry to miss your visit. But," he added, with one of his usual smiles, "I shall be at leisure this afternoon, and in the cool of the evening we can take a stroll. What say you?"

The doctor nodded.

"Apropos, *docteur*, suppose we have a little game of *monté* afterward at your quarters. I never permit gaming in mine, you know. The padre will not object; and I am confident our *compadre*, the Tuerto, will be delighted."

"As you please, captain," replied the medico, with a cold, indifferent air and averted face. "I will join you in the promenade, and I shall be ready to receive you in the evening."

"*Hasta luego, amigo!*" said Captain Brand, as he again stuck his cigar between his teeth, waved his hand in adieu, and walked to his boat.

"You don't love me, doctor," thought the pirate. "I don't fear you, captain," thought the doctor.

It was a touch of high art the way this notorious pirate pitched the bag of gold toward his coxswain, crying, "Catch that, Pedillo!" and then the almost girlish manner in which he pattered about the beach and held up his trowsers, so that he might not even get his slippers damp. Had that salt water been red blood, he would not have cared if his feet had been soaked in it. And then, too, the little exclamation of joy when he finally stepped into the stern-sheets, and sat down beneath the awning, while he stretched his smooth brown linen legs out on the cushions. Oh, it was certainly a touch of high piratical art!

"The old 'Centipede' is looking a little rusty after her late cruise, Pedillo!" throwing his head back to evade a curl of smoke, and casting his cold eyes like a rattle of icy hail at the coxswain. "But I am glad Pedro took your place"—puff, puff—"that knife-stab prevented you, of course"—puff—"and we shall have her all tight and trig again in a day or two."

"*Si, señor!*" said Pedillo, respectfully; "and how goes Señor Gibbs, *capitano?*"

The *capitano* rolled his icy eyes again at the coxswain, and replied, carelessly, "Why, Pedillo, our friend Gibbs came to see me when the 'Centipede' anchored, but almost before"—puff—"he had given me an account of his unfortunate cruise he fell down in a fit. The fact is, however"—puff, puff—"that, what with hard drinking and inflammation which set in on the stump of his lost leg, he has been in a very bad way"—puff—"quite in a dangerous condition indeed, requiring all my old Babette's care and attention"—puff—"but this morning the good padre went to see him, and he told me a while ago that he left him without fever, and altogether tranquil."

Pedillo's wiry mustaches twirled of themselves.

Meanwhile the boat skimmed lightly over the basin, and as the captain ceased speaking she ran alongside of the felucca. Don Ignaçio, with his bright single eye in full burning power, and a cigarette between his wrinkled lips, was on the deck of the vessel to receive his visitor; and as he saw the coxswain follow his superior with a weighty bag under his arm, his glimmering orb became brighter, if possible—as if it was piercing through the thick canvas of the bag, and counting, ounce by ounce, the contents—and putting out his fore finger, it was grasped cordially by the white hand of Captain Brand.

"*Como se va?* How goes it with my *compadre?* Stomach and head all clear after our long dinner of yesterday?"

The *compadre* said that his head was particularly clear that morning, and as for his stomach he had not yet inquired; but if the *capitano* had any doubts as to the former proposition, he had better step below and decide for himself.

In accordance with this ambiguous invitation, the visitor and commander disappeared down the small cuddy in the afterpart of the felucca, where was a low, stifling hole of a cabin, dank with stale tobacco-smoke, and smelling awfully of rats and roaches. There was a little round table in the middle, and on one side was a single berth, with some dirty bedding, which had not been cleaned, apparently, since the vessel was built. Light was shed from a skylight above.

Captain Brand gave a sniff of disgust as he entered this floating sanctum of Don Ignaçio, but, without remark, seated himself on a canvas stool, and waved a perfumed cambric kerchief before his nose.

Commander Sanchez, catching the inspiration, merely observed that it was a little close certainly, and not so spacious as the superb cabin of the schooner, and that sometimes, when lying in a calm off the lee side of Cuba, it was hot enough to melt the tail off a brass monkey; but yet it was his duty, and he did not particularly mind it.

Hereupon Captain Brand requested Don Ignaçio to produce his papers, and they were presently laid upon the table. For a few minutes the pirate was absorbed in running his cold eyes over the accounts—making pencil-notes on the margins, and comparing them with a memorandum he took from his pocket; but at last he threw himself back and exclaimed,

"*Compadre*, the account of old Moreno, at the Havana, is correct to a real—three hundred and twelve doubloons and eight hard dollars. Yours, however, has some few inaccuracies—double commissions charged here and there; all losses and sales charged to me, and all profits credited to you."

Don Ignaçio spread out the palms of both his hands toward his companion, as if to exorcise such unjust charges from the brain of his confederate.

"*O si, si, compadre!* it is as I state, and you know it is true; but, nevertheless, a few dozens of ounces more or less makes no difference; and, to make short work, I am ready to pay. But," said Captain Brand, laying a hand on the heavy bag of money beside him, "though I am quite ready to cancel my debts in hard cash here on the spot, yet, as I am bound on a long cruise—Heaven only knows where—I would prefer to keep the gold and pay you in something else."

Don Ignaçio threw his head back and fixed his eye like a parrot on the captain, waiting to hear farther.

"What have I on hand besides gold? Well, there are a few bales of Mexican cochineal, and English broadcloths, and some cases of French silks, which you can have at a fair market value; then there is all that collection of silver table-service, which you can take by weight; and, besides, lots of rare furniture, which you may set your own price upon—altogether much more than enough to pay Moreno and you both. What say you, *compadre?* is it a bargain? or shall I carry the stuff with me, and run the chance of disposing of it on the Spanish Main?"

It was a long time before the crafty old Spaniard could make up his mind whether to receive his pay in a simple portable currency, or take more bulky matter, with the hope of making double the money by the operation. Finally, however, his greed overcame his prudence, and he accepted the last proposition, with the understanding that the articles should be transferred to the felucca the next night.

"Ah!" said Captain Brand, with another sniff of disgust, as he spat on the dirty floor of the cabin, "I am glad the affair is settled, for I wouldn't remain another hour in this filthy hole for all the money—you have cheated me out of, you old rascal."

He said the last portion of this sentence to himself as he emerged from the cuddy.

“ But listen,,*amigo !*” he continued, as they both reached the deck. “ You will give me duplicate receipts on the part of Señor Moreno, so that I can forward one to him from the next port I visit. And, by the way, suppose you come on shore this afternoon for a stroll, and in the evening we will have a little game of *monté*—eh ?”

“*Cierto !* (certainly !)” returned the commander of the felucca; when Captain Brand, with his bag of gold intact under his arm, got into his boat and was pulled to the shore.

CHAPTER XXI.

TREASURE.

> "Gold! gold! gold! gold!
>   Bright and yellow, hard and cold,
>   Molten, graven, hammered, and rolled;
>   Heavy to get, and light to hold;
>   Hoarded, bartered, bought, and sold;
>   Stolen, borrowed, squandered, doled;
>   Price of many a crime untold—
>   Gold! gold! gold! gold!"

It was long past noon when the pirate returned to his island home, and the day was hot, for the sea-breeze had not made, and the tropical sun was pouring down its burning rays until the sand was roasting as in a furnace; the very rocks throwing off a trembling mirage of heated air, and the lagoon almost boiling under the fiery influence. The sailors, with aching heads and parched mouths, were swinging in their grass hammocks beneath the sheds; and, save the watchful vigilance of the men at the look-outs and battery, the little island was wrapped in repose.

Captain Brand, however, was as cool as a cucumber; and regardless of the heat, and indifferent about *siesta*, he drew the curtains of the saloon, and took some active exercise. First, however, he desired his faithful Babette to get out some camphor trunks and pack the contents of his splendid wardrobe. This operation was performed under the critical eye of Captain Brand himself, to which he personally lent his aid by stowing away, here and there, his caskets, trinkets, and treasures—those which had been presented to him by the unfortunate people who had the ill luck to make his acquaintance on the high seas, or in midnight forays on shore. Then the captain opened and rummaged cabinets, bureaus, and bookcases, making liberal presents to his trusty housekeeper; and, turning from that occupation, he had all his table furniture spread before him, when he made careful estimates of the value of the silver, china, and glass. This concluded, Captain Brand ordered Babette to furnish him a slight repast; and while it was preparing—the captain taking the precaution to bolt his handmaiden in her kitchen—he went quietly into his bedroom, and when he came out he bore heavy burdens in his muscular arms, all of which he laid conveniently near the trap in the floor. Then letting the hatch swing softly down, he lowered the heavy arti-

"HE CREPT FORWARD ON HANDS AND KNEES, THE BLAZING TORCH LIGHTING UP THE DAMP AND DRIPPING ROCKS."

cles by the silk rope, as he had Master Gibbs, though not so suddenly, going down himself as nimbly as a rat after them. In the vault
beneath, Captain Brand struck a light and set fire to a torch, which
blazed out luridly, and illumined the dark excavation and passages
like day. Going slowly on, with his burden in his arms, by the path
by which we traced the padre, he came to the outer door, which
opened into the fissure in the crag; and, after a vigorous effort, the
beam was raised, and he passed out. Once outside, he felt his way
cautiously, stepping clear of the stagnant pools beneath, and guarding his head from the jagged rocks above; and then, lighting his way
over the stones which had upset the equilibrium of Don Ricardo, he
crept slowly into an aperture on the right.

No serpents or venomous reptiles disturbed the pirate's progress;
for, though there were plenty of them coiled or crawling near, yet
their instinct probably taught them that he was a monster with a
more deadly poison than themselves, and whose fangs were sharper,
though his tongue did not hiss a note of warning. Captain Brand put
down his burden and crept forward on hands and knees, the blazing
torch lighting up the damp and dripping rocks, all green and slimy
from the tracks of the snake and lizard. Where the narrow fissure
seemed to end by a wall of natural rock, the pirate rolled aside a
large stone at the base, and scratching away the sand, a large copper
lock was displayed, in which, after pushing aside the hasp, Captain
Brand touched a spring, and it opened. Then, exerting all the force
of his powerful frame, a rough slab of unhewn rock yielded to the
effort, and rose like a vertical door slung by a massive hinge at the
top. Placing the large stone at the opening, so as to prevent the slab
falling to its place, the captain stood the torch within the opening,
and went back for his burden; then he returned, and squeezed himself with it into a small excavated, uneven chamber, where he sat
down.

"Nasty work," communed the pirate with himself, "but a safe
place to lay up a penny for a rainy day! Let me see. These two
bags of doubloons, and the small one my Gibbs brought me, with
those three, there, of guineas, and those sacks of dollars, will make
about ten thousand pounds. That will make me a nest-egg when I
retire from the profession and return to Scotland. They will have
forgotten all my boyish follies by that time."

Captain Brand alluded to forging his father's name, and other little peccadilloes of a similar nature.

"And I may be elected to Parliament—who knows? It is something of a risk, perhaps, to leave all this pretty coin here, but then
it's a greater risk to carry it in the schooner"—he argued both ways
—"and then, again, damp does not decay pure metal. But," thought
Captain Brand, "suppose somebody should discover this little casket

in the rock. Ah! that's not probable, for no soul besides myself knows of it, and even the very man who made the door did not know for what it was intended; besides, he died long ago."

Captain Brand had forgotten, in this connection, that the man who cut out the stone chamber and door, and fashioned the hinge and lock, took too much sugar in his coffee the morning the job was finished, and died in horrible convulsions before night. Oh yes, that incident had entirely escaped his memory!

Captain Brand, having now thoroughly reasoned the matter out, gave each of the bags lying on the sand a gentle kick to get a responsive echo from the coin; and then creeping out of the treasure-chamber, he withdrew the torch, removed the stone, and the heavy slab fell again into its place. Then clasping the lock, covering it over with sand, and rolling back the stone, he seized the torch and quickly returned to the vault beneath his saloon. There, putting out the torch by rubbing it against the stone pavement until not a spark was left, by the sunlight, streaming through the loopholes around, he passed to one side and began removing the cases of cochineal, silks, and what not, near to the strongly-barred portcullis door, which opened toward the basin fronting his dwelling. It was hard work, but Captain Brand seemed to enjoy it; and even after he had arranged the packages intended for shipment in his *compadre's* felucca, he began again. Going to the farther corner of the vault, he stopped before a strong mahogany door, and taking a key from his pocket, unlocked and threw it wide open. It was as black as night inside, floored and lined with wood, and emitting a choking atmosphere of charcoal and sulphur. Piled around the walls were some fifty or a hundred small barrels with copper hoops, and branded on the heads with the word "powder." Unmindful of the odor and the rather combustible material around him, Captain Brand again resumed his work, and rolled a large number of the little barrels toward the doorway, near the merchandise already there, saying to himself the while,

"I think that will about fill the 'Centipede's' magazine, and we must make a proper disposition of the remainder."

Hereupon Captain Brand, actively bent upon the work of disposing of his treasures, rolled out a dozen or two more of the little barrels. Strange to say, among the very few articles that were never presented to him, but actually bought of Señor Moreno, was this highly useful and indispensable material of powder, and he therefore set much store by it. And it was with a sigh of regret that the pirate stood the little barrels on their ends in a line across the great vault of the building, beneath kitchen, bedrooms, and saloon, and especially beside the square upright stanchions on which the interior of the building rested. Not content with this, he took a copper hammer and knocked in all the heads of the little barrels, and then, with a scoop of the same metal, he dipped out large quantities of the black material, and poured thick trains of it from barrel to barrel, sometimes capsizing one, but always particularly cautious not to rasp a grain of it beneath his grass slippers and the pavement. Then he took a piece of match rope, and sticking one end deep into a barrel, he just poked the other end out of a loophole, to be in readiness whenever Captain Brand should deem proper to touch his lighted cigar to it.

"There," said Captain Brand, "that piece of tow will burn about thirty or forty minutes, and then—stand from under!"

Ascending the hatchway again with the agility of a cat, he drew up and secured the trap, and in ten minutes afterward he was freshly attired in a nice pair of India panjammers, a grass cloth jacket and vest—with, of course, the usual knickknacks in his pockets—and seated at table, where his busy housekeeper had placed a broiled chicken and a bottle of old Bordeaux before him.

· CHAPTER XXII.

PLEASURE.

"But ever, from that hour, 'tis said,
　　He stammered and he stuttered,
As if an axe went through his head
　　With every word he uttered.
He stuttered o'er blessing, he stuttered o'er ban,
　　He stuttered, drunk or dry;
And none but he and the fisherman
　　'Could tell the reason why."

"Babette," said Captain Brand, as he tapped a spoon against his coffee-cup and puffed his cigar, while the stout dumb negress was removing the remains of the light dinner, "Babette, old girl, you know that we are going to leave here in a few days, and I should like to know whether you care to go with us or remain here on the island."

The negress made a guttural grunt of assent, and nodded her head till the ends of her Madras turban fluttered.

"Ho! you do, eh? Well, my Baba, I shall be sorry to leave you, for you will be very lonely here, and it may be a long, very long time before I come back."

Babette jerked her chin up this time, and did not grunt.

"It's all the same, eh? old lady! Well, I shall leave enough to eat to last you a lifetime; but you will have to 'change your quarters, my Baba, and live in the padre's shed, for I—a—don't think this house will be inhabitable long after I am gone."

The negress gave another grunt and nod of assent.

"Yes. Well, old lady, the matter is decided, then; but, in case you should have any visitors here after we have gone, you won't take any trouble to describe what you have seen here? No! That shake of your head convinces me—not if they roast you alive?"

The hideous sign of understanding that the woman expressed in her dumb way would have convinced any body without the trouble of uttering a word.

"*Bueno!*" said Captain Brand; "that will do for to-day."

Rising as he spoke, he stepped to a cabinet, slipped a large handful of doubloons in his trowsers pocket, put on his hat, and walked out.

The sea-breeze swept over the island with its full strength, making the lofty cocoa-nuts bow their tufted tops, the palm-trees rustle their broad flat leaves and clash the stems together. The mangroves bent, too, before the wind, and the sand eddied up in tiny whirls amid the great expanse of cactus, while the vessels swung with taut cables to their anchors. Even Captain Brand's hat nearly was blown off his dry light hair as he joined his *compadre*, Don Ignaçio, at the landing; and the sandy dust blinded—though only for a moment—that one-eyed individual's optic, and put out his cigarette as they struggled against the influence of the breeze. But yet they walked on in the direction of the sheds, and as they passed through the courtyard, where the men were lounging about in yawning groups or sitting under the piazza, playing cards—getting up and touching their hats as their chief passed—Señor Pedillo accosted him thus:

"*Capitano*, the people are thirsty, and desire a barrel of wine."

"Not a drop, Señor Pedillo—not so much as would wet the bill of a musquito! To-morrow at daylight let all hands be called, for we have work to do, and we must be quick to do it."

Pedillo slunk away, abashed by the positive tone of his commander; and Captain Brand, with his companion, passed on to the domicile of the padre and doctor. Pausing at the open door of the shed, they looked in. The padre was lying flat on his back on his narrow bed, with his mouth wide open, and snoring like a key-bugle with leaky stops; while his beads and crucifix—misplaced emblems in contact with drunkenness and debauchery—were reposing on his ample chest. The doctor was sitting beside his own couch, whispering words of childish comfort to the little boy, whose pale cheeks and brown curls reposed on the pillow of the bed. The poor child's thin, limp fingers rested like the petals of a drooping lily in the dark, bony hand of his friend, and his dim hazel eyes were turned sadly toward him.

"Holloa, *amigos!*" shouted Captain Brand, in a hearty voice. "We are losing the glorious sea-breeze. *Vamanos!* let us take a stroll to the Tiger's Trap."

Hereupon Captain Brand entered the room, and gave the padre a violent tweak of the nose, at the same time puffing a volume of cigar-smoke into his beastly mouth, which combined effort brought the holy father to life in a trice, choking and sputtering, as he arose, a jargon of paternosters, which an indifferent hearer might have mistaken for a volley of execrations, so savagely were they uttered.

"Take a sip of Geneva, my padre. There it is on the table. Ah! do you call half a bottle a sip? Well! Come, doctor, let us be moving."

Down by the narrow gorge of the inlet, and over the smooth rocks and shelly shore, the party took their way, Don Ignaçio leading with the amiable priest, on whom he glared with his malevolent

K

eye as if—he not being a person from whom money or its equivalent could be squeezed—the greedy old Spaniard would like to transfix him with a glance. In the rear came Captain Brand and the doctor, the former as gay as a bird—of the vulture species—and his companion grave, severe, and preoccupied. Stopping· as they reached the Tiger Trap Battery, where, after Captain Brand had made a close inspection of the guns, and held sharp confabs with the men who rose to receive him, he moved away a few steps, and, resting his body against the lee side of a projecting rock, removed the cigar from his frozen lips, and said,

"The 'arguments you have urged, monsieur, and the views you entertain, have a certain amount of reason in them. It is true you were deceived in coming here, but yet you swore to remain and not betray us when you did come. Well—ah! don't interrupt me; I divine what you are going to say—you did not know what our real character was. Perhaps not. Nevertheless, I can not consent to your going away with that old rascal, Don Ignaçio, there—that is, if he would·take you, which I think he would not, as your presence on board might compromise him with the Cuban authorities; and," went on Captain Brand, as he crossed his legs, and held his fine Panama hat on his head as a ruffle of the sea-breeze shot around the rock, " with respect to your remaining here on the island, you will only have that dumb old beast of a Babette for company; and it is highly probable that the English·or American cruisers will be down upon you before a change of the moon, and they might—a—hang you, perhaps, for a pirate. Ho! ho!"

" If Don Ignaçio declines to take me, Captain Brand, of course I can not go in the felucca; but, let come what will, I am resolved not to sail in the ' Centipede.' "

The pirate regarded the doctor for a moment with a cold, freezing look, not wanting, however, in a partial glimmer of respect and admiration, as he thus resolutely stated his determination; and then, putting his finger lightly on the doctor's arm, as he saw Don Ignaçio and the padre draw near, he said impressively, in a low tone,

"*Monsieur le Docteur*, do not make hasty resolutions. *I* command here, and my will is law. I will turn the matter over, however, in my mind, and give you a final decision before we part to-night. Now let us return. The sun is down, and the rocks are slippery."

" Well, *caballeros*, let us have a little social amusement," said Captain Brand, as he sat down at the table in the padre's and doctor's quarters, and wound up his splendid watch, the present from the Captain General of Cuba. "But bear in mind that we must break up at midnight, for our *compadre* here has a multitude of articles to get on board his felucca to-night, and I must be astir at daylight."

Did Captain Brand think, while he turned the key of that gold repeater, of the bloodstained wretch he had put to death in the morning, who was lying stark and stiff in his narrow, damp resting-place, or of the poor little sufferer who had been torn from his heart-broken mother sleeping near him?. Oh no, certainly not. Captain Brand was thinking of a little game of monté.

The padre lugged out a small store of dollars, and a gold ounce or two, and other stray bits of gold, down to quartitos or eighths of doubloons—all of it donations made him for remission of sins and absolutions, presented at one time and another from the pirates of his flock, such donations falling in pretty rapidly after a successful cruise, but dwindling away to most contemptible gifts long before his flock took to sea again.

Captain Brand was very liberal to his crew, dividing a great deal of money with them, but, since he rarely visited any foreign ports, they had little chance of squandering it; and in the end it served merely as a gaming currency to play with, and eventually coming back to him as contributions for stores, ammunition, rigging, and so forth. The captain, therefore, was a large gainer by the operation, as most of the articles in eating and drinking, and the vessel's outfit, were—as we know—generally presented to him, so that he was enabled to stow away the cash for future gratification.

Don Ignaçio Sanchez was likewise a moneyed man, and came provided with a long pouch of solid gold, which he made into little piles before him of the exact size of those of the captain. The doctor, however, declined to play, and sat an indifferent spectator of the game.

"Let us begin, *señores!*" exclaimed the Don, as he rapidly shuffled the cards, and his keen, black spark of fire lit up with animation at the rich prospect before him. "We are losing precious time. I'll be *banquero! Vamanos!*"

So they began. The cards were dealt, and the betting went on. The padre forgot breviary and beads in his excitement, and as his little pointings were swept away, he forgot, too, the sacred ejaculations he was wont to lard his discourse with, and he became positively profane. The captain won largely in the beginning, and jeered his *compadre* with great zest and enjoyment; but that one-eyed, rapacious old Spanish rascal was not in the least disturbed, and bided his time. At first the conversation was light and jovial, Captain Brand insisting upon the doctor describing minutely how he had hacked his friend Gibbs's leg off with a hand-saw, laughing hugely thereat, and wiping the icy tears from his cold blue eyes with his delicate cambric handkerchief. Then the fascinating game began to fluctuate, and the luck set back with a steady run into the piles of the banker. Captain Brand liked as little to lose his money as any other gambler in cards, stocks, or dice, and he was somewhat chafed in spirit; but what especially irritated him was losing it to that wrinkle-faced, one-eyed, greedy old scoundrel, with no possible hope of ever seeing a dollar of it again. As for the padre, he was dead broke; and since his friends would not lend him a real, and the banker did not play upon credit, he sat moodily by, and gloated over the winnings of the Tuerto, cursing his own luck and that of his companions likewise.

"Ho!" growled Captain Brand, "*maldito a la sota!* I have lost my last stake!"

Even while he spoke the poor little boy murmured in a sobbing voice, "Mamma, *chère* mamma!" and turned uneasily in his little nest from his fitful slumber.

"That crying imp again!" said the now angry pirate, as he hurled the padre's half empty gin jug in the direction of the couch, which crashed against the wall, and fell in a shower of glass splinters over the little sleeper.

The child gave one terrified shriek, and, starting from the bed in his little night-dress, now soiled and torn, he ran and threw himself on his knees before the doctor. Another bottle was raised aloft by the long muscular arm of the pirate; but, before you could wink, that arm was arrested, and the missile twisted from his grasp.

"For shame, you coward! Don't harm the boy. He will die soon enough in this awful den without having his brains dashed out."

"Ho, *Monsieur le Docteur!*" muttered the villain, looking as if he would like to taste the heart's-blood of the resolute man who stood before him, as he pushed a hand into his waistcoat pocket, "do you presume to call names and oppose *my* will?"

But, controlling his passion with a violent contortion of face that would have made one's blood run cold to see it, he changed his tone and said,

"Nonsense, doctor; you seem to take rather a strong interest in the brat—possibly an injudicious one; but, since he is my prize, you know, by law, come—what will you give for him? Ah! happy thought, we will play for him! There, deal away, *compadre*. *Sota* and *cavallo!* I take the knave again, and you ten doubloons against the boy on the horse."

The doctor said not a word, but nodded assent, and seemed absorbed in the game.

"*Presto!* Turn the cards, you old sinner! Quick! *Por dios!* horse has kicked me, and the knave loses! *Monsieur*, the brat is yours!"

Then starting up, Captain Brand hastily pulled out his watch, and said, "*Hola, caballeros*, the time is up! I must say good-night."

Don Ignaçio's brown thin fingers, like a dentist's steel nippers, laid down the cards, and carefully picked up his winnings, even to the smallest bit of the precious metal, and dropped it piece by piece into his long pouch, following them each with his glittering eye, like a magpie peering into a narrow-necked bottle, and smiling with his wrinkled old lips as the dull chink of the coin fell upon his ear. When he had performed this operation, he tied up the mouth of the bag as if he was choking somebody to death; and then, twitching something which was partly hidden in his sleeve, he arose in readiness to go out.

As, however, Captain Brand turned to follow his *compadre*, he looked carelessly toward the doctor, and said,

"By the way, monsieur, I have made up my mind with respect to our conversation to-day, and you *shall* remain on the island. No thanks. Adieu. Now, Don Ignaçio, if your men and boats are at the cove, we will make sharp work with your business. *Vamanos!*"

CHAPTER XXIII.

WORK

> "Skeleton hounds that will never be fatter,
> All the domestic tribes of hell,
> Shrieking for flesh to tear and tatter,
> Bones to shatter,
> And limbs to scatter,
> And who it is that must furnish the latter,
> Those blue-looking men know well!"

WHEN the pirate stood in his saloon on the morning subsequent to the pleasurable events of the Sunday previous, he, as well as his saloon, presented altogether a different aspect. The apartment had been stripped of all its rare and costly furniture, cabinets, candelabra, plate, china, and glass, and nothing of value was left save the camphor trunks on the floor, the cane-bottomed settee, a few chairs, and a table. All the beautiful things, ornamental as well as useful, had disappeared, even to the rich packages of merchandise in the great vault beneath. The late possessor, however, of all that worldly wealth did not appear to be at all discomposed, or to cherish the faintest pang of regret at his loss. In truth, he seemed to be relieved from an uncomfortable load of responsibility; and feeling assured, perhaps, that in roaming about the world he could collect a still more valuable collection—only give him time—and he would exercise his critical taste with every pleasing variety. It was thus he consoled himself as he stood there in his now denuded room, attired in a pair of coarse canvas trowsers, a red flannel shirt, with a short sharp hanger on his hip, and a double-barreled pistol in his belt—quite the costume in which he so singularly shocked Doña Lucia, whose lovely miniature once hung there on the wall in company with the other miserable victims of his lust.

Captain Brand had just entered his dwelling, having been up and actively occupied ever since we last parted with him. Now he had come for a cup of tea and dry toast; and, while Babette was bringing that simple breakfast, the pirate stood, tall, erect, and powerful, with one muscular arm resting high above his head on the side of the doorway, and the other lying lightly on the shark's-skin hilt of his cutlass, looking out to seaward—a very model, as he was, of a cool, prudent, desperate villain.

"Ah! there you go, you crafty old miser, in your guarda costa!

Take care, my compadre, of that reef. If that felucca's keel touches one of those coral ledges there won't be a tooth-pick left of her in ten minutes. San Antonio! but that was a close shave! How the sharks would rasp your bones, for there's no flesh on them! Grazed clear, eh? *Bueno!* now you're in blue water, you rapacious scoundrelly old wretch, and make the most of it."

Captain Brand waved his hand in adieu to the felucca, which, with the wind off shore, had crept through the coral gateway, and, with her great lateen sail and green glancing bottom, was rising and falling on the long swell as she slipped away to the eastward. He then gulped down his tea, made one or two savage bites at his toast, and again walked out to the veranda, descended the ladder, and took his course toward the basin.

There, too, the scene had changed; and instead of the tranquil, shelly shore, only agitated by the musical rippling from the pure little inlet, the faint cry of a sea-gull, or the chirps of the lizards in the crevices of the rocks across the basin, those sounds had given place to the nimble feet and voices of busy sailors. The "Centipede," also, had been towed from her moorings to a jetty which projected into the water from the shore, and there she lay, careened down, her keel half out of the water, with a dozen of her crew scrubbing her lean sides till the green-coated copper came flashing out in the sunlight like burnished gold. With her slanting masts lashed to the jetty, carpenters were engaged reducing the length of the fore-mast, and trimming out a spar for a new bowsprit. The long gun, with its carriage, lay near, and artisans were at work at a temporary forge, hammering out bolts and straps to replace those which were weakened by long service. On the shore, too, were a score or more of the piratical gang—Spaniards, negroes, Indians, Italians, and who not—ferocious-looking scoundrels, busy as bees, splicing and knotting ropes, stretching new rigging, cutting running gear from the coils of hemp or Manilla-grass rope, or making spun-yarn and chafing-mats; while beneath the low mat-sheds hard by, sail-makers were stitching away with their shining needles, making a set of square sails for the changed rig of the "Centipede," or repairing old sails. But this was not all; for in a shed beyond was the armorer, with a few hands, grinding pikes and cutlasses, and cleaning small arms; while farther still was the gunner and his mate, filling powder-cases for the long gun and swivels, and making up musket and pistol ball-cartridges.

In the midst of all these busy throngs moved Captain Brand, hither and thither, from vessel to forge, from sails to rigging, giving clear, sharp directions in various languages—commendation here, reproof there—inspecting with his own cold eyes every thing; judging of all; quick, active, ready; never at a loss for an expedient, and urging on the work like a thorough-bred seaman as he was, who knew his

own duty and how to make others do theirs. So went on the refit-
ting of the "Centipede," all through the burning hot tropical day;
and while the half-exhausted crew took a respite in the scorching
noon for dinner, still their leader toiled on. Or, if he took a rest, it
was in closely scrutinizing the progress made by his men, in puffing
a cigar like to a small high-pressure engine, or in clambering up the
steep face of the crag to the signal-station, where he would peer away
in all directions around the island—never missing the glance of a pelican's pinion or the leap of a fish out of water. Then he would return
to the cove and begin anew the work. It was no longer the elegant
Captain Brand, in knee-breeches, point-lace sleeves, and velvet doub-
let, seated at his luxurious table, groaning under splendid plate, fine
wines, and brilliant wax-lights, and dispensing a profuse hospitality,
but Captain Brand the pirate, in tarry rig, amid sailors, sails, and
cordage, munching a bit of hard biscuit at times, or a cube of salt
junk out of a mess kid, but ever ready, never weary, and always up
to the professional mark.

At the first gray blush of dawn on the following day Captain Brand
was astir again, and before the sun went down behind the waves the
schooner "Centipede" had been transformed into a brigantine, her
fore-mast reduced, new standing rigging fitted for it, with a new
bowsprit and head-booms, her rail raised four or five feet by shifting
bulwarks, and a temporary house built on deck over the long gun.
She was also painted afresh, with a white streak; and, with false
head-boards on her bows to hide her snakelike snout of a cutwater,
no one, unless in the secret, could have known that the clumsy box
of a merchantman lying there was once the low, swift, piratical
schooner which had made so notorious a name in the West Indies.
Still the work was driven on with scarcely any intermission—a few
hours' repose for the crew at night, and an hour for dinner in the
day; but as for Captain Brand, he never slept at all—a doze for an
hour or two, perhaps, on his settee in the saloon, and a cup of tea
in the morning, with cigar-smoke, satisfied his frugal requirements.
The next day, by noon, the water and stores were got on board the
brigantine, her magazine stowed, the dunnage of the crew transferred
from the sheds, the captain's camphor trunks on board and cabin in
order, the sails bent, anchors on the bows, and, swinging to a hawser
made fast to the rocks, the vessel was ready to put to sea at any
moment.

"Pedillo," said Captain Brand, as his vigilant gaze took in all
around him and then rested on the "Centipede"—"Pedillo, you may
warp the vessel down to the mouth of the Tiger's Trap so soon as
you've strewed some fagots ready for lighting in the sheds. When
you get to the Trap, tell the gunner to take a gang of hands and give
that battery a good coat of coal tar, plug the vents of the guns, and

bury carriages and all in the sand beside the magazine. Tell him to destroy the powder, and pitch overboard all he can't conceal; and let him bear a hand about it, for we shall sail with the last of the sea-breeze toward sunset.

"And, Pedillo"—here the pirate's voice dropped to a whisper—"come back after the vessel is secured, and bring that Maltese fellow without a nose with you. It will be as well, perhaps, for you to provide yourself with a few fathoms of raw-hide strips, as we may have occasion to use it. *Quien sabe?*"

Señor Pedillo's black wiry beard fairly bristled as he grinned understandingly at his superior; and, getting into a bit of a canoe at the jetty, he paddled off to the brigantine to execute his orders.

Meanwhile Captain Brand slowly bent his steps toward the house under the crag, and entered his spacious saloon for the last time. On the bare table, too, was his last dinner, served on a few odd dishes and cracked plates.

"Babette, old girl!" said he, as he sat down to this repast, "you have a bottle of good Madeira, and a flask of Hock left? No?"

The negress shook her head violently, made the sign of the cross, and by other telegraphic motions gave her master to understand that Padre Ricardo had dropped in, drained both bottles, and then had reeled off on board the brigantine.

"The drunken selfish beast!" muttered Captain Brand; "it will be the last taste of wine he will swallow for a long time."

The pirate was quite correct in his schemes for the padre's reform, for the next copious draught the holy father imbibed was the briny salt water from the Caribbean Sea.

"Well, my Baba, a drop of water, then! Thank you, old lady. Here's to your health while I am gone. There—you need not blubber so over my hand—good-by!" And so passed away from Captain Brand's sight the only creature in the wide world who loved him.

CHAPTER XXIV.

CAUGHT IN A NET.

"I closed my lids and kept them close,
And the balls like pulses beat;
For the sky and the sea, and the sea and the sky,
Lay like a load on my weary eye,
And the dead were at my feet."

CAPTAIN BRAND did not linger long over his frugal dinner, and when he had finished, as if he had not had enough exercise for the last three days, he began to walk with long nervous strides across the saloon.

"He called me coward, did he? and dared to lay his hands on me! By my right arm, my Creole doctor, I'll teach you not to call hard names again, and I'll paralyze your hands for all time to come."

The pirate's jaws grated like a rusty bolt as he hissed out these murderous threats; but as his eye caught the squirming green silk rope as he swung round on his heel in his walk, he paused and muttered,

"That bit of stuff may be of use. I'll take it by way of precaution."

Hereupon he rapidly unrove the cord and coiled it away in the bosom of his shirt. Then looking at his watch, he said, "Ho! the time approaches, and here comes Pedillo."

Lighting a cigar, he left his dwelling for the last time; and, after pausing to hear a report from Pedillo that his orders had been executed and the vessel all ready for sea, and whispering a few precise directions in return, Captain Brand mounted up the steep face of the crag again, and accosted the signal-man at the station.

"Any thing in sight?"

"Nothing to the eastward, *capitano;* but it has been a little hazy here away to the southward since meridian, and I can hardly see through it."

"*Bueno*, my man! give me the glass. You can go on board the brigantine. I'll take a last look myself."

While the signal-man scrambled down the crag, Captain Brand rested the spyglass on the trunk of the single cocoa-nut-tree, whose skeleton-like fingers of leaves rattled above his head like a gibbeted pirate in chains, and then he searched steadily along the hazy horizon. As he was about, however, to withdraw his eye from the tube, something—a mere dim speck—arrested his attention. Quickly dropping the glass, and as rapidly rubbing the large lens and carefully adjusting the joints, he raised it again, as a backwoodsman does his rifle with an Indian for a mark. For full five minutes the pirate stood as motionless as the crag beneath him, intently glaring through the tube at the speck in the distance. At last he let the glass fall at his side, and pulling out his watch with a jerk, he muttered to himself,

"It is a large and lofty ship; but, should she be a cruiser after me, she will find the bird flown and the nest empty. Ho, now for action!"

Springing down the precipitous declivity as he spoke, he paused a moment at a loophole of the vault beneath his dwelling, and puffing his cigar into a bright coal, he carefully twitched the match-rope which led to the train, opened the loose strands, and placed the fire to it. Waiting an instant till he saw the nitre sparkle as it ignited, he moved away with long, swinging strides toward the sheds. There, glancing through the now deserted halls the crew had occupied, where quantities of fagots, and kindling-wood, and barrels of pitch were standing, he continued on till he came to the quarters of the doctor. The doctor was standing at the open door on the thatched piazza, looking quietly at the brigantine, whose sails were loosed, and the vessel hanging by a sternfast, with her head just abreast the Tiger's Trap.

"Ah! *Monsieur le Docteur*, I have merely called to bid you a final adieu before I go on board; and as I have a few moments left, and a few words to say, suppose you walk with me toward the chapel. *Allons!* there is a suspicious sail off there," waving his glass in the direction, "and I wish to take a good look at her."

"Doctor," continued Captain Brand, as they reached the little esplanade facing the graves and church, "you will have no one left here on our island save our dumb Babette, and the chances are rather remote for your getting away, without, perhaps, some of the West India fleet should happen to drop in here, which I do not think probable. I rely, however, upon your keeping your oath, even if they do come, and not betraying the secrets you are acquainted with."

The pirate said this in an off-hand, friendly way, as he had his glass leveled toward the sail he saw in the offing.

"Captain Brand," replied the doctor, "I was deceived in coming here, as you well know; but I shall religiously keep my oath for the twenty years, as I swore to do. After that, if we both live so long, my tongue and arm shall speak and strike."

The pirate stepped back a little as he shut up the joints of the spyglass with a crash, and, with a scowl of hate and vengeance combined, he said, in a loud voice, while his cold eyes gleamed like a ray of sunlight on an iceberg,

"And I, too, keep my oaths; and, without waiting twenty years, I strike now!"

Even while the treacherous villain spoke, two swarthy, sinewy scoundrels crept stealthily from within the chapel, and, with the soft, slimy movements of serpents, as their leader uttered the last word, they sprang at the back of the doctor, and wound their coils around him, twining strong strands of raw-hide rope about his arms, legs, and body. 'Bound as in a frame of elastic steel, their victim was thrown, face downward, upon the sand.

"Be quick, Pedillo! the time is flying! Gomez, bring the corpse trestle from the chapel."

In a moment a wooden frame with legs, and stretched across with a bed of light wire, which had been used to carry the mortal remains of the pirates—and the poor women, too, beside them—to their last resting-places, was brought out from the little church. Then the bound victim was laid on it, face upward; again the hide thongs were passed in numerous plaits until the body was lashed firmly to the trestle.

"Place it on the edge of that rock there, with his head toward the cocoa-nut-tree. Take this silk rope, Gomez, and clove-hitch it well up the trunk. There, that will do. I myself will perform the last act of politeness."

Saying this, the pirate widened the noose of the cord, and, slipping it over the doctor's head, he placed the knot carefully under his left ear. The victim gave no groan or sigh, and his dark, luminous eyes were fixed on the blue sky above him in heaven.

"*Monsieur le Docteur,*" said Captain Brand, as he hurriedly looked at his watch and raised his hat, "I have but one word of caution to give you: if you struggle you will have your neck broken before you are stung to death! Talk as much as you like; but, as Babette is a long way off, and hard of hearing, I doubt if she comes to your assistance! Adieu!"

The retreating figures went leaping toward the inlet, and, as they rushed through the sheds, applied a torch to the combustible material deposited there, and then sprang on toward the Tiger's Trap. A few minutes afterward the doctor turned his eyes in that direction, and saw the sails of the brigantine sheeted home and run up like magic; and, taking the last breath of the sea-breeze on her quarter, the sternfast was cast off, and she slipped easily out of the gorge-like channel. Still, as those dark stern eyes watched the receding hull of the "Centipede," a sudden jar shook the island, a heavy column of white smoke rose from below the crag like a water-spout, and, spreading out like a palm-tree, came down in a deluge of timber, stones, and

"A DULL, HEAVY, BOOMING ROAR, THAT SHOOK THE CRAG TO ITS BASE, ANNOUNCED THE RUIN OF THE PIRATES' DEN."

dust, while sheets of vivid flame leaped out from the gloom, and an awful peal, followed by a heavy, booming roar, that shook the crag to its base, announced the ruin of the pirate's den. At the same time the red fires gleamed in fitful flashes from the sheds, and, rapidly making headway, all at once burst forth in wild conflagration, till the whole nest was wrapped in flames. The shock of the explosion and the fires killed the wind, and a lurid pall of smoke and cinders hung like a gloomy canopy over the island.

CHAPTER XXV.

THE MOUSE THAT GNAWED THE NET.

> "There passed a weary time. Each throat
> Was parched, and glazed each eye.
> A weary time! a weary time!
> How glazed each weary eye!
> When, looking westward, I beheld
> A something in the sky."

As the powder vomited forth its dreadful thunder, and as the stones and timbers from the blasted den were hurled high in air, and scattered by the explosive whirlwind far and near, some of the splinters and fragments came down in dropping hail upon the red-tiled sheds and the doctor's dwelling. At the first shock the lonely child started up in his little bed, and while the earth rocked and the stones came pelting and crashing on the roof, he screamed, "Mamma! mamma!" No loving echo came back to those innocent lips, and naught was heard save the crackling of the flame beyond, licking its tongue along the dry timber and roaring joyously as it was fed. "Mamma! *chère* mamma!"

Yet no answer, and still the savage flames came careering wildly on till the very stones of the court-yard cracked like slates, while the burning flakes and cinders loaded the air, and the eddying volumes of smoke reeled in dense clouds, and poured their suffocating breath into the room where the forsaken child was crying.

One more panting, helpless cry, and the little fellow instinctively flew through the open doorway, where, blinded and choking with the devastating element around him, he staggered feebly beyond its influence. Yet again a flurry of thick smoke lighted up the forked and vivid flames, and chased the child before it.

Oh, fond mother! in your poignant grief for the loss of your poor drowned boy, you were spared the agony of seeing him, even in imagination, struggling faintly before that tempest of fire and smoke, calling plaintively for her on whose tender bosom his head had rested, while his naked feet were cut and bruised by the sharp coral shingle beneath them. But onward and onward the boy wandered, and fortunately his footsteps took the path into a purer atmosphere which led toward the chapel. Here he looked timidly around at the lurid glare behind him, and then entered the church and sank down exhausted, his feverish, smarting eyes closing in slumber on the hard pavement beneath the image of the Virgin Mary.

Then came the close and sultry night—no murmur of a land-wind to drive the smoky canopy away—the black cinders falling in burning rain on basin, thicket, and lagoon, till even the very lizards and scorpions hid themselves deep within the holes and crevices of the rocks. Midnight came. The dim and silent stars were obscured by a veil of heavy clouds, and with a low, muttering sound of thunder, the vapory masses unclosed their portals, and the rain fell in torrents. The flames, now nearly satisfied with their work, leaped out occasionally from the fallen ruins, but were quenched by the tropical deluge, and smouldered away amid the charred and saturated timbers. Then the thunder ceased, the lizards and scorpions came from their retreats, the teal fluttered over the lagoon, and the noise of the waves bursting over the reef came again to the ear. Still there was no breath of air; the atmosphere was thick and damp; and out from the mangrove thickets and wide expanse of cactus, swarms of insects, musquitoes, and sand-flies in myriads went buzzing and singing in the sultry, murky night.

So dragged on the weary hours until day broke again, and the seabirds floated off seaward for their morning's meal, and the flying-fish skipped with their silvery wings from wave to wave, as the dolphins glittered in gold and purple after them below the blue water. No bright and blazing sun came over the hills of Cuba to light up this picture, but all was blight and gloom, with murky masses of dead, still clouds hanging low down over the island.

The little suffering boy, lying there on the coral pavement, with his head resting on the thin, delicate arm, with pale, sweet face turned half upward toward the Virgin, gave a feeble cry and opened his eyes. He rose to a sitting posture, with his little hands resting on his lap and little ragged shirt. Then, with his dim hazel eyes fixed upon the painting, while the tears coursed slowly down his pallid cheeks, he put forth his hands in a childish movement of supplication, and murmured again his tearful prayer, "Mamma! mamma!"

Presently rising, he turned his feeble footsteps toward the doorway, and as his eye caught the stone bowl of holy water standing on its coral pedestal near the portal, he bent down his feverish head and slaked his parched lips. Revived by this, he timidly looked out from the chapel, and shuddering as he beheld the gloomy wilderness around, he once more screamed in a thin piercing cry, "Mamma! oh, *ma chère* mamma!"

That was the last sad wail for help for many and many a long year that those infant lips were destined to utter; and when he again called upon that dear name, his manly arms would clasp a joyful mother to his swelling heart.

L

"Henri!" came back like an echo in a clear shout to the shriek of the boy. "Henri! Henri!" was reiterated again and again, each time in a voice that seemed to split asunder the canopy of clouds above.

The boy started and listened.

"Henri! Henri! this way to your good friend the doctor! Quick, my little boy!"

Now with the step of a fawn the child ran out upon the sharp sandy esplanade, and following the voice as he tripped lightly through the narrow pathway between the needle-pointed cactus, in a moment he stopped, with a look of horror, beside the trestle on which the bound and nearly naked man was stretched.

Ay, it was a sight to make a strong and stalwart man turn pale with sickness and horror, much less a baby boy of three or four years old. There lay the man, all through the dreadful night, with swarms on swarms and myriads upon myriads of stinging insects, biting and sipping, and sucking his life-blood with distracting agony away. Ah! think of the hellish torture often practiced by those bloody pirates upon their victims in the West Indies! The bound man's eyes were closed, the lips and cheeks puffed and swollen out of all human proportions, and the inflamed body was one glowing red and angry surface. No needle could have been stuck where the venomous stings of a thousand sand-flies or musquitoes had not already sucked blood. Ay, well might the child start back with horror!

"It is your friend the doctor, Henri," he said in French, still in a strong but kindly voice. "I can not see you, but get me a knife. No, my child, never mind—you can not find one; don't leave me."

Here the child timidly put his little hands out and brushed away the poisonous insects, and then touched the doctor's face.

"Ah! Henri, see if you can not slip that pretty silk rope over my head; yes, that is the way—*doucement*—easily, my child! Well, now, my Henri, you are weak and sick, my poor little boy; but listen to me—yes, I feel your little hands on my eyes. Well, bite upon that cord that goes across my throat. Bite till it snaps asunder! I am nearly choking, little one; but don't cry."

True, the strips of raw-hide, which had partially slackened in the rain that had washed the body of the victim, now began, to tauten again in the sultry heat of the morning, and lay half hidden in the swollen throat, stomach, and limbs of the tortured sufferer.

Henri's sharp little teeth fastened upon the strand, biting and gnawing, until finally it was severed, and the doctor gave a great sigh of relief.

"Blessings on you, my poor boy!" he murmured, painfully. "Now bite away on the strands which bind the arm. There! Don't! don't hurry! Rest a little, my child! Ah! it is well!"

"AH! HENRI, SEE IF YOU CAN NOT SLIP THAT PRETTY SILK ROPE OVER MY HEAD."

Again those sharp little teeth of a mouse had gnawed through the net which bound the lion-hearted man; the ends of the raw-hide drew back and twisted into spiral curls, and the right arm, though numbed and four times its original size, was free.

"Thanks be to God for all IIis mercies!" exclaimed the doctor, as with difficulty he raised his released arm to his face and pushed back the swollen lids from his closed eyes—"and to you, my little friend, for saving this wretched life!"

Waiting a few moments to recover his strength, the doctor made a mighty effort, and some of the coils whose strands had been cut by those little teeth yielded and gradually unrove, so as to leave the upper part of his body free. Then, while the child was once more cutting the lashings of his feet, he himself unfastened the knots of his left arm, and by a vigorous effort he tore the net from off him and sat upright. Clasping his numbed and swollen hands together, he turned his face and almost sightless eyes to heaven.

"May this awful trial serve as a partial forgiveness of my sins, and make me a better man!"

He paused, and laid his heavy arms around the child, while warm and grateful tears trickled down his cheeks. Slowly, and like a drunken man, his feet sought the sand, and then, weak, trembling, and faint, he staggered along the path, the boy tripping lightly before him, till he fell exhausted on the floor of the chapel.

"Water, my Henri! water!"

The child scooped it out from the stone bowl with his tiny hands and sprinkled it on his friend's face.

"There, that will suffice, my brave boy! Lay your cheek to mine!"

What a sight it was—that dark, swollen, yet powerful frame lying on the coral pavement, and the innocent child, like a dewdrop on the leaf of a red tropical flower, nestling close beside it!

CHAPTER XXVI.

THE HURRICANE.

"'Twas off the Wash—the sun went down—the sea looked black and grim,
For stormy clouds with murky fleece were mustering at the brim;
Titanic shades! enormous gloom! as if the solid night
Of Erebus rose suddenly to seize upon the light!
It was a time for mariners to bear a wary eye,
With such a dark conspiracy between the sea and sky!"

Past a September noon. The great canopy of dark, murky clouds fell lower and lower, until they nearly touched the earth, wrapping as in a blanket the single cocoa-nut-tree on the crag, and shutting out the light and air of heaven as they settled over the noxious lagoon, the mangrove thickets, and pure inlet. The sea-birds came screaming in from seaward, fluttering their wide-spread wings in the sultry atmosphere, and alighting on the smooth rocks, where they furled their pinions and put their heads together. The flying-fish no longer skimmed over the waves, and the dolphin and shark sank deep down in the blue water, or lay still and quiet beside the coral groves. The rolling, swelling ocean of the tropic, with its glassy, greasy surface unruffled by the faintest air, rolled heavily on until it struck the coral ledge, when, with a dull, heavy roar, it broke over in creamy foam, and came sluggishly in to the sandy beach. There the tiny waves lashed the shelly strand, and all was still again. No sun; no breeze; and even the birds, and serpents, and insects gasped for breath. The fish below the sea, the animated nature above, and the very leaves and vines of the forests and thickets knew what was brewing in the great vacuum around.

Slowly and painfully the man in the chapel regained his feet, and with the child by the hand, moved on to the farthest corner by the rude altar, where he sank down again, and, clasping the boy to his heart, waited in breathless awe. As if the powder and flames had not done their destructive work, the wrath of heaven was to be poured out over the devoted den of the pirates.

Then came a bellowing roar as a current of wind swept over the sea, cutting a pathway in the blue water, and scooping it up in an impalpable mist, hurrying on to the low beach of the island, and tearing the sand and shells up in heaps—and then a lull. Now, as if all the demons of winds had let loose their cavernous lungs from the

four quarters of the earth, and like the shocks of artillery, volley
upon volley, came the hurricane. The sea became one boiling, seething, hissing surface of foam, pressed and flattened by the weight of
the tempest, which laid the black rocks bare on the ledge, and drove
the water into both mouths of the inlet, until, with a crashing shock,
it met in the basin, and broke over and over the cove, and high up
the wall of rocks on the other side. Two or three streams of whirlwind meeting, too, over the island, drove the lagoon hither and
thither, catching up the white pond-lilies by their long stems, twisting off the dense thickets of mangroves by the roots, burrowing holes
in the sandy beds of the cactus, and shearing off their flat, thorny
leaves and needle points by the acre together; then a rushing whirl
around the cocoa-nuts, bowing their tufted tops at first till they nearly touched the earth, when, the stout trunks snapping like glass, they
would go pitching and tossing from base to crown, careering and
dancing aloft, borne away with sand and mangrove, cactus, flowers,
and sticks, into the flying.clouds before the hurricane. Then another
lull; and from the opposite direction again thundered the terrible
breath of the demons, sweeping thousands of sea-birds, with broken
pinions, screaming amid the gale, hurling them against the crag, strip-
ping the feathers from their crushed carcasses, and in a moment bu-
rying them a foot deep in clouds of sand. No more pauses or lulls
now in the hirtling tempest; but with a steady, tremendous roar,
which made the earth tremble, the rocks quake, and laid every vestige of vegetation flat to the ground, it came on mightier and mightier, and fiercer and fiercer,.with black masses of never-ending clouds
sweeping close down like dark midnight, as if heaven and earth had
come together. All through the gloomy day and through the night
this elemental war, with its legions of careering demons, continued
to lash the sea and smite the land; until, as if satiated with vengeance, the clouds belched forth in red lightning, vomiting out peal
upon peal of awful thunder as a parting salute, and then, moderating
down to a hard gale from another quarter, broke away. The blue
sky appeared, and the glorious sun once more came up in his majesty
over the distant hills of Cuba.

CHAPTER XXVII.

THE VIRGIN MARY.

"A weary weed, tossed to and fro,
  Drearily drenched in the ocean brine,
Soaring high and sinking low,
  Lashed along without will of mine;
Sport of the spoom of the surging sea;
  Flung on the foam, afar and near,
Mark my manifold mystery—
  Growth and grace in their place appear."

WITH the boy clasped to his heart, the doctor sat beside the altar of the chapel during all the direful strife without, shielding his little charge from the clouds of fine sand and rubbish that every few minutes came swirling within the temple, dashing the padre's candlesticks into battered lumps of brass on the pavement, and tearing to atoms the votive offerings hung around the walls by the pirates. But, as if in mercy to the trustful souls lying there, the Virgin Mary still looked down in sweet pity upon them, and the little chapel stood unharmed.

When at last, however, the hurricane's back was broken, and Æolus had reined up his maddened chargers and curbed their flying wings, and when all the demons of the wind had gone moaningly back to their caverns in the clouds, the doctor arose, and with the boy beside him, knelt devoutly before the altar while he uttered a fervent prayer of thanksgiving.

"Come, my Henri, now we may go out and see if we can find something to eat and drink. You are weak and hungry, my poor little boy; but you shall not suffer much longer."

That strong man, with the heart of a gentle woman, had no thought of how ill, and famished, and thirsty he himself was from the terrible torture he had endured. No, he only thought of the child who had saved him.

In front of the chapel the sand and bushes were piled up in ridgy heaps, the coral wall around the cemetery had been thrown down, while the flat head-stones over the pirates' graves had disappeared entirely. Not so, however, with the white slabs near by where those poor doomed women were lying; for the hurricane had spared their tombs, and a pall of pure white sand was sprinkled evenly over their remains. Bending over them was the trunk of the cocoa-nut, with its top stripped and its leafless branches quivering in the wind; while from below them streamed out the long, thin green silk rope which had so often served Captain Brand, the pirate, for his private executions. Near at hand lay the trestle on which the doctor had been stretched—caught by the base of the cocoa-nut column, and half buried in sand—while the cruel strips of raw-hide which had lashed the victim down were tied and twisted into a maze of complicated knots by the nimble fingers of the winds.

The doctor started, and his half-closed eyes shot out gleams of anger as he beheld the unconscious implements designed for his torturing murder; and leaving the child at the doorway to the chapel, he sallied out, detached the rope, loosened the trestle from its sandy bed, and placed them in a corner of the chapel.

Then carefully picking his way, with the boy in his great arms, over the trees and débris which obstructed the pathway, he speedily reached the site on which had stood the sheds of the "Centipede's" crew. Fire, water, and wind had done their work effectually, though the fire had partially spared the detached store-house and shed which he had shared with the infamous padre. All else was a ruin of loose blocks of stone, broken tiles, nearly buried in banks of sand. From a well in the once busy court-yard, and which had also escaped the devouring elements, the doctor drew a bucket or two of water, in which he slaked the boy's thirst and then his own, and afterward poured water over their bodies. Then, from a still smouldering beam which puffed out at intervals a thin curl of smoke from beneath one of the sheds, he lit a fire in the court-yard, while from the wreck of the storeroom he succeeded in rescuing some hard biscuit and a ham. This last he tore in shreds, and placing them on sticks before the fire, they were thus enabled to make a hearty meal, first providing for the wants of the child, however—soaking the biscuit for him, as if it were his first duty on earth. Again raising the boy in his arms, he passed from the ruined sheds and bent his steps toward Captain Brand's former dwelling. The road was heaped with shells and sand, strewed with shoals of dead fish and wounded or dying birds, while the wreck of a boat, mingled with the timbers and planks of the jetty to the basin, were lying pell-mell on the beach of the little cove. Casting his eyes around in search of the once spacious dwelling, with its vaults, veranda, and saloon, he could hardly at first trace a vestige of the structure. The powder, more destructive even than the hurricane, had tossed walls and building into a confused heap of rubbish; then came the wind and sand on top of the rocks which had tumbled down by the concussion of the first explosion, and then the water, packing all together as if no habitation had ever existed there. The doctor walked slowly around until he came to the angle where the kitchen once was, and there, three fourths hidden beneath a mass of blackened stones and charred timber, peered forth the white skeleton of a human being. The flesh had been seared and burned from the face and skull by the instantaneous flash of the powder, and there lay the remains of Babette, whitely bleached, as if she had been thrown a lifeless corpse on the sea-beach. A few yards below this frightful spectacle lay a number of shattered boxes and trunks, then a confused bundle of clothes, and a sandy saturated collection of kitchen utensils and crockery. Yes, the poor dumb woman, the creature and witness of many a cruel scene, ignorant or uncertain of the warning given her by the master she loved, had fallen another tribute to his long list of victims.

The doctor only waited long enough to select a few necessary articles from the heterogeneous heap before him, and then, with the child still clinging contentedly to his shoulder, he returned to the chapel.

BUILDING THE BOAT.

CHAPTER XXVIII.

THE ARK THAT JACK BUILT.

"Good heaven, befriend that little boat,
    And guide her on her way!
A boat, they say, has canvas wings,
    But can not fly away;
Though, like a merry singing-bird,
    She sits upon the spray."

The land wind sighed and murmured; the sea-breeze wafted its rustling influence over the waves; the long swells broke over the ledge; the inlet flowed pure and limpid; and the gulls and sea-mews floated gracefully over the reef, as if a hurricane had never poured its baneful wrath upon it or the lonely island.

Day by day and week by week, the man and boy, getting each hour stronger and better, worked and worked. He with his great arms hewing and sawing, and the child attending upon him like a shadow. By great toil and exertion the doctor had succeeded in placing some of the timbers of the jetty together as launching-ways, and on the cradle he had laid the wreck of the old boat. Then, with an old saw and some tools he found near the site of the mat sheds by the cove, he began to build the frail ark which was to carry him and the child from the hated island. From the storehouse, too, he obtained plenty of provisions to supply their wants, and old sails and rope he found in abundance. Babette's collection of worldly wealth provided them with linen and clothing, together with utensils for eating and drinking; and he had made their dwelling in the little chapel clean and habitable. Here they slept by night on an old sail, and soundly too, the sleep of repentance and innocence. With the early morning the man and the boy arose, and took their way to the cove. The little fellow was clean and tidy now, dressed in a little loose calico frock, and a queer contrivance of an old bonnet fashioned out of Babette's gear, and on his feet were a pair of little canvas slippers, stitched for him by his protector. After a bath in the basin of the inlet the fire was kindled, and the simple breakfast prepared. Then, while the strong man hewed, and sawed, and hammered beneath a temporary awning which covered the open workshop, the boy would pick up shells along the cove, or with a little rod and line, seated on a flat rock near by, jerk out fish from the basin to serve for dinner. Sometimes he would wander about in search of nails and spikes for the boat, or gather sticks for the fire, but never out of hail, and never beyond the watchful eyes of his friend. Yes, those watchful, kind eyes followed his slightest movements; and while the hammer was going in vigorous blows on the planks, or the axe chipping away a timber, his pleasant voice sang Creole songs to the child, or encouraged his innocent prattle. A loaded musket, which, with some ammunition, he had dug out from the wreck of his old quarters, stood leaning against an upright post under the shade, and woe to the man or beast that might have dared to approach the boy! In the burning heat of the tropical day the labor ceased, and the child either lay on his back on the soft sand beneath the awning, kicking up his little legs, watching the small gulls as they skimmed across the basin, or, with his brown curly head resting on the doctor's knees, slept sweetly. Happy and contented he was, too, with the return of health and strength; and if his budding memory looked back to her he had lost, and the recollection of his faithful Banou, it was only for a moment, and, like a childish dream, it passed away.

Every evening at sunset, when the work was done for the day, the doctor, with Henri in his arms and the musket on his shoulder, would climb the crag, and peer all around the island; but never a sail did he see from the hour the "Centipede" spread her canvas, while he lay helplessly bound on the trestle with the green noose around his neck. As the twilight faded, the sole human occupants of the island returned to the chapel, and when they had said a simple prayer, kneeling before the Virgin, they laid themselves down on their canvas bed to rest till the dawn. Many a silent hour in the watches of the tedious night did the doctor lie awake, while the cool sweet breath of the child fanned his cheek as he lay nestling beside him, pondering and wondering on the fate of his charge. He knew absolutely nothing about his history save that he had been pitched overboard from the brig the pirates were robbing; but what was the name or nation of the vessel, where from, or whither bound, he was in utter ignorance. He had questioned the leader Gibbs on that occasion after the chase by the corvette, when he had lopped off the brute's leg; but, what with suffering and drink, the ruffian had either forgotten the brig's name, or feigned to, and all he could impart was the belief that she was an English trader. Even from the boy, too, the doctor could elicit nothing of importance, though day by day he tried every means of leading the child's mind back to the past, but always with the same result.

"*Oui, ma chère mama! Bon Banou!*" and "*Ma petite cousine, Rosalie!*" These were the only words the little fellow had to link his fate with the future, and even they became fainter and fainter on his mind and tongue as the time passed on. With this delicate web around the destiny of the child, and that he spoke French, and had evidently been tenderly nurtured, the doctor was forced to be content.

Well, so the days and nights went by, and so the work went on, and the little ark began to assume a wholesome look, and to be capable of plowing the distant main. Then, when she was planked up, with a gunwale on, and half-decked over forward, she was calked, and the seams payed with pitch. When all ready for launching, early one morning the doctor and the boy went gayly down to the cove. There, as the first golden rays of the rising sun shot athwart the inlet, Henri stood up in the bows, and with a large pearl-shell of pure spring water, he waved his tattered bonnet round his curly locks, and with childish delight, as the vessel began to move, he emptied the shell of its sparkling treasure, shouting, as she slid off the ways into the basin, "*Ma petite cousine Rosalie!*" The builder, too, took off his hat and shouted, in his deep bass, till the rocks gave back the echo of "*Rosalie! Rosalie!*"

Thus was the ark launched and christened by her captain and crew, and there she rode on the basin, a little pinnace of about ten tons, which had been once used to carry anchors, chains, and stores about the harbor. A week or two more, and she was fitted with a single mast, stepped well in the bows, for a jib and one square lug-sail. Then ballast in bags of sand was laid along her keelson, and a couple of breakers of fresh water got on board, together with a quantity of cooked salt meat and hard biscuit stowed away under the half-deck forward—where, too, was a cozy little nest of spare canvas, with an oakùm pillow, for the boy! Yes, there lay the good ship "Rosalie," outward bound, with sails bent and gear rove, cargo on board, and waiting for a wind.

Meanwhile the doctor had tried her under sail, and satisfied himself that every thing worked well, and that she was in proper trim. Then he moored her within a fathom from the shore, and waited for a moon to light him on his voyage. Whither?

Carefully, too—like one who had passed a lifetime on the ocean, from the China Seas to the broad Atlantic, under the suns of the tropics as well as in the dim gloom of high latitudes—the doctor studied the clouds and watched their course, noting the flight of the birds in the air and the track of fish in the sea. At last the trade breezes began to blow regularly and steadily; the land winds, too, in the gray of the morning, fluttered timidly away out to sea, and the round pearly moon shone bright and mellow over rock and water.

"To-morrow, my brave boy, we shall sail away from the island. Ah! you clap your hands, eh? Yes, we shall go to find mamma!" This was said as man and child stood for the last time on the lofty crag, while the former ranged his dark eyes scrutinizingly around the horizon. Nothing in sight!

Once more to their chapel of refuge, where, for the first time in all their association, putting the child to sleep by himself, the doctor sat down on the trestle by the entrance, and, lighted by the brilliant moon, he caught up the tangled mazes of the hide net which had bound him, and sedulously applied himself to a task before him.

Any one who has seen the effect produced by a violent gale upon the tattered shreds of a shivered main-top-sail, bound up into the most tortuous knots that it is possible to conceive of, and so hard and solid that you might saw the canvas balls in slices like boards, may form some idea of the task the doctor had imposed upon himself to loosen the hide strands tied together by the furious fingers of the hurricane. Patiently and quietly, with no sign of temper, he applied himself to the work, and with nothing but a sharp-pointed spike to aid his hands, he began to unravel, bit by bit, the laced knots and bunches of raw-hide, without ever cutting a strand, until, as the moon sank glimmering down, the tangled mass lay in clear coils beside him — though in several pieces, where it had been severed by the teeth of that little mouse purring behind the altar—and the task was done. Then raising the trestle, he bore it within the altar, and with the now unraveled coil of hide, and the softer silk rope for a pillow, he again stretched himself upon what once had been his bed of torture.

For what possible object all this labor had been undertaken, or for what future purpose—vague they must have been—no one but the persevering man who did it can tell; and there he lay, no sound coming from his compressed lips till the day dawned. Then he arose, and, kneeling over the sleeping child, he again solemnly repeated the oath he had before taken in his hut—

"Sleeping or waking, on land or sea, I devote the remainder of my wretched life to returning this lost child to his mother. So help me God!"

The little boy stirred, as if the angels and the sweet Virgin were whispering their protecting power over him, and, with a smile dawning upon his rosy, dimpled checks, he raised the lids from his bright hazel eyes, and put his fat round arms around the doctor's neck. If two great drops fell upon that upturned innocent little face from the dark full eyes bending over him, they were not tears of sorrow! Oh, no! It was the dew of hope and trustfulness falling from the soul of a repentant sinner relying upon an all-wise Providence.

"Come, my Henri, say your little prayer of the morning, and we will go." The man had taught the child that little prayer which he himself had learned at his mother's knee.

Up again to the crag, and down to the shelly margin of the shore; and a long look the man gave at the ruin of shed and den, as he gently placed the child on a sand-bag in the stern-sheets of the ark.

Then he cast off the rope which held the vessel to the hated strand, hoisted the sail, and, as she bubbled along the inlet with the first sigh of the land wind, he stood at the helm with his bare head lighted up by the beams of the rising sun, and his lips moved in prayer.

On, noiselessly through the Tiger's Trap sailed the little pinnace till she bowed her rugged cutwater in the yielding waves, and with her square lug-sail swelling gently to the freshening breeze, she held her course to sea. I question much if the stanch brigantine, named the "Centipede," which had preceded her through this tiger's gorge, with all the ruffianly crew that manned her, and their villainous captain on her quarter-deck, stood half the chance of a prosperous voyage as the tiny ark, called the "Rosalie," which followed, with her noble, brave commander, and his weak and boyish mate. Who can tell?

M

END OF PART I.

PART II.

CHAPTER XXIX.

LAYING UP THE STRANDS.

"Ever drifting, drifting, drifting
On the shifting
Currents of the restless main,
Till in sheltered coves and reaches
Of sandy beaches,
All have found repose again."

IT was in the year of our Lord eighteen hundred and twenty-two, and in the broad and commodious harbor of Kingston, a great mercantile haven, crowded with shipping from all parts of the commercial globe; land-locked by reef and ridge, with the rocks and heights crowned by frowning batteries of heavy cannon; while beyond were spread the lower and upper town, in masses of low two-story buildings, with piazzas, bright green jalousies, stately palm, tamarind, and cocoa-nut-trees waving above them. At the mouth of the harbor strait, where stands Fort Augusta, lay a magnificent double-banked American frigate, with a broad blue swallow-tailed pennant at her main, standing out stiff, like a dog-vane, from the lofty mast, as the ship rode to the strong sea-breeze.

The stays and rigging came down from trucks, cross-trees, and tops in straight black lines, from the great length of lower masts and enormously square yards fore and aft; and from side to side, till they met the long majestic hull and taper head-booms; while below were two rows of ports, with the guns run out and the brass tompions gleaming in their muzzles. The awnings were spread in one flat extended sheet of white cotton canvas from bowsprit to taffrail, and from the wide-spread lower booms at the fore-chains boats were riding by their painters. Within a cable's length of the frigate's black quarter lay a low rakish schooner, like a minnow alongside a whale, with a thin little coach-whip streaming from her main-mast head, a long brass gun amidships, and looking as trig and tidy as a French maid beside her portly mistress.

The bell struck in twin notes *eight* on board the frigate, echoed back from the pigmy schooner in a faint, double succession of tinkles; the whistles resounded from deck to deck in ear-splitting notes, surging and chirruping all together, and then suddenly ceasing with a rattling beat of a drum and a short bellow of "Grog, ho!"

Between the guns of the main deck, and about the spar-deck battery forward of the main-mast, sat five hundred lusty sailors on the white decks around their mess-cloths, bolting hot pea soup after their grog, and chatting and laughing in a devil-may-care sort of a strain, as if the grub was good and the timbers sound, as they were, of the stanch frigate beneath them. No noise, no confusion, but just as polite and courteous, in their honest, seamanlike way, as half a legion of French dancing-masters, they whacked off the salt pork before them with their sheath-knives, munching the flinty biscuit, and all as happy and careless of the past and future as clams at high water. Ay, there they clustered, those five hundred sailors, in their snowy duck trowsers and white, coarse linen frocks, with the blue collars laid square back over their broad shoulders, exposing their bronzed and hairy throats, wagging their jaws, and ready at any moment, at the tap of the drum, day or night, to spring to the guns, and make the battery dance a jig as the solid iron food went amid sheets of flame toward a foe. Yes, and ready, too, in the gentle breeze or the howling tempest, to leap at the shrill pipe of the whistle from the busy deck or their snug hammocks, and, like so many monkeys, jump up the shrouds, lie out on the enormous yards while the frigate was plunging bows under in the tumultuous seas, grasp the writhing canvas in their sinewy paws, and wrap it up close and tight in the hempen gaskets. Man-of-war sailors, for battle, or gale, or spree, every one of them.

On board that little consort near were about forty more of the same sort, only older, more bronzed, and more deliberate and methodical in manner, sipping their pea pottage after blowing away the steam, cutting their pork after much reflection, and cracking their biscuit tranquilly. Their conversation, too, was slow and dignified, each word well considered before it came out, and never interrupting one another in a yarn, as did the younger harum-scarum chaps in the big ship near. But yet those weather-beaten old sons of Neptune, who had each one of them seen sights that would make your hair stand on end to think of, could handle that schooner when her low deck was buried waist-deep to the combings of the main hatch in angry water, and make that Long Tom amidships there spin round on its pivot, and never threw away idly one of its solid globular messengers. Ay, trust them for that.

Then honor to them all, those gallant tars who have fought the battles of our country by sea and lake, and upheld those Stars and

THE UNITED STATES FRIGATE "MONONGAHELA."

Stripes until they are respected to the uttermost ends of the earth! ·
Glory to them, ye wise legislators, who sit in council upon the nation's
wealth and grandeur! Think of the fearless arms that have shielded
your otherwise unprotected shores when circled in a ring of dreadful
fire from the guns of a haughty foe.

And you, too, ye rich traders! whose valuable cargoes roll hither
and thither over the trackless deep, cared for by those toiling tars
who fight and bleed for the flag that waves o'er your treasure—in
stinging gale, with frozen fingers, or under burning suns, with panting breasts—think of them when your noble ships come gallantly into
your superb ports, and unlade their floating mines of wealth into
your spacious warehouses, while you in your lordly mansions sip your
wine! Think of those arms grasping the shivering sail in the mighty
tempest, in the black night, and the coarse fare they eat, the sometimes putrid water they drink, and the hard beds they lie upon, while
you are reposing on downy pillows with your wives and little ones
beside you! Ah! take pity on the sailor, and scatter your shining
gold over him in his distress.

When the time comes, as come it may, when the cannon of a hos-
tile fleet are thundering at your ports; when your lumbering craft
are flying before the rapacious grasp of quick-heeled cruisers, and
fiery bombs are hissing through the pure air, bursting in your marble
palaces and blasting your stores of wealth to dust, *then* you will turn
with blanched faces to the sea, and wonder why you have so long
forgotten the noble hearts and stalwart arms that once were thrown
around you. But not before.

On the flush quarter-deck of the frigate, by the raised signal lockers' abaft, stood a bronzed old quarter-master, a spy-glass resting on
his arm, through which every minute he peered around the harbor,
giving an eye, too, occasionally to the half-hour glass, whose sands
dribbled steadily into the lower bulb on the locker beside him.

What cared he—no wife or child to cheer him! No cares save
but to see that the ensign did not roll foul of the halyards, that the
broad pennant blew out straight, that the half-hour glass did not
need turning, and that no boat approached the frigate without his
reporting it to the officer of the watch. Naught else save, perhaps,
whether the other old quarter-master, Charley Holmes, down below
there on the gun-deck, had wiped from his lips the moisture of the
midday grog, and would be up in time to take the relief while the
pea soup was warm. Nothing else.

The lieutenant of the watch briskly paced the solid deck, scrubbed
white as milk with lime-juice and molasses, the even seams between
the planks glistening like the strands of a girl's raven tresses as
his profane and rapid feet pressed upon them. What thought he in
his careless walk, with the gleaming bunch of bullion on his right

,shoulder, sword by his side, white trowsers, and gilt eagle buttons on his navy-blue coat?

He was thinking how his pittance of pay would support, in a scrimpy way, his poor mother and sister, who looked unto him as their only hope and refuge. And he thought, too, as he tramped that noble deck, made glorious by many a battle and victory in which he had borne a humble part, that his rich and powerful country would eventually reward him with increased pay and promotion. Were the single dollar which lay alone in his trowsers pocket, and the light mist which arose off there beyond the Apostles' Battery, opposite Port Royal Harbor, an evidence of one or a sign of the last aspiration? We hope not; but we shall see.*

Three or four midshipmen, too, pranced over that frigate's white quarter-deck, on the port side, in their blue jackets and duck trowsers. Little gay madcaps they were, scarcely well into their teens, with little glittering toasting-forks of dirks dangling at their sides, and ready for any lark or mischief.

And what thought those boyish imps of reefers? Did they trace the flight of that tropic man-of-war bird, sailing high up in the heavens, heading seaward, away into the distant future, through clouds and sunshine, rain and storm? And did they think, as they fluttered along the deck, that their own career might lead them in that direction, toward the star of promotion which shone so brightly near at hand, and was never reached; or else, by a chance shot, to come tumbling down with a crippled pinion, and hobble out their lives on shore? No. Those gay young blades, whose mothers were dreaming and sighing for them, had no reflections of that kind. They were chattering about the little frolic they had on their last liberty day, when the captain ordered them off to the frigate at sunset, and planning another for the week to come. Happy little scamps, let them dance their careless thoughts away!

"Two bells, sir," said the quarter-master to the officer of the watch.

"Very good! Young gentlemen, tell the boatswain to turn the hands to, and have the barge manned. Let the first lieutenant and the marine officer know that the commodore is going to leave the ship. There, no larking on the quarter-deck, Mr. Mouse!"

This last command was addressed to a tiny youngster who was hardly big enough to go without pantalettes, much less to wear a jacket and order half a hundred huge sailors about, any one of whom was old enough to be his great-grandfather. But yet that small lad did it, and could steer a boat, too, or fly about like a ribbon in a high wind up there in the mizzen-top, while the men on the yard were taking the last reef in the top-sail.

* This was written before the "Pay Bill" was passed.

"Go down to tho cabin, sir, and let the commodore and his friend know tho boat is ready."

Down tho ladder skipped Mr. Mouse, and while ho was gone, the guard, in their white summer uniform and cross-belts, stood at ease, resting on their muskets on tho quarter-deck, eight side-boys and the boatswain at tho starboard gangway, with tho first lieutenant and tho officer of tho watch standing near.

Presently there came up from tho after-cabin hatchway a fine, handsome man, in tho very prime of life, in cocked hat, full-dress coat, a pair of gleaming epaulettes, sword by his hip, and his nether limbs cased in white knee-breeches, silk stockings, and pumps. The one who followed him was apparently a much older man, with grizzled locks, a dark, stern face, and without epaulets. The first raised his hat as he stepped on tho quarter-deck—not a thread of silver was seen in his dark hair—and then both bowed to tho officers, who saluted them as they moved toward tho gangway. The boatswain piped, tho marines presented arms, tho drum gave three quick rolls, and the commodore went over, tho gangway, preceded by his companion.

CHAPTER XXX.

OLD FRIENDS.

"What though when storms our bark assail,
   The needle trembling veers,
When night adds horror to the gale,
   And not a star appears?
True to the pole as I to thee,
   It faithful still will prove—
An emblem dear of constancy,
   And of a sailor's love."

THE barge left the side of the frigate, a broad blue pennant with white stars on a staff at her bow, with fourteen handsome sailors to man her, all in clean white frocks and trowsers, with straw hats and flowing black ribbons around them, on which was stamped in gold letters, "Monongahela."

The double bank of white ash oars flashed in the rippling waves of the harbor as the barge was urged over the water, the current seething and buzzing under her bows, and bubbling into her wake as she flew on toward the town. In a mahogany box at the stern sat a bushy-whiskered coxswain, whose body swayed to the stroke of the oars, while his hand grasped the brass tiller as he steered amid the shipping. The commodore had settled himself down under the boat's awning on the snow-white covered cushions in the stern-sheets, and, with one foot resting on the elegant ash grating beneath, he began to talk to the grave gentleman who sat opposite to him.

"It is many a long year since I last visited this superb harbor, but I remember it as if it were yesterday. You never were here before, I think? No? Well, if any of the old set I once knew, when I was first lieutenant of the old 'Scourge,' are yet alive, we shall have a pleasant time!"

"One fine fellow," went on the commodore, "I know is. His name is Piron. I had a note from him as soon as the frigate anchored yesterday, and I shall ask him to dine sociably with me on board this evening. I hope you will join us."

The grave gentleman said that he had business which would detain him on shore all night.

The barge swept up to the mole, the oars were thrown up at a wave of the coxswain's hand, and came into the boat on either side like shutting up a pair of fans, while the boat-hooks checked her way, and she remained stationary at the steps of the landing. The awning was canted, the commodore and his friend got out and mounted the stairway, while the boat's crew stood up with their hats off. On the mole were four or five people in light West India rig of brown and white, and broad Guayaquil sombreros.

"Cleveland!" exclaimed a tall, handsome man, as he seized the commodore by both hands, "how glad we are to see you! Here is Tom Stewart, and Paddy Burns, and little Don Stingo, attorneys, factors, and sugar-boilers, all of us delighted to welcome you back once more to Jamaica!"

Crowding about the commodore, shaking hands and slapping one another on the back, standing off a step or two to see the effect of time on each other's appearance, laughing heartily with many a happy allusion to days gone by, those old friends and former companions, unmindful of the hot sun, stood there with their faces lighted up and talking all together.

"And you are a commodore, eh! Cleveland, with a broad pennant and a squadron? Ah! we have kept the run of you, though. Read all about that action you were in with the 'President,' and that bloody battle in the 'Essex' and 'Phebe' at Valparaiso, with Porter. And here you are again, safe and sound, and hearty!"

"And you too, Piron! The same as ever! Not tired of cane-. planting yet? But how is madame?"

"Lovely a girl as ever, Cleveland, but never entirely got over that sad loss of the little boy, you know. However, she will be overjoyed to see you. She's been talking of you ever since we saw your appointment to the station fifteen months ago. Apropos, we have her widowed sister with us, whose husband was killed at Waterloo, and our little niece who came from France—all out there at the old place of Escondido, where you must come and pass a week with us. Nay, man, no excuse! The thing is arranged, and it would be the death of Stingo, Tom Stewart, and Paddy Burns if you disappoint us."

"Well, Piron, I am your man, but not for a day or two, until I have made some official calls here on the authorities. Meanwhile, gentlemen, you all dine with me this evening on board the frigate, every mother's soul of you! Coxswain, go on board and tell my steward to have dinner for six. Stop at the schooner as you go off, and say to Mr. Darcantel that I shall expect him to join us. Now, my friends, that matter is arranged, and we will all go off in the barge at sunset."

"Dry talking, isn't it, Stingo?" said Piron; "so, commodore, come, and we'll have a sip of sangaree and a deviled biscuit to keep our mouths in order. But, halloo! where is your friend, Cleveland? that tall man in black? Parson or chaplain, eh?"

"No," replied the officer; "an old friend of mine, my brother-in-law, who takes a cruise with me occasionally; but he never goes in society, and has taken himself off, as he always does when we get in port. He is a glorious fellow, though, and I hope to present him to you yet. Never mind him now."

Arm in arm went the blue coat and bullion, locked in white grass sleeves, along the busy quays, crowded with mule-carts and drays for stores or shipping. Spanish dons, dapper Frenchmen, burly John Bulls, standing at warehouse and posadas, all with cigars in their teeth, which they puffed so lazily that the smoke scarcely found its way beyond the brims of their wide sombreros. Negroes, too, with scanty leg gear, and still scantier gingham shirts, having bales, or boxes, or baskets of fruit on their heads, never any thing in their hands, chattering and laughing one with another as they danced and jostled along the busy mart; then through the hot, sandy ruts of streets, pausing now and then to shake hands with some old acquaintance beneath the overhanging piazzas; sedan-chairs moving about, with a negro in a glazed hat and red cockade at either end of the poles, in a long easy trot, as they bore their burdens of Spanish matron, or English damsel, or maybe a portly old judge, or gouty admiral, on a shopping or business excursion to the port; so on to the upper town, where the dwellings stand in detachments by themselves —single or in pairs—with spacious balconies and bright green Venetian blinds, all surrounded by gardens and vines; with noble tamarind-trees, and cocoa-nuts swaying their lofty trunks, and rattling their branches and leaves over the negro huts and offices below. Here the party stopped, and, entering a house, were ushered into a cool, lofty room, where there were a lot of mahogany desks, and a single old clerk, who resembled a last year's dried lemon, with some few drops of acid juice for blood, perched up on a hard stem of a high stool, with four or five quill pens, like so many thorns, sticking out above his yellow leafy ears.

"All by myself here, Cleveland, as I told you. All my people are living out there at Escondido. ·Very little business doing just now, and Paddy Burns and Tom Stewart haven't had a suit or a fight for the last six months. Inkstands dry, and my old clerk, Clinker, there, has forgotten how to write English.

"However," went on Piron, as the party threw themselves back on the wicker arm-chairs, and enjoyed the breeze which fluttered merrily through the blinds, "the cellar isn't quite dry yet; and I say, Clinker, suppose you tell Nimble Jack, or Ring Finger Bill, to spread a little luncheon here, with a bottle or two of Bordeaux, or something of that sort!" The dried, fruity old gentleman dropped off his branch at the desk like a withered nut, and then, with a husky kind of shuffle, betook himself off.

"QUEER OLD STICK, THAT," SAID THE COMMODORE.

"Queer old stick, that!" said tho commodore, as he unbuckled his sword and laid it on tho table.

"Ah! ho grew here, and will blow away ono of theso days. My father used to tell mo that he looked just tho samo when ho first sprouted as ho docs now. But ho is a dear faithful old stump; and you must remember hearing, Cleveland, of that frightful earthquako hero in seventeen hundred and eighty-three, which killed so many pcoplo? Yes? Well, it was old Clinker who saved my sweet wife that is now—and her sister; though ho was nearly squeezed—drier, if any thing, than ho is now—in doing it. Ho lay, you know, Stingo, supporting tho whole second story of tho house for seven hours, pressed as flat as a tamarind-leaf, while they were getting thoso twin babies out of their cradle. Yes, God bless him!" Starting up, while a flush of feeling darkened his face—"but, what is more, ho threw himself precisely where ho did, as ho saw tho walls giving way, so that not a hair of those children should bo injured when tho beams camo down. My father has told mo since, that when they got a lever under tho timber and wedged old Clinker out, ho gavo a kind of cackle; but, in my opinion, ho has not drawn a breath from that day to this. And, generally, ho is a very taciturn old root, and rarely opens his rind; but latterly ho talks a good deal about tho earthquako; says ho's sure there'll bo another awful ono beforo an interval of forty years has passed, and wants us to go away. No objection, however, to coming back when tho thing is over, and then waiting forty years for another. Don't laugh, you Paddy Burns, for if ever tho '*Tremblor*' gives you ono little shake, you'll jump higher than you did when that ugly Frenchman ran you through your waistcoat pocket, and you thought it was your midriff. Now, Tom Stewart and Don Stingo, what aro you grinning about? Your teeth will chatter so fast at tho next quake that you won't, cither of you, bo ablo to deliver a charge to the jury over a false invoice, or suck another drop of old Antigua rum."

"But really, Piron," broke in tho commodore upon this voluble harangue, "do you give heed to these barkings of that old clerk?"

"Why, yes, Cleveland," replied Piron, with rather a gravo manner, "I do; and, moreover, my sweet wifo Rosalio out yonder, who has never got over her grief for tho loss of our boy, regards every word old Clinker says as so much prophecy; and tho upshot of tho business is, I have made up my mind to leavo tho island."

"For where, my friend—back to France?"

"No. Since tho war and the peace, with Bonaparte at St. Helena, France is no placo for an Englishman, even with a French father, and I am going to try América."

"Truly, Piron, I am charmed to hear it. But what part of América?"

"Why, I've bought a fine sugar estate at a bargain in Louisiana, and there we shall pass the remainder of our days."

"He! he!" sniggled Tom Stewart, while Don Stingo and Paddy Burns cackled incredulously; but, at the same moment, Ring Finger Bill and Nimble Jack, two jet-black persons, in loose striped ging-ham shirts and bare feet, with an attempt at a grave expression of thick-lipped coffee-coolers, the whites of their eyes turned up with becoming decorum, and preceded by the old twig of a clerk, who seemed to crackle in the sea-breeze as he again hung himself, stern on, to his stool of a trunk, entered the cool counting-house, bearing trays, fruits, and bottles, which they methodically arranged on the large table.

"Massa! him want small, red, plump snapper, make mizzible brile?" said Nimble Jack. "S'pose Massa Ossifa him pick shell of land-crab, wid crisp pepper for salad?"

"No, no! Put those cool water monkeys on the table and be gone! Come, Clinker, take a bite with us!"

Leaving this pleasant party to sip their claret and water, and nibble their midday food, while they rambled back to the past or schemed into the future, we will return to the frigate.

CHAPTER XXXI.

"The handsomest fellow, Heaven bless him! ·
  Setting the girls all wild to possess him,
    With his dark mustache and his hazel eyes,
    And cigars in those pretty lips—"

"That girl who fain would choose a mate,
    Should ne'er in fondness fail her,
  May thank her lucky stars if Fate
    Should splice her to a sailor."

"The 'Rosalie's' gig coming alongside, sir," reported the quarter-master to the officer of the watch.

"Very well. A boatswain's mate and two side-boys. Mr. Rat, have the barge manned, and send her on shore for the commodore. Mr. Martin, tell the boatswain to call all hands to furl awnings."

While these orders were being executed, the whistles ringing through the ship, the sailors lining the white hammocks, stowed in a double line, fore and aft, around the nettings of the frigate, in readiness to cast off the stops and lacings and let fall the awnings, the officer on deck stood near the gangway. At the same time there tripped up the accommodation-ladder, lightly touching the snowy man-ropes, a young fellow of about one-and-twenty, dressed in undress frock-coat, one epaulet, smooth white trowsers, and shoes. Catching up his sword in his left hand as he reached the upper grating of the ladder, he took off his blue, gold-banded cap, and half bounded, with a springy step, on to the frigate's deck.

Observe him well, young ladies, as he stands there; for of all the scarlet or blue jackets on whose arm you have leaned and looked up at with your soft violet, blue, or dark eyes, you never saw a young fellow that you would sooner give those eyes, or those warm hearts too, throbbing under your bodices, or who would drive you wilder to possess him, than that gallant young sailor standing on the "Monongahela's" deck. Ay, observe him well, that tall, graceful youth, with a waist you might span with one of your short plump arms; those slim patrician feet, that might wear your own little satin slippers; then that swelling chest and those elegantly turned shoulders, which will take both of your arms, one of these days, to entwine and clasp around them! Ah! but the round throat and chin, the smiling

N

mouth, half hiding a double row of even teeth, with the merest moonshine of a mustache darkening the short upper lip, and then those large, fearless hazel eyes, sparkling with health and fun, shaded by a mass of chestnut curls, which cluster about his clear open forehead! Ay, there he stands, "a king and a kingdom" for the girl who wins him!

"Well, Harry, give us your fist, my boy! How do you get on aboard your prize? Not so roomy as the old frigate, eh? And a little more work than when you were playing flag-lieutenant, eh? Well, glad to see you, but can't stop to talk. So jump down below there in the wardroom; the mess are just through dinner, and yours won't be ready for an hour yet. Come, bear a hand, or I'll let these awnings fall on your new gold epaulet."

The new-comer tripped as lightly down the ladder to the gun-deck as Mr. Mouse, and making another dive down to the berth-deck, exchanging a rapid volley of pleasantry with the midshipmen in the steerage, he opened the wardroom door and entered. There, in a large open space, transversely dividing the stern of the ship, with rows of latticed-doored staterooms on either side, lighted by open skylights from above, with a barrel of a wind-sail coming down between the sashes, and every thing, from beams to bulkheads, painted a glistening white, and the deck so clean that you might have rubbed your handkerchief on it without leaving a stain on the cambric, around a large extension mahogany table stretching from side to side, the cloth removed, decanters and wine-glasses here and there, and water-monkeys in flannel jackets hanging like criminals from a gallows from the beams above, sat the wardroom mess of the frigate.

"By all that's handsome, here's Darcantel! Why, Harry, we are delighted to see you!" exclaimed half a dozen voices; "come, sit down here and take a glass of wine with us!"

As the handsome young fellow entered the wardroom, all faces lighted up as they saw him. The old sailing-master, who seldom indulged in more than a scowl since he lost his right ear by the stroke of a cutlass in capturing the tender to the "Plantagenet" seventy-four off the Hills of Navesink; the rigid old major of marines, who pipe-clayed his very knuckles, and wore a stiff sheet-iron padding to his stock to encourage discipline in the guard; the dear, kind old surgeon, who swallowed calomel pills by the pint, out of pure principle, and who lopped off limbs and felt yellow fever pulses all through the still watches of the hot nights with never a sign or look of encouragement; and the staid old chaplain, who had often assisted the surgeon and helped to fill cartridges, contributing his own cotton hose for the purpose when those government stores gave out in battle, and who never smiled, even when committing a marine to the briny deep; the purser, too, prim and business-like, looking as if he were a complicated key with an iron lock of his own strong chest, calculating perpetually the amount of dollars deposited in his charge, the total of pay to be deducted therefrom, and never making a mistake save when he overcharged the dead men for chewing tobacco; and the gay, young, roistering lieutenants, who never did any thing else but laugh, unmindful of navigation, pipe-clay, pills, parsons, or pursers, though standing somewhat in awe of the sharpish, exacting executive officer at the head of the table—all welcomed, each in his peculiar way, the bright, graceful young blade who dawned upon them. And not only the mess were cheered by his presence, but also a troop of clean-dressed sable attendants, whose wide jaws stretched wider, while the whites of their eyes seemed painfully like splashes of whitewash on the outside of the galley coppers, as they nudged one another and yaw-yaw'd quietly away aft there in the region of the pantry.

"Here, my salt-water pet, come and sit down by me, where all those old fellows can see you! Steward, a wine-glass for Mr. Darcantel! What? you won't take a sip of Tinta, and you can only stop a minute because you are to dine with your uncle the commodore, eh? Well, I'll drink your uncle's health even if you don't!" said the first lieutenant, as he familiarly laid his hand on the young fellow's shoulder and drained his glass.

"Why, Harry, what the deuce did you come down here for?" squeaked out the purser, as he unscrewed his lips into a pleasant smile. "You've put an end to that interesting account the master was giving us of how he lay inside Sandy Hook for six months with a glass to his—"

"Mouth," broke in the surgeon.

> "It was Sam Jones the fisherman,
>   Who was bound to Sandy Hook;
> But first upon the Almanac
>   A solemn oath he took—
> That he would catch a load of clams!"

"Silence there, you roarer!" said the surgeon, as he popped a filbert into the wide mouth of the rollicking fourth lieutenant, which cut his song short off. "Yes, Harry, that's what you have done in coming here for a minute. But stay a week with us, and the master will tell it you again. We've heard it once or twice before."

The old grizzled sea veteran scratched the remains of his ear, and growled jocosely while nodding to young Darcantel.

"Ah! my dear boy, and I'll tell you how the surgeon and nip-cheese there were entertained by a one-eyed old Spaniard at St. Jago."

"Let's hear it!" roared every body except the medico and purser. "Out with it, master!"

"Well, messmates, when we were in the old 'Scourge,' a long time ago, one day we anchored in St. Jago de Cuba."

Here the surgeon and purser smiled horribly, and implored the grizzled old navigator not to go on; every body had heard that old story; he might fall ill with the *vomito pietro*, and would require pills; or else there might be found a mistake in his pay account, and he would like, perhaps, to draw for the imaginary balance not due to him, and to drink his grog and scratch the remains of his old ear, or turn his attention to the load of clams waiting for him at Sandy Hook! But, for mercy's sake, don't repeat that silly, long-forgotten yarn!

"Well, messmates, in less than an hour after we had anchored in St. Jago they went on shore, and made the acquaintance of a little thin, sharp old villain, with one eye, who invited them to make him a visit, and pass the evening on a fine estate he owned near the base of the Copper Hills, some distance—about four leagues, I believe—from the town. He was a most respectable person, very rich, and commanded a Cuban guarda costa to boot. The *capitano*, Don Ignaçio Sanchez—wasn't that his name, doctor? Oh! you forget—all right! Off they started with a guide, on hired mules; but when they pulled up at their destination they found the Don wasn't there, though they were handsomely entertained by the señora—a comely, fat, and waspish body, with very few clothes on—who cursed her Don for sending people to see her, and the visitors too for coming. However, as her guests had not dined, she fed them bountifully on a supper of the nastiest jerked beef and garlic they had ever smelled. You told me so, purser."

Both Pills and Purser had forgotten all about it, and thought it would be better to talk of something else; that there was plenty of good wine to drink in place of drying his lips on such dusty old rubbish.

"Well, messmates, after the supper the old lady demanded a little game of monté, and she insisted, too, on making herself banker, though she had no money on the table to pay with in case she lost—which she had no intention of doing. So she won every ounce, dollar, real, and centavo they had in their pockets! The doctor and purser told me they saw her cheat boldly; but yet she not only bagged all the money, but she won their mules into the bargain!"

Here those individuals confessed roundly—standing on the defensive—that the fat old señora had a false pack of cards always ready in her ample bosom, and had cheated them in the barest manner conceivable; but yet they had no appeal, and were inclined, out of gallantry for the sex, to behave like gentlemen, though she did drink aguardiente.

"Well, messmates, toward midnight that hospitable wife of the

Don began to abuse our friends for not bringing more cash with them when they visited ladies, and then fairly kicked them out of the house! Yes, you both told me so when I lent you the money to pay the boatmen, after being obliged to tramp all the way back to the port on foot, nearly missing their billets in the old 'Scourge.'"

"Go on, master! Tell us all about it; don't stop!"

"Well, messmates, I was on deck while beating out of the channel, and just abreast the Star Castle I saw a boat with two gentlemen in the stern, stripped to a girt-line, and howling at rather than hailing the ship. Bear in mind, doctor, the men refused to take either of you unless you gave them your coats and trowsers before shoving off. And don't you remember, Hardy, how they yelled at us, and we thought they were deserters from that English gun-boat in St. Jago? And how the captain arrested the pair of them when they got on board for going out of signal distance? This is the first time *I* ever told this yarn," concluded the old navigator, tugging away at the lobe of his lost ear.

The young lieutenants shouted, and the old major of marines, forgetful of his iron-stuffed stock, laughed till he nearly sawed his chin off, rubbing his chalky knuckles into his eyes the while.

> "But first upon the Almanac
> A solemn oath he took—
> That he would catch a load of clams—"

"The barge is coming off, Mr. Hardy, with the pennant flying, sir!" reported a reefer, in the midst of the conversation, to the first lieutenant, as he shoved his bright face through the wardroom door.

"Very good, Mr. Beaver; but hark ye, sir! the next time you go ashore in the market-boat, look sharp that the men don't suck the monkey. Three of them came off drunk this morning. And inform Mr. Rat and Mr. Mouse that if I see their heels on the cutter's cushions again, I'll take a better look at them from the main-top-mast cross-trees. You understand, sir? Steward, a glass of wine for Mr. Beaver!" Saying this, the executive officer, with Harry Darcantel, arose and went on deck to receive the commodore.

CHAPTER XXXII.

A SPLICE PARTED.

"Oh! for thy voice, that happy voice,
   To breathe its loving welcome now!
Fame, wealth, and all that bids rejoice,
   To me are vain!   For where art thou?"

"What is glory—what is fame?
That a shadow—this a name,
   Restless mortal to deceive.
Are they renown'd—can they be great,
Who hurl their fellow-creature's fate,
   That mothers, children, wives may grieve?"

THE drum rolled, the marines presented arms, the boatswain piped, the side-boys and officers took off their caps; and as the colors dropped with the last ray of sunset from the peak, and the broad blue day-pennant came fluttering down from the lofty main truck, Commodore Cleveland and his friends stood on the splendid deck of the flag-ship "Monongahela."

It must have been with conscious pride that the brave and loyal commander gazed around him on the noble frigate and her gallant crew. The white decks, the tiers of cannon polished like varnished leather, with the breechings and tackles laid fair and even over and around them; the bright belaying-pins, holding their never-ending coils of running gear—the burnished brass capstan—the great boom —board to the boats amidships with a gleaming star of cutlasses, reflecting a glitter on the ring of long pikes stuck around the mainmast near, all inclosed by the high and solid bulwarks; while towering above, like mighty leafless columns of forest pines, stood the lofty masts, running up almost out of sight to the trucks in the fading light, supported by stays and shrouds, singly and in pairs, and braided mazes—black, and straight, and taut—never a thread loose on rigging or ratlin—and spreading out as they came down in a heavy hempen net, till they disappeared over the rail, and were clenched and spliced, or seized and clamped to the bolts and deadeyes of the chain-plates outside. Holding up too, in mid heaven, on those giant trunks—like a child its toys—the great square yards of timber branches, laying without a quiver, in their black lifts and trusses, with their white leaves of sails crumpled and packed in smooth bunts in the middle, and running away to nothing on either hand at the tapering yard-arms.

Grand and imposing is the sight. And well may you wonder, ye land lubbers, why all that mass of timber, sails, and cordage, with its enormous weight, does not crush with the giant heels of the masts through the bottom of the ship like unto an egg-shell, and tear the stanch live-oak frame to splinters!

The commander of the frigate saw all this, and he beheld at the same time the clusters of happy sailors, sauntering with light step and pleasant faces up and down the waist and gangways; and he heard, too, the scraping of a fiddle on the forecastle, the shuffling, dancing feet, and the least notion of a jovial sea-song coming up from the gun-deck. Yes, it must have been a glorious pride with which that gallant officer gazed around him from the quarter-deck of the magnificent frigate.

Did he say to himself, "I am monarch of this floating kingdom; my will is law; I say but the word, and those sails are spread and the ship moves to wherever I command. My subjects, too, who watch my slightest look and whisper, with that flag above, will pour broadside upon broadside—ay, they have!—from those terrible guns upon whoever dares to cross my track. Yes. They will fight for me so long as there is a plank left in this huge ship to stand upon, and while there is a rope-yarn left to hold the ensign—ay! even until my pennant, nailed to the truck, sinks beneath the bloodstained waves?" Did the commander think of all this? Perhaps he did.

And yet, in all the pride of rank and power, bravely won and maintained in many a scene of strife and deadly conflict, with visions of honest patriotism and ambition for the future, did his thoughts go back long years ago into the shadowy past, and was his spirit in the silent church-yard, where the magnolia was drooping over a grass-green grave? The sweet mother and her baby boy—the girl who had so fondly loved him, and the child who played about his knees—oh that they could have lived to share the wreaths of victory which were hung around his brow; that they could have lived to see the sword his country-gave him, to twine but for one little moment their loving arms around his neck! No, the magnolia waves its white flowers over mother and boy, and they sleep on in their heavenly and eternal rest.

Did Commodore Cleveland, as a saddened flash of thought swept over his handsome face, while he stood on his quarter-deck, dwell on those scenes? Yes, we know he did. By day and night, in war and peace, in gale or calm, on deck or at banquet, in dream and action, the girl and mother he so dearly loved was close clasped to his heart, and the child still playing at his knee.

"Gentlemen, let me make you acquainted with the first lieutenant,

Mr. Hardy; and permit me also to present my nephew, Mr. Darcantel, captain, if you please, my friends, of the one-gun schooner 'Rosalie,' formerly the slaver 'Perdita,' cut out of a river on the Gold Coast by the young gentleman who stands before you."

"Rosalie! why that's the name of my niece," exclaimed Piron; "and she is prettier and whiter than your trim little craft, sir. But you must come with the commodore to Escondido, and judge for yourself. But, bless my soul! *you* resemble our Rosalie, even if your schooner don't. Why, look at him, Paddy Burns!"

Don Stingo, and Tom Stewart, and the Paddy did look at him, and all shook hands with him, laughing the while at Piron, and asking when old Clinker looked for another earthquake.

"Come, Piron, come, gentlemen, don't let us keep the soup waiting! By the way, Mr. Hardy, will you do me the favor to take a glass of wine with us after gun-fire?"

"Thank you."

"Suppose you bring little Mouse with you; I like children; and perhaps you will excuse the younker from keeping his watch to-night? A little extra sleep in hammock won't hurt him, you know."

And so Commodore Cleveland raised his hat, followed by the eyes of respect and devotion from officer and sailor, as he passed down the ladder and entered his spacious cabin.

CHAPTER XXXIII.

THE BLUE PENNANT IN THE CABIN.

"To Bachelors' hall wo good fellows invite
To partake of tho chaso that makes up our delight."

"Ask smiling honor to proclaim
What is glory, what is fame?
Hark! the glad mandate strikes tho list'ning ear!
'The truest glory to tho bosom dear,
Is when tho soul starts soft compassion's tear.'"

"Now, gentlemen, let mo get off this heavy coat and epaulets. There! all right, Domino! put the sword in its case, and give mo a white jacket. Choose your own places, my friends. Piron, sit here on my right; Henri, take tho foot of tho table."

These last words wero said in French; whereupon Piron started and whispered to tho commodore, "By George, Cleveland, is that youth's name Henry, and does ho speak French?"

"Hush, Piron, he may hear you. His mother was French, and ho speaks the language like a native. Sho died when ho was a baby, and ho doesn't like to allude to it. Come, steward, wo are all ready. Serve tho gumbo!"

The cabin of the frigate was divided by a light lattice-work bulkhead in two parts, running from quarter to quarter of the vessel. The after part had a large sleeping stateroom on either side, resting on tho quarter galleries, and opening on to another gallery which hung over tho stern of tho frigate. Inside, in tho open space, was a round table, cushioned lounges, a few chairs, with a bronze lamp pendent from a beam above, while taking tho curve of tho stern over tho after windows was a range of bookcases, half hidden by tho gilt cornice and curtains of tho windows. The entire fittings and furniture of cabin and staterooms, including tho neat Brussels carpet on tho deck, wero elegant and useful, though by no means luxurious. Tho forward cabin, where no carpet graced tho floor, was much more spacious. It took in the two after ports of tho gun-deck; and tho carriages and cannon within tho sills of tho ports wero painted a marble white, as wero tho ropes, in covered canvas, that held them. In a recess forward was a large mahogany sideboard, or buffet, the top fitted with a framework for glasses and decanters, which wero reflected from a large mirror let into tho bulkhead. In tho middlo of this space was the dining-table, lighted by a pair of globe lamps hanging from above, while neat racks for bottles and water-jugs, moving on sliding brass rods, were also suspended from the paneled beams and carlines of the upper deck ceiling. On the right—the starboard side—was a door leading into a roomy pantry, where the steward and Domino, and the servants of the commodore, bestirred themselves at dinner-time.

"So, my friends," exclaimed the commodore, "you wish to hear what became of me after I last parted with you?"

"By all means, Cleveland! we are all dying to hear, and—" Here Piron's appeal was interrupted by the heavy report of a bow gun, which gave a slight, though almost imperceptible jar to the frigate.

"Smithereens! Stingo! what noise is that?" exclaimed Burns.

"Only the nine o'clock gun, sir," replied Darcantel.

"Hech, mon!" said Stewart, "ye needna upset ma glass of auld Madeira in yer mickle fright, for I've seen the time when ye ha' laughed at the music in the report of a peestol and the ping of a bullet! But your nervous seestem seems to be unstrung ever since the sma' French dancing count untied the string o' your waistcoat with his rapeer."

"You don't think, Paddy, the commodore here is going to bang a forty-two pound shot into our stomachs after all the good prog he's filled them with?" added Stingo, *sotto voce*, while the rotund Milesian threw his head back and twinkled careless defiance at them all.

Just then the orderly swung the port-cabin door open, and standing up as rigid as a pump-bolt, with a finger to the visor of his stovepipe hat, in cross-belts and bayonet, he announced "Lieutenant Hardy and Midshipman Mouse!"

"Ah! Hardy, glad to see you!" rising as he spoke; "squeeze in there between Stewart and Burns, or Darcantel! Here, gentlemen, let me exhibit to you Mr. Tiny Mouse! Don't move, Piron; I'll make a place for him near me."

Saying this, the commodore took the lad affectionately by the hand, and as he sat him down on a chair at his elbow, and while the conversation went on with his guests, he said, in a kindly tone,

"Tiny, my dear, the first lieutenant tells me you are a good boy and attend to your duty. I hope you pay attention to your studies also, and write often to your dear mother. Ah!.you do? That is right; for you know you are her only hope since your brave father was killed. There, sir, you may swig a little claret, but don't touch those cigars."

"Come, Cleveland! Cleveland! you are forgetting your adventures, my boy!"

"Well, my friends, you shall hear them."

CHAPTER XXXIV.

"And how then was the devil dressed?
Oh! he was dressed in his Sunday's best;
His jacket was red and his breeches were blue,
And there was a hole where the tail came through."

"Hairy-faced Dick understands his trade,
He stands by the breech of a short carronade,
The linstock glows in his bony hand,
Waiting that grim old skipper's command!"

"THE last dinner I had in Jamaica, and a very jolly one it was, as you all know, was out at Escondido, where we kept it up so late that I only got on board the 'Scourge' at daylight, in time to get her under way with the land wind. Well, we were bound to windward, and for a week afterward we rolled about in a calm off Morant Bay, maybe twenty leagues off the island, and one morning we discovered a sail. She was a large merchant brig, heading any way, and bobbing about, as we were, in the calm. Toward noon, however, a light air sprang up, and we got within hail, and I went on board to say a word or two to the skipper, for we had news before leaving Kingston that that infamous pirate Brand, in his long-legged schooner 'Centipede,' had been seen off Guadaloupe; and, in fact, we had actually chased him off Matanzas three months before; so I was ordered to give the brig a warning, particularly as she had reported a suspicious craft in sight that same morning at sunrise. When I got on board of her I saw—"

Here Piron placed both hands to his face as he leaned his elbows on the table, and the commodore, checking himself, hurried on:

"Ah! well, we kept the brig in sight all day, and ran round her once or twice in the evening, but toward midnight the trade wind freshened, and, as the coast seemed clear, and we were anxious to make up for lost time in the calm, we gradually came up to our course, and went bowling away to windward.

"I remember going below at the time, and just as I was about to turn in, I heard a quarter-master sing out to Hardy there, who was junior lieutenant of the ship, and who had the middle watch, that he saw a light going up to the brig's gaff. In five seconds I was on the poop, where I met the captain.

" This is his only son, gentlemen, and a braver or more skillful sea-man never trod a ship's deck," said the commodore, as he passed his hand affectionately over the boy's head, who was sitting beside him.

But he forgot, perhaps, to say that he, Cleveland, had stood by the father when he was struck dead by a cannon-shot, and that after-ward he had the boy appointed a reefer, and, out of his own means, helped the widow to eke out her pittance of a pension. Yes, Cleve-land forgot all that as he smoothed the youngster's soft hair, while, with the men around him, he drained his glass in silence to the memory of his departed friend and chief. Then resuming, he went on:

"In less than no time after the light was seen—for you must know, gentlemen, that it was an understood signal between us—the 'Scourge' was flying off with a stiff breeze abaft the beam, the crew at quarters, and the boats ready to be lowered from the davits. When we ranged up alongside the brig, and even before, we felt certain that our misgivings would prove true, and so they did; and merely slamming a shot over her, and dropping a couple of armed boats into the water, we luffed round her bows, and there we saw that cursed schooner—venomous snake as she was—just hoisting her sails, and creeping away to windward.

"We let her have two or three divisions of grape, and followed the dose up with round shot. I am sure we hit her, and that pretty hard, for we knocked away her fore-top-mast, and we saw the splin-ters fly in showers from her hull. However, she was well handled, and lying nearer the wind than the 'Scourge,' when day dawned she was clear out of range, and leaving us every minute. So we up helm and ran down again to the brig, to see what mischief had been done and to pick up our boats.

"Ah! yes, you all know what had taken place, so I won't go over the details; but the same afternoon, after seeing the brig pointed straight for Port Royal, and while we were once more on our course, we fell in with a water-logged boat, in which were half a dozen dead and dying men. One, a mongrel Indian from Yucatan, who was frightfully torn by two or three grapeshot, before he died on board —as did all the others—gave us, in his confused dialect, some account of the pirate he had served under, and the haunt he frequented. As near as we could learn, the haunt was situated somewhere on the south side of Cuba, on a rocky island having a safe and secure inlet; but as he did not know the latitude or longitude, we were left some-what in the dark. The last words, however, the mangled wretch ut-tered, as the gasping breath was leaving his body, were, that the spot could be distinguished by a tall cocoa-nut-tree which grew from a craggy eminence in the middle of the island. We buried them all, pirates as they were, decently, and then we clapped on all sail on our course.

"Steward, another bottle of the old Southside that Mr. March sent me from Madeira! Here, Domino, take Mr. Mouse up gently, and lay him down on my cot in the after cabin. Dear little fellow, he is sound asleep; and mind you draw the curtains around him, lest he take cold from the draught of the stern windows!"

Rather a striking contrast this to the way Captain Brand, the pirate, treated the little Henri in the den there in the Doçe Léguas.

Well, gentlemen, for some weeks after these occurrences we sailed about the islands, touching here and there, until at last we arrived at the Havana, took in stores and water, and then continued the cruise. The orders were to beat up the south side of Cuba, where we expected to fall in with the Mosquito fleet and some English vessels, especially detailed to destroy two or three nests of pirates who had for some years swarmed in those seas and infested that coast. In the course of time we beat all around the south side of Cuba, and at last dropped anchor in St. Jago, where we learned from the English consular agent that five or six fellows, who had been wrecked on the Carvalo reef, were identified as having been part of a piratical crew who had plundered an English vessel with a free passport bound to Havana, and had been sent there in irons for trial.

"The truth was, that the Spanish colonial authorities had so long connived, winked at, or been indifferent to what was going on during the wars of the Continent, that they allowed these piratical hordes to exist and thrive at their very doors. The matter had already been brought to the notice of the administrador of the port, and all other ports as far along the coast as Cienfuegos, and in such a threatening manner, too, that the governor at St. Jago, fearful of having his town blown down, exerted himself in the arrest of the rascals I have alluded to, and likewise in procuring information by dispatching guarda costas along the south side of the island.

"Accordingly, the very morning we anchored I went ashore with the captain of the custom-house, where we met the deputy administrador and a little withered, one-eyed old rascal, who was in the colonial service, and who professed to know the haunt, or at least he said he thought he did, of that notorious villain Brand.

"I remember distinctly spreading a chart before him, and while he traced with the end of his cigarette a course for the captain to steer by, I stood near, watching him narrowly. But the fact was, that he had the very sharpest spark of an eye set, or rather standing out, beside his nose that any body ever saw in a human being's head; and instead of me watching him, he seemed to be looking straight through me, and divining my thoughts and suspicions. However, the spot he pointed out, and the way he described it, with a cocoa-nut-tree on top of a rock, and the passage through the reef, so nearly corresponded with the confused account the Yucatanese gave us before he died,

that the captain was entirely convinced we were on the scent, though
I myself was not more than half satisfied. The place indicated was
near the Isle of Pines, three hundred miles off; but, to make the thing
more plausible, that one-eyed old scoundrel was detailed to run along
the Doçe Léguas Cays, see what information he could pick up there,
and then follow down after us.

"That night, or early the next morning, we were off again, and ran
down the coast, with a good offing to keep the wind, until we got to
the ground, and passed in by Cape St. Francis, and doubled round
into the Bight of Pines. There we fell in with a whole fleet of English and American cruisers and schooner craft, who informed us that
they had searched every accessible spot where a man could walk dry-
shod upon, from Guayabos to the Isle of Mangles; that they had destroyed several old and deserted piratical nests, and hung two or
three ostensible fishermen by way of wholesome warning to their
allies the pirates; but that was all; and from what they had learned,
there did not seem to have been an established retreat in that maze
of cays and reefs for four or five years.

"So you see we had our cruise for nothing, and then the captain
agreed with me that we had both been most egregiously deceived by
the Spanish commander of the guarda costa. Well, we hauled our
wind once more, standing well out to sea, and after a tedious beat
of some days we again edged in toward the coast, somewhere near
the Boca Grande of the Twelve League Cays on the westernmost
side. It was in the morning when we made the land, and, steering
close in, we got a good slant off the shore, and kept the glasses going
from the topmost cross-trees down all through the day. For my
part, as Hardy may perhaps remember, I scarcely took the glass from
my eye for eight hours, and from the mizzen-top I feel quite sure that
there were not many objects, from the size of a blade of grass to a
mangrove bush, that I did not examine, from the coral reefs up to the
rocky heights, let alone the cocoa-nut-tree that we were in search of.

"Toward afternoon, however, the weather came up hazy, the wind
began to fall off, and the barometer began to exhibit very queer
spasms indeed, rising with a sort of jerk at first, and then dropping
down the tenth of an inch at a clip, with the atmosphere becoming
close and sultry, and the men gasping about the decks as if we were
about to choke at the next breath. It was during the hurricane
months, and the indications certainly should have led us as far as
our legs could carry us to open water, instead of being caught em-
bayed perhaps with half a thousand reefs around us on what might
prove a lee-shore; but, nevertheless, the captain decided to hold on
till sunset, and then make an offing. The breeze still held in the upper sails, and so we slipped on in smooth water till about five o'clock,
when I heard a fellow sing out from the main royal yard,

"'On deck there! I can see a tall cocoa-nut-tree on an island here on the port bow!'

"Before the words were well out of his mouth I too caught the object, and I knew at the first glance that it was the spot we were looking for. At the same time the haze lighted up a bit, and we saw the ridge of rocks and every thing as the haunt of that pirate Brand had been described to us. So, my friends, we were all alive once more on board the 'Scourge,' and the captain resolved to dash in upon the scoundrel's nest before he could have time to leave it.

"The engine was rigged and water spirted over the sails from the trucks down, to make the canvas hold the wind, and in an hour after we were within two leagues of the island, and just as the sun fell below the horizon we caught sight of the mast-heads of a large vessel sticking up over some bluff rocks near the bold shore. Not five minutes later the hull of the craft came slowly out from the gap, under all sail, and we discovered her to be a long and rather lumbering-looking brigantine, painted lead-color, and bearing no resemblance to the schooner we had twice chased before. Simultaneously, however, with her coming out into full view, as she rounded in her head-yards and got a pull of the main-sheet, with the breeze abeam and heading to the eastward, we beheld a great volume of white smoke spout up over the rock near the cocoa-nut-tree, with a vivid sheet of flame at the base, and before the vast column turned, like the crown of a palm-tree, in its descent, we were greeted by a dull, heavy roar, the concussion of which fairly made the 'Scourge' tremble. Then, as the white smoke partially broke away, an avalanche of rocks and timbers was scattered far and near, and nothing visible but a veil of dust and masses of heavy smoke. Nearly at the same moment of this explosion wreaths of heavy black smoke arose from another spot nearer to the gap, lit up in the fading, hazy twilight with forked red fires, and soon after a great conflagration burst forth, swirling flakes of burning cinders all over the island, and casting a lurid glare upon the water around us."

CHAPTER XXXV.

AND THE PITCH HOT.

> "He is born for all weathers;
> Let the winds blow high or blow low,
> His duty keeps him to his tethers,
> And where the gale drives he must go.
>
> "The wind blew hard, the sea ran high,
> The dingy scud drove 'cross the sky,
> All was safe lashed, the bowl was slung,
> When careless thus Ned Halyard sung."

SAID the commodore, with a knowing shake of his head, "Ah! gentlemen, if the fellow, whoever he was, who was creeping away so nimbly in that lazy-looking brigantine, with English colors at the peak, had written down in detail what he had been doing on that secluded nook of an island, and sent the information off to us in a letter, we could have read it without breaking the seal. We could have told him that that little scoundrel with one eye had purposely misled us, and had given him warning to quit his strong-hold; and that he had hastily got his plunder and people on board his vessel, blown up and set fire to his nest, and that the brigantine he was now on board of was once upon a time the notorious schooner 'Centipede!' Yes, we knew all that by instinct."

Piron sat with his eyes fixed upon the speaker, taking in every word as it fell from his lips, the teeth set close together and the hand clenched which supported his head on the table. Paddy Burns and Tom Stewart, too, looked eagerly that way, as did Harry Darcantel, while Hardy sipped his wine and puffed his cigar leisurely, as if he knew the tale by heart.

"It had fallen nearly calm. A light air perhaps in the royals, though nothing down below. But as we hauled down our colors at sunset, which had been hoisted to let the fellow know who we were, down came his also. Then there we both lay looking at each other. He knew by instinctive experience that we were the American corvette 'Scourge,' mounting eighteen twenty-four-pounder carronades and two long eighteens in the bow ports; for the brigantine had once or twice determined their exact calibres, and that we were the fastest cruiser, with the wind a point or two free, that had been seen in the West Indies for twenty years.

"Yes, he knew all about us, but he was still a little in doubt whether we knew all about *him*. He lay—unfortunately, perhaps, for him—a little beyond the range of our long guns, or else he might have been spared a good deal of time and uneasiness, and we a long chase and considerable risk. Ah! as the night came, the very fires he had kindled in his den on shore prevented his escape; for while the calm lasted the bright flames shone upon him with the glare of hell! There we lay all that night without moving a muscle or a mile until day dawned—and such a day as did dawn!

"Meanwhile the barometer had fallen an inch and a half, until the master began to believe the bulb leaked, and the mercury was dropping into the case. Then, through the murky gloom of daylight, with the sea one flat greasy surface, with never the splash of a fish to disturb it, while the lowest whisper of the topmen aloft could be distinctly heard on deck, as if we were hung in the vacuum of an exhausted receiver where a feather would drop like a bullet, suddenly there came a sound from the direction of the cays. Suppose, Burns, you saw a forty-two pound shot coming toward you, and without you dodged quick, your head would be flying off with it in the same direction?"

"Whist, mon!" said Stewart, with a groan, "dinna be calling up sic peectures of the brain, Cleveland. Paddy, there, ne'er thinks of ony meesals bigger than a peestol bullet."

"Well, my friends, we ran precisely a similar risk, though the cloudy embrasures over the island had not quite enough thunder to reach us. However, the brigantine knew what would follow as well as we did—better, perhaps—and before you could swallow that glass of wine she was stripped as bare as a bone, and down came her yards too, but keeping the sticks up, and spreading a patch of a storm stay-sail forward that you might apparently have put in your pocket. Her decks and rigging were crowded with men while she was doing all this, but the moment it was done, and well done too, they ran into their holes below like so many rats, and we could only see a man or two left on deck near the helm.

"All hands had been called on board the 'Scourge' at four o'clock, and, with the exception of securing the battery, every thing was ready to make a skeleton of the ship the moment we saw the brigantine begin; for she was a wary fish, and we had no idea of letting her give us the slip the third time. I had the trumpet, however, and with the captain at my elbow, the instant he saw that the brigantine was once more rigged nearly in her old way, he gave me the word, 'Now, Cleveland, work sharp!'

"With a hundred and twenty men aloft, jumping about like cats, the light sails, studding-sail booms, royal and top-gallant yards came down, the top-gallant masts after them, and the flying jib-boom rigged in. Then the top-sails close reefed and furled with extra gaskets, and so .with the courses; preventer braces clapped on, rolling tackles hooked, and the spare purchases set up by the lower pennants. Meanwhile the divisions on deck had got hawsers over the launch amidships, the chains unbent, the anchors lashed down on the forecastle, and the quarter boats triced well inboard and secured with the davits. At the same time the light stuff from aloft was got below, the hammocks piped down, and the carpenters slapped the gratings on the hatches, and stood ready with the tarpaulins to batten them down. I never beheld a smarter piece of work done afloat—not even, Hardy, in the 'Monongahela.'

"As I turned round an instant a hoarse, howling bellow struck my ear from the island, and I just caught a glimpse of the tall cocoanut-tree flying round and round in the air like an inverted umbrella with a broken stick; while at the same time the men from aloft had reached the deck, and, jumping to the battery, the guns were run in and housed, spare breechings and extra lashings passed, and life-lines rove fore and aft. After that, gentlemen, there was no farther need of a trumpet.

"You all know pretty well what sort of a thing a hurricane is, and the one I speak of must, I think, have given you a touch of its quality here in Jamaica."

"Ay, by the holy Moses! we remember it well, bad luck to it; and so does Tom Stewart and Piron there, for it didn't lave a stick of sugar-cane standing from Montego Bay to Cape Antonio."

"Yes," said Stewart; "and to show ye what a piff of wind can do, the whirl of it caught up an eighteen-foot Honduras plank, and laid it crosswise, like an axe, full seven inches into an old tamarind trunk standing in my garden, and then twisted off the ends like a heather broom! Hech, mon, ye may see it there now any day!"

Piron was thinking of the barks that were driving before that hurricane, with no thought of the damage done to his own plantations.

"Well, then, I shall spare you all prolix description of it; and you need only fancy a ship blown every where and every how except out of water—now with the lower yard-arms cutting deep into the sea like rakes, the lee hammock-nettings under water, the stern boat torn away into splinters, the main-top-sail picked, bolt by bolt, from the yard until there was not a thread left, and the lee anchor twisted bodily out of its lashings and swept overboard!

"Then a lull, while the sea got up and the ship dashed down on the other side on her bow; then staggering back and making a sternboard till the water was plunged up in a deluge over the poop. Recovering herself again, and almost quivering on her beam-ends, the guns groaning and creaking as the terrible strain came upon the breechings, with the shot from the racks bounding about the decks, dinting holes in the solid oak waterways big enough to wash your face in, and then hopping out of the smashed half-ports to leeward. The spar-deck up to your arm-pits in water, and every man of us holding on to the life-lines or standing rigging like grim death, while all the time the roaring, thundering yell of the hurricane taught us how powerless we were, by hand or voice, to cope with the winds when they were let loose in all their might and fury!

"Nor need I relate to you the scene presented below—mess-chests, bags, tables, crockery, flying from deck and beam to stanchion, smashing about in the most dangerous way, pell-mell, while the worst of the tempest lasted. But, gentlemen, the 'Scourge' had a frame of live-oak, to say nothing of two or three acres of tough yellow-pine timber in her, a good deal of fibrous hemp to hold the masts up; and, moreover, she was well manned, and, though I say it myself, she had a skillful captain and thorough-bred officers, in whose sagacity the crew could rely, to manage that old 'Scourge.'"

"That she had," exclaimed Hardy; "and the most skillful and the coolest of them all was the first lieutenant!" The "Monongahela's" executive officer here bounced off his chair as if he was prepared to fight any man breathing who did not subscribe to that opinion.

"Well, my friends, that awful hurricane continued for about twenty hours, from late one morning till the beginning of the next. As for day, there was none; for the sea and black clouds made one long night of it. Fortunately, too, we had been driven off shore, and when the murky gloom broke away, and we were able to look around, our first anxiety was to see what had become of the brigantine.

"Yes, and I truly believe, in all that turmoil of the elements, while we were on the brink of foundering and going down to old Davy's locker, that there was not an officer or man, from the captain to the cook, who was not thinking of that pirate, and hoping that he might go down first. I myself, however, felt a sort of confidence, as I was held lashed on the poop to the mizzen rigging, that the brigantine might be caught and whirled about—so long as she was above water—by the same blows of the hurricane that beat upon the 'Scourge;' and when the tornado broke, and some one sang out 'Sail ho!' I knew by instinct it must be the 'Centipede.'"

CHAPTER XXXVI.

THE CHASE.

"With sloping masts and dipping prow,
  As who pursued with yell and blow
Still treads the shadow of his foe,
  And forward bends his head,
The ship drove past, loud roared the blast,
  And southward aye we fled."

"Clap on more sail, pursue, give fire—
  She is my prize, or ocean whelms them all."

"So many slain—so many drowned!
  I like not of that fight to tell.
Come, let the cheerful grog go round!
  Messmates, I've done. A spell, ho, spell!"

"It was all hands again, gentlemen. The hurricane had settled down into a moderate gale from northeast, though it was some time before the awfully confused sea got to roll regularly. Then we judged ourselves—for reckoning and observation had been out of the question—to be a long way south of Jamaica, and even to the southward of the great Pedro Bank. We did not wait this time for the pirate to lead us in getting ready for a race, but we got up a bran new suit of top-sails and courses out of the sail-room, and, so soon as the men could go aloft with safety, they were ordered not to unbend the few tattered rags still clinging to the yards, but to cut away at once. Up went the top-sails and courses, and they were soon brought to the yards and set close-reefed, with a storm-jib to steady the ship forward. Presently we gave her the whole fore-sail and main-sail, and I think that even then, for some hours, but one half the corvette's upper works could have been visible as she plunged through the angry heaving seas.

"It left us dry enough, however, to pay some heed to the brigantine ahead of us. She was about four miles off, a little on our weather bow, and as she rode up—splendid sea-boat that she was—like a gull on the back of a mighty roller, we could see that her bulwarks—mere boards and canvas, probably—had been washed away, the house between her masts gone too, and, no doubt, her long gun, or whatever else had been lying hid under it. And now she was once more the

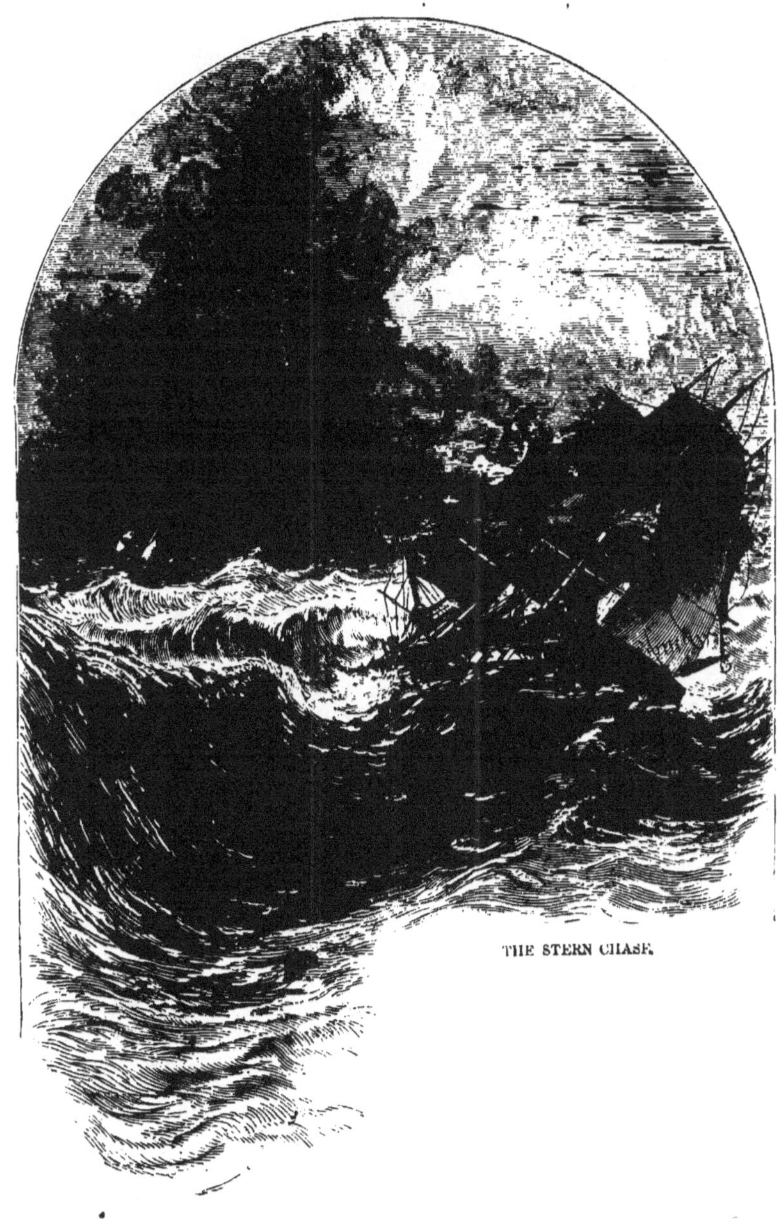

THE STERN CHASE.

schooner 'Centipede,' long and sharp, and without any rail to speak of, so that we could see her deck from the stem to her taffrail at every lurch she made. The only difference in her appearance was a short fore-mast with cross-trees, and a top-mast for square sails. Almost as soon as our top-sail sheets were hauled home, her own yards went up and the sail was spread, while with the bonnet off her fore-sail, the whole jib and a close-reefed main-sail, she went flying to the southward with the gale a point abaft the beam.

"Thus we went on, the sea getting more regular every hour, so that we could send up the top-gallant masts, get the yards across, shake a reef or two out, and put the 'Scourge' in order. The schooner needed no encouragement from us, but cracked on more sail until her long main-mast reeled and bent over, as she came up on the breaking ridge of a wave, like a whip-stalk. By noon the clouds had gone, and left us a clear sky, with the gale going down into a full top-gallant breeze, sending the corvette along good eleven knots. We got an observation for latitude, and five hours later we determined the longitude and our position to be a few leagues to leeward of the Sarrana Keys, with that bird of a schooner before us heading for the Musquito coast.

"If *we* had caught a cataract of water as it rolled over our bows in the morning, the schooner was taking *her* bath in the afternoon, for occasionally, for five minutes at a time, there was nothing seen of her deck, and only the masts and broad white canvas above, like jury-sticks out of a raft. But when she did slide up with her low, long hull shooting clean out of water, till nearly half her keel, with the copper sheathing flashing in the sun, was visible, she looked like a dolphin making a spring after a shoal of flying-fish. And then on her narrow deck we could see a few fellows lashed about the fore-mast, and a couple more abaft steering her like a thread through a needle.

"We began to gain upon her now, and whenever she kept a little away before the wind the gap between us closed more rapidly; for the ship could evidently outcarry the schooner, and, had the breeze freshened and the sea kept up, we could have run her under if her masts didn't go out of her, as we hoped and expected every minute they would. Gradually, however, she watched her chance and hauled up till she brought the wind barely abeam, and steered true for the Musketeers—a bad cluster of low keys nearly surrounded by as terrible ledges and reefs as any to be found in the Caribbean Sea.

"Her captain was evidently bent upon playing a desperate game, but, if he thought he would not find another ready to lay down the same stake, he was greatly mistaken! It was about sunset when we made the keys, and there we went—the schooner leading us about a mile—at a rate which would have made both vessels leap clear over the first ledge they struck, and perhaps have thrown summersaults of us into the bargain. I asked the captain, who had never left my side on the poop, if we should keep on.

"'Yes, sir,' he replied, 'so long as we have a gun and a plank to float it!'

"And, by Saint Paul! we kept on. And there was not a soul on board the 'Scourge,' from the drummer-boy up, who did not agree with the captain. How those villains on board the pirate relished this decision we could only surmise; but, at all risks, he held his course with a nerve that might have made the devil himself shudder.

"By this time the sun was well down, and a brilliant moon was riding high in the heavens; but, as bright as it was, the fellow who commanded that schooner required an eye as keen as an albatross and a hand as steady as an iron bar to guide his craft in the direction he was going—too late for either of us to think of hauling off.

"He must, too, have had a thorough knowledge of the reefs and keys, and trusted, perhaps, if he got clear himself, that the corvette, drawing eighteen feet water and ignorant of the channel, might touch something which would throw the game in his hands. Our men had the ropes stretched along the decks and the battery clear on both sides, so as to be ready to wear, or tack, or fire, as our pilot ahead might require.

"The reefs were to leeward of the string of low keys, which made the water comparatively smooth, though the wind still swept strongly over us and sang through the rigging; and it was here the 'Centipede' entered, going like wild pigeons the pair of us. The outer reef had a fair, deep passage, and so had the next; but the inner one presented but one narrow gateway, scarcely wide enough for a ship to scrape through, with the whole reef one uninterrupted fringe of black pointed rocks and roaring white breakers, which toppled over, and boiled and eddied like a thousand whirlpools into the smoother water inshore.

"As the 'Centipede's' stern gave a sharp pitching jerk when she entered this boiling gorge, we saw, in the moonlight, her head yards laid square, the fore and aft sails flowing in the sheets as she fell off with wide wings and the wind on her quarter, and flew down inside the reef.

"Five minutes after we too entered this maelstrom chasm, and, though the helm was hove hard up, and the after-sails shivered, yet, before the 'Scourge's' bows, going at the rate she was, could turn the sharp angle of that water-gate, her port bilge grated against a coral ledge, and grooved and broomed the planks and copper away like so much sea-weed! But yet that slight graze never stopped us a hair's weight, and, with additional sail, we rushed after our pilot, mile after mile, through reef, ledge, breakers, inlets, and keys, now braced sharp up, and again going free, until at last the fellow, having run us a dance of full ten miles, once more emerged into the open water, close jammed on the wind, steering nearly due east.

"There, Hardy!" exclaimed the commodore, "I am tired of talking; suppose you take up the thread of the yarn. Domino, another bottle of tinta!"

CHAPTER XXXVII.

THE WRECK OF THE "CENTIPEDE."

"Gun bellows forth to gun, and pain
  Rings out her wild, delirious scream;
Redoubling thunders shake the main,
  Loud crashing falls the shot-rent beam.
The timbers with the broadsides strain;
  The slippery decks send up a steam
From hot and living blood; and high
And shrill is heard the death-pang cry!"

"She struck where the white and fleecy waves
  Looked soft as carded wool;
But the cruel rocks they gored her side
  Like the horns of an angry bull."

PIRON turned his gaze toward the first lieutenant, moved away the full glasses of wine, which he had never raised to his lips since the commodore began, and, resting his bloodless cheek on his other hand, listened.

"It's vera interesting indeed." "Tear an' ages, boy! Fire away!" quoth the Scotchman and his Milesian crony in a breath.

Hardy threw his arm over the shoulder of Harry Darcantel as if it was a pleasant Corinthian column to lean upon, and, breaking off the ashes of his cigar on the rim of a wine-glass which he had specially devoted to that purpose, he forthwith began:

"I am quite confident, gentlemen, that I can not describe what afterward took place so well as Commodore Cleveland, but, at all events, I'll do my best. Nor do I remember very distinctly the events of the night after we got out of the Musketeers Keys; for I was pretty well fagged out myself, and all of us who had the watch below turned in to take the first wink of sleep we could catch for forty hours.

"The next morning, however, when I took the deck, I found the corvette under royals and flying-jib, with a fresh trade wind blowing from about east-northeast, and a smooth sea; though close hauled as we were, and going ten knots, the spray was flying well up the weather leech of the fore-sail. The 'Centipede' was about a mile and a half ahead, jammed on the wind, and trying all she could to eat the wind out of us; but, as the commodore there said at the time, he had thrown that trick away when he cut off eight or ten feet of his fore-mast, and made a brigantino of the craft, so that he could not brace his head yards sharper, or lie nearer the wind than we did.

"I remember, also, that two or three of the officers and half a hundred of the sailors were very anxious to pitch shot at the chase from the long eighteen in the weather bridle port; but the captain refused, and said we might lose a cable's length or two in yawing off to fire, and it would be better to save the powder until we could slam a broadside into him. But all the while that 'Centipede' was handled and steered in such a thorough seamanlike manner, and proved herself such a beautiful sea-boat, that I doubt if there was a man on board the 'Scourge' who would not have given a year's pay to have taken her whole, and only expended a spare top-mast studding-sail halliards for the necks of her crew.

"From the top-gallant forecastle we could see every thing that took place on the schooner's deck: sometimes a lot of fellows forward reeving some fresh gear, peering about the low bowsprit, or putting on a seizing to a traveler on the jib-stay; with a chap or two aloft stitching a chafing-mat on the lee backstays; and then aft a man shinning up the main shrouds with a tin pot hung around his neck, greasing the jaws of the main gaff, and twitching a wrinkle out of the gaff-top-sail, so that it would lie as flat as this dining-room table set on end.

"But always, from the very first moment we descried her—before the hurricane and afterward—there were two fellows abaft by the taffrail. One a large fat man, in a long dark dress, who appeared at times to be leaning over the rail as if he were sea-sick; and the other a spare, tall-built fellow, who sat there with a quadrant in his hands and smoking cigars, measuring the distance between the two vessels as if he were a government surveyor, and especially appointed to make a hydrographical chart of the Caribbean Sea. Occasionally, too, we could see him approach the binnacle, spread a chart on the deck at his feet, examine it closely with a pair of dividers in his hands, and then he would return to his seat on the taffrail, cigar in his mouth and quadrant to his eye as before.

"Nor were we idle on board the 'Scourge;' for when the breeze lulled we slacked up the lower rigging and stays, got down all extra weight and hamper from the tops, sent the watch below to the berth-deck with a round shot apiece in their hammocks, moved a couple of carronades about the spar-deck till we got the ship in the best sailing trim, and then we went skipping and springing through the water with the elasticity of an India-rubber ball.

"At noon the sailing-master reported the position of the ship to be two hundred and eighty miles from the nearest land, which was the Darien Coast. So all that day and all that night, with a moon to make a lover weep to see, we went bowling after our waspish

consort in hopes before long of taking the sting out of her. No kite
ever pursued its quarry with a keener eye than we did. No hound
ever leaped after a wolf with the froth streaming from his jaws and
blood-red thirsty eyes, than did the 'Scourge' chase that infamous
pirate. The delay only made our eyes sparkle and our teeth sharper
in expectation; for we knew we would have our prey sooner or later,
and it was only a bite and a pleasure deferred.

"The next morning and all the day there was no change to speak
of in our respective positions. The 'Centipede' went skimming on
over the water with every thread of canvas she could spread, reeling
over on her side at times when the breeze freshened, while the spray
flashed up joyously and sparkled in the sun, leaving a bubbling current of foam in her wake, which, before it had been entirely lost in
the regular waves of the sea, the corvette's sharp bows would plunge
into, and again make it flash high up to her fore-yard, and then go
seething, and hissing, and kissing her black sides until it rippled
around her rudder and was lost again in the wake astern.

" And all the time that man sat with a cigar in his mouth on the
pirate's taffrail, while Commodore Cleveland there stood with a spy-
glass to his eye on the poop of the 'Scourge.'

"You may imagine, gentlemen," continued Hardy, as he again
knocked the ashes off his cigar, " that going to sea is attended with
some few discomforts, such as battening down the hatches in a siroc-
co in the Mediterranean off Tripoli; a simoom in the China Seas; a
bitter northwest gale off Barnegat, with the rigging and sails frozen
as hard as an iceberg; but if a man can catch forty winks of sleep
once in a while, whether in a hammock, or on an oak carronade slide
with the breech of a gun for a pillow, he may manage to weather
through it. But from the moment we first saw that pirate till we
saw the last of him, neither the first lieutenant of the 'Scourge' nor
the commander of the 'Centipede' once closed their eyes, unless—
well, I won't anticipate."

. Piron reached over his hand and shook that of his friend Cleveland
convulsively.

"Vera weel, mon! vera weel!" "He's the very man to do it!"
said Stewart and Burns to Stingo, nodding backward at the commodore.

Another striking contrast to the hand-shaking, virtuous compact
between Captain Brand and his friend, the pious padre Ricardo! I
wonder if they are shaking hands now! Probably not.

Gentlemen," resumed Hardy, as he shook the ashes level in his
wineglass, as if he wished to preserve them to clean his teeth with
after smoking, "I will not detain you much longer. Both vessels
were making great speed, and long before sunset we had been keeping a bright look-out for the land. At last it was reported, trending

all around both bows, low and with a trembling mirage of pines and mangroves looming up, and a multitude of rocky keys dead ahead. We were steering directly for Las Mulatas Islands, a cluster then little known to any navigators save, perhaps, the buccaneers of the Gulf of Columbus, and perhaps, too, with the intention of running us just such another dance as our pilot had a night or two before. However, we were again all prepared to explore the unknown reefs; and, moreover, we got the starboard anchor off the bow, and bent the cables to that and the spare anchors amidships, so as to be all ready to moor ship in case our pilot required us to do so. And likewise the cutters were hanging clear from the davits—the same boats which had once before paid a complimentary visit to some of his friends—supposing he would like to entertain us in person.

"The sun went down again in a fiery blaze, and with its last ray there slowly rose to the main truck of the pirate a swallow-tailed black flag, with a white skull and cross-bones in the dark field. It fluttered for a moment out straight and clear, and then twisted itself around the thin mast, never more to be released by hands or halliards! That was the last glimpse those pirates ever caught of the murderous symbol they had so often fought and sailed under; and it was the last sun that a good many aching eyes ever looked upon who were sailing there in that half league of blue water. The moon, however, was riding bright and beaming, as clear as a bell, overhead, and that was all the light we cared for. The 'Centipede,' no doubt, would have preferred no moon at all, with a cloudy sky and a bit of a rain squall, to pursue the intricate navigation before her; but Heaven arranged the atmospheric scenery otherwise.

"'By the deep eight!' sang out the leadsman in the port chains. 'The mark five!' came from the opposite side. 'Another cast, lads —quick!' 'And a half four!' 'Six fathoms, sir!'

"'We must have stirred up the sand, Cleveland,' said the captain; but even as he spoke the man in the starboard chains cried, 'Three fathoms, sir!' and while each instant we expected the ship to bring up all standing, and the masts to go by the board, the other leadsman sung out, joyfully, 'No bottom with the line, sir!'

"Well, we were safely through that bed of coral, doing, no doubt, some trifling damage to the tender shoots and branches, as we flew through a narrow channel, with the waves breaking and moaning on the sandy shores over the keys, out into deep water again.

"Four or five miles beyond stood out a bluff rock, looking in the moonlight like a dozing lion with his paws crossed before him, ready to bound upon any who should approach his lair in the dense jungle of pines and tangled thickets which stood up like a bristling mane on the ridge behind.

"The 'Centipede' was now but a short half-mile ahead of us, her

deck alive with men, and manifestly ready for some desperate devil-
ment.   On her after rail, too, stood that man, tall and erect, his feet
steadied by the cavil of the main boom, a spy-glass to his eye, and
looking at the rocky lion now close aboard him, still with a cigar in
his mouth; and we thought we could even see the thin puffs of smoke
curling around his face.   Suddenly, too, we saw the spy-glass whirled
around his head, and at the instant the vessel fell dead off before the
wind, the great main-sail flew over with a stunning crash and clatter
of blocks and sheets as the wind caught it. on the other quarter, making the long switch of a mast to spring like a bow, while the weath-
er-shrouds slacked up for a moment in bights, and then came back
taut with a twang you might have heard a mile!   We could now
see, as the space opened behind the rock, another frightful jagged
ledge, on which the rollers were heaving in liquid masses high up a
precipitous rock, and where the channel was not a cable's length
wide, leading into a foaming gloomy inlet, where not even the beams
of the moon could penetrate!   I heard the captain say, in his old decided way,

"'Now for it, Cleveland!   You take the battery, and I'll look out
for the ship!'

"Then, gentlemen," said Hardy, with unusual animation, as he
waved his right arm aloft with an imaginary cutlass swinging over
his head, "came the word 'Fire!'

"Yes, the entire starboard broadside, round shot, grape, and canister, all pointed toward a centre, were delivered with one simultaneous shock—the hurricane a mere cat's-paw in comparison—which
shook the corvette as if she had struck a rock, while the smoke and
sheets of flame spouted out from the cannon, half hiding the black
torrent which gushed forth from so many hoarse throats; and as the
roar of the concussion was taken up in terrible echoes from the lion
on the rock, a peppering volley of musket-balls from the marines on
the poop and forecastle made a barking tenor to the music.

"Meanwhile the helm of the 'Scourge' was hove hard down, and
as she just swirled, by a miracle, clear of the ledge under our lee,
and came up to the wind with the sails slamming and banging hard
enough to send the canvas out of the bolt-ropes, the courses were
clewed up, every thing aloft came down by the run; anchor after
anchor went plunging to the bottom, and before the cables had fairly
begun to fly out of the hawse-holes with their infernal jar and rattle,
high above the sounds of flapping sails, snapping blocks, running
chains, and what not, came another clear order, 'Fire!'

"Then pealed out the port broadside at a helpless, dismasted hulk
within two hundred yards of our beam, rolling like a worm-eaten log
on the top of a ruffled broad roller, going to break, in ten seconds,
on the ledge, whose pointed rocks stood up like black toothed fangs

to grind its prey to atoms! But before the fangs closed upon it our own teeth gave it a shake; and as the breath of our bull-dogs was swept aft by the fresh breeze, we could see the sluggish mass almost rise bodily out of water as it was torn and split by the round iron wedges, the fragments flying up in dark, ragged strips and splinters with squirming ropes around them, looking, in the moonlight, like skeletons of gibbeted pirates tossed, gallows and chains, into the air, and then coming down in dips and splashes into the unforgiving water.

"A minute later, all that was left of the shattered hull fell broadside into the open fangs of the ledge, which ground it with is merciless jaws into toothpicks. But in all the lively music and destruction going on around us—which takes longer to tell than to act—we heard no human voice save one, and that came in a loud, terrified yell amid the crunching roar of the ledge,

"'*O Madre! Madre dolorosa!*'

"This, gentlemen, was the last sound that came from the piratical schooner 'Centipede.'"

P

CHAPTER XXXVIII.

VULTURES AND SHARKS.

"Oh ho! oh ho!　Above! below!
Lightly and brightly they glide and go;
The hungry and keen on the top are leaping,
The lazy and fat in the depths are sleeping!"

"Ah! well-a-day!　What evil looks
Had I from old and young;
Instead of the cross, the albatross
About my neck was hung."

WHEN Hardy had concluded his part of the tale, he stuck the stump of his cigar into the wine-glass of ashes, as if he had no farther use for either, moistened his throat with a bumper of tinta, and almost unconsciously passed his left arm around Harry Darcantel's neck.

Stingo drank two bumpers, as if he had a particularly parched throat; but Paddy Burns and Tom Stewart, strange to relate, never wet their lips, and passed their hands in a careless way across their eyes, as if there were moisture enough there—as, indeed, there was; feeling, as they did, in the founts of their own generous natures, for their dear friend who sat opposite.

Piron's head rested, face downward, on his outspread hands, and a few drops trickled through his close-pressed fingers, but they were not wine.　And as he raised his head and looked around the board, where glowing, sympathizing eyes met his, he said, in a low, subdued voice,

"I trust I may thank Heaven for avenging the murder of our child!"

Even as he uttered these words, his gaze rested on the face of Darcantel; and striking the table with a blow that made the glasses jingle, he started back, as he had done on the frigate's quarter-deck, and exclaimed,

"Great God! can it be possible that that boy was saved from the clutches of the drowned pirate!"

Not so fast, good Monsieur Piron—not so fast.　Your boy was saved, and Captain Brand was not drowned.　So keep quiet for a time, and you shall not only see that bloody pirate, but hear how he departed this life; only keep quiet!

Paddy Burns said, with a violent attempt at indignation, " Wirra, ye spalpeen! is it thinking of old Clinker and his 'arthquake ye are?" While Tom Stewart ejaculated, "Hech, mon! are you for breaking the commodoor's decanters and wine-glasses, in the belief that ye are the eerthquak yersel?" Stingo, who was more calm, and a less excitable Creole, merely murmured, "Commodore, we want to hear more of what took place, and then what became of you for the past sixteen or seventeen years."

"You shall hear more if you are not tired, gentlemen, though I have very little to add to what Hardy has already related of the 'Centipede.' Steward, let the servants turn in; and brew us, yourself, a light jorum of Antigua punch! Now, then," said Commodore Cleveland, "I'm your man!

"After we had scaled the guns on both sides of the 'Scourge,' as Hardy has told you, the captain thought it an unnecessary trouble to lower the boats to pick up the chips floating about the mouth of the channel; and, besides, it would have been a bit dangerous, since the sea was coming in savagely, boiling about the ship, with a very uncertain depth of water around and under us; and, moreover, we had our hands full the best part of the night in reeving new running-gear, bending a new sail or two that had flapped to pieces when every thing was let go by the run in coming to anchor. However, before morning, we were in cruising trim once more, and ready to cut and run in case it was expedient to lose our ground-tackle, and get out of what we afterward learned was the Garotte Gorge. But by sunrise the wind fell away into a flat calm, and with the exception of the long, triple row of rollers heaving in occasionally from seaward, we lay as snug and quiet as could be.

"After breakfast the quarter-boats were lowered, and Hardy took one, and I got in the other, and we pulled in toward the jaws of the channel, between the Lion Rock and the ledge on the opposite side.

"There were still a good many fragments of the wreck, which had escaped the reacting current out to sea, floating about on the water; some of the timbers, too, of the hull were jammed in the black gums of the ledge, shrouded in sea-weed and kelp, as if all had grown there together. Farther on was part of the fore-mast and top-mast, swimming nearly in mid-channel, anchored as it were by one of the shrouds —twisted, perhaps, around a sharp rock below. The top-sail was still fast to the yards, hoisted and sheeted home, and laid in the water transversely to the masts, just as it fell under the raking fire of our first broadside, jerking over the main-top-mast with it.

" A myriad of sea-birds, from Mother Carey's chickens to gulls and cormorants, and even vultures and eagles from the shore, were clustered on the wreck as thick as bees—screaming, croaking, and snapping at each other with their hard beaks and bills, while thousands more were hurrying in from seaward, and either swooped down over the ledge, or tried to find a place on the floating spars.

"The gorge, too, was alive with barracoutas and sharks, leaping out of water, or with their stiff triangular fins cutting just above the surface, and sometimes even grazing the blades of the cutter's oars. I pulled slowly toward the wreck of the fore-mast, and hooked on to the reef-cringle of the fore-top-sail. The birds did not move at our approach, and one old red-eyed vulture snapped on the polished bill of the boat-hook, leaving the marks of his beak in the smooth iron. Down in the clear green depths, too, the water was alive with ravenous fish, and we could see at times hundreds of them with their heads fastened on to some dark object, rolling it, and biting it, and pulling every way, with now and then the glance of a clean-picked bone shining white in the limpid water as the mass was jerked out of our sight.

"The bowmen, however, attracted my attention, and one of them sang out, as he pointed with his finger, 'I say, Mr. Cleveland, here's the captain and his priest lying in the belly of the top-sail!'

"I walked forward, while the men fired a few pistols to scare away the birds, and looked in. There, about a foot below the water, lay one drowned man and half the body of another, who had evidently been cut in twain by a twenty-four pound shot at the stomach, leaving only a few revolting shreds of entrails dangling beneath the carcass. The other corpse was a large, burly, fat man, wrapped in a black cassock, with a knotted rope to confine it at the midriff, and around his thick bare neck was a string of black beads, holding a gold and ebony crucifix, pendent in the water. The eyes of the one with half a body had been picked out by the gulls, but he still possessed a fang-like tusk, sticking through a hare lip under a fringe of wiry mustache, which gave me a tolerable correct idea of his temper even without seeing his eyes. The truck and shivered stump of the main-top-mast, too, with the piratical flag still twisted around it, lay across his chest; but, as we approached, an eagle seized it in his beak, and, tearing it in tattered shreds, flew aloft, with the remains of the parted halliards streaming below his talons.

"The large lump rolling slowly over beside him had the crown of the head shaved, and the mouth and eyes were wide staring open, as if it was chanting forth a misericordia-for his own soul. As I stood gazing at these revolting objects, and while the men were firing pistols and slashing the oars and boat-hooks around to drive away the greedy birds, a huge pelican, unmindful of powder or ash, made one dashing swoop into the sail, and as he came up and spread his broad pinions—nearly as broad as the sail itself—he held in his pouch the crucifix from the padre's neck, and as he slowly flapped his great wings and sailed away, with the beads dropping pit-a-pat-pat on the

glassy surface of the water, a cloud of cormorants, gulls, and vultures took after him to steal his plunder.

"At the same time the sharks—many of them resting their cold,
sharp noses on the very leech of the topsail—waiting like hungry
dogs for a bone, with a thousand more diving and cutting in the
water beneath, at last cut through the canvas belly of the sail, and,
before you could think, the floating corpses were within their serra-
ted jaws. In another moment the bodies rose again to the surface
outside the sail and wreck; then another dash from the monsters,
and a greedy dive and peck from the birds; a few bubbles and shreds
of black threads, and that was the last of those wretches until the
sea shall give up its dead.

"As for Hardy, he pulled higher up the gorge, and examined the
rocks and pools on both sides, but saw nothing living or dead, and
we both returned to the ship."

Had Dick Hardy landed at the flat rock where the eddy swept in
under the Lion's paws, he might have seen the footprint of a man,
with a straw slipper in it; and following the track a few yards farther, he would have passed his sword through a villain lying bleeding in a mangrove thicket; and found, too, in his belt, snugly stowed
away, a lot of gleaming jewels, with a sapphire gem of priceless value
on the finger of his bloody hand. But never mind, Hardy! You
will hear more of that man one of these days, and you will have no
cause for regrets—though he will, perhaps; and, meanwhile, let him
wander in quest of fresh villainies over Spanish South America.

"Well, gentlemen," resumed Commodore Cleveland, "although I
have doubts whether the mangled carcass we saw in the sail was the
captain of that notorious 'Centipede,' yet I felt confident at the time,
and do now, that it was scarcely possible for him or a man of his crew
to have escaped our fire and the water and rocks combined. So that
evening, when the land-wind made, we tripped anchor and sailed
away from the coast of Darien."

"Come, my friends," said Piron, in a low, tremulous voice, rising
as he spoke, "we must not push Cleveland too far to-night, for it is
getting late, you know, and they keep early hours on board men-of-
war."

"No hurry, Piron! I'll talk to you all night, if you have the patience to listen to me. No? Then I'll have the boat manned." He
touched a bell-rope which hung over his head, and the cabin door
opened. "Orderly, my compliments to the officer of the watch, and
desire him to call away the barge."

While some of the gentlemen in the forward cabin left the table,
and stood about in groups chatting till the boat was reported, Piron
put his arm around the commodore's belt, and they moved aft into
the starboard stateroom. Little Mouse was lying sound asleep on

the elegant cot, with all his clothes on, but with a smile on his lips, and dreaming, maybe, of the dear widowed mother he would one of those days make proud of him.

"Cleveland, my old friend, tell me more of that young Darcantel!"

"Hist! Piron, don't wake little Tiny! There's nothing to tell more than he is my adopted nephew, and the son of the gentleman who occupies that stateroom opposite. But when we go out to Escondido I'll tell you about his father, who has led a very adventurous life."

"Well, good-night! You will bring young Darcantel with you, and this little rogue, too, here in the cot. My wife and her sister will be delighted to see you all. Good-night!"

As the "Monongahela's" bell struck eight for midnight, the commodore's guests got in the barge and pulled toward the shore.

At the same time, a light gig, with handsome Harry Darcantel, went alongside the "Rosalie," and Commodore Cleveland turned into his friend's cot opposite, leaving small Mr. Mouse to sleep his dream out till morning; while, as the barge ran up to the landing at Kingston Harbor, and a gold ounce was slipped into the old coxswain's honest paw, what did they all think about? Good-night!

CHAPTER XXXIX.

ESCONDIDO.

"They bore her far to a mountain green,
　To see what mortal never had seen;
　And they seated her high on a purple sward,
　And bade her heed what she saw and heard;
　And note the changes the spirits wrought,
　For now she lived in the land of thought."

"'Twixt Africa and Ind, I'll find him out,
　And force him to restore his purchase back,
　Or drag by the curls to a foul death,
　Cursed as his life."

HIDDEN in a cleft of the hills of Jamaica, fifteen hundred feet above that blue tropical sea below, on the brow of a cool valley, where that bounding stream of white water rushes from the tall peak in the sky in tiny cataracts, till it forms a pool there, held in by the smooth rim of rocks, where the cane-mill is lazily turning its overshot wheel, with the spray flying off in streaming mist, and the happy blacks stacking the sugar-cane in even fagots as they unlade the huge carts with solid wheels cut out of a single drum of a cotton-tree; the six or eight yoke of oxen ahead ruminating under the shade of the tropical foliage, with never a switch to their tails; while the lively young sea-breeze comes flurrying up the valley, whistling among the coffee bushes below, bending the standing cane on the slopes, rattling the tamarinds, cocoa-nuts, and plantains, and then climbing with noisy wings up the mountain, is lost with a whirl in the heavy cloud which obscures the lofty peak.

Below the mill, where the mule-path crosses the foaming torrent by the shaky bridge, which stands on cocoa-nut stilts, and never yet has been thrown down by an earthquake, nestling under a precipitous crag, stood the mountain seat of Escondido. Vines and parasitical plants, mingled with scarlet creeping geraniums, made a living wall of dewy green and red on the face of the hoary rock, falling over here and there at some projecting acclivity in leafy torrents, and then forming a glowing green cornice along the topmost edges of the height.

The buildings stood on a flat esplanade below, looking down the gorge as from the apex of a triangle, and taking in the overseer's houses on the plantations, with their cone-shaped roofs, the fields of cane and coffee groves, the cataract between, down to the white snowy beach at the sea-shore, and the blue water crested by waves as far as the sight could reach.

The main house was square—standing on stilts, too, like the shaky bridge—the lower part fenced in by straight bamboos, of one story, with a broad roomy veranda going all round, where half a dozen grass hammocks were slung between the windows which opened into the dwelling. A great airy saloon and dining-room faced the valley, while six or eight cool bedchambers looked out from the rear up at the green wall of the precipice, and down on the sparkling stream of the mill.

But there were no loopholes for musketry, nor vaults and dungeons.

The sun had long passed the tall peaks of the blue mountains above, and the shadows had fallen down the valley until even the patch of white pebbly cove at the shore had become dim; and no sounds were heard save the rustling of the sea-breeze, the splash of the torrent as it fell off from the rickety old wheel of the cane-mill, mingled with the shrill cries and songs of the negroes as they unloaded the carts.

Yes; but there *were* other sounds—the low, sweet tones of women's voices—inside the villa of Escondido. Two lovely matrons were sitting within that lofty saloon, hand clasped in hand, and gazing with glowing pride upon a lovely girl, who waved lithe as a lily on its stem before them.

It is about seventeen years since we last saw this charming trio. And now look at them, old bachelors, and tell me if, while old Time has been scraping the hair off your own selfish heads, and pinching the noses, too, of the ancient maids beside you, has not the scything old wretch spared these lovely matrons? Look at their rounded forms, those soft dimpled cheeks, and those bands of brown tresses, kissing the pear-shaped ears before they are looped up in one magnificent knot of satin at the back of the head. Look at them, you miserable old procrastinators, and then kneel down before the ancient damsels you have sneered at, even if they have the pelican gout and a crow's-foot at the corners of their eyes! They are better than you are, any day; so bear a hand, send for the parson—and now stand back.

But come here, my young gallants, and take a peep at that Bordelaise demoiselle standing before those fair matrons. Strange to say, she is nearly a blonde, with large blue eyes, so very blue that—fringed with lashes that cast a shade over the cheek—they seem almost black. Then, too, that low, pure forehead, with great plaits of hair going round and round her elegant head like a golden turban, and thin hoops of rings quivering in the pearl-tipped ears. Tall and waving in figure, as maidens are; with slim, arched feet, dimpled at the ankle; and round, tapering fingers too, with a wrist so plump and soft that no manacles of bracelets could press it without slipping off the ivory hand. Dressed she was in a light mousseline, coyly cowering in loose folds around her budding bosom to the slender waist, where, clasped by a simple buckle of mother-o'-pearl, it fell flowing in gauzy, floating waves to her feet. Look at her, my gallants, for she is Rosalie!

"They are coming to-day, my aunt; and Uncle Jules says that our dear old Captain Blunt has just arrived at Kingston, and is coming with them."

"What else, my daughter?"

The girl held a letter before her face, maybe to hide a little blush which suffused her cheeks.

"Why, mamma, he writes that the spring-cart, with Banou, was to start overnight with the ' traps'—that means trunks, I suppose— and that—"

"What, Rosalie?"

"That there is a handsome young officer, the nephew of Commodore Cleveland—*merci*, mamma! some of Uncle Jules's nonsense!"

No such great nonsense, after all, mademoiselle, when your uncle Piron tells you to keep that fluttering little heart safe within your bodice, for there are thieves in blue jackets in the island of Jamaica. Strange, too, as she spoke—with her animated face, large blue eyes, and graceful, wavy figure—how much she resembled both those lovely women, with their darker coloring, who sat smiling sweetly upon her.

"Oh! here comes Uncle Banou. Well, my good Banou, what news of your master?" said Madame Piron, as she put out her hand to the black, who raised it respectfully to his lips.

"He will be here with his friends at sunset, eh! And Mademoiselle Rosalie must place the gentlemen's things in their rooms, and see that the billiard-house has some cots made ready in it."

"Nothing more?"

"No, madame."

"*Allons!* Rosalie, we have no time to lose."

Winding through the mazes of the tropical forest, over the broken stony road, leading through a brilliant labyrinth of wild fig and acacia, plume-like palms, white shafts of silk and cotton, and lance-wood, mahogany, and ebony, parasitical plants in green and red, with endless varieties of gay flowers strung and laced in superb festoons on trunk and branch; singing birds and paroquets making the forest alive; while, mingled with the delicious fragrance of orange-blossoms, cinnamon, and pimento, the fresh breeze wheeled through clump and leaf, changing the hues of plant and flower from white to crimson, green, purple, and gold, as Nature painted them in gorgeous dyes.

Through this brilliant vegetation, along the uneven road, came the sound of horses' feet, with hearty shouts and laughter; and presently appeared a cavalcade, mounted on mules and horses, all making the forest ring with merriment.

Ahead came Tom Stewart, on a small, sure-footed pony; and beside him Mr. Tiny Mouse, reefer, on a high mule, with a scrubbingbrush mane, looking like a fly pennant at the mast-head of the frigate, kicking his little heels into the old mule, as if that mule minded it even so much as to shake his long ears! Then straggling in the centre were Darcantel, Stingo, and Paddy Burns; and behind them came a tall, muscular man, on a mettled barb, which he controlled by a touch of his little finger. And at his side, on the most diminutive of the donkey breed, with feet touching the ground, clung stout Jacob Blunt, the sailor, in a more dreadful trepidation than he had ever known on board his old teak-built brig, lying there in the Roads of Kingston; while the rear was brought up by Piron and Commodore Cleveland.

"Now, you little madcap, look sharp when we turn the curve of the mountain, and you'll catch a peep at Escondido; and don't you pinch that old mule again on her back, or she'll pitch you up into that silk cotton-tree."

"If it pleases Providence to restore me safely to my dear old 'Martha Blunt,' I'll take my davy never to sit astride of any d— brute on four legs again!" This mild vow came from the lips of Jacob Blunt, and he honestly meant every word he said.

"Give us another jolly song, Stingo; it will keep your throat clear for the claret."

"For the sake of my old timbers, sir, and as you vally my wife's blessing, don't sing! There, you infarnal beast, you've yawed sharp up to this ere bush, and put my starboard glim out forever! I say, Don Spanisher, don't sing—*I'm* going fast enough!" shouted the poor skipper, as he passed his paws around the little brute's neck, with his hat over his eyes.

"Colonel," said Burns, as he reined up, and gave the perverse little donkey a cut with his whip, which elicited another hoarse roar from the old sailor as the animal half doubled himself up, and then ambled away like a yawl in a short sea, until he came up to the people ahead, when he stood stock-still and brayed maliciously, "have you another cigar, colonel? Thankee! Fine scenery this about here —never visited Jamaica before? Ye have been off the island, eh? It's a nate little spot Piron has there, that it is; and the whole of us will be mighty sorry to lose him. Is he going to lave? Yes, he is; and, what is worse, he is going to take his swate wife and her sister.

Is the sister handsome? Begorra! handsome? Why, man, she's a beauty! And didn't I crack the elbow-joint of that ugly, abusive divil, Peter Growler, for saying he had seen a gray hair in her head, when I know it was only a loose thread from her lace cap—and me in love with her all the time. Bad luck to him! he's never fired a pistol since."

Here Paddy Burns's small eyes twinkled as he slowly raised the stock of his riding-whip at a slender lance-wood-tree about twelve yards off, and gave the lash a sharp crack.

The person on the spirited barb almost unconsciously put his right hand in his pocket.

Take care, Paddy Burns; the colonel has a cool hand and a colder eye, and has made a study of pistols—cannon and swivels too, perhaps. Knows the cutlass exercise as well, and has had considerable experience in bullets, knives, and ropes. Has murdered women—lots of them. Wouldn't stick at killing a child with a junk bottle. And as for men—pshaw! Keep a bright look-out, Paddy. Why, he'd drown your mother if you had a sister to love. For didn't he drag his own old father and mother down to a dishonored grave? and do you think, you brave, honest little Irishman, that he would sleep a wink the less sound for putting you to death? Bah! man. Shoot all the game you spring, but don't waste powder on a tiger or a shark. You would like to take a mutual shot with him, though? Of course you would—who doubts it? But then, gentlemen fight gentlemen; and this colonel at your elbow is a scoundrel, miscreant, villain, assassin, and—pirate! So you can't take a crack at him, Paddy Burns.

CHAPTER XL.

PAUL DARCANTEL.

"From the strong will, and the endeavor,
That forever
Wrestles with the tide of fate;
From the wrecks of hope far scattered,
Tempest shattered,
Floating waste and desolate."

"WELL, Piron, as I have told you, after the peace was made in 1815, I had command of a brig, and took a cruise on the coast of Brazil. After that I was appointed to a thirty-six gun frigate—the old 'Blazer'—and went, for three years, to the East Indies, and round home by the Pacific. When we were paid off I made a tour in Europe with that boy's father, Dr. Darcantel, and—"

"But you promised to tell me, Cleveland, something about him."

"Nothing easier; and, if we have half an hour before we get to Escondido, I will give you all I know, in a general way, of his history. Yes? Well, then, Darcantel is descended from one of the oldest and best Creole families in our State of Louisiana, and the plantations of my family and his father were contiguous to each other on the Mississippi, some leagues up the coast above New Orleans. We had the same tutor when we were children, and we grew up from infancy to boyhood together. He was passionate and ungovernable even as a child; but as he was the heir to a large estate, and his father dead, his weak mother humored and allowed no one to curb him. I myself, one of a numerous family, was put in the navy, and I went away on cruise after cruise, and did not get home again to the old plantation for full seven years. I was a man then, had seen some active service, and I held a commission as a lieutenant in the navy.

"In the mean while, Paul Darcantel, who had taken, at the time I left, a strong fancy for medicine and surgery, had been sent to France to begin his studies. How he applied himself we do not know; but with a large letter of credit he spent a great deal of money; and we heard that, with great talents and wonderful skill in his profession, he was yet unfitted for close application, and plunged madly into the vortex of dissipation around him. I heard, too—or at least my brothers told me—that his extravagances had seriously impaired his

fortune, and that his duels had been so numerous and desperate as
to make his name dreaded even in Paris. On one occasion, at a café,
he had cut a bullying hussar's head clean off with his own sabre for
knocking a woman down; and in another duel, where he had detected a French count cheating him at cards, he shot his nose off for
a bet. With this unenviable reputation, and at the urgent solicita-
tions of his agent, after years of absence he returned to his ancestral
home. We met as of old—it was Paul and Henry—and though still
the same restive, hot-headed spirit as he had ever been, he yet always
listened patiently to what I said, and I could, in a manner, control
him. He paid very little attention to his property, however, and
when he did go to the city to consult with his factor or trustee, he
got into some wild frolic, duel, and scrape, and came back worn out
with fatigue and dissipation. He was a fine, stern-looking youth in
those days, with great muscular power, which, even with the endu-
rance put upon it by gaming and drinking, seemed not to be lessened.

"After one of these visits to New Orleans, where his long-forbear-
ing agents had at last awakened him to a bitter sense of his delin-
quencies, and when mortgage upon mortgage were laid with all their
shocking truth before him, he returned and came to me. With all
his vices and faults, he was truthful and generous. He told me all,
and how he would try to do better, and soothe the declining years
of his too indulgent mother.

"I always had great faith in the companion almost of my cradle,
and I loved him, I think, better than my own brothers. Well, he
spread all his affairs before me, and in my little den of an outhouse
on the plantation we both went systematically over the papers.
We were two days and nights at the business; and when, at last, I
showed him that he would still, with a little prudent economy, have
a fair income, and eventually, perhaps, redeem his hereditary property, he burst out in a wild yell of delight, and hugged me in his arms.
When he had put away the papers, I said,

"'Paul, you know I am engaged to be married, and I have not
seen my sweetheart for two whole days; she has a sister, too, prettier than my Fifine, whom you have never seen since we were boys
together. Come, will you go with me? We can pull ourselves
across the river.'

"He hesitated; and it would have been, perhaps, better had he
refused to accompany me, for dreadful misery came of it."

The commodore gave a deep sigh, and touched his horse with the
spur.

"I don't know, though, Piron; there is a fate marked out for us
all, and we should not exclaim against the decrees of Providence.
Paul went with me across the river. There, on the bank, was a
little bower of an old French-built stone house, where dwelt the last

of a line of French nobility who dated back to the days of Charlemagne. It was an impoverished family, consisting of a reckless brother and two sisters, who, with a few acres of sugar-cane and some old faithful servants, managed to make both ends meet, and to support the establishment in a certain air of elegance and comfort to which they had been accustomed. They were of a proud and haughty race—the brother a disdainful and imperious gentleman, smarting and brooding over the reverses of his family, and rarely visiting his neighbors. His sisters—and they were twins—were trustful, happy girls, and Josephine had been my childish love."

Here Cleveland bent over his saddle-bow, and if the quiet old horse he bestrode believed the large drops which fell upon his sleek neck came from the clouds, or the drooping foliage of the forest, that animal was never more deceived in his quadruped life. We know that fact, for it stands upon the angelic record.

"Well, my dear Piron, as we entered the little saloon where Fifine was seated at the piano, playing the sweet airs she had sung to me when a little bit of a girl, and her beautiful sister bending over a table near, absorbed in a book, while the candles under the glass shades lighted up her dark passionate eyes and brunette complexion, Paul approached her. It was not love at first sight, because they had played together when children; but it was such a love as only begins and dies with man or woman. The brother came in soon afterward, but there was no love exchanged between him and Paul, and they met in a manner which seemed to revive the early dislike they had entertained one toward the other in boyhood.

"So the time passed, and in the course of a few months Josephine and I were married, and our home was made on my own old place. Still, night by night, in storm, calm, or freshet, Paul pulled himself in a skiff across that mighty river, and we could see the lights shining to a late hour in the little bower. He had changed a great deal, for he loved with the whole force of his fiery and impetuous nature. Pauline loved too, though still she feared him. The brother, however, bitterly opposed their union, and stormy scenes arose. Josephine and I did all we could to put matters on a happy footing, but Jacques, the brother, grew more determined as his sister refused to cast off her lover, till at last his feeling against him broke out into open scornful insult; and though Paul still persisted in seeing Pauline, yet we feared that the impetuous spirits of the two men would, at any moment, burst out into open violence.

"Darcantel, however, controlled himself, avoided as much as possible any altercations with Jacques, applied himself to the duties of his plantation, and always promised me that he would wait and see if time would not induce the brother to give his consent to the marriage. Meanwhile Paul's mother died. A year passed. Fifine gave

me a little boy, who was called after me, and then I went again to
sea. Nearly three years later I returned, and the very night before
I reached the plantation a dreadful tragedy had occurred. I might,
perhaps, have prevented it had I been there, but it was ordered otherwise.

"It seems that two days previously Jacques wrote to Paul—I saw
the letter—and it was something painful to read; for he not only re-
capitulated his vices and follies, but he taxed him with being a ruined
gambler, who had brought his mother in sorrow to the grave, and
ended by swearing, in the most solemn manner, that if he dared again
to speak to his sister or darken their doors, he would shoot him like
a dog!

"That evening, as usual, the skiff pursued its way across the river,
and late at night when it returned there was a fluttering white dress
in the stern. Scarcely, however, had the skiff left the bank than a
boat shoved out from the other side manned by four negroes, and
came swiftly over in pursuit. What afterward transpired I heard
from an old married couple of servants who had passed their lives
with the family. It appears that Paul, with Pauline in his arms, had
barely reached the hall of the great house, and was giving orders to
close the doors, when Jacques rushed in with a naked rapier in one
hand and a pistol in the other. Paul adjured him, by all he held sacred, not to attack him, as his blood was up, and, unarmed as he was,
he would do him a mischief. Pauline, too, implored him by a sister's
love to desist; but seeing him still advance, as she partially shielded
Paul, she told him that the man she loved was her husband.

"Blinded with haughty rage, this last admission rendered him ungovernable, and he lunged with all his force at Darcantel. Paul par-
ried his rapid passes, though receiving some sharp thrusts in his arm
and shoulder, and still supporting his drooping, terrified wife on his
left arm till, by a quick spring, he got within Jacques's guard, and,
seizing him by the wrist, wrenched the weapon from his grasp. This
was enough to make the brother totally insane by passion from baffled revenge, when he leveled his pistol and fired. There was a faint
cry with the report, and a groan from Jacques as the sword went
through his body and heart, till the hilt struck hard against his ribs
as he fell, a dead man, on the marble pavement. But the bullet from
his pistol had pierced the fair forehead of his sister, and she lay a
bridal corpse in her husband's arms. It was horrible.

"I spare you all the afflicting details, Piron, and will only add that
Paul left the plantation that night, and when I got home I found an
envelope post-marked 'New Orleans,' inclosing a paper, which con-
stituted me his sole executor, and leaving our little boy his heir. I
had but a short leave of a month, and duty called me again away.
It was on the anniversary of the day the tragedy occurred, after an-

other long interval of four years in the 'Scourge,' that I again returned, and then there was wailing and moaning in my own dwelling. My poor Josephine had never recovered from the shock; she drooped away like a lily, her little boy by her side, and both died during my absence."

What makes the strong man's eyelids quiver and voice tremble—those eyes that have looked calmly on death and carnage in every shape, with his deep, calm voice cheering on the men to battle at his side? Ah!

"It was midnight, and I walked out to the little grave-yard where my fathers had been buried, and bending my steps to a cluster of magnolias on a little mound by itself, I—I—a—kneeled down beside the sod where reposed all I had loved on earth! I do not know how long I remained there, but presently I heard a groan near by, and a tall man rose up from where he had been stretched, face downward, on the ground, and I beheld Paul Darcantel! I could hardly recognize him at first, for he seemed fifty years older than when we had last parted.

"'Cleveland,' he said, in a hollow, choking voice, 'forgive me! I am a changed, and, I trust, a better man. I have been drawn to this holy spot by the same errand which brought you hither, and though I did not expect to meet you, yet I am glad of it now. Speak, and say you forgive me, and you will shed a ray of hope and salvation into the heart of one who will suffer unto the end! Speak!'

"Old memories crowded around me, and I saw before me the child in the cradle, and with our arms round each other's necks as we played together. I forgot, for the moment, the sisters lying there —bride, mother, and baby-boy. The magnolias bowed their white flowers in the light of the waning moon, and we fell again into each other's arms.

"After a time he said, 'My only friend, I have brought home with me a little helpless boy; he is named Henry, after you, and will take the place of the lost little one lying here. Whoever of us survives shall inherit that estate. Come with me and look at him!'

"He led me to the other mound, and there, beside the tree, a beautiful child lay calmly sleeping, wrapped in a sailor's jacket, with his curls escaping from a straw hat, and the head resting on one arm on the grave beneath him.

"'Be good to him,' Paul went on, 'for the sake of those we have lost ourselves! His mother's name was Rosalie.'

"He stooped down as he said this, and, raising the boy in his arms, he kissed him passionately, and then put him gently in mine. 'Let him kneel sometimes at this grave, my friend, and pray for me.'

"In another moment Paul Darcantel had gone. The little fellow partly woke, and put his arms affectionately around my neck, and whispered 'Mamma! mamma!' That dashing, brave young fellow ahead there was once that boy.

"Well, I took the child to the house, where my good mother and sisters went wild over him, and there he passed a happy boyhood. Years went by, and he grew apace, the pride and delight of us all; and as he evinced the greatest fondness for me and the accounts I gave him of my life at sea, I had him appointed a reefer in the navy. Since that he has seen a great deal of service; been distinguished in action; and, on shipboard as well as on shore, liked and respected by all who know him.

"In the mean while his father went away, nobody knew whither, for years and years. He wrote to me, however, and to his son, from all parts of the world; and when I made the tour in Europe I spoke about, Darcantel was my companion. But while there he passed a retired life, never went into society, but visited every hospital in every sea-port from the Mediterranean to Aberdeen in Scotland; for he is not only a surgeon, as I have reason to know, of wonderful skill, but a thorough-bred seaman too; and when he has been with me on board ship there is no one whose opinion of the weather, or other nautical matters, do I place greater reliance on. I could tell you of half a dozen times when his advice to me has saved serious damage. And during all these years Darcantel's estates, under the careful supervision of my eldest brother, have been redeemed from their load of debt, and now he enjoys a noble income—or, rather, he spends nothing on himself, but devotes it to widows and orphans, and sick or worn-out sailors.

"In the seventeen years which have gone by since he brought his child to me he has made several visits of a month or two's duration to the plantations, but only when Henry was on leave from duty. Then it was a pleasant sight to see them both together, and the touching air of affection which bound the youth to his father. Henry, from a child, often went and prayed beside the grave under the magnolias, and to this day he believes that his own mother lies buried there. Perhaps it is as well that he should cherish this early belief; for I may tell you in confidence, Piron, that we believe there at home that he is the illegitimate offspring of some erring passion of Darcantel, though none of us have ever learned it positively from his father's lips. He is not a person to be questioned by any one, not even by me; and as he seems anxious to throw a thick veil over the past, we never venture to draw it aside.

"When, however, I was appointed to my present command, Darcantel desired to sail with me, and see the West India Islands, which he had not visited for an age. I was only too happy to have him, especially as Harry there—whom I love like a father—was named to the little schooner he had cut out in Africa on his last cruise, and ordered to join my squadron. But whenever we get into port his father goes quietly on shore; passes his time, I think, among the sailors of the foreign shipping, spending money freely among the deserving, and again coming back in his calm, stern way. He told me, however, Piron, yesterday, that perhaps he might accept your kind invitation to come up here, though not for some days. By George!" said the commodore, "that must be Escondido!"

Piron sighed as if a pleasant dream had vanished.

CHAPTER XLI.

INSTINCT AND WONDER.

" ' Ho ! sailor of the sea !
   How's my boy—my boy ?'
  ' What's your boy's name, good wife,
    And in what good ship sailed he ?' "

" Through the night, through the night,
  In the saddest unrest,
Wrapped in white, all in white,
  With her babe on her breast,
Walks the mother so pale,
Staring out on the gale,
    Through the night !"

As the cavalcade trotted round the curve of the peak, and then walked the cattle down the steep zigzag road of the beautiful valley, the commodore said, "But, Piron, tell me who that large man is with the black hair and blue eyes."

" Why, Cleveland, all I know of him is that he landed at Kingston in a vessel from the Isthmus of Panama, and is going to Cuba on his way to England. He came to me, hearing that I was the consignee of old Blunt's older brig, bound to New Orleans, and so home, to know if he could be dropped at St. Jago, where he has some property or debts to collect; and since the old skipper has no objection, he has taken passage in the brig when she goes with me and my family. I have since met him—he calls himself Colonel Lawton—at dinners of our set, and he seems to be an Englishman or Scotchman. Tom Stewart thinks the latter from his accent, and for his liking for snuff; but Paddy Burns differs, and believes he don't like snuff, but only takes it to show his splendid box. Any way, he speaks all languages, Spanish, French, Italian, and English, and can talk slang in them all like a native. He has served, too, from his own account, with Bolivar there on the Spanish Main; and he was with Cochrane in that desperate affair of cutting out the 'Esmeralda' in Callao Bay. A very amusing, entertaining vagabond he is, and I asked him to join us to make the acquaintance of my people on our last frolic to the valley; but, somehow, I am rather sorry that I gave him a passage with us in the brig, for I don't altogether like his looks."

"Neither do I, Piron; his hair is too black for his light blue eyes. However, we must make the most of him."

Over the shaky bridge of the torrent, where Jacob Blunt prayed earnestly for Martha Blunt, and d—d his donkey as if he had never rocked on water before; Mr. Mouse, with a last tiny kick on the saddle-flaps of his lofty mule, tumbled off; Colonel Lawton swinging himself from the saddle of his barb as if he had been part of him; Tom Stewart, Paddy Burns, and Don Stingo sliding off any way; Harry Darcantel trying to descend in fine style, and failing miserably; Piron and the commodore doing the thing leisurely; Jacob Blunt pulled off bodily; while the laughing blacks took the beasts and led them away.

There were three pair of eyes that watched all this grace and clumsiness from the windows of the saloon. Two pair of dark ones smiled, and the pair of blue opened until they seemed like azure globes, and then they closed until the fringe of chestnut lashes nearly hid them from sight.

"Colonel Lawton, do me the favor to follow my old friend Banon—you too, Captain Jacob, and Lieutenant Darcantel and Mr. Mouse; Paddy Burns and Stingo, here, will show you your quarters in the old billiard-room. Come, commodore, the rest of us will find quarters in the casa."

An hour later the saloon and sala were all alight, and the sashes of the jalousies closed, for it was cool at times up there at Escondido. There, too, stood the party of gentlemen, Mr. Mouse being a prominent figure in the background. Then came a rustling of robes, and as the great folding doors swung open, the three ladies lit up the saloon in a halo of loveliness with brighter rays than were shed from the wax-lights in the chandelier. Two fair hands were placed in those of Cleveland, and the look which accompanied went back to the happy morning on the old brig's deck, away off there to sea.

"Oh, monsieur, I can not say how glad I am to see you once more! Let me present you to my sister, Madame Nathalie Delonde, and *our* daughter. Ah! my dear Captain Blunt, both your children before you again, and you have come to take us away."

"Colonel Lawton, *ma chère*," said Piron.

"And, mesdames," said the commodore, "let me also present my nephew, Lieutenant Darcantel, and Mr. Mouse."

What caused that woman to start as the girl took the tiny reefer by the hand, and impulsively clasped those white hands together, while her heart beat in yearning throbs, and her bosom rose and fell like billows by the shore? Why did she then raise one hand to her fair neck, and, as if in a dream, feel for the golden links of the chain, with the other hand pressed to her panting heart for the locket which once reposed there? How was it that, bewildered by a mother's instinct, she gazed at the youth before her, and then turned her eyes hopelessly around in search of her husband in the crowd?

"Yes, madame. This is my nephew, Henry Darcantel."

"Ah! Henri! Excuse me, *monsieur*. I am charmed to see you!"

Why, now, did the touch of his hand make her heart beat faster, and send a thrill of joy through her frame? Only be a little calm, madame, for a while longer, and don't be sad and ponder all night, like your good Jules Piron does habitually. Wait; Jules will tell you all *he* knows when you are alone to-night.

The doors of the sala were thrown open. The broad pennant leading with Madame Rosalie; the military chieftain marching beside Madame Nathalie, much to the animosity of Paddy Burns. Then Mr. Mouse convoying mademoiselle, to the infinite disgust of the commander of the "Rosalie," one-gun schooner, formerly the "Perdita." But what made that old negro in spotless white, standing at the door, jerk his head back and open his great eyes till there was no black left in them? And why did he blunder about the table afterward, and pour wine over the colonel's richly-laced coat, while staring like an ogre at the young blue-jacket opposite? That old Banou, perhaps, did not like to see his young mistress too much attended to by every gay scamp who came near her. Oh no; of course not. But then, if that brawny negro in white had only known over whose arm and mutilated hand he was pouring light wine in his abstraction, he would have crammed that heavy cut decanter in powdered glass splinters down the chieftain's throat. There would have been claret of a different color spilled then—quantities of it. You needn't feel in your pockets, colonel, or look round the sala to see if perchance there is a green silk rope squirming from the ceiling. We don't keep any of those pretty things out at Escondido. So go on with your dinner, you cold-eyed scoundrel, and tell all the lies you can to that lovely woman at your elbow; how you wanted to save Bolivar's life, and it was saved without you. Don't forget, either, to tell her how that patriot had you drummed out of his army, suspecting you of having assassinated the officer near you in the confusion of battle, and robbing him of his watch to replace the one presented to you by the captain general. Paddy Burns is watching you, Colonel Lawton, and that whole-souled little Irishman is not the man to be trifled with. Now remove the covers. But take care, Banou— you nearly twitched off the military gentleman's hair. Tom Stewart saw it, and he noticed, too, a broad red seam, like the track of a musket bullet—honorable wound, no doubt—under your black glossy wig.

Mr. Mouse had fallen desperately in love with the perfumed damsel beside him, and he knew she was up to her rose-tipped ears in love with him, oh! fifty fathoms deep; but his mother liked girls, and he would leave her half-pay! Still he didn't forget his adoration for the roast duck; and he slyly swigged some Madeira too, with a wary eye on the broad pennant through the flowers of the épergne. Talked, too, did that reefer—ay, chattered—and said that the quiet young officer on her left was very well liked in the steerage, and commanded a pretty little craft named the "Rosalie." She knew that before, did she? Well, his father was a cold, stern man, but he was kind and generous, and had been very good to his poor mother, God bless him!

Commodore Cleveland talked in a low tone, all through the dinner, to the lady who did not eat at the head of the table, but who occasionally rested her white hand, with a trustful reliance, on the great tanned-leather paw of Jacob Blunt, that honest mariner not wishing to talk to any body, man or woman. That ancient mariner was mentally cursing donkeys; speculating how he should get back to the "Martha Blunt" brig, in Kingston harbor; and praying for Martha Blunt, wife, riding at single anchor near Plymouth beach. Piron took wine with every body, said a word or two all around the table, and talked to Tom Stewart about certain business matters connected with the plantation when he had gone.

Then came the last course, and the dessert of delicious fruits, which quite stopped Mr. Mouse's mouth, and even his palpitating heart ceased beating; while Mademoiselle Rosalie nibbled some lady-finger biscuit, and bent her graceful head to listen to the music of the earnest lips beside her.

We told you, miss, how it would be; and, in spite of the warning, there you are—the color coming and going over your girlish cheeks, and never saying a word! "What a couple that would make!" thought Madame Nathalie. And what a resemblance in expression there is between them—he with his dark hair and eyes, and she fair and blue. Be careful, my sweet Rosalie! And so thought her sister and her sister's husband; Stingo, too, old Banou, and every one save Tiny Mouse, who had no rivals but Rat, Beaver, and Martin, and he could take the wind out of their sails any day.

The party of ladies rose from the table, and leaving the men—all except the captain of the "Rosalie" and Mr. Mouse, who would have remained had he not seen a shake of the broad pennant's finger—went into the saloon. Then there was a brilliant prelude on the piano, a touch of a guitar by stronger fingers, an air from an opera, a song or two, much conversation—while Reefer Mouse slept on the sofa—and coffee. Then it was late; every one was fatigued, *bon soirs* were said, and the party—coffee and all—separated.

CHAPTER XLII.

TRUTH AND TERROR.

> "In slumbers of midnight the sailor-boy lay,
>   His hammock swung loose at the sport of the wind;
> But watch-worn and weary, his cares flew away,
>   * And visions of happiness danced o'er his mind."

> "And how the sprites of injured men
>   Shriek upward from the sod;
> Ay! how the ghostly hand will point
>   To show the burial clod;
> And unknown facts of guilty acts
>   Are seen in dreams from God!"

In a great square room, standing, as usual, on cocoa-nut stilts, which had once been used for a billiard-room, were half a dozen iron-framed cots, ranged along the walls, in which some of the Escondido's guests were to bivouac. Every thing, however, was tidy and comfortable; snow-white bedclothes and gauze musquito nets, lots of napkins and ewers, and things for bathing behind a screen of dimity curtains; and not forgetting a large table—vice the billiard-table—in the centre, on which stood plenty of sugar and limes, cinnamon and nutmeg, bottles and flasks, red and white, and—very little water, in jugs.

The occupants of this bivouac had turned in, and the lights had been doused. Conversation, however, was kept up, especially by the thin little voice of Mr. Mouse, who, having enjoyed a nap in the early evening, and having been danced and tumbled about on the trip to the lodge by Harry Darcantel, who was in tiptop condition, the reefer was as wide awake as a blackfish. Don Stingo chanted a few convivial airs and snored; so did Jacob Blunt, with a spluttering groan intermixed; and Paddy Burns fell off into a doze, saying blasphemous words addressed to the world at large, with a mutter against the military, hoping he might look at a Bolivian patriot edgewise with a friend and companion of his, Mr. Joe Manton, at his side; he would put an end to any more lies about charges of cavalry, and cutting out frigates in Callao Bay. That Paddy Burns would, though he didn't wear a wig and a large sapphire on the only finger he had left on his left hand, and with a diamond snuff-box, too! Presented to you by a connection of your family, was it? Take a pinch out of it? D— him, no! Begorra, the snuff is not Lundy Foot's, and the box is brass, sir, brass!

"I say, Mouse, keep quiet, will you, and let me go to sleep!" Harry Darcantel did not think of going to sleep; that was a fib he told the reefer; he wanted merely to shut his eyes and dream of— you know who—a tall, graceful girl with blue eyes and light hair, who looked at him once or twice such looks that there was no sleep for him for ever so long. What did she say? Why, she never opened her pouting lips to show those even pearly teeth. She only looked out of those soft blue eyes. That was all!

"Mr. Darcantel, I think of getting married."

"The d— you do! And who to, pray?"

"Why," said Mr. Mouse, as he rolled over and kicked the sheet off his slate-pencil built legs, "I haven't made up my mind; but do you know that that pretty girl up there at the big house has taken quite a fancy to me, and when you were presented to her mother she gave me *such* a squeeze of the hand! Oh my!"

Here Mr. Mouse's narrative was cut short by a pillow hitting him plump on the mouth, clean through his musquito net.

"Very charming young lady, Mr. Mouse," said a quiet voice, in a cool tone, on the other side of him; "she did seem to take a violent fancy to you."

Mr. Mouse rolled over, and then, sitting up in his cot, replied, "Yes, sir! and that was her mother sitting by you when the big nigger in white capsized the wine over your sleeve, and nearly pulled your a—hair off."

Look out, Mr. Mouse! If that man there beside you once gives a twitch at your curls, he'll pull something more than hair—perhaps a little scalp with it!

"Oh!" was the sound that came back.

"Yes, sir; and the other beautiful lady next the commodore is her sister. She had a son just mademoiselle's age, who was murdered by pirates off Jamaica ever so many years ago, and Commodore Cleveland chased them in a ship he was first lieutenant of—my father commanded the ship—she was the old 'Scourge.'"

"Hold your tongue!" came from the cot where the spare pillow was thrown from.

"Ho!" said the military chieftain; but if the room had not been so dark, the way his eyes opened and emitted an icy glare of surprise would have made Tiny Mouse shiver with cold.

"Oh dear, yes, colonel, I heard the commodore tell all about it the other night on board the frigate. He thought I was asleep, but I kept awake through the best part of it."

"The best part of it?"

"Why, sir, how an old one-eyed Spaniard deceived my father, and

sent him on a fool's errand from St. Jago down to the Isle of Pines, and afterward how the 'Scourge' chased the piratical schooner in a hurricane for ever so long, clear away to the coast of Darien, where they blew her out of water, and killed every scoundrel on board!"

Not every one, Mr. Mouse. There is the very greatest of those scoundrels grinding his teeth and glaring your way at your elbow.

"What was the name of that cape, Darcantel, where the schooner was destroyed? No, I won't be quiet; the colonel wants to hear all about it. There's a good fellow, tell me!"

"Garotte Cape."

The listener slowly raised the mutilated hand, and put the finger with the sapphire ring to his throat, evidently not liking the name of that cape, for it caused a choking sensation to utter it—"Ho! Cape Garotte!"

"Yes, sir; and Darcantel's father here once chartered a vessel, and went all the way down there to explore the place, and was gone fifteen months! Wasn't he, Darky?" said the boy, familiarly.

"Mouse, I tell you what it is, if you don't shut up that little flytrap of yours, I'll make Rat lick you when you go on board!"

"Rat lick me?" said Tiny, as he jumped straight up in the cot; "I gave him and Martin a black eye apiece only on our last boat-duty day for saying your father, the doctor, had killed his brother-in-law in a duel!"

"Hush, my dear little fellow! you did a very foolish thing. There, say no more on that subject; it gives me pain, my Tiny. So talk on as much as you like."

"My dear friend," exclaimed the lad, in a broken voice; as he plunged through his net and put his arms around Darcantel, "I wouldn't grieve you for the world; but do you suppose, little as I am, that I wouldn't fight for the doctor, who is so kind to me, and has done so much for my poor dear sweet mother?"

Here there was a sob as he wound his arms closer round his friend's neck, and cried like a child, as he was.

"Well, never mind, Tiny; go to sleep, now! I am not angry. There, turn in!"

"I won't speak another word to-night, Harry, for any soul breathing—little fool that I am!"

"I beg your pardon, monsieur," said the colonel, in French, with a slight quiver on his tongue, "but did your father really go all the way down to Darien out of mere curiosity?"

"Yes, sir, he did go there to see if by any chance one of the pirates had escaped; and he traveled, too, a good deal about among the Indians, making inquiries."

"Ho! and did he pick up any information there?"

"Why, sir, I am not positive, but I believe that he got a hint that

a European had wandered over that country who had been wounded in the head and hand, and was almost naked; but the natives could give him but very meagre accounts. He continued on, however, down the Isthmus, on the Pacific side, by sea, as far as Chili, when he went into the interior to Peru, crossed the Andes, and followed down the Orinoco to Para, when he sailed again for England."

"Oh! no other motive than curiosity?"

"Perhaps he had; for he once told me he had some old scores to settle with the man who commanded the pirate, and if he was alive he felt quite sure he would, one of those days, put him to death. My father, sir, is a very determined person, and never forgets an oath."

"Truly, monsieur, you interest me. But what sort of a man in appearance is your father—a doctor, I think you said?"

"He is a tall gentleman of about fifty, sir, though he looks much older; for he has suffered deeply in early life, when my mother—a —died; but I shall have the pleasure of introducing him to you, colonel. He is now on board our frigate at Kingston, and told me he would be up here to-morrow or the next day."

"Ah! thank you extremely, Monsieur Darcantel. I shall have— a—much curiosity to see him."

No more words that night; but much thinking and moving of thin lips, and eyes staring in the dark, wide open. There was low grating of teeth, too! And a man lay in that large room on a narrow cot, surrounded by a gauze net; and, so far as mental torture went, it was not unlike a trestle net we once saw without gauze, where a gaunt frame was stretched, with myriads of sand-flies, mus-quitoes, and stinging insects sucking his heart's blood. Sometimes the eyelids closed, as if they were a film of ice forming over the blue cold orbs within; and again the fabric cracked, and they were wide open once more. They could read, too, those frozen orbs; and like heavy flakes of snow falling on bloodstained decks, till it covered with a weight of lead the stark, stiff corpse beneath, they yet tried to pierce into the dark region beyond. And the heart beat with a slow and measured tramp, like a moose crunching through the sharp, treacherous crust of snow, and then stood stock-still! Had a letter, traced with the fingers of an icicle, been congealed a hundred feet deep in the heart of a toppling iceberg on the coast of Labrador, those eyes could have read it as clear as day!

"You infamous pirate, Captain Brand!" it began—"the son of the man who destroyed the 'Centipede' and her crew, and the boy whom your brutal mate tore from the mother you saw at dinner to-day, are near you! That calm, stern, determined doctor, too, whom you laced down on the trestle for poisonous insects to kill, has been on your track for the past seventeen years, and will soon hold you in his iron gripe! There will be no mercy then!"

Tho eyes closed, tho heart stopped beating, and tho thin lips and tongue, as dry as cartridge-paper, now took up tho strain, while tho mutilated hand clutched convulsively, as if thero were fifty fingers fingering knives and pistols.

"Shall I assassinate my old doctor, and run tho risk of being arrested and hung? No! IIo thinks mo dead, and I will go back to tho island, redeem my treasure, and pass tho remainder of my life tranquilly in the highlands of Scotland!"

Don't be too sanguine, Colonel Lawton; for, though your ten thousand pounds in gold is still in tho vault, yet there is Don Ignaçio Sanchez, whoso estates have been confiscated, and who has just got out of ten years' imprisonment in the Moro of IIavana, glad to savo his neck from the iron collar, and, without tho little jewel-hilted blade up his sleeve, is now turning about to see how ho may redeem his lost fortunes. Don't be an hour too late, I pray you, Captain Brand, for that sharp eye of Don Ignaçio has already, perhaps, looked at tho shiny cleft in tho crag, and thinks ho knows what lies hidden there! Oh, si! nothing but mouldy beans and paper cigars to live upon for ten years, and fond of more substantial food, even though it were yellow greenish gold, mildewed by damp, but yet solid and refreshing. *Cierto*—certainly! *Quien sabe*—who knows?

But be careful, Don Ignaçio! Don't take your old wife with you on that projected expedition, for you have treated that old woman —who resembles a rotten banana—badly! You havo won back in monté all she ever won by cheating, besides tho half ounces you used to givo her for the Church—cheated her by drawing two cards at a time when you saw tho numerals with that spark of an eye, and when you knew that she would win if you drew fairly! Yes, you have, you old sinner, for more than two score of years! And sho hates you now—though you don't think it—worse than you did Captain Brand! Have an eye to that old banana!

So passed that short night—long enough, however, for somebody —and before tho fresh land-wind had woko np to creep down the valley, there was a mettled barb, with open nostrils, galloping up the broken road as if ho had the devil on his back—as perhaps ho had, or Colonel Lawton, or Captain Brand, possibly all three, but it makes very little odds to us.

CHAPTER XLIII.

PEACE AND LOVE.

> " And many a dim o'erarching grove,
>   And many a flat and sunny cove;
>   And terraced lawns, whose bright cascades
>   The honeysuckle sweetly shades;
>   And rocks whose very crags seem bowers,
>   So gay they are with grass and flowers."

It was a delightful breakfast with the merry party at Escondido as they sat under the wide, cool piazza in the shade, with the sun throwing his slanting rays through the vines and clusters of purple grapes, and through the orange-trees, where the yellow fruit was fast losing its fragrant dew—all the men once more in summer rig, and the ladies in flowing muslin and tidy caps.

"My dear," said Piron to his wife, " we have lost one of our guests, Colonel Lawton; he went away at daylight this morning, and left a message to me, and compliments to you all, that business of importance, which he had forgotten, demanded his immediate return to Kingston."

There was no sorrow expressed by the lady or her fair sister, and even the men treated it with indifference, except Mr. Burns, who remarked, as he snapped a tooth-pick in twain, that, for his part, he was glad the fellow had gone; he didn't like his looks at all at all, though he did make himself so fascinating to the beautiful widow who sat next him.

"Ah! Monsieur Burns, think you I would prefer a scarlet coat when—"

"You might get a blue!" broke in Paddy, with a comical twinkle of his eye, as he winked in the direction of Commodore Cleveland, who sat opposite.

"No, no," exclaimed the pretty widow, hastily, as she shook her finger at her despairing admirer, "that is not what I was going to say—when those red coats there from England killed my poor husband at Quatre Bras."

"Ah! yes, my dear—bad luck to them! But an Irishman would never have been so cruel, you know, though, 'pon me sowl," went on Paddy, as he stuck a fork in an orange and began to divest it of its peel, West India fashion, to present it to the matron beside him, " I fear I should like to kill any man who loved ye, Madame Nathalie, myself."

" What a droll man you are, Monsieur Burns," replied the widow, laughing outright, " when you know you would prefer a jug of Antigua punch, any day, to me. Stop, now! didn't you say, at your grand dinner in Kingston, that you would never allow a woman to darken your doors ?"

" I—a meant—a black woman, my dear; as true as me name's Paddy Burns, I did !"

" What are you two laughing at, my sister ?"

" Why, here is Mr. Burns making love to me at breakfast, and before night he will be abusing me for not pouring enough rum iñ his punch !"

" That's his caractur, Madame Nathalie; for I, Tom Stewart, am the only person he ever loved, and he sometimes offers to shoot me for giving him unco' good advice."

" Howld yer tongue, ye divil ye! and you too, Stingo, or the pair of ye shall niver taste another sip of the old claret. Ye've ruined me cause entirely! But I'll lave ye me property, madame, when I'm gone."

" He's been talking of going, Nathalie," said Piron, " for the last twenty years, and has left his estate to at least thirty women, to my certain knowledge; but he hasn't got off yet, and—"

" Tom Stewart, ye miserable limb of the law! make out me will this very night."

Jacob Blunt unclosed his salt-junk mouth, and roared out in a peal of laughter that would have shivered his old brig's spanker, and caused, perhaps, Martha Blunt, sposa, to have spanked him, Jacob, had she heard and seen that mariner wagging his old bronzed face at the lovely woman facing him.

Mr. Tiny Mouse, who could not touch bottom on his high chair, with his little heels dangling about, forgetful of discipline, fairly kicked the broad pennant on the shins of his white ducks, screaming joyously; the three women made the piazza vibrate with their musical trills; Stingo and Stewart choked; Cleveland and Darcantel were amused; and old black Banou looked at his master, and grinned till his double range of teeth seemed like a white wave breaking at the cove. And then Paddy Burns took up the chorus, and after one or two Galway yells his friends took him up, thumped him smartly on the back, and stood him up against one of the posts of the piazza to have his laugh out. When he did, however, recover the power of speech, he wiped his eyes and looked around till they rested on Madame Nathalie, when, with his white napkin held up like a shield beside his rubicund visage, he spluttered,

"By me sowl, Tom Stewart, I mane what I say; and Paddy Burns's word is his bond!"

Ay, and so it was, you generous, whole-souled Milesian! And you did this time make a will. Tom Stewart and Stingo witnessed it, with handsome legacies therein set forth; and when one night you tumbled down—Well, we won't mention the particulars; but Paddy kept his word.

As the party rose from the breakfast table to get ready for a stroll down to the mill and around the plantation, one fair woman's hand was placed with a confiding, friendly clasp in that of Monsieur Burns; and then, as a graceful girl reached up to pull down her great flat straw hat from the post, Paddy Burns kissed her on the forehead, and she returned it too, as if she knew how to perform that ceremony even before people. Mr. Reefer Mouse had some thoughts of getting jealous, and calling Mr. Burns out, at ten paces, ships' pistols, and all that sort of thing; but the round, red-faced gentleman kissed him too, declaring the while, as he held him aloft, that he was first-rate kissing—that he was; nearly as good as mademoiselle, which quite disarmed Tiny's wrath, and then he hooked on to the damsel's delicate flipper, and tripped away with her down the valley.

Harry Darcantel exchanged a nod—not of defiance—with Paddy Burns, as much as to hint that those were not dangerous kisses—oh, not at all; and passing his hand over his brown mustache, he followed after the couple before him. Yes, Harry, Tiny's legs will get tired soon, and he will be hungry, and come back to old Banou for luncheon, while you will be putting aside the coffee bushes, and imploring mademoiselle to keep her straw hat about her lovely face, and not to get tanned by the sun. And when she turns her humid eyes toward you, you begin to believe the sky is never so blue as those eyes!

Tom Stewart, Stingo, and Burns never walked; they preferred lounging about the veranda, smoking cigars, and talking over the price of sugar and coffee, together with minor matters connected with factors' profits and suits at law. Jacob Blunt leaned over the bridge, thinking of the "Martha Blunts," brig and wife—not unfrequently confounding the two together—thinking this was to be his last voyage by land or sea, and that young Binks, his mate, should take command, and steer that old teak-built vessel carefully—oh, ever so keerful—or else the old hulk might come to grief.

Piron and his wife going mournfully down the valley—she with her mother's eyes gazing far out to sea, and he with his strong arm around her, whispering words of consolation; both looking, night and morning, out over the blue water, from chamber and piazza, and seeing nothing but a breaking wave and a baby-boy drowning beneath it—nothing more!

Madame Nathalie and Cleveland went on gallantly ahead—he with his blue pennant flying, and she with a black silk widow's ribbon around the frill of her cap, and a broader band about that muslin waist—talking of those they had both lost years ago, and trusting they were in heaven, as they believed they were; hope to meet again themselves in Louisiana, and see a great deal of one another in time to come—not a doubt of it! Yes, the cruise was more than half over, and he was quite tired of the sea. She, however, thought the sea beautiful, and never tired of looking at it. True, not rolling on top of it all the time—liked to sleep without rocking.

When the sea-breeze came fluttering up the gorge again, through the canes and the coffee-trees, and shaking up the superb foliage of the tropical forest, with the brilliant feathered tribes nestling close together on the lofty branches, and before the first salt breath had been exhaled in the clouds about the topmost peaks of the Blue Mountains, thousands of feet in the air, the party at Escondido had again returned to the broad piazzas, where, with blinds open, and swinging in cool grass hammocks, the men took siesta, while the ladies sought the pretty bowers within.

So passed one happy day, like the one gone before; and before the close of the week Dr. Darcantel joined the party, to take the place of Colonel Lawton; and a few days after old Clinker crackled up, very dry and thorny, with parchment in his pockets to take inventories, and do musty business generally.

Then the fair women, escorted by the navy men, and the Droger and Stingo, took their departure for the town house and ships in Kingston, leaving Paddy Burns, and Tom Stewart, and Clinker with Piron to close up matters, prior to his leaving the island. Paul Darcantel said he would remain with them likewise, since he had got through his business in Spanish Town and Port Royal, and wanted quiet. Madame Rosalie was the last to leave; and before her husband lifted her into the saddle, they stood together on the piazza, she looking with that still yearning gaze over the sea, and seeing nothing but breaking waves. That was the last look from Escondido!

CHAPTER XLIV.

SNUFF OUT OF A DIAMOND BOX.

"Hark! a sound,
  Far and slight,
Breathes around
  On the night;
High and higher,
Nigh and nigher,
Like a fire
  Roaring bright."

"Not a word to each other; we kept the great pace—
Neck by neck, stride by stride, never changing our place;
I turned in my saddle and made its girths tight,
Then shortened each stirrup, and set the pique right;
Rebuckled the check-strap, chained slacker the bit,
Nor galloped less steadily, Roland, a whit."

ANOTHER week rolled on. Old Clinker had pounded the parchment down as flat as last year's palm-leaves, rustling himself like the leaves of an old book, and began to squeeze out a few dry remarks about earthquakes. He at last got Paddy Burns, who was a round, fat man, with much blood in him, in such a state of excitement, by talking about cracks, and yawning chasms, and splits in the earth, clouds of dust, sulphureous smells, and beams falling down and pressing people to powder over their wine, that Paddy declared he thought he was swallowing sawdust and eating dried codfish at every sip of Antigua punch and suck of orange he took.

Tom Stewart, likewise, said he couldn't sleep a wink for quaking, and had cut a slice clean out of his chin while shaving, because his glass shook by a slamming door, and he thought his time had come.

Darcantel said nothing, but he took a quiet fancy to old Clinker, and talked for hours with him of the effect earthquakes had upon ships, and especially of general matters connected with the shipping interest, being withal very particular with regard to the appearance of the crews.

Piron looked grave, and heard the old clerk out, as if dried fruit were better than fresh, and limes sweeter than oranges.

Well, they were all sitting over their dessert at their last dinner at Escondido, for they were all going to leave old Clinker in the morning.

"HIS RIGHT ARM POISED WITH CLENCHED HAND ALOFT," ETC.

"Well, Clinker," said Piron, kindly, "don't let us talk any more about the earthquake. You told me yesterday that you had a note from Colonel Lawton, saying he would not take passage in the brig with us to New Orleans, as his business obliged him to leave before we could sail?"

Clinker choked out something like "Yes," as if it were the last sound a body could sigh with three or four hundred tons on his back.

"I'm dooced glad to hear it, Piron; for your military friend didn't enlist my fancy at all, and I don't believe any more of his patriot sarvice than I do in Clinker's earthquake. That colonel is a baste; and if my words prove true, I'll lave a thousand pounds to old Clinker there."

Paddy Burns's words did prove true; and old Clinker was with him when he gave a quake the earth had nothing to do with, it being entirely of an apoplectic nature; but he got the thousand pounds nevertheless.

"For once in your life, Burns, I agree with ye; and if that military mon went to shoot grouse with me in the Hielands, I'd tramp behind him, and keep both barrels of me gun cocked. The devil take his black wig and his green eyes! and he passing himsel' aff for a Scot, too! Tut, mon!"

"By the way, Clinker," said Piron, during a pause in the conversation, "if the colonel is not going with us, I must take him back his magnificent snuff-box he forgot when he left us so suddenly the other morning. Here it is, with the letters of his name on it in brilliants. I thought it too valuable to send by one of the blacks, and I kept it to carry myself."

How singular it was that the colonel should have forgotten his royal treasure! Keep your wits about you, Captain Brand, or one of these days you'll be forgetting your pistols.

"Given to him by a connection of his family, was it, Paddy? Weel, mon, let's take a peench for the honor of Sackveel Street, and then push it along to Meester Darcantel."

The doctor was sitting in his calm, grave way, listening to the disjointed words—like dry nuts dropping on the ground—from the shriveled lips of Clinker; but as he abstractedly put his fingers in the box, and turned his eyes languidly as he pushed down the lid, he gave a bound from his chair—with the box clutched in his left hand—giving a jar to the room and table that even made Clinker believe the forty-year earthquake had come before its time.

Standing there, with his tall, majestic figure, like a statue of bronze, his right arm poised with clenched hand aloft in a threatening attitude, his dark, grizzled locks bristling above his head, the black eyes flaming with an inhuman light, as if prepared to crush, with the power of a god, the pigmies around him, he said, in a deep low voice, which made the glasses ring and shudder,

"Who owns this bawble?"

"It belongs to a Colonel Lawton who has been staying here!" exclaimed Piron, quickly and hurriedly.

"What sort of man?" came again from those terrible lungs, without relaxing a muscle of his frame.

"A square-built, tallish fellow, of about feefty, with greenish-blue eyes, a black wig, and a glorious sapphire ring on the only finger of his left hand!" roared Burns and Stewart together.

Again came the jar of the earthquake to make the building, table, glasses, and all shake, as Paul Darcantel strode with his heels of adamant out of the sala and to the veranda; then a bound, which was heard in the room; and after five minutes' stupid silence Banou appeared.

The buckra gentleman had torn rather than led his master's barb from the stable, and scarcely waiting for a saddle, had thrown himself like an Indian across his back. There! his master might hear the clattering of the hoofs up the steep.

"The mon's daft—clean daft, mon!" "Be me sowl, it's the only pair of eyes I iver wouldn't like to look at over me saw-handled friend, Joe Manton!" "He's taken the box with him," crackled Clinker.

But that was the last that Paddy Burns, or Stewart, or Clinker ever saw of man or box. Piron rose and listened to the sound of the receding hoofs from the veranda; and when he resumed his place his lips were sealed for the night. *He* saw, however, and the rest of them heard a good deal about the man and the box in time to come.

Did that blooded horse, as he dashed round the curve of the peak, with his thin nostrils blazing red in the dark night, know who his rider was, and on what errand he was bound? It was not snuff that distended those wide nostrils as he plunged down the broken road, through the close, deep forest, over rocks and water-courses, without missing a step with his sure, ringing hoofs; and mounting the sharp gorge beyond with the leap of a stag, his mane and tail streaming in the calm, thick night; the eyes lanterns of pursuing light, flashing out before his precipitous tread in jets of fire, as his feet struck the flinty stones, with a regular, enduring throb from his heaving chest, as an encouraging hand patted his shoulder and urged him onward.

Down the mountain again, with never a shy or a snort—the horse knowing the rider, and the man the noble beast; the lizards wheetling merrily, and the paroquets on the tree-tops waking up to chatter with satisfaction. Then into the beaten track along by the seashore, the horse increasing his stride at every minute, the spume flying in flakes from his flaming nostrils, and the man bending to his hot neck, smoothing away the white foam, until, with a panting stagger, horse and rider stood still in the town of Kingston.

"Here, my boys, rub this your master's horse down well, and walk him about the court-yard for an hour. There! Take this between you!"

One last pat of the steed's arched neck, a grateful neigh as the dark face pressed against his broad head, and Paul Darcantel strode away in the gray light of the morning.

"Gorra mighty! Nimble Jack, look at dis! Bress my modder in hebben, it am one gold ounce apiece, sure as dis gemman's name Ring Finger Bill! De Lord be good to dat tall massa!- Him must hab plenty ob shiner to hove him away on poor niggers!"

Even while the tall man strode on toward the port, and as the happy blacks were chattering over their yapper, and walking the gallant steed up and down the paved court-yard, a dull, heavy-sailing Spanish brigantine was slowly sagging past Gallows Point and the Apostles' Battery, when, creeping on by the frowning forts of Port Royal, she held her course to sea.

Very different sort of craft from the counterfeit brigantine, with clean, lean bows, slipping out from the Tiger's Trap one sultry evening before a hurricane, which went careering, with a sea-hound after her, down to the Garotte Gorge. Different kind of a crew too; and Captain Brand must have remarked the contrast, with his keen, critical, nautical eye—that is, if he chanced to sail in both brigantines, as there is much reason for believeing he did—with great disgust, on board the dirty, dumpy old ballahoo now just clear of Drunkenman's Cay, and heading alongshore for Helshire Point, bound for St. Jago de Cuba.

CHAPTER XLV.

LILIES AND SEA-WEED.

"Oh leave tho lily on its stem!
  Oh leave the rose upon the spray!
  Oh leave the elder bloom, fair maids,
    And listen to my lay!"

"When descends on the Atlantic
    The gigantic
    Storm-wind of the equinox,
  Landward in his wrath he scourges
    The toiling surges,
  Laden with sea-weed from the rocks."

By day and night, under sun or moon, and in breeze or calm—by the resounding shore—on the rippling water—in saloon and grove, picnicking and boating—under vine or awning—all around in the whirling waltz, the measured contra-danza—amid the tinkle of guitar or trill of piano, the rattle and crash of the full band on board the frigate—gently rocking on the narrow deck of the "Rosalie," or down in the brig of teak, there was ever a white arm linked in the arm of blue—now timidly, then with a confiding pressure—now a furtive look of blue eyes into dark, then a fixed, steady gaze from the brown to the light—here a palpitating pause, and then the blue arms wound around the waving stem—two white arms clasping, with a passionate caress, the neck of the weed—and, yes! the lily floating on the white cheek of the pond had been caught by the strong weed, and with the reacting tide was going out to sea! Ay! the sailor had won the maiden!

But while the lily rocked hither and thither on the pond, with its blond leaves and petals of blue, and its pliant stem in danger at every tide, did the fond mothers watch it from the bank? That they did, thinking of the time when they were lilies of the pond themselves, with no fears of danger near. But at last it came, and, like blooming flowers, they swung to and fro in the rain, dropping a tear or two from their own rosy leaves—more in dewy sorrow than in fear—and waiting for sunshine; bending their beautiful heads of roses the while one toward another, peeping out with their dark violet eyes, and listening, as the wind shook them, with a tremble of apprehension, and clinging hopefully to the straight support on which they reclined.

By day and night, in burning sun with not a drop to drink, and in the sultry night with no morsel of food to eat—through the searing sand in the streets and lanes, down by the quays—to every vessel in the crowded harbor—in every hotel and lodging-house in Kingston—up and down Spanish Town—away off to Port Royal—occasionally going on board the frigate for gold, then on shore again—in ribald wassail and drunken dance, gaming hells especially, and low crimping houses, maroon and negro huts, and wretched haunts of vice—scattering gold like cards, dice, rum, and water—no end to it—in large yellow drops too—and still striding on, questioning, gleaming with those revengeful eyes—never resting brain or body, without drink or meat—went Paul Darcantel.

Oh, Paul, that cowardly villain saw you from the very moment you took that pinch of snuff out of his blue enameled box—ay, even before, when you walked your mule slowly up the broken road, while a goaded barb was curbed back in the gloomy forest till you had passed, with his rider's finger in his waistcoat pocket. And in all your ceaseless wanderings, by day and night, that now timid, terror-stricken villain has been following you; dodging behind corners—under the well-worn cloths of monté banks—in the back rooms of pulperias—hiding in nests of infamy—every where and in all places steering clear of you.

Oh, Paul! what a deceived man you are!

And while you are doing all this, just turn your eyes out to the calm spot off Montego Bay, where that leaky old brigantine is bobbing about. The dirty, surly *capitano* kicking and beating the hands from taffrail to bowsprit, particularly one great tall fellow, without a hat, and but a few dry thin hairs to shield his skull from the scorching sun; cursing him, as he puffs a cigarette, for being the most idle scoundrel of a skulk on board! But he—the scoundrel!—laughing with a hollow laugh up the sleeve of his filthy shirt, with never a dollar in his belt or an extra pair of trowsers in the forecastle, with bare feet, and still, cold eyes, now turned to green—eating nasty jerked beef and drinking putrid water—never sleeping for vermin—kicked and cuffed about the decks.

But yet he smiled with a devilish satisfaction, Paul, for he has escaped *you*, and was bound to St. Jago de Cuba! From there he would charter—steal, perhaps—a small boat, and run over to the Doçe Léguas Cays, where there were ten thousand pounds in mildewed gold!—if nobody had discovered it, which was not probable—and he—the scoundrel!—would gather it up in bags, and slink away to some other part of the world.

You must be very quick, Captain Brand, for the leaky brigantine does not sail so fast as the "Centipede," and your ancient compadre, Don Ignaçio, is just out of prison. His old, fat, banana wife is very sorry for it, but that's none of your business.

And you, Doctor Paul! don't you pity that flying, dirty wretch, with his mutilated hand, and soul-beseeching gaze out of those greenish frozen eyes, where a ray of mercy never entered, but whose icy lids fairly crack as your shadow stamps across them?

No, not a ray of pity or mercy for the infamous villain; not even a twitch of the little finger of his bloody, mutilated white hand! No, not the faintest hope of pity! He shall die in such torments as even a pirate never devoted a victim.

But you are worn out, Darcantel; your prey has escaped you. The people think you mad, as you are, for revenge; and though your stride is the same, and your frame still as nervous as a galvanized corpse, yet flesh and blood can not stand it. Go on board the "Monongahela," and talk to that true friend whose counsels you have ever listened to since you were rocking in your cradle; or take that noble, gallant youth in your arms and console him—for he needs consolation—and think of the mouse who gnawed the net years and years ago.

Well, you will, Paul Darcantel; but before you do, you will step into that jeweler's shop and buy a trifle for old Clinker there, out at Escondido. You want a ring, the finest gem that can be found on the island of Jamaica. There it is—its equal not to be bought in the whole West India Islands, or the East Indies either.

"I gave a military man an ounce for the setting alone, but the sapphire-looking stone may be glass. He was going to sail the next morning in a Spanish brigantine for St. Jago de Cuba, and wanted the money to pay his bill at the lodging-house adjoining. The señor might take it for any price he chose to put upon it."

What made that old dealer in precious stones and trinkets turn paler than his old topaz face as he yelled frantically for his older Creole wife? The señor had seized the ring as he broke his elbows through the glass cases which contained the time-honored jewelry, and dashed a yellow shower of heavy gold ounces over the floor of the little shop, smashing the glass door of that too in his exit! And when the little toddling fat woman appeared in the most indecent dress possible to conceive of, with scarcely time to light her paper cigar, she exclaimed,

"*Es lunatico, hombre! ay, demonio con oro!* A crazy man—a demon with gold!" And forthwith she picked up the pieces and looked at them critically to be sure of their value. "*Son buenos, campeche!* All right, old deary; we'll have such a podrida to-day! Baked duck, with garlic too! So shut the door. There's the ounce you gave the officer man for the ring, and I'll guard the rest."

That old woman did, too; and that very night she won—in the most skillful way—from her shaky old topaz, in his tin spectacle setting, his last ounce, and locked all up in her own little brass-nailed trunk for a rainy season for them both, together with their daughter's pickaninnies.

Paul Darcantel whirled and spun round the corners and along the sandy streets till he reached the landing, moving like a water-spout, and clearing every thing from his track. There he sprang into the first boat he saw, seized the sculls, despite the shrieks and gesticulations of the old nigger whose property it was, and who jumped overboard with a howl as if a lobster had caught him by the toe, and paddled into a neighboring boat, where, with the assistance of another ancient crony, they both let off volley upon volley of shrieks, which alarmed the harbor, while the boat went shooting like a javelin toward the men-of-war.

However, those old stump-tailed African baboons found a gold ounce in their boat after it had been set adrift from the American frigate. What a jolly snapping of teeth over a tough old goose stuffed with onions that night, with two respectable colored ladies and a case bottle of rum beside them! You can almost sniff the fragrant odor as it arises, even at this distance. I do, and shall, mayhap, many a time again, in lands where stuffed goose and comely colored ladies abound.

CHAPTER XLVI.

PARTING.

"The very stars are strangers, as I catch them
  Athwart the shadowy sails that swell above;
I can not hope that other eyes will watch them
  At the same moment with a mutual love.
They shine not there as here they now are shining;
  The very hours are changed.   Ah! do ye sleep?
O'er each home pillow midnight is declining—
  May one kind dream at least my image keep!"

There had been a small party on board the "Monongahela" the night before to bid the commodore good-by—all old friends of both parties—the Pirons, Burns, Stewart, Stingo, and Jacob Blunt. Clinker was not there, for he never went where it was damp, and if he got musty it must be from mildew on shore. The "Martha Blunt," under the careful management of young Binks, the mate, with Banou and all the baggage on board, was being towed by two of the frigate's boats down the harbor, with her yards mast-headed, all ready to sheet home the sails when the black pilot should say the land-wind would make and the passengers to come on board.

The lights were twinkling from lattice and veranda in the upper and lower town, the lanterns of the French and English admirals were shining from the tops of their flag-ships, and the revolving gleams from the beacon on the Pallissadoes Point flickered and dazzled over the gemmed starlit surface of the water. The awning was still spread on the after-deck of the "Monongahela;" and there, while the officer of the watch paced the forward part of the deck with the midshipmen to leeward, the sentries on the high platform outside and on the forecastle, the party of ladies and gentlemen stood silently watching and thinking.

There is no need explaining their looks or their thoughts; we know all about them. How Paddy Burns and Tom Stewart, with little Stingo, were going over the time, thirty years or more back, when with Piron there, boys together, they all swam on the beach of that fine harbor. The old school-house, too, with the tipsy old master, who whacked them soundly, drunk or sober; their frolics at the fandangoes in Spanish Town; their transient separations in after life on visits to France or the Old Country; the hearty joy to meet again and drink Jamaica forever. And now their companion in tropical heat and mountain shade was going to part with them, and sail away over that restless ocean, never, perhaps, to meet again!

Even old Clinker, as he sat on his stem by the old worm-eaten desk, with his dried old lemon of a face lying in his leaves of hands—with no light in the dark, deserted old counting-house—looked out between his fibres of fingers and saw the cradle, with the sleeping twins within it, while the rafters pressed him as flat as the old portfolio before him. And now, as a drop or two of bitter juice exuded from his shriveled rind, he saw those lovely twins floating away, never more to be saved from an earthquake by old Clinker.

Mr. Mouse, likewise, was wide awake, and hopping about with a kangaroo step, a little in doubt why Miss Rosalie was so pale, why those blue eyes were so dim, and why she said to him "Go away, little one," with a quivering, tremulous voice and hand. Mouse told Rat, and Rat told Martin and Beaver, that the poor girl was in love with him, Tiny, and that he would make it all right one of these days, when he got an epaulet on his little shoulder.

Softly, like the cool breath of a slumbering child, came a faint air from the land. The bell of the frigate, clanging in its brassy throat, struck for midnight. The sentinels on their posts cried "All's well!" The old brig was letting fall her top-sails, and the sound of the oars in the cutter's row-locks ceased.

"Cleveland," said Piron, quietly, "while the ladies and our friends are getting into the barge, come down with me in your cabin. I wish to have a parting word with you."

So they go down.

"Now, my dear friend, you have seen as well as I how wildly those young people are in love with each other; so has my wife and her sister; and, indeed, *my* sweet Rosalie seems more in love with him than our niece. I have not had the heart to put a thorn in the path of their happiness, and God grant it may all come right. But, Cleveland, you know that we come from an old and noble stock, where the bar sinister has never crossed our escutcheon, and I can not yet make up my mind to an immediate engagement. This our niece has consented to—Stop, Cleveland, hear me out. I do not, however, carry my prejudices to any absurd extent, nor have I spoken on this subject to the girl, and only to her mother and my wife; but I wish you to explain the way we feel, in your own kind manner, to your friend's son. Say to him what a trial it has been to us—how we all love him"—he pressed his handkerchief to his eyes—"and after he has learned all, if he still persists in urging his suit when the cruise is over, he shall have our consent and blessing. Time may work changes in them both; and meanwhile I shall not mention the matter to our little Rosalie, as we fear for the consequences."

"Spoken like a true father and a noble gentleman, my dear Piron!

I have thought as you and your excellent wife do on this matter; but, like you, I have not had the courage to give even a hint of warning to Henry. I shall, however, break the matter gently to him, and send my coxswain for his father also, whom I have not seen for a week, and who, they tell me, has been raging about Kingston ever since he ran away from you at Escondido. His son loves him devotedly, and a word from him will do more than I could say in a lifetime."

"The ladies are in the barge, commodore," squeaked Midshipman Mouse, as he popped his tiny head into the cabin.

"Very well, sir. And tell Lieutenant Darcantel that I wish to see him to-morrow morning, before church service. Come, Piron!"

On the lower grating of the accommodation ladder stood the commodore, with his first lieutenant, as the barge shoved off.

"I am heartily obliged to you, Commodore Cleveland," said Jacob Blunt, "for your kindness to me; and if Mr. Hardy will permit, I'll give the boats' crews a glass of grog for their trouble in towing the old brig."

Certainly! Jacob knew what was proper under the circumstances, and liked a moderate toss himself after a hard night's work as well as the lusty sailors in the boats, and the youngsters, Rat and Martin, who steered them.

So the barge shoved off, with no other words spoken, though there were white handkerchiefs wet with women's tears, and red bandanas, too, somewhat moist; while following in the barge's wake went a light whale-boat gig, pulled by four old tars, who could make her leap, when they had a mind, half out of water, for it was in those brawny old arms to do it. But now they merely dipped the long oar-blades in the water, and could not keep up with the barge.

They knew—those corrugated old salts—that their gallant, considerate young captain there in the stern sheets, with the tiller-ropes in his hands, who steered so wildly about the harbor, had something more yielding than white-laced rope in his flippers; and that the sweet little craft under white dimity, with her head throwing off the sparkling spray as she lay under his bows, was in no hurry to go to sea—not caring much, either, to what port she was bound, so long as she found good holding-ground when she got in harbor with both bowers down, and cargo ready for another voyage—not she!

Finally, old Jacob Blunt, master, again in full command of brig "Martha," with Mr. Binnacle Binks catting the anchor forward, all sail made, sheets home, and every thing shipshape, with a fresh, steady land-wind, and a light gig towing astern, went steering out to sea, bound to New Orleans by way of the Windward Passage.

At the first ray of sunrise the gig's line was cast off; and with the waves breaking over her, those four old sons of Daddy Neptune bared their tattooed arms—illustrative of ships, anchors, and maidens—and bent their bodies with a will toward the harbor.

"Take keer, sir, if it's the same to you, or we'll be on that ledge off the ''Postles' Battery.' It looks jist like that 'ere reef in the Vargin's Passage as I was wunce nearly 'racked on, in the 'Smasher,' sixteen-gun brig."

"No fear, Harry Greenfield."

"Beg your parding, Mr. Darcantel, but that 'ere wessel you is heading for is that old clump of a Spanish gun-boat; our craft is off here, under the quarter of the 'Monongahcelee.'"

"Oh yes, Charley; I see the 'Rosalie.'"

What made these old salts slew gravely round one to the other, as their sixteen-feet oars rattled with a regular jar in the brass row-locks, and shut one eye tight, as if they enjoyed something themselves? Probably they were thinking of a strapping lass, in blue ribbons, who lived somewhere in a sea-port town long years ago. But yet they loved that young slip of sea-weed, whose head was bent down to the buttons of his blue jacket, his epaulet lopsided on his shoulder, his sword hilt downward, and his brown eyes tracing the lines of the ash grating where pretty feet had once rested, while he jerked the tiller ropes from side to side, and his gig went wild by reef and point toward the "Rosalie."

When the gig's oars at last, in spite of her meandering navigation by her abstracted helmsman, trailed alongside the schooner, and while her crew were cracking a few biscuits and jokes on deck, with the sun high up the little craft's masts, her captain hurried down to his small cabin, and changed his rig for service on board the frigate.

CHAPTER XLVII.

DEVOTION.

" To walk together to the kirk,
    And all together pray,
While each to his Great Father bends—
Old men and babes, and loving friends,
    And youths and maidens gay !"

"Farewell! farewell! but this I tell
    To thee, thou wedding-guest,
He prayeth well who loveth well
    Both man, and bird, and beast!"

SUNDAY morning in Kingston harbor. The deep-toned bells from
cathedral and church were wafted off from the town; the troops at
Park Camp marching with easy tread to their chapel; matrons and
maidens, with bare heads, fans, and mantillas, going along demurely;
portly judges, factors, and planters trudging beside palanquins of
their Saxon spouses; negroes in white; Creoles in brown, cigarettes
put out for a time; while swinging censers and rolling sound of organs and chants, or prayers and sermons from kirk and pulpits, told
how the people were worshiping God according to their several be-
liefs.

On the calm harbor, too, and in Port Royal, lay the men-of-war,
the church pennants taking the place of the ensigns at the peaks, the
bells tolling, and the sailors—quiet, clean, and orderly—were attending divine service.

On board the "Monongahela" the great spar-deck was comparatively deserted—all save that officer with his spy-glassing old quarter-master, and the sentries on gangway and forecastle. The ropes,
however, were flemished down in concentric coils, the guns without
a speck of dust on their shining coats, the capstan polished like an
old brass candlestick, and every thing below and aloft in a faultless
condition.

As Harry Darcantel came rather languidly over the gangway, and
went down to the main deck, where the five hundred sailors in
snowy-white mustering clothes were assembled, Commodore Cleveland beckoned to him with his finger as he stood talking at the cabin
door to his first lieutenant.

" Hardy, I do not feel well this morning; make my excuses to the chaplain, and go on with the service. Come in, Harry. Orderly, allow no one, not even the servants, to enter the cabin—except Dr. Darcantel, in case he should come on board."

The stiff soldier laid his white-gloved finger on the visor of his hat. Then the chaplain, standing on his flag-draped pulpit at the main-mast, with those five hundred quiet, attentive sailors seated on capstan-bars and match-tubs between the silent cannon, and no sound save his mild, persuasive voice, as he read the sublime service from the good lessons before him. Then, after a short but impressive sermon, adapted to the comprehension of the honest tars around him, with a kindly word, too, for the sagacious officers who commanded them, he closed the holy book and delivered the parting benediction.

As he began, a shore boat, in spite of the warning of the sentry at the gangway, came bows on to the frigate's solid side, and as she went dancing and bobbing back from the recoil of the concussion, a tall, powerful man leaped out of her, and, by a mighty spring, caught the man-ropes of the port gangway, and swung himself through the open port of the gun-deck. Bowing his lofty head with reverential awe as the last solemn words of the benediction were uttered by the chaplain, he joined, in a deep, guttural voice, the word "Amen," and strode on and entered the cabin.

The curtains were closely drawn of the after cabin, even to shut out the first whisper of the young sea-breeze which was fluttering in from Port Royal; and there stood that noble officer, with his strong arm thrown around the gallant youth—the picture of abject woe—talking in his kind, feeling accents, trying to console him, painting the sky bright in the distance, and begging him, by all the love and affection he bore him through so many years, to be a man, and trust to his good conscience and his right arm to cleave his way through the clouds and gloom which surrounded him.

"There, Henry, you are calmer now. Sit down here in my stateroom, and while you think of that fond girl, give a thought to that poor bereaved mother, Madame Rosalie, who loves you for the resemblance she thinks you bear to her little boy, who was murdered by pirates just seventeen years ago off this very island."

"What do you say, Cleveland?" said a voice behind him, with such deep, concentrated energy that the commodore fairly started. "What did you say about a lost child and a Madame Rosalie?"

Paul Darcantel stood there in the softened crimson light, with his sinewy, bony hands upraised, his gaunt breast heaving, with unshorn beard and tangled, grizzly locks, the iron jaw half open, and his dark, terrible eyes gleaming with unearthly fire.

"Speak, Harry Cleveland! For the wife you have lost, speak!"

"My dear, dearest friend, do be calm! Why have you been so long away from me? I wanted you here, but you did not come.

Our poor boy has had *his* first lesson in this world's grief, and I have felt obliged to tell him all—yes, every thing! That the grave he has so often wept over, under the magnolia, does not contain his mother; and that—"

"Merciful God!" said Paul Darcantel, sinking down on his knees, with his hands clasped together, while the first tears for more than twenty years streamed from his agonized eyes. "There is a Providence in it all! That boy is not my son! I saved him from the pirate's grasp, and that woman must be his mother!"

Lower and lower the lofty head bent till it touched the deck, the bony hands clasped tight together, and those eyes—ah! those parched eyes—no longer dry!

"Paul, Paul, what is this I hear? For the love of heaven and those angels who are waiting for us, speak again!"

"My father—my more than father, I am not illegitimate, then! No such shame may cause your boy to blush for his mother?"

While strong and loving arms raised the exhausted man from the deck, and while he becomes once more the same determined Paul Darcantel, and with hand grasped in hand is rapidly recounting unknown years of his existence, let us leave the cabin.

CHAPTER XLVIII.

ALL ALIVE AGAIN.

"Among ourselves, in peace, 'tis true,
    We quarrel, make a rout;
And having nothing else to do,
    We fairly scold it out;
But once the enemy in view,
    Shake hands, we soon are friends;
        On the deck,
        Till a wreck,
    Each common cause 'defends."

Down in the steerage, where a bare cherry table stood, and upright lockers ranged around, with a lot of half-starved reefers devouring their dinner—not near so good or well served as the sailors' around their mess-cloths on the upper decks—with a few urchins utterly regardless of steerage grub, and a dollar or two in their little fists, all nicely dressed in blue jackets and white trowsers, waiting for the hands to be turned to and the boats manned, to go on shore for a lark.

Abaft in the wardroom, two or three of the swabs, the surgeon's mates, and the jaunty young marine lieutenant were getting into their bullion coats and fine toggery, and buckling on their armor to do sad havoc among the planters' families in the evening, away there in Upper Kingston. As for the first lieutenant, the purser, the fleet surgeon, the sailing-master, and the old major of marines, they had been ashore before, and didn't care to go again; growling jocosely among themselves on board the frigate, and glad to get rid of the juvenile gabble.

Presently, and before the hands were turned to from dinner, the cabin bell rang so violently that the orderly's brass scale-plate fixtures on his leather hat fairly rang too as he opened the sacred door.

"Tell the first lieutenant I want him."

The dismayed soldier forgot to lay his white worsted finger on his visor as he slammed to the door and marched out on the gun-deck.

"Mr. Hardy, unmoor ship! Hoist a jack at the fore and fire a gun for a pilot! Get the frigate under weigh, sir, and be quick about it!"

"Ay, ay, sir!"

S

As Hardy rapidly passed his old cronies, who were tramping along the deck as he mounted the after-ladder, he said, with a nod,

"By the Lord! I haven't seen the commodore in such a breeze since he blew that pirate out of water at Darien."

In a minute the "Monongahela's" bell struck two, and the boatswain and his mates, piping as if their hairy throats would split, roared out, "All hands!" and a moment later, "All hands unmoor ship!"

"What does that mean?" said a cook of a mess to Jim Dreen, the old quarter-master, who had just come down from his watch.

"Mean? why, you lazy, blind duff b'iler, it means that I've lost my blessed dinner."

"Hallo!" says Rat to Beaver, "what's that? Unmoor ship on my liberty day! I swear I'll resign!"

No you won't, reefers, but you'll trip aloft as fast as your little legs will carry you—Mouse in company—up to the fore, main, and mizzen tops, and squeak there as much as you like; but jump about and look sharp that nothing goes wrong, or Mr. Hardy will be down upon you like a main tack.

Bang from the bow port and the union jack at the fore!

"God bless my soul, fellows, this is the most infernal tyranny I ever heard of!" came from the wardroom; "all of us engaged to dine and dance in Kingston this evening, and—"

"It's 'All hands up anchor, gentlemen!'" and away they all went.

Down went the mess-kids, and down came the awnings, and up came the boats to their davits; in went the bars to both capstans, the nippers clapped on, and the muddy cables coming in to the tunes of fifes; while above the running gear was rove, the Sunday bunts to the sails cast off, and the five hundred sailors dancing about on the decks, spars, and rigging of that American double-banked frigate, as if they could always work her sails and battery to the admiration of their good commodore there, who was looking at them from the quarter-deck.

"Massa captan," said the shining ebony pilot, in his snowy suit, as he took off his fine white Panama hat, "dis is de ole pilot, sa, Peter Crabreef—name after dat black rock way dere outside. Suppose you tink ob beating dis big frigate troo de channel? Unpossible, wid dis breeze!"

"Peter Crabreef," said the old sailing-master, to whom these observations were addressed, "you had better not give such a hint to that gentleman there in the epaulets; for if you do, you'll never see Mrs. Crabreef again! You had better keep your wits about you, too, and plenty of water under the keel, for the commodore is fond of water!"

"Sartainly, massa ossifa! I is old Peter, and never yet touch a nail of man-of-war copper battam on de reefs!"

On board the pigmy black schooner near, half a dozen old salt vet-
erans were squinting at the flag-ship and holding much deliberate
speculation as to what all the row meant. Old Harry Greenfield,
however, with Ben Brown, who were the gunner and boatswain of
the little vessel, observed that, "In the ewent of our bein' wanted,
ye see, Harry, it will be as well to have the deck tackle stretched
along for heavin' in, and get the prop from under the main boom."

Even as they spoke, a few bits of square bunting went up in balls
to the mizzen of the frigate, and, blowing out clear, said, as plain as
flags could speak, "Prepare to weigh anchor!"

At the same moment the "Rosalie's" gig came bounding like a
bubble over the water with the tall gentleman beside the young
commander in the stern sheets. There was a great, nervous, bony
hand now holding his, but with as an affectionate pressure as the
soft dimpled fingers he himself had held the night before. Gig
not steered at all wild now, but going as straight as a bullet to the
schooner.

The stirring sounds of the fifes as the sailors danced round with
the bars in the capstans, with a beating step to keep time to the
lively music, were still heard on board the frigate, and then came
from the forecastle,

"The anchor's under foot, sir!"

"Pawl the capstan! Aloft, sail-loosers! Trice up! Lay out!
Loose away!" Almost at the instant came down the squeaks from
aloft of, "All ready with the fore! the main! the mizzen!" "Let
fall—sheet home! hoist away the top-sails!"

Again were heard the quick notes of the fifes on both decks, and
in less than five minutes more the anchors were catted, and the
"Monongahela," under a cloud of canvas, began to move.

But where was the "Rosalie," late "Perdita," all this time? Why,
there she goes, with never a tack, through the narrow strait, lying
over under the press of her white dimity like a witch on a black
broomstick, as she shoots out to sea.

And who is that tall man, on that narrow deck, clapping on to
sheet and tackle, though there was no need of assistance, or skill, or
seamanship to be displayed on board that craft, except by way of
love of the thing? And why does he, during a pause when there
was nothing more that could possibly be done, stand by the weather
rail, shaking a great huge old seaman by both hands till he almost
jarred the schooner to her keel?—Ben Brown, the helmsman, whom
you have heard of on board the "Martha Blunt," who, by some accidental word he dropped near to the tall gentleman, caused that hand-
grasping collision.

It was not another five minutes before the other thirty-nine old
sea-dogs knew all about every body, and where they were bound,

and so on. They did not care a brass button for the thousand silver dollars they were to have from the tall gentleman—not they! They wanted merely to lay their eyes along that Long Tom amidships, and to have a cutlass flashing over their shoulders—so fashion! Pistols and pikes! Fudge!

But where was the " Martha Blunt?" Oh, that old teak brig was bouncing along past Morant Point, with a good slant from the southward, pretty much where she was some seventeen years before, with a few more passengers in her deck-cabin, reading their Bibles, and praying for those who go down to the sea in ships on that Sabbath day—one looking with her sad eyes out of the stern windows, and another doing the same, and both thinking of the same boy who had been dashed out of one of those windows; and though both of them knew the other's thoughts, yet they did not dream they were thinking of the same person at the time.

And where was the Spanish brigantine, with the exacting *capitano*—who was a slaver in dull times—and his pleasant mate, who would think no more of sticking a knife into you than he did of kicking that skulking, icy-eyed sailor on board—detesting as he did the entire Saxon race ever since Cadiz was bombarded—and feeding him on rotten jerked beef? There were no prayers, only curses, on board that brigantine as she dropped anchor in St. Jago that fine Sunday morning.

And where was our ancient one-eyed mariner, formerly in command of the colonial guarda costa felucca, the " Panchita," named after his fat banana of a sposa? Oh, the Don—simply Ignaçio now—had had a quiet confab with the deputy administrador all about some treasure which he knew was concealed, and where—for he had seen with his bright eye the light of a torch in a cleft of a crag—and he would go shares with that official if he would give him a little assistance.

"*Oh, cierto!*" Why not? And there was an old launch, with a torn lateen sail, which Columbus might have been proud to command; and, in this fine weather, he might sail back to Port Palos in her.

Oh yes! But, to keep all secret, he would merely take old Pancha, his wife, for crew. And so, with a few bundles of paper cigars, and some dried fish and water—the only property they possessed, save his eye and a pack of cards, and those valuables rescued with difficulty—they sailed the night before the blessed Sunday. *He* never came back, though. No blame attributable to the eye—that was as bright and wary an old burning spark of suspicious fire as ever; but then old Pancha held the cards, and this time she won. Very singular it was, *cierto.* If Ignaçio had not gone back again for another bag which was not there, why, the *sota* of a knave being the next card—Ah! we won't anticipate.

But we are all alive yet, except those murdered women, whose white coral head-stones still stand up there in the cactus, and poor Binks, and those slashing blades of the poisonous, many-legged "Centipede," who were eaten by the sharks—all alive the rest of us, and wide awake!

CHAPTER XLIX.

THE ROPE LAID UP.

"The captain is walking his quarter-deck
With a troubled brow and a bended neck;
One eye is down the hatchway cast,
The other turns up to the truck on the mast."

"The breeze is blowing—huzza, huzza!
The breeze is blowing—away, away!
The breeze is blowing—a race, a race!
The breeze is blowing—we near the chase."

WELL, the positions of all hands were simply these. The icy-eyed man, without snuff-box, or ring on that mutilated flipper, with two under pockets in his shirt, and something in them, a pair of filthy old canvas trowsers, and no hanger by his side, where there had been so much hanging in the good old times, slipped overboard like a conger eel, and swam on shore at St. Jago de Cuba. Without a *real* of wages—for he was to work his passage—and because he didn't feel inclined to work, the *capitano* in command assisted his agile subordinate to kick him all the voyage.

Had, however, the mate presented that cold eel his knife for a moment before he jumped overboard and squirmed to the shore, that cuchillo' would have found a redder sheath than the crimson sash which usually held it. Fortunately perhaps for the mate, he was not of a generous disposition, save with kicks and ropes'-ends, or else he might have regretted his philanthropy.

So soon as the icy-blue man had congealed, as it were, in the sun until he was quite dry and frozen again, he slunk away to the ditch of the old fort, where he thawed till nightfall, and then entered the town; hanging round the pulperias, smacking and cracking his parched lips for a measure of aguardiente, only two centavos a cup, and not caring for that fine, generous, pale, amber-colored old Port sent to him by the good Archbishop of Oporto! But, not having the copper centavos—though his own coppers stood so much in need of moisture—he continued to skulk on.

Presently, coming to the wide streets and to the outskirts of the town, he spied a large mule, ready caparisoned for the road, hitched to the door of a house, waiting for his owner to mount him. The icy green-eyed individual, disgusted for the time with blue salt water, aud being, as we know, a capital cavalry-man—in dashing charges among the patriots, and caprioling also up the Blue Mountains to Escondido—thought he would take another gallop on the dry ground, just to keep his hand and little finger in; so he quietly cast off the mule's painter, and flung his canvas legs over the beast as if he belonged to him. And so he did; for he told the man at whose place he passed an hour or two that night, and who thought he knew the master to whom the mule had once belonged, that it had been presented to him by an old friend, whose name—as had the mule's—escaped him.

All this time the one-eyed man, with his banana woman, Pancha, were creeping along the water part of the land—with the Peak of Tarquina in sight—toward Cape Cruz, bound round that peninsula, and so on to the Doçe Léguas Cays; while the man on the mule navigated by the Sierras del Cobre of St. Jago, steering by bridle for Manzanillo, and then to take water again for the same secret destination.

The cargo that both expected to take in there was about ten thousand pounds sterling in mildewed coin of various realms and denominations; but it was there, and would pass current any where.

So they sailed and navigated. It was tedious work, though; and it took a week for the old launch with the torn sail to get into the Tiger's Trap—fine weather, and no sea—and there make fast to the rocks. At the same evening hour the mule with his passenger planted his fore feet, like a pair of kedges over his bows, in the fishing village near Manzanillo, and foundered bodily, going down with his freight slap-dash in the mud. The passenger, however, escaped, and skulled along by the shore, where he fell in with a poor fisherman who was about to shove off in his trim, wholesome bark for professional recreation on the Esperanza bank.

Glad was old Miguel Tortuga to have a strong man to assist him for the privilege of joining in a sip of aguardiente and catching a red snapper or two; so they jumped on board and spread the sail.

Had old Miguel, however, seen the sharklike eyes of his assistant in the sunlight, or dreamed what a snapper was about to catch *him*, he would not have gone fishing that night, and it would have saved him much tribulation at daylight the next morning, when he was picked off a small rock by a fisher acquaintance of his from Manzanillo.

But we have nothing to do with old Miguel; and need only say, to console him, that his stanch boat went safely through the blue gateway of the roaring ledge of white breakers, and late Sunday night lay calmly in the inlet abreast Captain Brand's former dwelling.

To go back again for a week, the "Monongahela"—double-banked leviathan as she was—came plunging out to sea from Kingston, ev-

ery man and boy, from Jack Smith on her forecastle to Bill Pump
in the spirit-room, and from Richard Hardy to Tiny Mouse, knowing from the first plunge the frigate made what they all sailed
for.

With her proud head toward the east, she went dashing on past
the White Horse Rocks, and woe to the small angry waves which
did not get out of her way, for she smashed them contemptuously in
foaming masses from her majestic bows, sending them back in sparkling spray and bubbles to hiss their angry way to leeward in her
wake. On she went, far off to sea, where the trade wind was stron-
gest, disdaining gentle zephyrs near the land, with her great square
yards swinging round at every watch while beating to windward—
the tacks close down, yards as fine as they would lay, and the heavy
sheets flat aft.

Every evening the surgeon, the purser, the chaplain, the major, and
the old sailing-master were in the cabin, going over the chase of a
certain pirate in a schooner "Centipede" away down on the Darien
Coast, with Cape Garotte there under their lee, and the vultures and
the sharks grinding the bones and tearing the flesh of the half of a
man with the tusk gleaming out of his wiry mustache; and the padre, with his eyes staring wide open, and the crucifix, borne away
by the carnivorous birds of prey.

All of those dreadful particulars, together with matters that had
gone before—of a lost boy, a heartbroken mother, and a murdered
mate, Mr. Binks, on board the brig "Martha Blunt"—the party at
Escondido, the snuff-box, and Paul Darcantel—all about him, too,
from the tragedy on the plantation, his despair, and reckless life afterward, when he served in slavers, where he did something to allay
the sufferings of the poor wretches; and afterward how he was tre-
panned to the "Doçe Léguas," went a cruise with Mr. Bill Gibbs,
whose leg he hacked off with a hand-saw, not knowing at the time
about the locket; the little child he had saved; how that child had
saved him from his torture on the trestle with his mouselike teeth;
how he had wandered the wide world over searching and searching
for the mother of that boy!

And there the boy was—the manly, brave young fellow now—
whom officers and sailors had always loved, flying away with the
dark doctor—no longer Darcantel, but Harry Piron—with his fond
father and mother in the distance, and the sweet girl he adored with
her blonde head resting in her mother's lap.

Ay, every soul in the ship knew all about it, and talked of it, and
drank to the happiness of the young couple—all save Dick Hardy,
who moved energetically about the frigate's decks, with his eyes
every where, below and aloft, prompt, sharp, and quick, quite like
Cleveland, there, beside him, when they were together in the old

THE OLD WATER-LOGGED LAUNCH.

"Scourge" during the hurricane, and chased, to her destruction, the "Centipede."

"Sail ho!" sang out the man on the fore-top-sail yard.

"Where away?"

"Right ahead, sir. A brig on the starboard tack!"

Ay, the old "Martha Blunt" bouncing along under all sail, squaring off at the short-armed seas, and striking them doggedly, as she beat up for the Windward Passage between Hayti and Cuba.

But there was an old sea-bruiser of a different build, who wore the belt in the West Indies, and was after that sturdy old brig with teak ribs for a hearty set-to; and when she came up alongside, in the friendly sparring-match which ensued while both squared their main yards, and lay for an hour side by side, there was considerable conversation; so much talk, in fact—boats going to and fro, mingled with roars and shrieks, and clasping of hands on board the brig—never a sound on board the ship—that the blue pennant fluttered in such a way it was hard to tell whether it was Jacob, or Piron, or the sweet wife, or mademoiselle, or her lovely mother, who threw their arms around that pennant's truck.

Then yard-arm and yard-arm, the frigate with her canvas canopy of upper sails furled, and the brig in her best bib and tucker, they both filled away and moved side by side.

For a day or two they went on, talking and laughing to one another in these friendly shakes of the hand over blue water, until one day, the brig being to windward, she came upon an old water-logged launch, with a broken mast and a torn sail hanging over her side.

It fell calm, and Jacob Blunt ordered young Binks to get into the yawl and tow the boat alongside, and to be smart about it; for the breeze might make so soon as the fog rose, and the commodore was not the man to be kept waiting in a big frigate. Mr. Binks was smart about it, and presently he returned—though there was no hurry, for the calm lasted a long time—with his water-logged prize.

There was no human being in this prize; but when she came alongside, and a yard tackle was hooked on to let the water drain out of her, Jacob Blunt and the people on board gave a pleasant yell of astonishment.

It was not the soiled pack of Spanish cards, or the few bundles of saturated paper cigars floating about, which caused this excitement. No, it was several canvas bags lying there in the stern sheets, strapped with strands of a woman's red petticoat to the empty water-cask beneath the thwarts; and not one of those canvas bags, or what was in them, injured in the least by salt water. Very carefully were those bags—and they were weighty—lifted on board the brig, over the rail where the pirates swarmed some long years ago, on to the quarter-deck; and then there was another joyous shout from Jacob Blunt, as when he had hailed the trade wind in that long past time.

"By all that's wonderful, here is my old bag of guineas, and some few Spanish milled dollars! Look at the mark, my darlings!"

Another weighty bag was set aside for Mrs. Timothy Binks, and the rest were devoted, with some large doubloon reservations for crew, to Martha Blunt and Jacob Blunt in their declining years.

Then, the weather being still calm and foggy, Jacob and his passengers went on board the double-banked frigate for church service, where they all prayed with much hope and thanksgiving for what had passed and what was to come; and then they went into the commodore's cabin, where they remained ever so long a time.

Let us go back this same week again—a very long seven days it has been for every body, particularly so for the icy-eyed man, who was extremely anxious, as he kicked and lashed his mule, and kept looking round the south side of Jamaica, from Portland Point to Pedro Bluff and San Negril, throwing a ray of cold frost there day and night, expecting that tall doctor to come striding along in that deep water, heading due north.

And at last the dark figure hove in sight, in the schooner "Rosalie" —the sweet little craft skimming exultingly over the seas, kissing them occasionally with both her dainty, glistening cheeks, reeling joyously over on her side, with her tidy dimity laced and spread in one flat sheet of white, while the slender arms bent like whalebone to the freshening breeze, and she left the dancing bubbles sparkling and flashing lovingly in her wake.

Two hundred miles to go, and the breeze fell from fresh to light, until at last, shrouded in a thick fog, one Sunday morning, when there was no air at all, only a flat calm, the sea as smooth as a glass mirror with the quicksilver clouded.

Then out sweeps, my lads! Ten of a side, and two of those bronzed old lads at each sweep! All except the two after ones, where Ben Brown and the tall doctor handled one apiece.

Thus, with sails down and bare arms, the light little "Rosalie" continued gliding rapidly over the mirrored surface—a little ashamed of herself, perhaps, at being seen in such a scanty rig—while her commander guided her graceful course, and Harry Greenfield peered about forward to see that no harm should arrest her dainty footsteps.

Presently was heard the toll of a bell. The sweeps paused, the hide gromets resting on the tholl-pins, and the water raining from their broad blades.

"That must be a man-of-war off here on the quarter," exclaimed the young officer at the tiller, "ringing for church."

The old seamen at the sweeps unconsciously took off their hats, wiped the sweat from their brows, and listened.

"It can hardly be the 'Monongahela,'" said Ben, "though p'raps she took more of a breeze to wind'ard, off the island."

Still the schooner glided on noiselessly over the sea, until, a minute later, Harry Greenfield sang out,

"Port, sir! or we'll be plump into a vessel here ahead."

The helm was put down, and the "Rosalie" sheered off to starboard within a biscuit toss of a large brig.

"By my grandmother's wig!" said Ben, "that's the old 'Martha Blunt!'"

"Henri," said Paul Darcantel, in French, in his deep voice, "the last request I shall ever make is to keep on. There is not a moment to lose!"

"Give way, men!" shouted the officer, in 'a decided tone, as the words came with a stifled gasp from his heaving breast, while the sigh that followed was drowned in the splash of the sweeps in the water as they again chafed in their gromets, and the foam flashed away from the blades astern.

But there was another splash. A white object sprang with a bound over the brig's quarter, dipping below the surface of the calm sea, and when it came up, two great flippers, with a large black head between them, struck out like the paws of an alligator, breasting the water with a speed that soon brought him within a few fathoms of the schooner's low counter. Then, seizing hold of the slack of the main sheet, which was thrown to him, he came up, hand over hand, as if he could tear the stern frame out of the schooner. A vigorous grasp caught him by one paw, and, with the other laid on the taffrail, he leaped on deck as if his feet had pressed a springboard instead of the yielding water.

Again, as in the olden time, he held his little Henri aloft in his giant arms; but this time it was Banou who was dripping from a souse, and not his little master.

"Give way, my souls! Another thousand dollars if we get up to the Key before dark!" said the deep, low tones of the tall doctor.

"Good Lord!" roared a voice from on board the brig, now shut up again all alone in the fog—"if that old nigger has not gone and jumped overboard, my name's not Binks!"

"All right, Mr. Binks; Banou is safe! Send a boat on board the 'Monongahela,' and report that the schooner 'Rosalie' has passed ahead," went back in a clear note.

It was some considerable time before Binks could believe that he had not been hailed by David Jones himself, for he had seen nothing, being at the time in the lower cabin reading his Bible, and writing his name, "Binnacle Binks, Master of brig 'Martha Blunt,'" on the fly-leaf; and he was only disturbed in this praiseworthy occupation by a heavy body plunging overboard, and by one of the drowsy crew, who had, with his comrades, been sleeping near, reporting that circumstance with his eyes half shut.

Then young Binks took considerable more time to get a boat lowered, and send her, with the cabin-boy, to the large frigate close on his beam, whose bell had just struck seven.

The boat, too, with four sleepy hands to pull her, took considerable time to find the ship, and then the whistles were piping to dinner, and all the good people from the brig, with the flag-officers, had retired to the commodore's cabin for luncheon.

When Jacob Blunt heard the news, regardless of sherry and cold tongue, he himself got in his boat, leaving his passengers in an excited frame of mind, but rather comfortable on the whole, and returned to the teak bosom of his " Martha."

There he took young Binks firmly by the shoulder, and walked him aft to the rail where his father—long since dead and murdered —had been used to sit and sing sailor ditties.

Then he impressively told him that "this 'ere sort of thing wouldn't do! even if he was a readin' the Bible, which was all very good on occasion, sich as clear weather out on the broad Atlantic; but in fog times, when schooners was creepin' about in among the Antilles, and partick'larly off Jamaiky or the south side of Cuby, mates and men should be wide awake and lookin' every wheres. And harkee, Binnacle! when you commands this 'ere old brig, or maybe a bran-new ' Martha Blunt,' and me and my old woman lying below together in narrow cabins, you must bear in mind these my words! Well, my boy, don't rub that 'ere sleeve over your eyes no more, and it will be all right."

Young Binks promised "that from that 'ere minnit he would never sit on no rails, or sip no grog, or even read his old mother's Bible when he wos on watch, but always be as keerful as if there wos no lady passengers or children on board, or bags of shiners in the lower cabin stateroom—that he would! And his blessed old second father might take his davy he, young Binks, would never be caught foul again."

Meanwhile the girlish schooner tripped away far out of sight, and when the fog lifted and the breeze came to blow it to leeward she was once more tidily dressed in snowy white, and splashing the water from her black eyes, as the last rays of the setting sun showed her the Tiger's Trap in the distance.

"Henri, my boy, put your arms around me again as you did when I lay in torture on the trestle on that island. Have no fears for me; we shall meet again. There! now listen to me. Here is a packet which I wish you to carry to Porto Rico with this letter. The old judge is alive, I think, to whom this letter is addressed, and it may perhaps soothe his declining years. I wish to take your little gig, with Ballou and Ben Brown—no more force—and if, as I believe, that villain has returned to his former haunt, I will fulfill my oath to its very letter. Meanwhile, so soon as we have shoved off, while the breeze still holds, run down to the frigate—she is not three leagues off—and you will be in your yearning parent's arms, and those of the girl you love, before they sleep. There! I know you will think of me. Farewell!"

CHAPTER L.

ON A BED OF THORNS.

> "An orphan's curse would drag to hell
> A spirit from on high;
> But oh! more horrible than that
> Is the curse in a dead man's eye!"

> "O Heaven! to think of their white souls,
> And mine so black and grim!"

"Ho, ho!" said Captain Brand, as he stretched out his straight legs in their canvas casings on the sand of the little cove, "safe and sound, and not a soul to share this nice supper of that good old man Miguel!

"Ho, ho!" continued he; "here at last! No Babette to cook for me—no 'Centipede'—nothing but that stanch little boat presented me by that generous fisherman, who, I fear, is drowned by this time. Well, let us enjoy ourselves! Excellent real snapper this! Sausage rather too much garlic perhaps; but the brown bread and the aguardiente unexceptionable. Blaze away, my little fire; your sticks cost me much labor to dig out of my once comfortable house, but you are better than gunpowder any day.

"Just to think of the years that have passed! That great bank of sand there over the sheds, nearly as high as the crag, where my brave fellows once caroused; the young cocoa-nut springing up on the crag itself—not a vestige of my old habitation left, or the bright blades or pleasant guests to dine with me!"

Here there was something of the old cold murderous scowl on the captain's face as he twisted the point of his nose.

"Ah! yes, there may be my wary-eyed Sanchez left, though the last I heard of him he was in the Capilla dungeon of the Moro. And that"—grating his teeth, and glaring with his icy eyes at the fire, as if those two blocks of ice would put it out—"cursed doctor who pursues me!

"Well, well, neither of those old friends are here yet, and before another sun sets I shall bequeath the old den to them both! Ho, ho! with those solid bags of clinking metal, I shall leave them as much sand and rocks as they choose to walk over. What a sly devil I was to stow that treasure away for a rainy day! Never told a living being! Poisoned the fellow, too, who made the lock! Capital joke, 'pon my soul!"

This was the very last of the very few jokes that Captain Brand over enjoyed.

"And, now I think of it, I wonder if my thirsty old mate's bones are yet lying there in the vault. What *was* his name? such a bad memory I have! Oh! Gibbs—Bill Gibbs—with one leg! Ho, ho!"

Here Captain Brand drained some more aguardiente out of a cracked earthen pot, and slapped his fine legs with rapture.

"And those dear girls who married me! Lucia, too!"

The dirty wretch started as the wing of a sea-bird swooped down over the pure inlet; and he thought he saw a white fore finger beckoning him on to his doom.

"Pshaw!" said he, smoothing down his filthy tattered shirt with the finger of his mutilated left hand, "how nervous I am! But what a bungle Pedillo made of that marriage! And my good Ricardo, too! What a feast the sharks must have had on his oily, well-fed carcass! Misericordia! Ho, ho! I believe I'll bid my friends goodnight."

Captain Brand stretched himself out at full length on the shelly strand, his boat secured by a clove-hitch round his right leg, which rode calmly in the little inlet; his bald head, with the few dry gray hairs on his temples, resting on Miguel's sennit hat, and the thin scum of frosty eyelids drawn over his frozen eyes—cracking their covering at times—until at last the pirate, aided by fiery aguardiente, slept.

A few late cormorants and sea-birds sailed over him in his fitful slumber, and uttered a cold cry, as if their pecking-time had not come yet, but would shortly, as they sought their silent retreats on the wall of rocks opposite.

And Captain Brand dreamed, too—of the old laird, his father, in prison; his mother weeping over forged notes; the sleeping, unsuspecting people he had treacherously murdered; the pillages he had committed; the men he had slain in open conflict; those he had executed with his own private cord; the poor woman who had died in worse torments, when, indeed, even knife or pistol, rope or poison, would have been a mercy; the agony and sufferings of those who survived them; with all the concomitant horrors which make the blood run cold to think of, and which made the pirate's almost freeze in his veins—living years in minutes—did Captain Brand, as he lay there on the chill sand in his troubled nightmare of a sleep.

"Ah! *Dios! Dios!*" chattered the Señora Banana Pancha, at the other outlet to the inlet, rolling over on the ledge of the rocks at the Tiger's Trap.

"What has become of my Ig—Ig—nacio—the one-eyed old villain who has persecuted me for forty years? Why did I cut the old launch adrift before I got in myself? And here I am alone and des-

T

olate on this cursed island, and my Ig—Ig—naçio—bless spark of an eye—not come back to me! Ah! *Dios! Dios!* what has become of the little man? He will kill me, *cierto*, when he comes back and finds the boat gone with all the money, which nearly broke his thin back to bring here; but, *Dios! Dios!* I am dying of thirst, and not a shred of dried fish or jerked beef has gone into my old mouth—"

Yes there has, Doña Pancha, for just then a piece of hawser-laid rope—rather dry, perhaps, for mastication—was placed across your crying mouth that you might bite upon, if you would only stop your old tongue.

For while you were screaming on the rocks, and yelling for your Ig—Ig—naçio, who went back for the last bag of gold that wasn't there, a light gig glided in like a blackfish, and a bigger blackfish jumped up and stopped your old mouth, Pancha, with that bit of hide rope. But if you will keep quiet, Pancha, and not exorcise Banou for the Evil One, that old nigger will give you a cup of liquid not known in the devil's dominions, and treat you also to some white biscuit to nibble upon.

Ah! you will, eh? and tell all about that thin curl of smoke, which you believe to have been made by that coal-eyed Ig—Ig—naçio, away up there by the inlet? Now keep quiet again, old Lady Banana; and while your screaming mouth is gagged, don't cut this small gig away, or else she may navigate herself out to sea, as did your Ig's launch, and you be left desolate again.

The tropical night was still; the lizards wheetled, the breakers roared on the outer ledge, the ripples washed musically on the shelly shores, the alligators flapped about on the surface of the lagoon, the insects buzzed around the mangrove thickets; and as the gray dawn of morning appeared, and the rain began to fall, a steaming hot mist arose, through which the sea-birds flapped their wings and sailed away in search of their morning's meal. The sharks and the deep-sea fish, however, lay still and motionless low down by the base of the reefs, and watched with their cold, round eyes. Captain Brand, too, arose, and, opening *his* green-bluish eyes, smoothing his moulting feathers, and splashing his fins in the wet sand, took an observation.

This was the rainy day for which Captain Brand had laid by all that money to spend it in!

It was a Monday morning—Black Monday for Captain Brand—when, after divesting his leg of the clove-hitch, he secured old Miguel's boat to a large stone, and then, according to his own ancient practice, he clambered with difficulty up to the venerable crag. Captain Brand had no spy-glass, and there was a good deal of rain falling, but yet he thought he saw a large ship, a brig, and a small schooner in the offing.

So Captain Brand scrambled down again, a good deal disconcerted, knowing it would be hours and hours before those vessels got up to the island, even were they so inclined ; but, nevertheless, he bestirred himself. Fortifying his inner man with the last half pint of aguardiente for breakfast, which quite refreshed him, he went to work.

First, he took Miguel's copper coffee-pot, into which he emptied that disciple of the net's shark-oil jug, which Miguel himself used for a torch to attract the fish. Then, with a strip of old canvas—part of one leg to Captain Brand's trowsers ; to such straits was he reduced—seized like a ball on the end of a stick, and a match-box, he was all ready for Black Monday's work.

Captain Brand, however, made one serious omission ; he snugly stowed away his beautiful pistols in a locker of the boat to keep them dry, never having been wet but twice before in all his marine excursions—the first time at Cape Garotte, and the next when he jumped overboard from the brigantine at St. Jago. He set great store by these valuable implements, for they had done him good service in time of need. Miguel came into possession of them afterward, and sold them almost for their weight in gold.

But, for the first time, Captain Brand forgot his personal friends and bosom companions. It was a great oversight ; and he was extremely sorry when it was too late to go back for them. However, with the copper oil-pot dangling from his little finger, where the sapphire once shone, and the torch-stick in the other hand, he marched boldly over the sandy ridges toward the crag.

But, Captain Brand, there had been three pairs of open eyes watching you through every mouthful of snapper you snapped, and every drop of fiery white rum you swallowed. Ay! and while you tossed about on the shelly beach, with the red glow of the embers of the fire lighting up your cold-blooded, wrinkled face—while, twisting your nose, you muttered ho! ho's! of murderous satisfaction—there was not a bird that swooped over you, or a lizard on the rocks with jet beads of eyes, that watched you so sharply as did those attentive beholders from the crag.

And when you made your observations from the young cocoa-nut clump, those watchers retired down the opposite side, and two of them clambered through a hole in the roof of the decaying little chapel, while the other moved to the little cemetery of coral gravestones, and there scooped a place in the sand and cactus behind the one cut with the letter L.

Captain Brand meanwhile came on, picking his way through the dense cactus, which lacerated his legs, and sadly tore the remains of his loose canvas. The rain came down in torrents, the thunder growled and crashed as the tropical storm burst over the island ; and just as a vivid sheet of forked lightning seemed to stride the crag, and the awful peal that followed shook it to its base, Captain Brand crept for shelter within the cleft of the rock, and sat down to prepare for a more extended research.

He may have been gone twenty minutes; but when he again emerged the rain had ceased, the clouds were breaking away, and the gentle sea-breeze blowing, while Captain Brand looked a thousand years older. He seemed to have borrowed all the million of wrinkles from his compadre, in addition to those he already possessed. The thin lids of his frozen green—now quite solid—eyes had apparently exhaled by intense cold, and left nothing but a stony look of horror.

What caused our brave captain to reel and stagger as he plunged with a bound out into the matted cactus, without his tattered hat, like a wolf flying from the hounds? Had he trodden on a snake, or seen his compadre, or had that white finger waved him away? Yes, all three. But the interview with his one-eyed compadre had shocked him most.

On he came, driving the hot, wet sand before him, toward the Padre Ricardo's chapel. There he paused for breath, though it was only by a spasmodic effort that he could unclose his sheet-white lips, where his sharp teeth had met upon them, and held his mouth together as if he had the lockjaw, while he snorted through his nostrils.

"Ho!" he gasped, "the spying old traitor has sacked the cavern, and the gold must have gone in that launch I saw the night I came over the reef. Ho! the traitor has found the torture I promised him; but I would like to have killed him a little slower."

Here Captain Brand, having regained some few faculties and energy, moved on beyond the church, till he came to the white coral headstone, where he stood still.

It was his last walk on deck or sand! Shading his still horror-stricken eyes by both hands, he glared to seaward.

"Ho, ho! there you are, my Yankee commodore, with that old brig under convoy, and that pretty schooner! Reminds me of my old 'Centipede.' *Bueno!* there are other 'Centipedes,' and I must begin the world anew. I am not old; here is my strong right arm yet; and who can stop me?"

Captain Brand made these remarks in a loud tone, as if he wanted the whole world to hear him; and as if he had failed in early life, and come to a strong resolution to retrieve his past errors.

As he waved his strong right arm aloft, while, in imagination, blood rained from the blade of his cutlass after cleaving the skull by a blow dealt behind the back of an unsuspecting skipper or mate, suddenly he paused, and the arm fell powerless at his side, where it hung dangling loose like a pirate from a gibbet on a windy night.

He caught sight of the old broken cocoa-nut trunk to which he had hitched the green silk rope, with its noose around his victim's neck, and he endeavored to prevent himself falling to the sand.

"Ho!" he choked out, his jaws rattling like dry bones, "I see it all now. The column was snapped just where the rope was hitched, and the trestle must have been torn to pieces by the hurricane. Ho, ho! That's the way my man escaped, to dog me all over the world. Ho! I have no time to lose; he may be here at any moment."

This was the last connected speech that Captain Brand ever made in this world, or in the world to come, perhaps, for at the last word Paul Darcantel rose in all his revengeful majesty before him. With folded arms he bent his dark, stern eyes upon the pirate, wherein the revenge of twenty years was gleaming with a concentrated power.

"You palsied villain! the oath I took to you, and for which I have been accursed, expired yesterday! I took another myself, when we stood here last together, and I am come to fulfill that oath, and—strike!"

His terrible voice and words came back in an echo from the crag, and they seemed with their intense energy to pierce and shrivel the man before him into sleet. And the pirate would have fallen had not two huge, black, lignum-vitæ paws grappled him about the body, pinioning his arms to his sides as if they had been bolted through and through, while at the same moment another pair of tough, sea-weed flippers wound a lashing round his straight legs, and they laid him gently down on the sandy esplanade.

"The trestle, Banou. And you, Ben, bring the hide strands, the faded old cord, and that black altar-cloth!"

The pirate lay on his back, his eyes wide open—for he could not shut them, since the lids had gone in frost—but the solid balls, light green now in the light, rolled from side to side. He recognized the old apparatus too, though it was in different hands than those of Pedillo and his confederate; and he saw, also, that, though the pale green rope was rotten, yet his knowledge of nautical matters taught him that it yet might bear a taut strain, and that those coils of hide thongs never gave way by any amount of tugging, and he saw as well that they had been recently dipped in grease.

But what was to be done with that rotten, moth-eaten old cloth, which the men used to play monté on on Saturday nights in the sheds, and on which the good padre played *his* cards likewise in the chapel? It was not to keep the cold air away from him, or shield his half-naked body from the poisonous insects. Then what could it be for?

"Lift him up, men, and when you lash him down, leave only that little finger free!"

Ben Brown squatted himself on a stone beside the bier, and with his cutlass unbuckled and laid on the sand, and sleeves rolled up, be-

gan his work as if he had a chafing-mat to make for the dead-eyes of
the frigate's lower shrouds, and, though in a hurry, still intended to
make a neat job of it. He had a small and rather sharp-pointed marline-spike, too, which he wore habitually, like a talisman, round his
neck, and which stood him in hand in the intricate parts of his task.

Taking in at a glance the exact amount of hide stuff he required,
he middled the coils, and passing each strand fair and square, his old
bronzed arms went backward and forward, under and over—sometimes pricking a little hole by accident in the pirate's own thin hide
as he passed the strips by the aid of his marline-spike, but always
apologizing in his bluff, rough way, though without squirting tobacco-juice into his victim's face, as did Mr. Gibbs to Jacob Blunt.

"Beg pardon, ye infarnal pirate! but that stick will do ye no
harm. It'll heal much sooner than the iron spike one of yer crew
drove through both cheeks of my watch-mate when you gagged him
on board the brig.

"I say, old nigger, hand us a little more of that slush, will ye?
this 'ere strand won't lie flat. Thankee, old darkey! Kitch hold
on that lower end, will ye? and draw it square up between his pins,
and straighten out that 'ere knee-joint a bit—so fashion.

"I wouldn't hurt ye, you ugly villain, for a chaw of tobaccy.

"Warm work, shipmate! suppose you just toddle down to the
boat for that 'ere grafted bottle lyin' in the starn sheets, and bring a
tin pot of fresh water with you; the gentleman might be thirsty, you
know. I am—Benjamin Brown, of Sandy Pint, seaman."

So Benjamin plaited Captain Brand, late of the "Centipede," down
on his bier; not a thong too little, or one in the wrong place. A strand
between each of his toes, and the big ones turned up in quite an ornamental way, and worked around with a Turk's-head knot.

"Breathin' works all reg'lar, too, no bit of hide bearin' an onequal
strain over his bread-basket. Throat and jaw-tackle in fair talkin'
order, little finger free; and there, Capting Brand, jist let old Ben
reward ye, good for evil, ye child-murdering scoundrel, for the lick
your mate gave him with the pistol on the head, by placing this
soft pillow of green silk rope under your bare skull. There! a little this side, so as ye can look at your finger, while I pass this broad
piece of stuff over your ear. Don't ye look at me, ye infarnal scoundrel, or I'll let this 'ere copper spike slip into one of yer junk-bottle
glims!

"Now," continued Ben, "I'll take a spell till the doctor and the
old nigger come back."

Ay, the job was done, and the mat over the dead-eyes of the
shrouds!

During this neat and seaman-like operation Paul Darcantel wandered away on the tracks of the flying wolf till he came to the cleft

"NOW CAPTAIN BRAND KNEW WHAT WAS COMING."

in the rock. There he picked up and lighted the torch and stalked on. Presently he came to the stones before the low cavern, and pushed his way in with the blazing torch before him. Had Paul Darcantel had nerves, they would have shaken at what he saw; but having none to shake, he calmly fixed his eyes upon the sight.

There lay the head of the ancient Ignacio, caught, as he tried to creep out of the treasure-chamber, by the falling of the stone slab. It must have been sudden, for the stump of a paper cigar was still seized in his wrinkled lips, while the snake-like curls twined about his ears, and his wary eye looked out with its usual suspicious intensity, and seemed to throw out a spark of fire in the reflection of the torch. Rising from a coil in a slimy bed of sand before the head was a venomous serpent, with his graceful neck curved into the broad flat head, all like an ebony cane, straight, motionless, and elegant to the curved top—fascinated by that single living orb of the dead man.

The human intruder left this well-matched pair to their own venomous devices, and winding his way on, he soon came to the open door to the vaults. A powerful kick smashed in the door of the dungeon, and while the rusty bolts were still ringing on the stone pavement, Paul Darcantel entered the loathsome chamber.

He saw nothing at first save a few fragments of broken crockery and a rusty metal pot—not even a rat. But flaring the torch down upon the mouldy floor something sparkled in the light. This he snatched, and it was the long-lost locket and chain which had last rested around the baby-boy's neck.

When the doctor strode back to the esplanade of the chapel he found Benjamin Brown and Banou taking a friendly sip out of the tin pot.

"Well, sir," said Ben, as he got on his pins and strapped on his cutlass, "there he is, sir! and as neat a piece of cross-lashing as ever I did. He looks as if he growed there, jist like a hawk-bill turtle a-bilin' in the ship's coppers, only he can't paddle about.

"I did it marciful, too, sir, and tried to convarse with him, in case he had any presents to make to his friends.

"Why, sir, and would you believe it? I offered to pour a drop of grog—mixed or raw—down his tight mouth, but he never had the perliteness to thank me or ax me a question, but only looked wicked at me. Consarn him! if he had only winked, I wouldn't mind it!" said Ben, with much indignation; "but, howsever, I don't b'lieve he's any think to leave or any friends left!"

But Captain Brand, though speechless without being tongue-tied, and unable to wink, still thought. And what did the doctor propose to do with him in case he was not to be stung to death by insects, sand-flies, musquitoes, and what not?

"Lift the trestle for the last time, men, and stand it here over this thick bed of cactus, so as the little finger may touch the letter on this white tomb-stone."

Now Captain Brand's doubts were relieved, and he knew what was coming. Oh ho! ho!

"There! that is right! Now collect stones and rocks, and wall this trestle up solid to the edge of the frame, so that a hurricane can't loosen it."

Big Banou went to work now, and presently his job was done—coral rocks, and loose head-stones of pirates, well packed down with sand, made the sides of the living tomb. Then the black pall was drawn over the body, and they left the pirate to his inevitable doom.

Soon the three executioners reached the Tiger's Trap.

"Banou, take this locket and chain—ah! you know it well—to your young master. Brown, the two thousand dollars will be placed in your and Greenfield's hands for distribution among the schooner's crew; make a good use of it! Tell the commodore that I shall take an old woman we have found here away with me in a stolen fisherman's boat to Manzanillo, and within the year I shall be at home! There! shove off, my lads!"

As the gig skimmed through the Tiger's Trap, Paul Darcantel, with the widow of Ignaçio, sailed out by the Alligator's Mouth, and as they crossed that roaring ledge, the sun sank in its unclouded glory in the west, and the young moon, with its thin pearly crescent, looked timidly down upon the island.

And the night passed, and the next and the next, with scorching days and blazing suns between them; while the mangrove, the palm, the cocoa-nut, and the cactus—ah! that luxuriant plant throve apace—shooting up its steel-pointed bayonets two inches of a night in thorny needles as thick as pins in a paper, growing clean through the hide of ox or man like blood, till their hard-edged leaves met resistance, when, turning flat side up, they put forth a score for one of the needle bayonets! No escape from them. From shoulder to heel one long, hopeless agony. The fierce sun flaming down, absorbed by the black pall of death! The moon glimmering in pale white rays of splendor through the moth-eaten holes upon the finger and the white tomb-stone! All the day and all the night!

Was it a dream, Captain Brand? No, a frightful reality! Don't you feel a fresh thorn at every slow pulse of the heart they are aiming at? And don't you hear those dread croakings of gulls and cormorants flapping in the air, who have left their prey on the reef to join the vultures in their feast on the shore? You may almost catch the grating sounds of the rasping jaws of the sharks as they crowd into the inlet, and rest their cold noses on the shelly cove where you slept!

Flesh and blood, and pinions and beaks can endure it no longer.

A cloud of carnivorous birds swoop down at last, snap the black pall in their talons and bills, and fly fighting and screaming away with it. Another cloud, darker than the rest, light upon the body, and while the needle-points pierce the palpitating heart, and the breath flutters on the still clenched lips and nostrils, the eyes are picked out, and the flesh is torn piecemeal, hide strands and all, till nothing is left but a hideous white skeleton, with the long bony finger pointing to the letter L.

The lizards wheetled on the rocks, the alligators lashed the lagoon amid the steaming mist of the mangrove roots; the sharks and birds returned to the reefs, the cocoa-nuts waved their tufted tops, the palms crackled in the shower and gale, and the pure inlet murmured musically on the shelly shore for years and years over and around the deserted key, until the whitened bones crumbled into dust, and were borne away by the four winds of heaven.

The hemp has been tarred and spread, the strands twisted, and the rope laid up. The knots have been turned in between good sailors and bad—between pirates and men-of-war's-men—and here Harry Gringo hauls down his pennant until his reading crew care again to take a cruise with him in blue water.

THE END.

Davis's Carthage. Carthage and her Remains: Being an Account of the Excavations and Researches on the Site of the Phœnician Metropolis in Africa and other adjacent Places, under the Auspices of Her Majesty's Government. By Dr. N. Davis, F.R.G.S. Profusely illustrated with Maps, Wood-cuts, Chromo-Lithographs, &c., &c. 8vo, Cloth, $3 00.

Burton's Central Africa. The Lake Regions of Central Africa. A Picture of Exploration. By Richard F. Burton, Capt. H.M.I. Army; Fellow and Gold Medalist of the Royal Geographical Society. With Maps and Engravings on Wood. 8vo, Cloth, $3 00.

Barth's North and Central Africa. Travels and Discoveries in North and Central Africa. Being a Journal of an Expedition undertaken under the Auspices of H.B.M.'s Government in the Years 1849-1855. By Henry Barth, Ph.D., D.C.L. Profusely and elegantly illustrated. Complete in 3 vols. 8vo, Cloth, $9.

Cumming's South Africa. Five Years of a Hunter's Life in the Interior of South Africa. With Notices of the Native Tribes, and Anecdotes of the Chase of the Lion, Elephant, Hippopotamus, Giraffe, Rhinoceros, &c. By Gordon Cumming. With Illustrations. 2 vols. 12mo, Cloth, $2 50.

Wilson's Western Africa. Western Africa: Its History, Condition, and Prospects. By Rev. J. Leighton Wilson, Eighteen Years a Missionary in Africa. With numerous Engravings. 12mo, Cloth, $1 25.

> Mr. Wilson, an American missionary, has written the best book I have seen on the West Coast.
> —Dr. Livingstone, *Rivershire, W. Africa*, Feb. 20, 1803.

Discovery and Adventures in Africa. Condensed Abstracts of the Narratives of African Travellers. By Professor Jameson, James Wilson, and Hugh Murray. 18mo, Cloth, 50 cents.

The Life and Adventures of Bruce, the African Traveller. By Major Sir Francis B. Head. 18mo, Cloth, 50 cents.

Lander's Niger Expedition. Journal of an Expedition to explore the Course and Termination of the Niger. With a Narrative of a Voyage down that River to its Termination. By R. and J. Lander. Engravings. 2 vols. 18mo, Cloth, $1 00.

Urquhart's Pillars of Hercules. The Pillars of Hercules; or, A Narrative of Travels in Spain and Morocco in 1848. By David Urquhart, M.P. 2 vols. 12mo, Cloth, $2 50.

Owen's Voyages. Voyages to explore the Shores of Africa, Arabia, and Madagascar: performed under the Direction of Captain W. F. W. Owen, R.N. 2 vols. 12mo, Cloth, $1 50.

Mungo Park's Central Africa. Travels of Mungo Park, with the Account of his Death, from the Journal of Isaaco, and later Discoveries relative to his lamented Fate, and the Termination of the Niger. 18mo, Cloth, 50 cents.

MADAGASCAR.

The Last Travels of Ida Pfeiffer: inclusive of a Visit to Madagascar. With an Autobiographical Memoir of the Author. Translated by H. W. Dulcken. Steel Portrait. 12mo, Cloth, $1 25. (Uniform with Ida Pfeiffer's "Second Journey round the World").

Three Visits to Madagascar, during the Years 1853-1854-1856. Including a Journey to the Capital, with Notices of the Natural History of the Country and of the Present Civilization of the People. By the Rev. William Ellis, F.H.S. With a Map and Wood-cuts from Photographs, &c. 8vo, Cloth, $3 00.

HARPER'S WEEKLY FOR 1864.

Harper's Weekly is devoted to Art, Literature, General Information, and Politics. It will contain a carefully condensed and impartial record of the events of the day, pictorially illustrated wherever the pencil of the Artist can aid the pen of the Writer. In Politics it will advocate the National Cause, wholly irrespective of mere party grounds. Its Essays, Poems, and Tales will be furnished by the ablest writers of both Continents. A new Novel, by Mr. George Augustus Sala, entitled "QUITE ALONE," will, by special arrangement with the Author, appear in the Weekly simultaneously with its publication in Mr. Dickens's "*All the Year Round*." The Publishers will see to it that the current Volume shall justify the favorable opinions expressed by the loyal Press upon the Volume which has just closed.

Extracts from Notices by the Press.

"Harper's Weekly is the best publication of its class in America, and so far ahead of all other weekly journals as not to permit of any comparison between it and any of their number. Its columns contain the finest collections of reading matter that are printed. Thus, if you look into the Volume for 1863, you will find that its stories, and miscellaneous articles, and poetry are from the minds of some of the leading writers of the time. Its matter is of a very various character from elaborate tales and well-considered editorial articles to the airiest and briefest jests, good-humored hits at the expense of human follies, which proceed from the liveliest of minds. It is a vigorous supporter of the war—discussing all questions that concern the contest in which we are engaged with an amplitude of perception and a breadth of patriotism that place it very high indeed on the roll of loyal and liberal publications. Its illustrations are numerous and beautiful, being furnished by the chief artists of the country. Most of the illustrations are devoted to the war, including battle-pieces, scenes made renowned by great events there occurring, and portraits of eminent military and civil leaders. Even a person who could not read a line of its letter-press could intelligently follow the history of the war through 1863 by going over the pictured pages of this volume."—*Evening Traveller* (Boston.)

"Harper's Weekly, besides being a literary paper of the first class—the only one among American or European Pictorials with a definite purpose consistently and constantly carried out—is at once a leading political and historical annalist of the nation."—*The Press* (Philadelphia).

"Harper's Weekly. — In turning over its pages, we were struck anew with the fidelity with which it delineates passing events: a true picture of the times. The scenes of the war, portrayed by the graphic pencils of artists on the battle-field and in the camp, are re-produced in excellent wood-cuts with marvelous promptness and accuracy. The letter-press furnishes an appropriate accompaniment to the illustrations; presenting a pleasing variety, sprightly and entertaining. We can not wonder at the popularity of the *Weekly* when we observe the spirit and enterprise with which it is conducted."—*Journal* (Boston).

"Harper's Weekly for 1863.—From a careful examination of this work, as it came out in its weekly form, we can honestly advise our readers to purchase the stately and pictured volume. We dare not say how many duodecimo volumes of matter, and of good and interesting matter, it contains. As a record of the events and opinions of the past year, and as literally a picture of the time, it has a permanent value, while its wealth of excellent stories and essays makes it an endless source of entertainment. The original editorial articles are of a very high order of merit, and relate to subjects which attract the attention of all intelligent and patriotic minds. Soundness of thought, liberality of sentiment, and thorough-going loyalty find expression in the most exquisite English. Altogether, we should say that *Harper's Weekly* is a necessity in every household."—*The Transcript* (Boston).

"Harper's Weekly and Magazine, with their immense circulation, are grandly loyal and influential. The *Weekly* especially has been true to the cause; and while it gives in admirable correspondence and accurate pictures a complete illustrated history of the war, with all its battles, incidents, and portraits of generals, it has splendidly enforced by argument and example its principles. Closer reasoning is not to be found than that to which its editors might fairly challenge answer."—*City Item* (Philadelphia).

Notices of Harper's Weekly.

"HARPER'S WEEKLY, of which the Seventh Volume is now issued in neat, substantial binding, shows the industry and zeal with which the cause of the Union has been maintained in its columns during the year 1863. It has continued to increase the fervor of patriotic sentiment as well by its appropriate pictorial illustrations as by its able editorial leaders commenting on the events of the day. In its present shape, the journal furnishes copious materials for the history of the war, and can not fail to find a place in public and private libraries as an important volume for permanent reference."—*Tribune* (New York).

"HARPER'S WEEKLY *for* 1863—a journal of the year, kept in the most interesting way; and as we turn over the pages we revive many now almost forgotten sensations, and see, bit by bit, how history has grown. The volume closed and bound up becomes history; but it would not be just to this publication to omit a remark on the influence which it has exerted during the year, and which it continues to exert. An illustrated journal like *Harper's Weekly*, which circulates, as we have heard, over one hundred and twenty thousand copies per week, chiefly among families, and which has probably a million of readers, has necessarily a great influence in the country. The *Weekly* has consistently and very ably supported the Union, the Government, and the great principles to develop which the Union was founded. Unlike most illustrated journals, *Harper's Weekly* has displayed political and literary ability of a high order as well as artistic merit. Its political discussions are sound, clear, and convincing, and have done their share to educate the American people to a right understanding of their dangers and duties. In its speciality—illustrations of passing events—it is unsurpassed; and many of the pictures of the year do honor to the genius of the artists and engravers of this country. Thus complete in all the departments of an American Family Journal, *Harper's Weekly* has earned for itself a right to the title which it assumed seven years ago, 'A JOURNAL OF CIVILIZATION.' "—*Evening Post* (New York).

HARPER'S WEEKLY.—This periodical merits special notice at the present time. There is probably no weekly publication of the country that equals its influence. More than one hundred thousand copies fly over the land weekly: they are read in our cars, steamboats, and families. Our youth especially read them; and as *the* family newspaper of the nation, its power over the forming opinions of the next generation of the American people is an important item.

It is abundant, if not superabundant, in pictorial illustrations—a means of strong impression, especially on the minds of the young. Both by its illustrations and its incessant discussion of the occurrences and questions of the war it is a "current history" and "running commentary" on the great event, and there is probably no literary agency of the day more effective in its influence respecting the war in the families of the common people. Most happy are we then to be able to say that this responsible power is exerted altogether on the side of loyalty. No paper in the land is more outspoken, more uncompromising for the Union, for the war, for even the policy of the President's "great Proclamation." When the rebellion broke out we did the publishers the injustice of some anxious fears about their probable course on the subject.

Steadily have they kept up with the Providential development of its events and questions; not only abreast of them, but, in important respects, ahead of them. No periodical press in the nation deserves better of the country for its faithfulness and "pluck" in all matters relating to the great struggle. And we should do it injustice were we not to add that, with its outright loyalty and bravery, it combines commanding ability. The editorial leaders which it continuously flings out against all political traitors and flunkies strike directly at their mark. They are evidently from pens both strong and polished. On even the astuter subjects of policy, finance, &c., it is eminently able. And it makes no mistake in supposing its readers capable of an interest and of intelligence in these respects. American families look keenly into such questions, and with such a really educational force as this paper wields, it is especially right and commendable that it seeks to elevate the common mind to the higher questions of the times. The American people will not fail to notice and to remember the courageous and patriotic course of *Harper's Weekly* in these dark times of hideous treason, and of more hideous, because more contemptible, semi-treason.—*The Methodist*, N. Y.

TERMS.

One Copy for Four Months	. . . . $1 00
One Copy for One Year	. . . . 3 00
Two Copies for One Year	. . . . . . 5 50
"Harper's Weekly" and "Harper's Magazine" one year	5 50

An Extra Copy of either the Weekly or Magazine will be supplied gratis for every Club of TEN SUBSCRIBERS, at $2 75 each; or, Eleven Copies for $27 50.